TOOK

A Ghost Story

MARY DOWNING HAHN

The Beginning

The old woman stands on the hilltop, just on the edge of the woods, well hidden from the farmhouse below. Two men and a woman are getting out of a car that has a sign for Jack Lingo Realty painted on the side. The old woman has seen plenty of Realtors in her time. She doesn't know this one, but she remembers his pa, old Jack Lingo, and *his* pa, Edward, and the one afore him, back and back through the years to the first Lingo ever to settle in this valley and take up the buying and selling of houses.

Though young Lingo doesn't know it, Auntie is helping him sell that house to the man and the woman in the only way she knows – muttering and humming and moving her hands this way and that way, weaving spells in the air, sending messages as she's always done. Messages that make folks need things not worth needing. Dangerous things. Things they regret getting.

You might wonder why Auntie wants this man and woman to buy the house. Truth to tell, she doesn't give a hoot about them. They're ignorant fools, but they have something she wants, and she aims to get it. It's almost time for the change, and they've come on schedule, just as she'd known they would.

"New for old," she chants to herself. "Strong for weak, healthy for sickly, pretty for ugly."

When the man and the woman follow young Lingo into the old Estes house, Auntie sways back and forth, grinning and rubbing her dry, bony hands together. Her skirt blows in the wind, and long strands of white hair whip around her face. With a little hop and a jig, she turns to something hidden in the trees behind her. "Won't be long now, my boy. We'll get rid of the old pet and get us a new one to raise up."

Though he stays out of sight, her companion makes a noise like a hog when it's hungry—a squealing sort of snort that might be a laugh, or it might be something else altogether.

Auntie gazes down at the rundown farmhouse and

outbuildings, the overgrown fields, the woods creeping closer year by year. From the hill, she can see the missing shingles in the roof, the warped boards riddled with termites and dry rot, the cracks in the chimney.

Almost fifty years have passed since the Estes family left the place. Nobody has lived there since then. Local folk avoid the place. They scare their children with stories about the girl, the one before her, and the one before her, back and back to the very first girl. Fear keeps them out of the woods and away from the cabin on Brewster's Hill. Those children know all about Auntie and her companion.

But newcomers always show up, city people who've never heard the stories. If the valley folk try to warn them, they scoff and laugh and call the stories superstitious nonsense. They come from places where lights burn all night. They don't heed the dark and what hides there.

It all works to Auntie's advantage.

Down below, a door opens, and Auntie watches young Lingo lead the man and woman outside. Even though they speak softly, Auntie hears every word. They aim to buy that tumbledown wreck of a house, fix it up, and live there with their children, a boy and a girl, they tell him. It's just what they want—a chance to get away from their old life and start anew in the country. They'll get some chickens, they say, a couple of goats, maybe even a cow or a sheep. They'll plant a garden, grow their own food.

The man and the woman get into the Realtor's car, laughing, excited. Auntie spits into the dirt. Fools. They'll find out soon enough.

She listens to the car's engine until she can't hear it anymore. Then she snaps her fingers and does another jig. "It's falling into place just like I predicted, dear boy, but don't you say a word to her back at the cottage. She ain't to know till it happens."

Her companion snorts and squeals, and the two of them disappear into the dark woods.

To wait.

ONE

It was a long drive from Fairfield, Connecticut, to Woodville, West Virginia—two days, with an overnight stay in Maryland. My sister, Erica, and I were sick of the back seat, sick of each other, and mad at our parents for making us leave our home, our school, and our friends.

Had they asked us how we felt about moving? Of course not. They've never been the kind of parents who ask if you want to drink your milk from the red glass or the blue glass. They just hand you a glass, and that's that. Milk tastes the same whether the glass is blue or red or purple.

Going to West Virginia was a big thing, something we should have had a say in, but no. They left us with a neighbor, drove down there, found a house they liked, and bought it. Just like that.

They were the grownups, the adults, the parents. They were in charge. They made the decisions.

In all fairness, they had a reason for what they did. Dad worked for a big corporation. He earned a big salary. We had a big house, two big cars, and all sorts of other big stuff—expensive stuff. Erica and I went to private school. Mom didn't work. She was what's called a soccer mom, driving me and Erica and our friends to games and clubs and the country club pool. She and Dad played golf. They were planning to buy a sailboat.

But then the recession came along, and the big corporation started laying people off. Dad was one of them. He thought he'd find another job fast, but he didn't. A year went by. One of our big cars was repossessed. Erica and I went to public school. We gave up the country club. There was no more talk about sailboats.

The bank started sending letters. Credit card

companies called. Dad and Mom were maxed out financially. The mortgage company threatened foreclosure.

So we had to sell the house. I can understand that. But why did we have to move to West Virginia? It was cheaper to live there, Dad said. Erica and I would love it. So much space—woods and fields and mountains. He took to singing "Country Roads," an old John Denver song about West Virginia, putting lots of emphasis on "Almost heaven, West Virginia." He also informed us that the license plates said "Wild, Wonderful."

So here we were, on an interstate highway, with nothing to see but mountains and woods, wild but not wonderful, in my opinion. It was like being in a foreign country. How would I ever get used to all the nature surrounding us?

Beside me, Erica was talking to the doll Mom had given her—not because it was her birthday or anything, but because she was so unhappy about leaving Fairfield.

That's rewarding bad behavior, if you ask me. I was just as unhappy as my sister, but since I didn't cry myself to sleep and mope in my room and refuse to eat, all I got was a pair of binoculars and Peterson's *Field Guide to Birds of North America*. Dad thought I might like to identify the birds we were sure to see when we went hiking. Well, maybe I would, but still, that doll was ten times more expensive than my binoculars. It came with a little trunk full of clothes. There were even outfits in my sister's size so she and the doll could dress alike. It had its own bed, too. And its hair was red just like Erica's and cut the same way.

All the time we were in the van, Erica talked to the doll. She tried all its clothes on and told the doll how pretty it was. She hugged it and kissed it. She even named it Little Erica.

It was making me sick. But every time I complained, Erica got mad and we started quarreling and Mom turned around and blamed it all on me. "Leave your sister alone, Daniel," she'd say. "She's perfectly happy playing with Little Erica. Read a book or something."

"You know I can't read in the car. Do you want me to barf all over that stupid doll?"

At last we turned off the interstate. The roads narrowed and ran up and down hills, crossed fields, passed farms, and tunneled through woods. We glimpsed mountains and swift rivers. The towns were farther apart and smaller, some no more than a strip of houses and shops along the road.

By the time Dad finally pulled off an unpaved road and headed down a narrow driveway, the woods around us were dark. In the van's headlights the trees looked like a stage set lit by spotlights.

The van bounced over ruts and bumps, tossing Erica and me toward and away from each other. "Stay on your side, Daniel," Erica said, "and stop banging into me and Little Erica. We don't like it."

"That doll doesn't care — she's not real."

"She is so!"

"Be quiet, Daniel," Mom said.

"It's not my fault," I said. "Instead of blaming me, tell Dad to slow down."

Just then we came out of the woods, and I got my first view of the house. It stood in the middle of a field of tall grass — weeds, actually. Even in the dark

I could see that the place was a wreck. The porch sagged under the weight of vines growing up the walls and across the roof. Tall, shaggy bushes blocked most of the windows on the first floor. Shutters hung crooked. Some were missing altogether. I was sure it hadn't been painted for a long time.

Erica was the first to speak. "It's scary."

"What's scary about it?" Dad asked.

"It's dark." She hugged her doll tightly. "The woods are scary, too. And there aren't any other houses."

"Wait until morning, Erica," Mom said. "It's lovely in the daylight. You'll see."

"And we have a few neighbors down the road," Dad added.

How far down the road? I wondered. And what were they like?

Dad and Mom got out of the van and headed toward the house. Erica ran to catch up and slipped her hand into Mom's. I followed them, breathing in the unfamiliar smell of the woods and listening to night sounds. Wind rattled branches and hissed through the weeds in the field. A shutter banged against the side of the house. An owl called from the woods.

At the same moment, something made the hair on my neck rise. Sure that someone was watching us, I turned around and stared down the dark driveway. I saw no one, but I shivered — and not because I was cold.

Arrival

The old woman stands on the hilltop, at the edge of the woods, well hidden from the farmhouse below, just as she did before, but now it's a dark, cold night, lit by the moon. All around her, bushes and branches rattle in a wind that carries autumn's breath. But she isn't cold. She leans on her staff and peers toward the road.

"They're coming," she calls to her companion. He snorts and continues snuffling about in the dead leaves for good things to eat.

Headlights bounce down the driveway. A big car stops by the house. Even in the dark a person can see that it's a ramshackle wreck of a place, ready to topple with the first strong wind that comes its way.

The car doors open and the interior lights come on. She sees the girl, just the one she needs. The child gets out, clutching a dolly. The old woman sniffs fear. The girl is scared of the dark and the old house. She doesn't want to live here. Well, she won't live here long, will she?

The girl's name is blown by the wind across the dark field and laid at the old woman's feet. Erica. Air-ric-cah. She likes to draw the name out, especially the last syllable.

"Air-ric-cah, Air-ric-cah," the old woman whispers. The name glides lightly through the air, a rustle of black silk thread, and winds itself into the girl's ear.

She sees the girl tense and look around, move closer to her mother.

"Yes," the old woman hisses. "You'll do. Air-ric-cah, Air-ric-cah."

She does one of her little jigs and calls to her companion. "Time to go, dear boy. We'll see her soon, don't you worry. She's the one, she's ours."

As the family enters their new home, the old woman and her companion wrap themselves in darkness and make their way home.

TWO

While we waited on the porch, Dad fished a big old-fashioned key out of his pocket. With a lot of effort he finally got it to turn in the lock. Moonlight followed us inside and cast our shadows across the dusty floor. In front of us, stairs led to the second story.

Mom flicked a switch, and the shadows fled. To the right was the living room, or maybe the parlor, empty now except for a fireplace. Three tall windows with old-fashioned wavy glass reflected us standing in the hall, slightly distorted, like people in a fun house.

"Where's our furniture?" Erica asked.

"It's coming tomorrow," Mom told her.

"But where are we sleeping?" she asked, sounding a bit tearful.

"Don't you remember?" Dad asked. "We brought our camping stuff—sleeping bags, foam mats, pillows, blankets."

"Can I sleep with Mommy?"

"Of course you can." Mom put her arm around Erica and hugged her.

I was getting pretty tired of Erica's clinging behavior. "What's wrong with you?" I whispered. "You never used to act like this."

"I never had to live in the woods before." She turned to Mom. "Are we going to eat wild berries?"

"Of course not, sweetie," Dad said. "Whatever gave you that idea?"

"That's what happens sometimes in stories."

"Well, this isn't a story, Erica," Mom said.

Dad got an ancient gas stove going, and Mom heated a pot of water. When it boiled, she dumped in noodles and heated a jar of marinara sauce.

We ate our first meal in the house picnic style in front of the fire. Erica snuggled beside Mom and shared her food with Little Erica. The food stuck to the doll's face, and Erica tenderly wiped her clean with a napkin.

Later, we all crawled into our sleeping bags and watched what was left of the fire fall into ash. The lights were out, and the moon shone in through the tall windows. I heard Erica whispering to the doll.

Sometime during the night I woke up. I'd drunk too much soda at dinner, and now I needed the bathroom. I eased out of my sleeping bag and got to my feet. Dad snored, Mom slept like a dead woman, and Erica murmured as if she were dreaming.

I tiptoed across the floor and eased the front door open. It was easier to pee outside than find my way upstairs to the bathroom.

The moonlight was brilliant and the stars were clustered thickly over my head, more than I'd ever seen in Fairfield. After I finished what I came out to do, I stood on the porch and gazed at the dark mass of woods bordering the fields. The night was cold, but as I turned to go inside, I was stopped by a sound in the darkness—a howl, which might have been the wind in the trees but was scarier. Much scarier. I shivered and edged toward the door, but before I stepped inside, I looked back. Something moved at the edge of the woods. Its head gleamed in the moonlight, as white as bone. I heard the howl again, louder this time, and stumbled backward, slamming and bolting the door.

"Daniel," Mom called sleepily, "what are you doing up in the middle of the night?"

"I went outside to pee. Something in the woods howled." I slid into my sleeping bag, shivering with cold and fear.

"Shh," she whispered. "You'll wake up Dad and Erica."

"Didn't you hear it?"

She shook her head. "It was probably an owl or a fox."

"No. I saw it," I told her. "It was as tall as a man, and its head shone in the moonlight."

Mom smoothed my hair. "Go back to sleep, Daniel. There's nothing out there. It's dark, you're in a strange place, and your eyes were playing tricks on you."

I moved a little closer to her. Maybe she was right. She must be right. Monsters didn't roam the woods anywhere but in fairy tales. I closed my eyes and practiced breathing slowly and deeply, but it was almost daylight by the time I fell asleep.

When I woke up, sunlight filled the living room. Just as Mom had said, whatever I'd heard and seen in the dark had a natural explanation—night noises most likely, animals going about their nocturnal business, embellished with my imagination. Moonlight and shadows play tricks on you.

The moving truck arrived before we'd finished breakfast, and Mom put us all to work. We picked our bedrooms first. Mine overlooked the woods, which were not quite as close to the house as I'd thought the night before, but close enough for me to see a deer pause at the edge of the trees and then vanish into the shadows. The lawns in Connecticut were overrun with deer, but this was a wild deer and therefore more noble than the ones who ate our shrubbery and our flowers and the vegetables Mom tried to grow.

Erica's room was across the hall from mine, at the front of the house. Mom and Dad were next to her. The bedroom beside mine was reserved for Dad—his office, he called it. At the end of the hall was a small room, probably a sewing room, Mom said, or a nursery. She claimed it for her weaving. "The loom will fit just right under the windows," she said.

The moving men spent most of the day tramping around the house, upstairs and down, putting furniture where Mom told them to. When they finally drove away, Mom gave us our next tasks. Unpack our clothes and belongings and put them away.

I finished first and stopped in Erica's room to see how she was doing. Her clothes lay in a heap on her unmade bed. Her boxes of toys and books sat in the middle of the floor, where the moving men had left them, still taped shut. Erica sat on a window seat, her back to me. She held Little Erica.

"We don't like it here," Erica whispered to the doll. "It's a bad, scary place, no matter what they say. You and I know, but nobody believes us."

Little Erica had nothing to say that I could hear, but my sister bent her head close to the doll as if she were listening to her. "Yes," she murmured. "Yes."

I hated to interrupt the weird conversation, but I stepped into the room and said, "Mom told you to put your stuff away, but you haven't even started."

Erica whirled around. Her red hair swung like

a flag. And so did the doll's. "I'm never going to put anything away until we go home."

"*This* is home now." I picked up a box labeled SOCKS AND UNDERWEAR and pried off the tape. "I'll help you."

"Leave my things alone!" Erica laid the doll down and snatched the box away. "Get out of my room, Daniel. We don't want you here."

"What's going on?" Mom stood in the doorway.

"I was just trying to help her unpack."

"I don't want him to help," Erica said. "I'm leaving everything just like this until we go home."

"Honey, we *are* home." Mom tried to hug her, but she pulled away.

"Home is Connecticut," Erica whispered. "Not *here*."

Mom made a gesture toward the door. "Leave this to me, Daniel."

As I left the room, Mom shut the door. I lingered in the hall for a moment. Mom was talking softly. Erica was crying.

I found Dad in the basement in front of a huge furnace that looked like something you'd find on the

Nautilus, all dials and levers and doors and pipes. A submarine engine only Captain Nemo understood. Steampunk in every way.

"Let me see," Dad mused. "It's September. Hopefully, I'll have time to figure out how this monster works before we need it."

I pictured a long, cold winter, with the four of us huddled around the fireplace to keep warm.

"Or maybe I can call somebody from the oil company," Dad went on, "and he can explain it to me."

We stood side by side and looked around the basement. It was dark and dank and musty. The ceiling was so low Dad could barely stand up straight. Pipes festooned with cobwebs hung even lower. The only light was a bare bulb hanging by a cord from a crossbeam. The floor was dirt, the walls stone. The damp air smelled as if it had been trapped down here since the house was built.

"Once I establish myself as a photographer," Dad said, "we'll fix this basement up. Replace the furnace with something new that I can understand. Put in some windows, maybe a sliding glass door. I could even build a darkroom and get out my old film cameras."

While Dad was picturing a darkroom and sliding glass doors, I was imagining a murderer carrying his victims down the steep, rickety steps and digging graves in the dirt floor.

"I'm going outside," I told Dad. "I could use some fresh air."

Leaving him poking around in the junk piled in every corner, I found Mom at the kitchen table, busy sorting napkins and tablecloths. Erica was sitting near her, reading *Bedtime for Frances* to Little Erica. Neither of them noticed me, so I slipped out the back door to do some exploring.

The house looked even worse in daylight. Peeling paint exposed bare gray wood. A gutter dangled from the eaves, and a downspout lay in the weeds. Judging by the number of shingles I saw on the ground, the roof probably leaked. The porch floorboards were warped, the railing was loose, and the steps tilted to one side.

Behind the house, I discovered a small tumbledown barn almost hidden under a tangle of wild grapevines, honeysuckle, poison ivy, and brambles. All around it grew a jungle of pokeberry weeds taller than I was. Poisonous berries hung from the red stalks in black clusters, like grapes. Sticking up from the weeds were two doorless refrigerators, an old plow, an ancient Ford pickup truck, several rusted air conditioners, and a mildewed sofa. The town dump, I thought, right in our own backyard.

What were Dad and Mom thinking when they bought this place? Had they lost their minds? We'd never get the house fixed up, let alone clear the junk out. I felt like packing my belongings and siding with Erica. Maybe between the two of us we could persuade Mom and Dad to go back to Connecticut.

THREE

The next day, we went to Home Depot. We couldn't afford to paint the outside of the house yet. That would have to wait. But we could afford to make the inside look better.

I chose blue for my room, and Erica chose lavender for hers. Mom and Dad picked shades of beige for everything else, except for the kitchen, which was to be yellow. A bright, cheerful color, Mom said.

It took a week to paint the house. All of us, even Erica, helped scrape and sand and clean the walls. When we finally finished, the place looked more like home—our pictures on the walls, our furniture in the rooms, our books on the shelves. We ate dinner at our dining room table using our plates and glasses and silverware. We ate breakfast and lunch at our kitchen table. Mom's collection of teapots appeared on a shelf in a kitchen. Dad helped her set up a loom in the little room upstairs. He organized his office and arranged his pipe collection in his barrister bookcase. He hung his diploma from UMass.

In my room, I lined up my books on a shelf Dad made for me. I kept my Star Wars figures and my puzzle collection on their own shelves. Posters of Spider-Man and Captain America hung on one wall. A movie ad for *The Hobbit* hung between the windows on the opposite wall. I was beginning to feel at home.

Erica finally unpacked her boxes and hung up her clothes. She folded underwear and socks and T-shirts and put them in bureau drawers. She arranged books and found places for her dolls and stuffed animals.

When she was finished, her room looked exactly like her room in Fairfield—her lavender checked curtains fit the new windows and the paint matched her old walls. The only difference was the view—woods and fields and mountains instead of green lawns and neighbors' houses.

The next week, Mom enrolled Erica and me in school. It was our first trip to Woodville itself. The shopping center on the outskirts of town had a Home Depot, a Walmart, and a Piggly Wiggly grocery store, as well as a nail salon, a liquor store, an insurance agent, a bank, Joe's Pizza, and a real estate office with faded photos of houses for sale taped to the windows. What more did we need, Dad asked.

Whatever it was, we wouldn't find it in Woodville. Except for a used-clothing store, a bar, and a thrift shop, the buildings on Main Street were boarded up. Even the graffiti was faded.

Narrow streets ran uphill from one side of Main Street and downhill from the other side. Dogs barked as we drove by. A gust of wind blew newspapers down the street. We didn't see a single person. The whole town could have been abandoned, as far as I could tell. Except for the dogs, of course.

"Next time we'll take the scenic route," Mom said, "if there is one."

She turned off Main Street and drove uphill through a neighborhood of old houses that were slightly nicer than the ones we'd seen so far. The Woodville School was at the top of the hill—kindergarten through eighth grade, which meant that Erica's second grade classroom and my seventh grade classroom would be in the same building. The school was made of dark gray stone and had tall, narrow windows; a steep flight of steps led to the main entrance, a big black door. It might as well have been named the Bastille School for bad boys and girls.

Erica clung to Mom's hand. "I don't want to go here. It's ugly."

"Don't be silly." Shaking her hand free, Mom pulled open the door. "It will be fine," she added. "Just give it time."

I knew by the uncertainty in her voice that she didn't believe her own words. But what could she do? It was the only school in town.

Mom led us into an office filled with old-fashioned dark furniture. A thin woman looked up from a typewriter and did a funny thing with her mouth, which I think was meant to be a smile. Her hair was pulled tightly back from her face, and she wore a plain black dress with long sleeves. She scared Erica and made me nervous. Even Mom looked uncomfortable. According to the sign on her desk, she was Miss Danvers, school secretary.

"You must be Mrs. Anderson," she said to Mom. "And you are Erica and Daniel, if I'm not mistaken. Welcome to Woodville Elementary."

While Erica and I sat side by side, as silent as mutes, Mom filled out forms. Miss Danvers returned to her typing. I watched, fascinated by the sight of a real live person using an antique instead of a computer.

"Their official transcripts should arrive any day," Mom said as she handed Miss Danvers the completed paperwork.

A bald man with a gray mustache stuck his head out of an inner door and smiled at us. "I'm Mr. Sykes, the principal. I hope you two will enjoy our school — a bit smaller than you're used to, I'm sure. Not as up to date, maybe, but —" The phone in his office rang, and he excused himself to answer it.

I knew sarcasm when I heard it.

Miss Danvers led the three of us down a hall. The walls were grayish green and bare. No bright paintings, no starred reports, no posters. The closed doors to classrooms were unadorned too. It was very different from the schools I'd gone to in Connecticut.

Miss Danvers stopped at a door labeled SEVENTH GRADE. "Wait here," she told Mom and Erica.

Opening the door, she ushered me into the room. The teacher was a large woman with a stern face. She looked at me as if I were an invasive species.

The kids in the room stared at me. They sat in old-fashioned one-piece desks arranged in straight rows from the front to the back of the room. No artwork. No projects. Just the flag and a faded portrait of George Washington. The blackboard was made of slate, and sticks of chalk and erasers lay on the ledge beneath it. It looked like a classroom from an old black-and-white movie.

I glanced over my shoulder. Mom was staring into the room in disbelief. "Daniel, this is Miss Mincham, your teacher," Miss Danvers said. Turning to the class, she added, "Boys and girls, Daniel's from Connecticut, that little state near New York City."

Their eyes flicked over me, taking in my khaki pants, turtleneck sweater, and parka—standard clothing in either Pine Ridge or Carson Middle

School, but not here. The uniform for both boys and girls seemed to be jeans and T-shirts, old and faded and either too big or too small.

A boy in the back of the room snickered. He must have been fifteen or sixteen years old, from the size of him. Two girls whispered to each other and giggled.

Miss Mincham rose to her feet, an awe-inspiring sight. Almost six feet tall and weighing about two hundred pounds, she frowned at the boy in the back row and the two girls. Then she told me to take a seat in the back row—the empty one next to the giant boy.

The class was studying history. Miss Mincham called out events from the Revolutionary War and asked kids to supply the dates when they happened. I've never been good at remembering stuff like that, so I didn't do any better than the rest of them. When she shifted the subject to math, she sent us to the blackboard for drills in long division. English consisted of reciting rules of grammar. And geography was naming capitals of foreign countries.

In the cafeteria, a kid knocked my lunch tray out of my hand and pretended it was an accident. In gym class, a bunch of boys cornered me in the locker room and shoved me around, sneering at my clothes and my snobby accent. Ignoring their behavior, the gym teacher blew his whistle and yelled, "Okay, that's enough, out on the floor, let's play some basketball." I was bumped into, tripped, and hit on the head with the ball—all accidentally of course.

By the end of the day, I hated Woodville School. I found Erica, and we boarded the bus that would take us home. The driver was a woman named Mrs. Plummer, the first nice person I'd met all day. She told us our stop was the last one. "It's a long ride," she said.

As we rumbled along narrow roads, uphill and down, letting kids off at farms and trailer parks along the way, the boy behind me kicked the back of my seat, and his friend said things like "I'm from Connecticut and I'm better than you," in what he thought was a good imitation of the accent I never knew I had.

Finally, there was only one kid on the bus beside Erica and me. Despite the lurching ride, he staggered up the aisle and sat down in front of us. Leaning over the back of the seat, he stared at us. He was maybe ten years old, a scrawny boy with dingy blond hair and sad brown eyes. He looked as if soap was not used in his house, either on him or on his clothes.

"My stop is the last one," he said. "Did you forget to get off?"

"No," I said. "We're the last stop."

He shook his head. "There's no stop after mine."

"We just moved here," I told him. "We live on a farm, just over the bridge."

His eyes widened. "You live on the Estes family farm?"

I shrugged. "Maybe. I don't know who used to live in our house."

I glanced at Erica, who was staring at the boy.

"Is something wrong with where we live?" she asked.

"It's where the girl disappeared," he said.

"What girl?"

I nudged her. "Don't listen to him. He's just trying to scare us."

He looked at me. "I'm not lying, if that's what you think. Just ask anybody about Selene Estes. They'll tell you." He shoved his face close to Erica's.

"Something got her and drug her away and nobody ever saw her again."

Erica drew back, her eyes fearful.

"Nothing dragged her away," I told him. "She got lost and fell off a cliff or something."

"Hah," the boy said. "That's what you think. There's things out in these woods people from Con-neck-ti-cut ain't never heard of."

With a grinding of gears, the bus stopped and the boy got off. I looked out the window and saw him standing by the road, making a face at me. Then we jolted and bumped and swayed around a curve and up a hill, leaving him and his stories behind.

The bus made its next and final stop at the end of our driveway. As we got off, the driver, Mrs. Plum-mer, leaned out the door and called, "Don't believe anything Brody Mason tells you. He's a born liar, that boy."

As the bus drove away, Erica turned to me. "Do you think a girl disappeared from our house?"

"Of course not," I said. "You heard what the bus driver said. Brody or Brady, or whatever his name is, is a liar. He was trying to scare you."

"He did scare me." She fumbled to adjust the shoulder strap on her backpack. "He wasn't lying, Daniel, I could tell."

I straightened her strap for her. "Listen, Erica, that boy was definitely lying. And do you know why? The kids here don't like us. We're outsiders. That's why they're so mean."

Erica turned to me, her eyes bright with tears. "My teacher, Mrs. Kline, is mean, too, even meaner than Miss Davis back at public school in Fairfield. She kept me in at recess and made me write one hundred times 'I will not daydream in class.' The girl who sits behind me whispered that I'm ugly. At lunchtime, all the girls laughed at me and said I talk funny and wear weird clothes. They wouldn't let me sit at a table with them either."

"It was exactly the same in my class," I told her. "I got beaten up in gym, and my teacher called me stupid because I didn't know the capital of Rhodesia or the exact date George Washington crossed the Delaware, let alone rules of grammar, which nobody ever taught me."

"Maybe Mom will teach us at home."

I shook my head. "No. She'll just tell us to be

patient and the kids will start liking us. You know, all of a sudden they'll realize how nice we are. Even if we do come from Connecticut."

"You don't believe that, do you?"

"No," I said. "In fact, I don't think even Mom believes it."

Erica frowned. "Do you hear noises at night?"

I looked at her, surprised by the sudden change of subject. "Do you?"

"Sometimes I hear a sort of whispering. Almost like somebody's calling me. It sounds like this—*Air-ric-cah, Air-ric-cah*."

She said it in a low, scary voice—a weird, drawn-out version of her name.

"It's just the wind," I told her. "Hear it blowing in the tops of the trees? It sounds like it's whispering up there."

Erica shook her head. "No, it's not like trees or wind. It's my name. Then it whispers other things. I can almost make out the words, but not quite."

She broke away from me then and ran to meet Mom on the front porch, her red hair flying in the breeze, her backpack bouncing.

I followed her slowly, thinking about what she'd

said. I was sure that Erica had imagined the whispering voice, but when I looked at the woods behind the house, I felt my chest tighten with anxiety. In the late-afternoon light, the shadows of the trees stretched across the field. The woods were already dark, and the mountainsides were in shadow.

Mom waved to me from the porch, and I broke into a run, suddenly eager to be inside, safe from whatever might be hiding in those woods—things that didn't exist in Connecticut.

FOUR

After dinner that night, Erica told Mom and Dad about the boy on the bus and what he'd told us. Our parents agreed with me. This was an old, old farm, and no one had lived in the house for a long time. It was exactly the sort of place that inspired people to make up stories.

"It must be a country version of an urban legend," Dad said. "Like the man with the—"

Mom stopped him with a sharp look.

"The man with a what?" Erica asked.

"The man with a monkey," I said, to rescue Dad. I definitely didn't want him telling Erica about the man with the hook. In fact, I myself didn't want to hear that story, not here, not at night, not when anything could be out there howling in the dark, watching us through the tall living room windows Mom hadn't gotten around to covering with curtains.

"Does the monkey disappear?" Erica persisted.

"Of course not," I told her. "He and the man run away from the circus and live happily ever after in a tarpaper shack."

Erica laughed. "And they eat wild berries for breakfast, lunch, and dinner?"

Dad winked at me. "Exactly!"

Erica snuggled beside Mom on the couch and listened to a chapter of *The Moffats,* a book Mom loved when she was Erica's age. And still did.

But when it was time for bed, Erica said, "I don't want to go upstairs. It's so dark outside my window."

"Daniel's right across the hall from you," Mom said, "and Dad and I are in the next room."

"Will you come with me, Mommy?" Erica asked. "And tuck me in and sit with me till I fall asleep?"

Dad sighed. "Give in now, Martha, and it'll be the same every night."

Either Mom didn't hear him, or she ignored him.

Scooping Erica up as if she were still a baby, she carried her upstairs.

Dad shook his head. "Your mother is spoiling that child."

I shrugged, opened my odious social studies book, and began memorizing the imports, exports, and native products of Germany. What a waste of time Woodville School was. My textbook had been published thirty years ago.

When I passed Erica's door later, I heard my sister say, "Are you sure it's just a legend?"

"Yes," Mom said. "Please stop worrying about it. No one disappeared. A girl named Selene never lived here. That boy was a liar."

The next morning, Erica and I sat in the front of the school bus, right behind Mrs. Plummer. The bus slowed for the second stop, and Brody got on. Erica stared out the window, pretending not to see him, but I gave him a dirty look. He made an ugly face, sat down behind us, and began kicking the back of my seat.

As the bus filled with kids, Brody told them where Erica and I lived.

One girl said she never walked down the road past our driveway. Her friend claimed that her big sister and some of her friends drove up the driveway on a dare. It was few years ago, when no one lived in the house.

"They heard people crying and wailing and calling Selene's name. They didn't see nothing, but they got out of there fast."

Erica pressed her fingers in her ears and hummed, but I listened to every word. If I was dumb enough to believe their stories, a family named Estes lived on the farm about forty or fifty years ago, maybe more, no one was sure. It was before they were born, but their parents or maybe their grandparents remembered it. They had a daughter named Selene, and she disappeared when she was seven years old, and no one ever found her. One girl said she was *took*. Maybe it was the demons in the woods, a boy suggested. Maybe Old Auntie the conjure woman up on Brewster's Hill got her, Brody said. Or, worst of all, a girl said, Old Auntie's razorback hog, the one called Bloody Bones, ate her up.

Nobody agreed about who took Selene, but they all agreed she was never found.

By the time we arrived at school, Erica was trembling. We waited until the bus was empty and then got up to leave.

Mrs. Plummer stopped Erica. "Don't let them scare you," she told my sister. "It's just a yarn people been spinning for years, not a speck of truth in it. A girl named Selene disappeared, but she wasn't 'took.' There's no conjure woman and no Bloody Bones."

She rummaged in her purse, pulled out a pack of Life Savers, and handed it to Erica. "Help yourself. You, too."

We each took one and thanked her. "They're not really bad kids," Miss Plummer said. "Just nobody's taught them manners. They've grown up as wild as bears in the woods. Give them time. They'll get friendly when they're used to you."

A week passed, and another week followed, but those kids didn't get used to Erica and me. They didn't even try. Luckily, Mrs. Plummer saved the seat behind her for us, so no one could say or do anything to us without getting kicked off the bus.

Even so, they found ways to torment us with stories of Selene Estes. A whisper here, a comment there, a note or a drawing passed to us.

When we were off the bus, with no Mrs. Plummer to protect us, the boys continued to knock me around on the playground and the girls whispered about Erica. Unlike Mrs. Plummer, our teachers never noticed. Or maybe they just didn't care.

Mom and Dad didn't have any more luck in Woodville than we did—the adults disliked them for the same reasons the kids disliked Erica and me. They were especially offended by our failure to join the only church in town. We weren't only outsiders, we were godless outsiders.

As far as jobs went, neither Dad nor Mom found a position in Woodville. Not that there was much to choose from.

Dad finally got a job at Home Depot, where he wore a big orange apron and helped people find tools, paint, garbage cans, plumbing supplies, and whatever else they were looking for, most often the restrooms.

Soon after, Mom landed a position as a receptionist at the real estate office on the other side of the parking lot from Home Depot. Nobody there cared where my parents came from or if they went to church. The people who worked at the shopping center were practically all outsiders themselves, from cities such as Charleston. In Woodville, they claimed, you'd never be accepted if you weren't married to your cousin. Dad laughed at this, but Mom said it was an ignorant way to talk.

On weekends Dad and I got into the habit of spending our free time roaming the woods and fields, following trails made long ago by trappers and hunters. He was forever stopping to take a picture of a lichen-covered boulder or a mossy log, a tangle of branches, a gnarled tree, a hawk or a crow in flight, but I didn't mind. I loved being in the woods with him.

Neither Mom nor Erica went with us. Mom had too much to do, she said, and Erica had no interest in the great outdoors. While Mom busied herself weaving, Erica sat nearby, re-reading the Little House on the Prairie books or playing with Little Erica. Sometimes she drew picture stories in her sketchpads; sometimes she painted with watercolors. She seemed perfectly content until the day ended. When night came, she grew fearful and clung to Mom. She still spoke of hearing scary whispers in the dark corners of her room.

On this particular day, a Saturday, Mom was

working at the Realtor's office. Erica didn't want to stay at home alone, so she agreed to go with Dad and me. Although it was sunny, the wind was brisk, so we pulled on heavy sweaters and wrapped scarves around our necks. Erica dressed Little Erica in a sweater that matched hers and wrapped a bandanna around the doll's neck.

The wind ripped leaves from the trees and filled the air with whirling gold. Dad tried to capture the last of the foliage, but the color had peaked and many of the trees were bare.

His camera swinging from its strap, his hiking stick in hand, Dad chose a trail that led uphill, winding around boulders and outcrops of trees. After a while we came to a steep drop-off on one side of the trail, not exactly a cliff, but high enough to do serious harm, maybe even kill you, if you fell. Just looking down, down, down at the rocks far below was enough to make me step back toward the safe side of the trail, far from the edge.

Erica froze and clung to Dad's hand. "I'm scared of high places," she whispered. "Can we turn around and go home now?"

Leaving Dad to convince Erica that he wouldn't

let her fall, I ran ahead, bounding from rock to rock. If I'd been looking where I was going, I might not have tripped on a tangle of roots half hidden in the fallen leaves, but the next thing I knew, I was flat on the ground on my belly. Struggling to get my breath, I looked through the weeds at a chimney pointing like a finger at the sky.

Scrambling to my feet, I followed an overgrown path to the ruins of an old log cabin that was slowly sinking into the earth. Overgrown with dying vines, shielded by brambles, its walls tilted and sagged. Part of the roof had collapsed under the weight of a fallen tree, but the stone chimney was straight and true.

"Dad, Erica!" I yelled. "There's an old cabin here!"

They made their way through the weeds and undergrowth, Dad leading and Erica following, clutching her doll as if she might be in danger.

We walked around the cabin. Dad took dozens of pictures from every possible angle. He even got down on his stomach to get a different perspective.

"Can we go inside?" I asked.

"I don't see why not." Laughing, Dad knocked at the door. "Just in case."

When he pushed the door open, a buzzard flew out. Dad and I leaped out of its way, and Erica screamed.

"It's just a big bird," Dad told her. "A black buzzard. Nothing to be scared of."

The buzzard landed on a limb and hunched there, staring at us in disapproval. Suddenly he lifted his wings and took off, vanishing into the sky like a streak of black feathers shot from a bow.

"Quoth the buzzard, 'Nevermore,'" Dad said.

Erica looked worried. "Can we go home now?"

"Don't you want to go inside?" Dad asked.

"No." She peered into the darkness beyond the door. "Somebody might be hiding in there."

"Oh, come on." Dad took her hand and led her through the doorway, which was so low he had to stoop to go through it, and I followed close behind.

A little daylight filtered through the vines covering the windows, layers and layers of them twisted together like tangled ropes. The dirt floor reeked of mold. The air smelled of rot and decay and old ashes. I shivered in the damp cold. Suddenly I wanted to go back outside where the sun shone and the air was fresh.

"It smells bad in here," Erica whispered. "Please, Daddy, can we go home?"

"Let's explore first," Dad said. "You never know what you might find in an old place like this."

Although I would never have admitted it, I didn't want to be inside the cabin any more than Erica did. Cobwebs hung like curtains from the rafters; things scuttled in the shadows—mice, insects, I guess. Weird funguses grew in the dampness. What if we dislodged something and the rest of the roof caved in? We'd be buried alive.

While Erica waited in the doorway, I took a few steps into the cabin. Dad unearthed old bottles, broken pottery, chipped plates and cups—artifacts, he said, to take home and photograph. He was particularly pleased to come across the skulls and bones of several small animals—foxes, raccoons, squirrels, he guessed, that had sheltered and died there.

The little bones were too much for Erica. She retreated to a low stone wall on the edge of the woods and sat in the sun, her head close to her doll's head, having one of her imaginary conversations.

I didn't like the bones any more than my sister did. I didn't like the moldy smell or the damp cold

47

either. In fact, I didn't like anything about the cabin, and I wished Dad would finish taking pictures and get out of there.

"I'm going outside," I told him, "to keep Erica company."

"Okay. I'll be done in here soon, just a few more minutes." With his back turned, he busied himself poking around in a broken-down cupboard, going through things that once belonged to a long-gone stranger.

I sat beside Erica on the wall, glad for the sun on my back and the smell of autumn leaves.

"I want to go home," she said.

"Me, too."

"I wish his camera battery would die."

"Yeah. How many pictures can he take, anyway? There's nothing in there but trash and broken stuff."

"And bones." Erica swung her legs harder, banging her heels. "I don't like bones."

While she smoothed Little Erica's hair, I watched a fuzzy brown caterpillar crawl slowly over the stones. He had a wide black stripe across his back, and I tried to remember if that meant a cold winter was coming.

The longer I sat on the wall, the more I noticed

rustling noises in the woods behind us. An animal, I told myself, moving around in the fallen leaves and underbrush. I turned and peered into the trees, but saw nothing. My neck itched. Someone was there. Maybe Brody and his friends had followed us.

Erica moved closer to me. "Do you hear it now?" she asked.

"Hear what?"

"The whispering." She dropped her voice so low I could barely hear her. "Air-ric-cah, Air-ric-cah—it's calling me. Who is it? What does it want?"

Despite the sun, I felt as if a shadow had passed over us. Even though I couldn't hear the whisper, I sensed that something was behind us in the woods, hidden, watching us. If I told Erica that, she'd be even more scared, so I said, "Nothing's calling you, Erica. You're imagining it."

"You must be deaf." Erica turned away from me and hugged the doll.

At last Dad came out of the cabin. Erica and I waited silently while he prowled around, taking pictures of anything and everything that stayed still long enough—glassless windows, splintered boards, the dark doorway, the chimney, tall weeds, tangles of thorns. He even lined up the things he'd found inside and took pictures of them arranged like still lifes on the wall. A little skull, a cracked plate, a few dead leaves, gloomy stuff.

Finally Dad said, "Come on, let's go." You'd think Erica and I, not him, were the ones who'd wanted to stay. He waved at his collection of junk. "We'll come back later with a bag and get this stuff."

Frankly, I hoped Dad would forget about coming back. I didn't want those things in our house. They'd belonged to someone once. Someone most likely dead by now. The past clung to them like a stain you couldn't wash away.

We headed down the trail toward home, with Erica and me just ahead of Dad. We went slowly, cautiously, watching our step on the steep trail. Sometimes it's harder to go down a hill than to climb it.

Dinner did not go well that night. Mom was upset about her job. Receptionist, ha. A glorified typist, that's all she was. Her boss was stupid and bigoted. He treated her like a servant—do this, do that, fix the coffee, go to Piggly Wiggly, pick up some pastries.

"Oh, you think that's bad," Dad muttered. "Try moving crates of stuff around a store the size of

Home Depot and some manager with a high school education tells you you're doing it wrong. Me doing it wrong. *Me* with an M.B.A. You think I like working there, wearing that big orange apron?"

I ignored them and tried to choke down the stew Mom had spent the afternoon cooking. When I complained that the meat was tough, Dad snapped that tough meat was all we could afford.

"It's got fat in it," Erica said.

"Well, then don't eat it." Dad pushed his chair back and left the table.

"Where are you going, Ted?" Mom asked. "You haven't finished your dinner."

"I'm an adult," Dad said. "I don't need permission to leave the table."

We sat in silence and listened to him climb the stairs. The door to his den closed. He'd spend the rest of the night in there, photoshopping his pictures.

Mom stared at his unfinished dinner. Erica hugged her doll and gazed into space. No one said anything. The shadows of the old house gathered around us.

FIVE

Dad spent more and more time staring at his computer instead of working on his photography. Mom sat in front of her loom and watched the bare trees sway in the wind, but she didn't touch the rug she'd begun weeks earlier. She drank coffee and smoked, an old habit she'd gone back to. It calmed her nerves, she claimed.

She played Joan Baez albums and sang along with sad ballads about death and sorrow. She knew all the words.

Worst of all, she lost interest in cooking. Ever since the night Erica and I complained about the stew meat, she'd begun buying canned soup and canned stew and frozen dinners that she cooked in the micro-wave. We ate grilled cheese sandwiches at least three nights a week.

Once in a while she came home with a rotisserie chicken from Piggly Wiggly or a pizza from Joe's. As if that were a treat. Back in Fairfield, we went out for pizza at gourmet places. We'd never have eaten one of Joe's pizzas, full of salt and fat and topped off with runny sauce and rubbery cheese.

Nobody said anything about the food. Nobody, not even Erica, complained. We sat at the table and ate what was on our plates. Our conversation con-sisted of requests for salt or pepper.

Dad worried about money and the leaking roof and dripping faucets. When he wasn't at Home De-pot, he wandered around the house making lists of repairs, but instead of doing them, he played games on his computer, something he'd always said was a waste of time.

Erica roamed the house with Little Erica. When I tried to talk to her, she had nothing to say. Every question produced an "I don't know" or a shrug of her shoulders.

Her conversations with the doll grew longer and more frequent. It made me both sad and angry to watch her living this strange imaginary existence. Sad because she used to be a happy, normal kid with real friends. Mad because she persisted in isolating herself from the family, which caused problems between Mom and Dad.

One day, before our parents came home from work, Erica and I were alone in the living room, trapped inside by a cold November rain. As usual, my sister was whispering to Little Erica. I slid closer to hear what she was saying, but she stopped talking and frowned at me as if I'd interrupted a private moment.

I was in a bad mood. I'd flunked another geography test. Someone left a sheet of notebook paper taped to my locker: "*Selene is gonna getcha.*" A boy named Caleb Rice tripped me in the hall and got a big laugh out of the kids who saw me take a tumble and drop all my books.

"That doll can't hear a thing you say," I said crossly.

"What do you know about dolls?"

"What everybody knows—everybody but you. They aren't alive."

"Think what you want." Erica smiled as if she knew things I didn't.

"Tell me one thing she can do that a real person does."

"She listens to me. Nobody else does. She talks to me, too. Nobody else does that either."

"Prove it," I said. "Make her say something."

"Little Erica only talks to me."

"You're such a liar." Disgusted with her and myself, I looked out the window. The van was coming down the driveway, its headlights slicing through the dark. "Mom and Dad are here."

Erica shrugged and started combing Little Erica's hair. "I wish I had a sister like *you* instead of a brother like Daniel." She spoke to the doll just loudly enough for me to hear.

The back door opened, and Mom and Dad came in, bringing the cold evening air with them. From the way they acted, neither speaking to nor looking at each other, I knew they'd been quarreling.

Back in the good old Connecticut days, they

hardly ever argued, but now it happened so often they barely spoke to each other without one making the other angry. Usually it was the house. The leak in the roof had gotten worse, and we had to set buckets out to catch the rain. Cold drafts sneaked in through every crack. Dad had figured out the furnace, but the house was never warm. Mom said we lived in a barn.

They were too busy arguing to pay much attention to either Erica or me. I don't think they realized how miserable we were. Or how much they'd changed.

At dinner that night, I said, "Maybe we should go back to Connecticut. Not Fairfield but someplace cheaper, like Bridgeport."

"Bridgeport?" Mom put down her fork and stared at me. "Do you really think we'd be happier in *Bridgeport?*"

"I don't know." I looked at her. "But the schools might be better."

"Doubtful," Dad said.

"They have Home Depots there," I said. "Lowe's, too."

"Oh, that's an inducement," Dad said. "I could

wear my nifty orange apron and show investment bankers where the restrooms are."

"Never mind." I left the table, only to hear raised voices behind me. Erica slunk past me and went to her room.

The days passed, rushing us toward winter. The house got messier. Books piled up in odd places. Newspapers and magazines littered floors and tabletops. Dirty dishes sat in the sink until we ran out of plates and then someone washed them. Nobody did the laundry until we needed clean underwear or socks. Dust balls collected under beds and furniture and in the corners of rooms.

I spent more time in the woods. The weather was turning colder, and the tall trees rocked and swayed over my head, making that sad sound bare branches make when the wind blows through them. I could see the mountains now, ridge after ridge, blue in the distance.

I didn't worry about getting lost—I always carried a compass in my pocket—but sometimes the woods scared me. Maybe it was the solitude, maybe it was being in the presence of so many tall trees, but I'd find myself looking over my shoulder. I'd stop and listen. Branches sawed and scraped against each other. A twig snapped. The bushes rustled. I never saw anything, and I never told anyone, but sometimes I thought something was following me.

I'd think of the man—or whatever I'd seen—on the edge of the woods that night. I'd never seen him again, but what if he was following me, watching me from hidden places, waiting for the right opportunity to—to what? To kill me? Kidnap me? Harm me in some way?

I told myself not to be silly, it was just squirrels or birds rustling the bushes or the wind blowing high and lonesome over my head, but a little voice from a dark part of my mind kept whispering, *What if it's something else? What if it's something dangerous? What if Brody wasn't lying about the things in the woods?*

One afternoon I took the wrong trail and came out of the woods two or three miles down the road from our house. It was already late, and while I walked, the sun dropped below the top of the mountains. Soon I was stumbling along in the dark, wishing

I'd brought a flashlight, wishing I had a dog. I'd asked Dad if we could go to animal rescue and get one, but he said we couldn't afford an extra mouth to feed. He'd looked so depressed, I never asked again.

In the thick dark of the woods, I heard the rustling, snuffling sounds of a large animal nosing in the fallen leaves. I smelled something disgusting—rotten leaves, mildew, decay. A bear, it must be a bear. I'd seen black bears on my hikes, but never so near that I could smell them.

Just as I was about to run, I heard a car behind me. I moved to the edge of the road. An old Ford slowed to a stop. The driver rolled down his window.

"What are you doing out here all by yourself?" he asked. "It's getting dark, and look at you, wearing jeans and a black jacket. You're lucky I saw you."

I backed away. The man was a stranger, and I was alone on a dark road. He could grab me and throw me into his car and drive away.

Which was worse—being kidnapped or being attacked by a bear?

"You must be the kid who lives in the old Estes place," the man said. "You want a ride home?"

I shook my head. My feet were tangled up in vines, and I was scared that I was trapped. "That's okay. I like to walk," I stammered.

"In the dark? Who knows who might come along and get you?" Then he laughed. "Oh, I see, you think *I'm* going to get you. Is that it?"

He opened the car door. The overhead light came on, and I saw an old man with white hair. "I'm Mr. O'Neill from up the road a ways. I know your dad, Ted Anderson. Nice fella. Helps me carry stuff to my car at Home Depot. Come on, get in before you get yourself run over."

Mr. O'Neill looked harmless. He knew Dad's name and where he worked. "Thanks," I said. Lurching out of the vines, I slid into the car.

"What were you doing way out here?" he asked.

"Hiking," I told him. "I took the wrong turn on one of the trails."

"Lucky I came along. You won't catch me traipsing around in the woods all by my lonesome. Hasn't anybody told you about Bloody Bones?"

"Bloody Bones?" I laughed. "That's just a silly old scary story about a monster coming up the steps one at a time to get you."

"That's not the real story. Not by a long shot. There's a lot more to Bloody Bones than that." He peered at me. "You ever come across an old, fallen-down cabin up on a hill?"

"My dad and my sister and I went there once. Dad took pictures of it."

"Well, that cabin once belonged to Old Auntie. She was a conjure woman. You know what that is?"

"A witch?"

He nodded. "Well, Old Auntie lived by herself, save for this big old razorback hog she kept as a pet. She took that mean, ugly critter with her everywhere she went. Some folks said that hog walked on his hind legs like a man, and I believe he did."

He pulled into our driveway and let the engine idle. "Well, one day Old Auntie couldn't find her hog anywhere. She searched high, she searched low—no sign of him. So she got out her conjure pot and made a potion she could see things in. And you know what she saw?"

I shook my head.

"She saw this nasty old feller that lived up in the mountains. He'd been hunting razorback hogs. One of the hogs he caught was her pet. That sneaking, thieving rascal slaughtered all the hogs and skinned them and carved off their meat and threw what was left in a heap. In that pile, Old Auntie saw her hog's bald head and bloody bones. So she cast a spell to summon him back from the dead. His bones put themselves together and rose up on their hind feet. His skull jumped on top of the bones, and off he danced. On the way to the sneaking, thieving rascal's house, he got some claws from a dead bear, some teeth from a dead panther, and a tail from a dead raccoon."

Mr. O'Neill paused to look at his watch. "It's later than I thought. Guess I'll have to make a long story a mite shorter. The hog killed that lying, thieving rascal—tore him clean apart with the panther's teeth and ate him up. Then he dug his grave with the bear's claws and brushed the ground smooth with the raccoon's tail. He left that lying, thieving rascal's bones up there in the rocks all by himself. Folks round here say you can still hear him howling and moaning and screaming when the wind blows just right."

Even though I knew it was just a story, one I'd heard around a campfire at Boy Scout camp, Mr. O'Neill had a way of making it sound real. The dark woods and the lonely road and the wind swaying the treetops added a lot to the telling, or maybe it was because I was already half terrified, but the old man definitely had a knack for scaring people.

Trying to hide my fear, I asked him what happened to the hog.

"Well, he dressed himself in that lying, thieving rascal's overalls and went home to Old Auntie, raccoon tail and all."

He paused a moment. "From then on, he became known as Bloody Bones. There's not a child in this valley who's not scared of him."

"It's just an old story kids tell," I muttered, but my heart beat a little harder than normal at the idea of Bloody Bones. Suppose he was what I'd heard and smelled. What if he was just about to pounce on me when Mr. O'Neill came along and saved my life?

"And I tell you Bloody Bones still roams the woods," Mr. O'Neill said. "He got a liking for human flesh when he ate that lying, thieving rascal."

"Oh, sure." I tried hard not to look past the headlights into the unknowable dark surrounding the car. If Bloody Bones hid in the trees, I didn't want to see him.

"Don't you *Oh, sure* me, son." Mr. O'Neill looked hard at me. "To this day, people have a way of disappearing in these woods."

He leaned across me and opened the door. "You mind getting out here? I'm a little late for an appointment in town. Or would you rather I drive you all the way home?"

I sat in the brightly lit car. The headlights faded into the night a few feet up the driveway. The woods were dark, and the wind was blowing through treetops as bare as bones. Who knew what was out there?

"I walked pretty far today," I said in a low voice. "And I'm really tired. Would you mind driving me to the house?"

Mr. O'Neill chuckled and said he'd be glad to, seeing as how I was too tired to walk up the driveway. I could almost hear quotation marks around *tired*.

When the car stopped at the end of the driveway, I saw my sister looking out the window at us. She held Little Erica up so she could see, too.

"That your little sister?" he asked.

I nodded.

"She's a pretty little thing," he said. "Take good

care of her, son. Don't let her go wandering off like . . ." His voice trailed off.

"Like Selene?"

"Oh, you heard that story, did you?"

"From Brody Mason."

Mr. O'Neill sighed. "He's a sad case, that boy. His mama died a few months back, and he and his daddy are having a hard time. No telling what he'll tell you, but in the case of Selene, it's the honest-to-God truth."

"Did she really disappear?"

"Yes, she did. No one found her. No one knows what happened to her." He paused a moment. "Lord, that was fifty years ago."

"Did you know her?"

He nodded. "I knew the whole family. She and my daughter Eleanor were best friends. She played at our house or Eleanor played at her house almost every day. It just about broke Eleanor's heart when Selene vanished."

"What happened to the Estes family afterward?"

He sighed. "They moved about a year later. By then, they knew she wasn't coming back. We never knew where they went. After what happened, I reckon they didn't want anything to do with this place."

I had more questions, but Mr. O'Neill looked at his watch again and said, "Time for me to hit the road, son."

I got out of the car. "Thanks for the ride."

"Glad to do it. Say hi to your dad for me."

When I opened the kitchen door, Mom asked who brought me home.

"Mr. O'Neill. He knows Dad."

"He's a nice old fellow," Dad said. "I enjoy talking to him at work."

Mom frowned at me. "What have I told you about taking rides with strangers?"

"He wasn't a stranger, Mom. You heard Dad. He knows him."

"But *you* didn't know him," Mom said. "He could have been lying. He could have kidnapped you. Promise me you'll never do that again!"

"Now, Martha," Dad said. "We aren't in Connecticut anymore."

"No, we certainly aren't." With that, Mom yanked a frozen pizza out of the oven and called Erica to the table.

I was dying to ask Dad if Mr. O'Neill had ever told him about Bloody Bones, or if he'd talked to him about Selene Estes, but Erica was sitting across the table, picking at her food and smearing dabs on Little Erica's face. She had enough trouble sleeping without imagining Bloody Bones sneaking up the stairs to get her.

I figured it was best to keep quiet and eat my dinner. I'd ask Dad later, when he was alone.

But after dinner Dad secluded himself in his den. Mom stood at a living room window, a cigarette in her hand, and stared into the darkness. Erica sat on the couch and watched Mom. "Will you read to me, Mommy?" she asked.

"Not right now, Erica." Mom left the window and went to the kitchen.

My sister and I looked at each other. "She's crying," Erica said.

I sat down beside her. "I know."

"Nobody's happy anymore," Erica said.

"Yeah, I've noticed."

"It's this house. We never should have come here." She leaned toward me. "Do you ever feel like something bad will happen?"

I could have said *All the time, every minute,* but I kept my thoughts to myself. "Like what?" I asked.

Erica gazed past me into the fire blazing on the hearth. "I don't know, just something." She smoothed Little Erica's hair. "Those whispers," she added. "They're getting louder. They keep me awake at night. Are you sure you never hear them?"

"Like I told you, it's just the wind or the floorboards creaking. Old houses make lots of noises."

"The wind doesn't say people's names."

Mom came back and sat down beside Erica. Picking up *The Middle Moffat,* she asked, "What chapter are we on?"

As Mom began to read, I studied her face. Her eyes were red, and so was her nose. I wanted to ask her what was going on between her and Dad. Were they getting divorced? But I knew she'd say, *Don't be silly, Daniel. Nothing's wrong. Everyone has arguments sometimes.* That's the problem with families—too many things no one wants to talk about.

Since I wasn't interested in the Moffat family, I left Erica and Mom snuggled under a blanket and climbed the stairs to the second floor. Down the hall, a strip of light shone under Dad's door. I heard explosions and gunfire, which meant he was playing one of his war games.

Downstairs, Mom and Erica laughed about something Rufus Moffat said.

I'd never felt so alone in all my life.

The Dolly

It begins with a whisper in the dark, always the girl's name, always long and airy. The old woman blows it through keyholes and cracks. She guides it upstairs and down until it finds the girl's ear and nestles there. Air-ric-cah . . . No one can hear it but the girl.

The girl has trouble sleeping, she's fearful, she withdraws and spends most of her time with the dolly. Perfect. The old woman gives the dolly a sweet voice. The dolly uses her sweet voice to tell the girl she loves her, but no one else does. She tells the girl she understands how she feels, but no one else does. Especially her brother. He hates her, doesn't she know that? Hasn't she always known that?

The girl tells the doll how unhappy she is. The children at school are mean to her. They laugh at her clothes, they laugh at the way she talks. On the playground, they gather in groups and turn their backs. Her brother is mean to her too. Her parents pick on her. They love her brother more than they love her. The doll agrees with everything the girl tells her.

One day, when winter is closing in and the nights are long, the dolly tells the girl she wants to go to the woods. The girl is afraid of the woods, she never goes there. She stays inside by the fire where it's warm. She reads to the dolly, she talks to the dolly, she shares her unhappiness with the dolly.

But the dolly insists. She has secrets she will share with the girl, but only if they are outside in the woods where no one can hear and no one can see. "If you really love me," the dolly says, "you'll do as I ask. If you refuse me, I'll stop talking to you. I'll be what your brother says I am—a lump of plastic. Is that what you want?"

Of course it's not what the girl wants. She puts on her parka and her hat and her gloves, and she goes out into the cold with the dolly. The wind blows her name through the air. It's taken up by a flock of crows and passed on into the darkness – Air-ric-cah, Air-ric-cah . . .

The dolly shows her a path. "This must be a secret," she warns the girl. "You mustn't tell anyone what we see or do here."

And so it continues.

SIX

As the days passed, Erica and I spent less and less time together. While she spent her afternoons reading and drawing and playing with her stupid doll, I roamed the woods, exploring trails and searching for hawks. Thanks to my binoculars and Peterson's *Field Guide to Birds of North America,* I could identify red-tailed hawks, sharp-shinned hawks, and Cooper's hawks. I knew the difference between black buzzards and turkey buzzards. Once, I'd even seen a bald eagle.

At first I tried to persuade Erica to come with me, but she'd said no so often, I gave up asking. Fine.

Let her mope around the house with Little Erica. It was obvious she'd rather talk to a doll than to me. Pretty insulting, I thought.

On the school bus, we sat next to each other, but we didn't talk to each other and no one talked to us. Erica stared out the window, as if she expected to see something in the woods. I stared straight ahead, trying not to listen to the other kids laughing at the snobs from Connecticut.

One day after school I left the house in such a hurry I forgot my binoculars. I'd been watching a red-tailed hawk for a few days, and I needed the binoculars to see him in the woods. Annoyed at myself, I hurried home just in time to see my sister disappear into the woods on the other side of the house.

I stopped where I was, puzzled. Erica hated the woods—what was she up to? Maybe I should follow her and find out. Hadn't Mr. O'Neill told me to keep an eye on her?

Keeping a good distance between us, I walked as silently as if Erica were a bird I didn't want to frighten away. She'd taken a narrow path that meandered through the woods like a deer trail, circling around boulders and trees. Every now and then she stopped and stared into the underbrush as if she were looking for something.

Finally she came to a clearing and sat on a fallen tree. Cuddling her doll, she began whispering, just as if someone was with her—not the doll, but a person. I peered into the bushes around her, but I didn't see anyone. At least I don't *think* I did—it was more like I sensed a presence.

But no, that was crazy. All I heard was a whisper of wind prying leaves from branches. All I saw were shadows. I backed away from Erica. If she wanted to sit in the woods and hold imaginary conversations, let her. Why waste my afternoon spying on her?

Without making a sound, I crept away, retrieved my binoculars, and went in search of the red-tailed hawk.

By the time I came home, it was almost dark. Erica was sitting on the couch reading to Little Erica, exactly what she'd been doing when I'd left the house.

I lit the fire and sat beside her. "Have you been here all afternoon?"

She looked up from her book. "Of course. Where else would I be?"

"It's such a nice day, sunny and everything, I thought you might have gone outside to play for a while."

The doll regarded me with her usual blank stare, but Erica frowned at me. "You know I hate the woods."

I was about to accuse her of lying but then decided against it. Maybe I'd follow her again tomorrow, just in case I'd missed something.

Suddenly Erica leaned toward me and asked one of her typical out-of-nowhere questions. "Do you ever have secrets, Daniel?"

"Sometimes. Why? Do you?"

"Maybe," she said softly. She smiled and gazed into the fire.

"What do you mean 'maybe'? Either you do or you don't."

Instead of answering, Erica began reading to the doll again. "'Once upon a time a woodcutter had two children, a boy named Hansel and a girl named Gretel—'"

"About your secret," I said, "the one you may or may not have. Has it got anything to do with the woods?"

"I'm reading to Little Erica now," my sister said. "Don't interrupt me."

I wanted to snatch the book out of her hands and throw it into the corner and hurl the doll after it. Instead, I left my sister and the doll on the couch and went to the kitchen to make myself a peanut butter sandwich. As I ate, I heard Erica reading "'Nibble nibble, mousekin'" in a scary witch's voice, much deeper and raspier than her normal voice. I almost got up to see if someone else was in the living room.

The Secret

The old woman waits in the woods, but you wouldn't recognize her. She has taken the form of the girl in the cabin. She watches Erica sit down on a log, just where the dolly tells her to sit. Good. The girl is biddable. She does as she's told.

The old woman comes closer. She smiles shyly and waits for Erica to notice her.

"Who are you?" Erica is startled, but not afraid, as she would be if the old woman had come as herself.

The old woman wears a gray plaid dress with a round collar. Her hair is red and curly. Her face is sweet and sad.

"I come to be your friend." The old woman speaks in a soft, childish voice that soothes the girl.

"I don't have any friends," Erica whispers.

"You got yourself one now." The girl sits on the log beside Erica. "That's a mighty pretty dolly you got. Can I hold her?"

Erica holds the dolly tighter. "She's very special."

"Please." The girl reaches for the dolly. "I ain't never seen a dolly so pretty as that."

Erica looks distrustful, but the dolly whispers, "Let her hold me, it's all right."

Reluctantly, Erica hands the little girl her dolly.

"Oh, I wish I had me a dolly like this one," the little girl says.

Rocking the doll in her arms, she croons a little song. The tune is familiar, but Erica can't make out the words.

Later, when Erica goes home, she doesn't remember what happened in the woods. It's a secret, even from herself.

After that, the old woman in her little-girl shape meets Erica in the woods every day. She tells her she lives with her sweet old auntie in a pretty little cabin on the tippity top of a hill. "She loves me ever so much," the old woman says in the little-girl voice. "More'n anybody ever did."

"More than your mommy and daddy?" Erica asks.

"My mama and daddy never loved me. They made me work hard at chores and beat me black-and-blue and made me sleep on the floor by the fireplace 'cause I was so bad."

"My parents would never do that."

"Oh yes, they would. Parents never love their little ones. They can't wait to get rid of them. You'll see. One day they'll get fed up with you and start treating you bad, just the way mine did."

Erica stares at her, and the little girl smiles. Things are going well. Erica believes everything the girl tells her. "They already love your brother more than you."

"It's true," Erica says. "They've always loved Daniel best."

"My auntie's keeping an eye on you," the little girl says in her sweet little, false little voice. "She loves you even though you don't know it yet, and she aims to rescue you and bring you to her cabin, where me and you will live like sisters."

The little girl pats Erica's hand. "Come live with us

afore they start into beating you and scolding you and making you sleep by the fire. Why, they could kill you dead one night."

Erica draws back a little. "You're scaring me."

The little girl says, "There ain't nothing to be scared of. Come away with me, and I'll keep you safe."

"Will I have to go to school?"

"School? No indeed. Old Auntie got no use for school. She'll teach you all you need to know."

Erica nods her head. Yes, she'll come with the little girl. And stay with her and Old Auntie. And never go to school again. Maybe not today, maybe not tomorrow. But soon.

The old woman sees the brother watching from the woods. He can't see her, but he knows someone is there. "I must go," she whispers to Erica, and slips away into the woods.

SEVEN

The next day, I left the house with my binoculars and my bird book, but instead of going to the woods, I hid in the tall weeds near the house and waited. It was a colder day and windy, but in a few minutes Erica ran out the back door, darted across the yard, and disappeared into the woods.

She took the same path, turned off into the clearing, and sat on the fallen tree. Her bright blue scarf blew in the wind, and her red hair swirled.

Hiding behind a tall maple, I watched her closely. Once in a while she whispered to the doll, but for the most part she neither moved nor spoke. She sat still and stared into the woods—waiting, I thought, but for what? Definitely a girl with secrets. No "maybes" about it.

The wind yanked the last of the leaves from the trees and sent them flying through the air. They rustled and sighed and sank to the ground in brown and yellow heaps. Some settled in Erica's hair and on her shoulders. Others landed on Little Erica.

Nothing distracted my sister. Not the falling leaves. Not the squirrel chattering on a branch over her head. Not the crow cawing from the top of a dead tree. She sat so still, I thought she must be holding her breath.

Suddenly she stood up and took a step or two toward the dead tree. She held the doll tightly and whispered to her.

While I watched Erica, I glimpsed a shadow drifting toward her through the trees—dark and formless, like a wisp of fog or smoke. I couldn't tell what it was—an old woman, a little girl, an animal—something small and dangerous, I could sense it. Behind it was something else, something worse, a shadowy, bony thing, taller than a man.

"Erica!" I shouted. "Stop, don't go near it! Run!"

My sister turned to me. "Daniel! What are you doing here?"

The shadow, or whatever it was, vanished, but I grabbed Erica and started pulling her away. "What's wrong with you? Can't you see? There was something there!"

"Let me go!" she screamed. "Let me go!"

"No. You're coming home, right now!"

"My doll," she cried, "my doll."

Little Erica lay on the ground where my sister had dropped her, her face in the leaves.

"I have to get her!" Erica twisted and turned, kicking me, flailing her arms. "She wants her! She'll take her!"

"Who wants her?" I yelled. "Who'll take her?"

Erica didn't answer, but she struggled even harder to get away from me, crying and screaming. Holding her was like holding a cat that doesn't want to be held. She didn't have claws or sharp teeth, but she managed to bite me twice and scratch my face.

But I didn't let her go. And I didn't pick up the doll.

Out of the woods at last, I saw Mom and Dad

getting out of the van. When they saw me hauling Erica through the weeds, they hurried toward us.

"What's going on?" Dad shouted. "Are you all right?"

With a burst of strength, Erica broke away and ran to Mom and began a sobbing account of what happened. "I was playing in the woods," she cried, "and all of a sudden Daniel grabbed me and started dragging me home. He said I wasn't allowed to be in the woods. He made me leave Little Erica there — she's lying on the ground all by herself."

Dad and Mom looked at each other. "You take care of Daniel," Mom said to him. "I'll get Erica into the house. She's hysterical."

"No." Erica began struggling again. "I have to get Little Erica. I can't leave her there!"

"It's almost dark," Dad said. "We'll get the doll tomorrow."

"No, no! I'll never see her again." Erica thrashed about wildly, more like a cat than before.

"Take her to the house, Ted," Mom cried. "I can't hold her!"

Dad got a firm grip on Erica, picked her up,

and carried her toward the house. Her shrieks finally stopped when the back door closed behind Dad.

Mom turned to me. "What's this about? Why wouldn't you let her get the doll?"

"There was something in the woods, something dark and scary." Words tumbled out of my mouth. I didn't think about what I was saying. I didn't try to stop myself. "I had to get her away from it."

Mom looked at me as if I'd lost my mind. "What are you talking about?"

"I don't know. I saw it. I was scared. I thought it was going to grab Erica. She was just standing there, like she was paralyzed or something."

Mom put her hands on my shoulders and gave me a little shake. "Daniel, how often do I need to tell you? No one is going to take you or Erica. No one is going to disappear."

I took a deep breath and tried to calm down. I wanted to believe Mom. I hadn't seen anything in the woods. Neither had Erica. It was all my imagination. Selene Estes had disappeared, but she hadn't been taken by Bloody Bones. He was a legend, he wasn't real. I couldn't have seen him.

But no matter what I told myself, I knew I'd seen

something. I couldn't explain it. I didn't know what it was, but it had been there.

After Erica cried herself to sleep, I talked Dad into going to the woods with flashlights to look for the doll. I didn't want to leave the house, but I felt bad about leaving Little Erica in the woods. That doll was just a hunk of plastic to me, but to Erica she was almost a real person.

When we opened the back door, a gust of wind blew leaves into the kitchen. They skittered across the floor and settled in corners as if they'd been waiting to come inside.

It took all of Dad's strength to pull the door shut behind us. The night was biting cold. An almost full moon lit the field.

At the edge of the woods, we turned on our flashlights. The wind tossed the trees, and their shadows danced over the path, crossing and crisscrossing the ground, making it hard to see.

I stayed close to Dad and aimed the flashlight at the ground. Nothing looked familiar. It was as if we'd taken a different path, one you could find only at night. I heard noises in the undergrowth. I imagined creatures you'd never see in daylight scurrying through the dead leaves. I kept my eyes on the path so I wouldn't see anything in the shadows on either side of me.

After we'd walked for half an hour or so, Dad stopped. His flashlight probed the dark, picking out one tree, then another. An owl was caught in the beam for a moment, its eyes huge and shining. Without giving me time to identify him, he flew soundlessly into the woods.

"Are you sure we're going the right way?" Dad asked.

"I think maybe we passed the clearing," I admitted. "I don't remember it being this far."

"I told you we should wait until morning to look for that doll."

I shone my flashlight behind us. "It all looks the same in the dark."

"So I noticed," Dad said.

We turned around and walked back the way we'd come. Dad studied every tree, every boulder, every fallen log.

He asked the same questions over and over. "Is this it? Does that tree look familiar? Do you think we're close?"

My answer was always the same. "I don't know."

After a while, Dad came up with new questions. "Did you scare Erica on purpose? Why didn't you stop and let her get the doll? Were you teasing her? Bullying her?"

"No," I said. "No. I saw something, Dad. I thought—"

He shook his head. "You *saw* something. All this because you *saw* something. What's wrong with you? I've been all over these woods and never seen anything out of the ordinary."

Bumbling and stumbling ahead of me, Dad thrashed at dry weeds and dead vines with a stick. Everything was my fault—my fault Erica was hysterical, my fault the doll was missing, my fault we couldn't find the clearing, my fault we were wandering around in the woods freezing our butts off.

"I give up," Dad said. "The doll's gone, and your sister is heartbroken. You should feel really great about that."

Dad had never talked to me this way. He got mad so easily now. So did Mom. Erica was unhappy and secretive and strange. I was miserable in school. And lonely. Nothing was right.

Without speaking to each other, Dad and I left the woods and trudged across the field. In the cold and windy dark, the house looked warm and inviting. Lights shone from the windows, smoke rose from the chimney, but it was like a mirage. Up close, inside the house, the warmth and happiness vanished.

No one spoke at breakfast. Mom slammed bowls of cold cereal down in front of Erica and me. She and Dad had already eaten and were getting ready to leave for work.

Before she left, Mom hugged Erica. "Please don't look so sad, sweetie. You and Daniel can look for Little Erica when you get home from school. In the daylight, you're sure to find her."

Erica didn't say anything. She sat with her head down, her cereal untouched, tears trickling down her cheeks.

"Erica, I promise I'll find her," I said. "I don't know what got into me. I thought—"

"That's enough, Daniel," Mom said. "Forget about what you thought you saw in the woods. You're just making matters worse."

"But Mom—"

Outside, Dad blew the horn, already annoyed.

"I have to leave." Mom grabbed her purse and fumbled with the zipper on her parka. The horn blew again.

"All right, all right," Mom muttered. To me she said, "Find the doll. Erica's very upset. She cried all night."

The door slammed shut, and the van drove away, its tires spraying gravel. I took Erica's untouched cereal and put our bowls and glasses in the sink. "We have to leave in ten minutes," I reminded her.

She nodded, but she didn't move from the table.

"Aren't you going to brush your teeth?"

No response. I did what I had to do in the bathroom and returned to find Erica sitting exactly where I'd left her.

I took her parka and mine off the hook. "Here, put this on."

Erica got up slowly and allowed me to help her with her jacket. "You should at least comb your hair," I told her. "You look terrible."

"Who cares what I look like?" Erica pulled on her mittens and a knit cap Mom had made for her. "Everyone at school hates me."

"Where are your schoolbooks?"

"I don't know."

I looked around and saw her book bag on the floor by the front door. From its weight, I knew her books were inside. "Did you do your homework?"

"No." Erica slipped the straps over her shoulder and followed me outside. The wind was cold and damp and smelled of winter.

Silently we walked down the driveway. Now that the trees were bare, we could see farther into the woods, all the way to the road.

"Erica," I said, "did you see anything in the woods? A sort of dark shape, a shadow maybe?"

"No."

"But you were sitting on that log, staring into the woods as if you were talking to somebody. And then you got up and walked straight toward whatever it was."

She shook her head. "That's what *you* thought I was doing."

"Well, what were you doing?"

"Nothing."

I wanted to shake the truth out of her, but I took a deep breath, counted to ten, and finally said, "You told me you had a secret. Is it something you do in the woods? Someone you see? Or talk to? Do you still hear whispers in the dark?"

Erica looked at me at last, her pale face closed tight. "A secret is something you don't tell anyone, Daniel. That's what it means."

"Does Mom know?"

"I just told you. It's only a secret if you don't tell anyone." With that, Erica ran down the driveway ahead of me.

I picked up a stone and threw it into the woods as far as I could. *Thonk*. It hit a tree and bounced off. I was frustrated. No matter what I asked, Erica would not give me an answer. Somehow, my seven-year-old sister was getting the best of me.

I caught up with her at the end of the driveway. Shivering in the wind, we waited silently for the bus. I'd given up talking to her. What was the point?

EIGHT

As soon as we boarded the bus, Mrs. Plummer noticed Erica's mood. "What's the matter, sweetie? You get up on the wrong side of the bed or something?"

Or something, I thought.

"It's my doll, Little Erica, you know—the one I told you about. My brother made me leave her in the woods, and now she's gone."

Mrs. Plummer turned around and looked directly at me. "Why on earth did you do something like that?"

As usual, I was being blamed. "It's kind of complicated," I said. "I thought, well, I won't tell you what I thought. It's dumb, and you wouldn't believe me. Let's just say I made a mistake, and I'm really sorry and I'll find the doll after school."

"He won't find her no matter how hard he looks." Erica turned her face to the window and pressed her nose against the glass. "She's been took," Erica whispered to herself in a voice so low I scarcely heard her.

Mrs. Plummer looked at me in the rearview mirror. "What makes you think I won't believe you?"

"My parents don't." She was slowing down to pick up Brody. With him getting on the bus, I couldn't tell her what I saw.

"Tell me later," Mrs. Plummer told me.

As usual, Brody gave me a nasty look as he walked past. He was heading for a seat at the back of the bus where he and his friends sat.

Ignoring him, I looked straight ahead, and Erica looked out the window. We rode in silence all the way to school.

My day was no worse than usual. A B-minus on a history report because I'd gotten a date wrong. A bloody nose in basketball—an accident of course. And so on and so on.

The bus ride home *was* worse than usual because

Erica still refused to speak to me. Without her to talk to, I had to listen to rude comments about my sweater, my haircut, my shoes, and who knows what. I wondered how the kids on the bus had entertained themselves before I'd had the bad luck to move to Woodville.

After Brody got off, Mrs. Plummer glanced at us in the rearview mirror once or twice, but she didn't have anything to say until she stopped at the end of our driveway. "I hope you find the doll, but be quick about it. It gets dark early, and I don't want you getting lost in the woods."

She shut the door and drove away, heading home, I guessed, to her husband and kids. We stood at the side of the road and looked down the driveway. The trees were a tunnel of darkness already.

"Let's go straight to the woods and look for your doll," I said.

"She won't be there," Erica said in the flat little voice she'd been using all day.

"Yes, she will." I took her hand to hurry her along, but she pulled away and ran ahead.

I chased her through the field's tall weeds and into the woods. In a few minutes I came to the dead tree, the clearing, and the fallen log. How had Dad and I missed it last night?

Erica waited for me, empty-handed. "She's not here."

"She must be." I ran around looking in piles of fallen leaves, under bushes, behind logs, even leaving the clearing to search the woods.

Erica stayed where she was, her arms folded across her chest, shivering.

"I don't understand it." I pointed to the place where I'd last seen Little Erica. "She was right there." I kicked at the leaves, scattering them, thinking the doll had to be under them.

Erica hugged herself as if she still held the doll in her arms. "She's been took."

"'Took'? That's how the kids in Woodville talk, not you and me. We say 'taken.' And besides, who took her?"

"Selene." The name dropped from Erica's lips like a stone. "The girl who lives on the tippity top of a hill with her old auntie."

"Are you crazy or just a liar? Selene disappeared fifty years ago. Nobody's seen her since."

Honestly, I wasn't as sure as I tried to sound. My

feeling of being watched, the darkness of the woods surrounding the house, Erica's behavior, the tension between Mom and Dad, the unhappiness we'd all sunk into—everything was wrong. Maybe, just maybe, it all tied in with Selene Estes. Or something else—I didn't know what.

My brain was muddled. My hands and nose were cold, and I wanted to go home, light the fire, and play games on my iPad.

Erica stared into the woods, at the very spot where I'd seen, or thought I'd seen, the shadow thing.

"You saw something yesterday," I said. "I know it."

"Suppose I did?" Erica's pale face looked spooky in the dim light, her eyes too big for her face and shadowed with dark circles.

"What did you see?" I stood over her. "I want to know!"

"It's a secret. I made a promise, I—" She was crying now.

Angry and frustrated by her silent, secret ways, I pulled her to her feet and shook her. Not hard, just a little. "I'm serious. There's something going on, and I need to know what it is."

"Let me go, let me go!" Erica struggled to get

away. It was just like the day before, and I was fed up.

"Tell me!" I shouted. "Tell me the truth, you little liar!" I let go of her and shoved her so hard she fell on her back in the leaves.

Scrambling to her feet, she glared at me like a wild thing. Her hair hung in her face; leaves clung to her jacket. "I hate you, Daniel! No matter what you do, you can't make me tell. Never never never!"

She spun around and dashed into the woods.

"Come back here!" I yelled.

I ran after her, slipping and sliding on fallen leaves, tripping on roots hidden beneath the leaves. A branch she'd brushed aside flew back and hit my eye. Its thorns clawed my face.

Smarting from pain, I shouted, "Go on, then, stupid! Run. You'll be sorry if you get lost and it's dark and cold and . . ." I stopped yelling because I couldn't hear her crashing through the bushes anymore.

Fine, I thought. *I brought her home yesterday. I'm not doing it again. Let her find her own way back, maybe it'll teach her a lesson.*

I turned away and followed the path back to the house. It was practically dark, and a cold wind hissed through the dry weeds. Erica wouldn't stay long in the woods. She probably knew a shortcut. When I got home, she'd be there, sitting on the couch, smirking because she'd beaten me. Mom would never know I'd let my sister run off into the woods without me.

The Taking

The old woman returns to the clearing and waits for Erica and her hateful brother. She leaves the dolly hidden in the woods near her cabin. She has another use for it.

She hears them coming before she sees them. Their voices are loud and angry.

The hateful brother can't believe the doll is gone, but Erica knows who took it. *That girl,* she tells him. *The one who lives with her auntie on the tippity top of a hill.* They fight, and the hateful brother pushes his sister. She falls backward into the leaves. Now she knows he hates her. She must find the cabin and the girl.

She scrambles to her feet and runs away from him. The old woman makes sure he gives up and goes home.

She lets Erica run until she's too tired to go farther. She watches Erica sink down on the ground and cry. She waits until the trees thicken with shadows. The wind blows harder, its breath as cold as death. Bloody Bones snuffles and snorts in the dead leaves, looking for grubs or voles, anything juicy or crunchy.

Erica hears him coming closer, step by shuffling step. She whimpers and cries and curls herself into a ball.

When the old woman is sure that Erica cannot run or put up a fight, she steps out of the woods in her own shape. Her ragged cloak billows around her gnarled body. Strands of white hair stream across her bony face. She stands over Erica, leaning on her staff, older than old, crueler than cruel, as wicked as the devil hisself.

"Air-ric-cah," she croons. "Air-ric-cah, come to Auntie."

Erica looks up. The old woman takes her arm and pulls her roughly to her feet. "You belong to me now. No one wants you but me, no one loves you but me. They've forgot all about you, and you've forgot all about them."

Smiling to herself, the old woman drags Erica through the woods to her cabin. She has what she wants.

NINE

When I slammed into the kitchen, Erica wasn't there. I called out, just in case, but there's something about an empty house. You always know when you're alone.

I pictured her taking her time coming home, sulking, mad, hoping I'd worry about her. Little brat. I couldn't stand my sister anymore. I was sick of her. Sick of her scenes. Sick of the doll. I hoped we'd never find it.

I smeared a thick layer of peanut butter on a piece of bread, poured myself a glass of cider, and went to my room to play games on my iPad. But for some reason I couldn't concentrate. The silence of the house pressed against my ears. A clock ticked. The refrigerator turned off and on. A gust of wind rattled the windowpanes. Noises you never heard except when there were no other noises.

I closed my iPad and went to the window. Where was Erica? I walked down the hall to her room. Maybe she'd been hiding there all the time, playing a trick on me. Yes, that must be it. She'd beaten me home, run upstairs, and hidden. It was just the sort of prank she'd pull.

Fully expecting to see her sitting on her bed, laughing at me, I flung open the door and flicked on the light. A row of stuffed animals sat on the window seat, staring at me with shiny round eyes.

I called my sister's name. I looked under her bed and in the closet, expecting her to jump out and scare me. No Erica.

As I turned to leave the room, I saw the van's headlights coming down the driveway. With a half-formed hope that Erica would be with Mom and Dad, I ran down the back stairs to the kitchen and opened the door before Dad had a chance to fumble with his key.

"Well, thanks, buddy." Dad brushed past me and set a case of wine down on the counter with a thud.

Mom was right behind him, balancing a stack of carryout cartons from Lucky's Chinese Restaurant. "No pizza tonight. Moo goo gai pan for you and me and Erica."

"And General Tso's chicken for me." Dad turned to the cupboard to get dinner plates. "Go fetch Erica so we can eat before the won ton soup gets cold."

"Why are you just standing there?" Mom asked. "What's wrong? Where's Erica?"

"She—" I took a deep breath, then started again. "She's not, she's, she's not—"

Mom left the kitchen. "Erica," she called. "Erica!"

Dad grabbed my shoulders and spun me around to face him. "What's going on, Daniel? Where's your sister?"

"She's not here, Dad. I don't know where she is. We had a fight. She wouldn't come home with me— she, she ran off—"

"She *ran off?*" Dad stared at me. "Why didn't you go after her? How could you let her run off?"

"I tried to stop her, Dad, but she was mad just like yesterday, and I—"

His eyes lit on the jar of peanut butter and the loaf of bread I'd forgotten to put away. "You came home and ate a sandwich? Is that what you did?"

"I thought she'd be here any minute. I never imagined she'd do something like this."

Mom reappeared. "She's not in the house, Ted."

Dad grabbed my shoulders again, harder this time. "Where did you last see her?"

"In the clearing. We were looking for the doll, but she wasn't there, and Erica wouldn't come home with me. She got mad. She said it was all my fault, and then she ran away from me, and I got mad at her and came home."

Dad swore softly. "Martha, you stay here in case she comes back. Daniel, grab your jacket and a couple of flashlights."

I followed Dad out into the cold, dark night. The wind was blowing harder now, and the trees sent wild rocking shadows across the driveway. In the woods, Dad began calling Erica. I joined in.

Erica, Erica, Erica. Her name bounced from tree

to tree, caught by the wind, tossed into the sky. But she didn't answer. She didn't come.

"Where are you?" Dad called, his voice scraped raw from shouting.

Are you, are you, are you, the trees repeated. Creatures in the underbrush rustled. An owl screeched.

Our voices sounded small in the noisy darkness.

We called her name again and again. We waved our flashlights in hope that she'd see their bobbing light. We were hoarse from calling. And desperate when she didn't answer.

The faint trail gave out, and we began circling back to the house without realizing it until we saw the lights in the windows.

"We need to call the police," Dad said. "We don't know the land the way they do. We'll get lost ourselves if we keep going."

Wordlessly, we made our way home. Mom was on the front porch, shivering in her warmest down coat. "You didn't find her?"

"No." Dad stopped to hug her. Mom clung to him. They stood there whispering to each other, as if they'd forgotten about me. I waited, shifting my weight from one frozen foot to the other, afraid Bloody Bones might be watching us from the trees.

Not that I believed he actually existed, not in my world, the real world, the five-senses world. But with the wind blowing and the moon sailing in and out of clouds like a ghost racing across the sky, I could almost believe I'd crossed a border into another world, where anything could be true—even conjure women and spells and monsters.

The police came sooner than we'd expected. We heard their sirens and saw their flashing lights before they'd even turned into the driveway. Four cars and an ambulance stopped at the side of the house. Doors opened, men got out. A couple of them had dogs, big German shepherds who pulled on their leashes, excited. Flashing lights washed the living room walls with red and blue.

"Why did they bring an ambulance?" Mom clung to Dad, her face a strange ashen color.

He frowned at the scene outside. "It's standard procedure when something like this happens."

Something like what? I wondered. No one was hurt. We didn't need an ambulance. Unless they thought—but no, Erica wasn't hurt, she was just lost. They'd find her fast with those dogs. I'd tell her I was sorry I got mad at her. I was scared, that was all. Scared of what? An old folktale? I shivered as a draft of cold air came creeping into the house. At my age, how could I be scared of a bogeyman?

Two policemen came inside and went upstairs. I heard their shoes clunking overhead. A policewoman sat down with us at the dining room table. She had questions: Erica's full name and age, a description of her and the clothes she was wearing, and the circumstances of her disappearance.

"Daniel was supposed to walk home from the school-bus stop with Erica," Mom said in a shaky voice, "but they had a fight, and, and—" She faltered and tried to brush away her tears.

The detective turned to me. "What was the fight about?" She'd been jotting things in a little notebook, and now she sat looking at me, waiting, her pen poised. She had stubby fingers and close-cut fingernails, no polish. No makeup either. A plain face, short hair. Not very friendly. Small, hard eyes. The name on her badge said Detective Irma Shank.

I told her what I'd told Dad, still leaving out any

mention of things in the woods or Selene Estes. My hands shook, and one leg jiggled without my being able to stop it.

"So he came home and ate a peanut butter sandwich," Mom said when I'd finished. "Then I imagine he went upstairs to play a game on his iPad. When we came home, he panicked and told us what happened."

While Mom talked, Detective Shank watched me, still jotting things down. "Is that what you did, Daniel?"

"Yes, but I thought Erica was playing a trick on me. She does things like that."

She looked at Dad and Mom, and they nodded. "Sometimes Erica is very willful," Dad said. "She's not happy here."

I wanted to say, *That goes for all of us,* but I kept my mouth shut.

"Where did you live before you moved here?"

"Fairfield, Connecticut," Dad said.

Detective Shank leaned across the table. "I know your daughter's only seven, but do you think she'd try to go back there?"

Dad and Mom looked at each other and shook their heads. None of us could picture Erica going to Connecticut. She had no money, and even if she did, what ticket seller would let her get on a bus all by herself?

"She's high-strung, fearful," Mom said. "I can't imagine her being outside in the dark—she's *afraid* of the dark. She sleeps with a light on." Now Mom began to cry in earnest. "She must be so scared. And so cold."

A policeman came inside. "We need something Erica has worn recently so we can set the dogs on her trail."

"And a recent photograph," Detective Shank added.

Dad went upstairs and came back with a pair of red socks Erica had worn the day before. Mom gave the police one of a recent set of school photographs.

"Beautiful little girl," Detective Shank said. "But such a sad expression." She looked at us with narrowed eyes, as if she were blaming us for everything.

The policeman went outside with the socks.

Through the window, I saw the dogs sniff the socks before the police led them into the field.

"I can't believe this is happening," Mom said. "It's like a nightmare."

"I know. I know." The detective patted Mom's hand. "Would you like tea?"

Mom nodded, and the woman went to the kitchen.

"Make yourself useful, Daniel," Dad said. "Show her where things are."

"Please don't blame me for this, Dad."

Dad looked around the room. "I don't see anyone else to blame."

In the kitchen, I went to the cabinet over the stove and got out cups and saucers. Detective Shank had already found tea bags and put the kettle on the stove.

While we waited for the water to boil, she looked at me. "When you and Erica were fighting, did you hit Erica, Daniel? Knock her down or hurt her somehow?"

Her question really upset me. Did she suspect me of harming Erica in some way or leaving her unconscious in the woods?

"I shoved her," I admitted, "and she fell down, but not hard. She jumped up and ran away from me."

"Are you sure that's all you did?"

"I'd never hurt my sister."

"Of course you wouldn't. Not on purpose." She looked at my face closely and touched the scratches on my cheek. "Did Erica do this?"

"It was a branch. She pushed it out of her way, and it swung back and hit me. The thorns scratched me, not my sister."

"What were you fighting about?"

"I told you. She was mad about the doll. She said it was my fault it was gone."

"Why did you prevent Erica from picking up the doll yesterday?"

"It was almost dark. We had to go home."

"I don't understand what difference it would have made to pick up the doll."

I started crying. I couldn't help it. "I should have let her get the doll. She really loves it. I wish I had, but I, I—I don't like being in the woods when it's dark."

The teakettle started whistling while I was trying to explain. Mom heard it, I guess, and came to the door. "What's going on?" she asked the detective. "Daniel's a minor. You have no right to question him without my permission."

"I'm just trying to understand why the doll was left in the woods yesterday, ma'am. It seems peculiar."

Mom turned off the stove, and the kettle's shrill whistle stopped. She put an arm around me, and I leaned against her, incredibly grateful for her protection. I'd begun to think that my whole family, as well as everyone else in Woodville, hated me, including Detective Irma Shank.

"I was scared," I finally admitted. "I was scared to stop for the doll."

"What were you afraid of?" Detective Shank shook her head, as if she didn't believe me. "You don't look like the sort of boy who's easily scared."

"I thought I saw something in the woods, in the shadows," I told her. "I was scared it was coming after Erica and me."

Detective Shank seemed unconvinced. Probably she'd already decided I had more to do with Erica's disappearance than I was saying.

Mom spoke up. "The children have been nervous, anxious. They're not used to living in the country with no neighbors. It's so dark at night. They're imaginative. They, they—"

Mom held me tighter. She was crying again. "Daniel has told you all he knows. Please spend your time searching for Erica. She's out there in the cold, and you're sitting here questioning Daniel as if you suspect him of harming his sister."

Detective Shank got to her feet. "Children often know more than they let on," she said with a glance at me. "I'm trying to understand all the aspects, ma'am. Believe me, I want to find your daughter as much as you do."

With that, the detective left the house and joined the police, who were now searching the shed.

"Do you still want tea, Mom?"

She nodded, and I made us both a cup. "Do you think Dad wants one?"

"He's outside, no doubt making a nuisance of himself." Cup in hand, she went to the window and stared past the reflection of the kitchen into the darkness beyond. "Where can she be, Daniel?"

Suddenly Dad barged into the kitchen with a couple of cops. He was holding Erica's knit hat, the one she'd worn yesterday. "One of the dogs found it caught on a branch," he said, "about a mile from here. A mile! How could she have gone that far?"

Mom took the hat and pressed it to her face. Crying softly, she continued to gaze into the darkness beyond the window.

"Where are the dogs?" I asked. "Are they still on Erica's trail?"

Dad gestured toward the squad cars and the ambulance still parked near the house. "Out there. They lost her scent not long after they found the hat."

I stared at Dad. "But they'll find her, right?"

"Yes, of course. Tomorrow they'll ask for volunteers to form lines and search the woods. It'll be better in the daylight. They can . . ." His voice dropped, and he stared out the window. "I can't believe this."

Before the police left, the officer in charge told us to get some sleep, to hope for the best. Erica was probably lost, but with the help of volunteer searchers, they'd find her tomorrow.

I can't speak for my parents, but I doubt they

slept much that night. I certainly didn't. For hours, I sat at my bedroom window, willing Erica to find her way out of the woods.

I'll never tease you again or get mad at you, I promised. *Just come home. Please, Erica, please come home. I'm so, so sorry.*

TEN

In the gray light of dawn I woke to the sound of voices in the kitchen. Mom was serving coffee to the volunteers who had brought doughnuts and Danish pastries and sticky buns. The whole house smelled like sugar, but I had no appetite for any of it.

Mom gave me a cup of hot chocolate. "Drink it," she said. "It's cold outside. Take some doughnuts or something."

She was pale, her eyes red and puffy from crying, and she was smoking. A woman from the Realtor's office told her to go back to bed, she looked terrible, but Mom insisted she was fine. "We're going to find Erica today," she said.

To please Mom, I took a doughnut and went outside. The police were talking to a bunch of people I didn't know, telling them what was expected of them. Form lines, walk an arm's length apart, examine every inch of ground. "If you see anything that may be connected with Erica, stop and call a policeman. Do not move it, do not touch it, leave it *in situ,* and wait for a policeman."

I edged away toward the woods. No one noticed me go. I had a crazy idea I could find Erica myself, be a hero, make up for leaving the doll and all that it had led to.

In the clearing where I'd last seen my sister, a crow perched in the dead tree. He cocked his head at me, cawed, and flew away. I sat down on the log and tried to think about where Erica might have gone.

I sat there for a while, but no ideas came to me. I stood up and called her, again and again, until my voice was as hoarse and raspy as a crow's. Her name rang in the air, bounced from tree to tree, echoed back to me. But she didn't answer. Nor did she come running out of the woods, her red curls in a tangle, her parka muddy—breathless, cold, hungry, elated to see me, Daniel, her rescuer.

"You won't find her that way."

I spun around, startled to see Brody standing a few feet away. He wore a ratty fringed suede jacket that looked as if it had once belonged to his mother. His bony knees stuck out of holes in his jeans, and his hair straggled over his eyes.

"What are you doing here?" I asked him.

"My dad's in the search party, so I thought I'd come along over and see what's going on. I heard you calling your sister's name. I doubt she'll hear you, no matter how loud you yell."

"She might hear me. Nobody knows how far away she is. She could be trying to find her way home right now. She could have fallen into a hole or something."

He edged closer to me, shuffling through leaves as he came. "Listen," he said in a low voice, "there's stuff about this place you don't know, stuff nobody's told you, mainly because you're such a stuck-up snot."

I stared at him suspiciously. His nose was running, and his eyes had a moist, pink look. If I was such a stuck-up snot, what did he want with me? Why was he here?

"What kind of stuff?" I found myself lowering my voice too.

He shrugged and took a quick look around. His eyes lingered on the dead tree. "You know what happened to Selene Estes, right?"

"You told me about her. Remember? On the bus—the first day I came to school."

Brody was almost whispering now. He kept looking at the dead tree. "Well, folks are saying your sister's been took, just like Selene was. And you won't ever see her again."

Took—there was that word again—how had Erica picked it up?

"Don't be so stupid, Brody. Selene disappeared more than fifty years ago. Whoever took her is dead by now—and so is Selene."

"Maybe," Brody said, "maybe not."

"Next you'll be telling me Bloody Bones took her."

"Nah, Old Auntie's got her. Ask anybody in Woodville. They'll tell you."

"Old Auntie lived a long time ago," I said. "She's definitely dead. If she even existed—which I doubt."

Brody shook his head. "She lives way back in the woods, up on Brewster's Hill. Every now and then somebody sees her at night, walking along the highway, collecting dead things. Her and Bloody Bones. That's what they eat. Roadkill."

"I don't believe you."

"You want me to take you to her cabin?" Brody asked, his eyes still boring into mine. "That's where everybody thinks she kept Selene. Maybe that's where your sister's at."

"I know where it is. I've been there with Dad and Erica. It's an old, falling-down ruin—nobody lives in it."

"In the daytime, yeah, but at night it looks like it used to."

"That's crazy," I said.

"I'm going up there," he said. "You can come if you like. Or not. Makes no matter to me what you do." He turned and started walking away.

I followed him. The fringe on his jacket blew

in the wind. The little beads sewed to it rattled and bumped together.

"What do you mean at night it's like it used to be?" I asked him.

"I mean," he said slowly, without bothering to look at me, "that it looks like it did when Old Auntie was alive."

"You just told me she's alive. Now you're saying she's dead?"

"No. What I'm saying is Old Auntie's a haunt come back from her grave."

I grabbed Brody's arm and made him stop and look at me. "Do you expect me to believe that?"

He shrugged. "Believe what you like." He turned his back again, but I wasn't through with him.

"This is what I think," I said. "You're dragging me up here to play some kind of trick on me. Which is really awful because my sister is missing and the whole town is looking for her and you're taking advantage of that to get me to go with you. I bet your friends are already up there, getting ready to scare me or something. What kind of kid are you?"

Brody backed away from me. "I'm not up to

anything. I want to help you find your sister, that's all."

We'd reached the steep part of the trail. The trees had thinned out, and the wind was blowing hard enough to knock me over the edge of the hill.

"Ghosts, monsters, places that are ruins in the daytime, but not after dark," I said. "It's all stupid lies, fairy tales. I'm going back to the house. Maybe they've found my sister."

"We're almost there," Brody said. "At least take a look."

I hesitated, stuck between climbing downhill and climbing uphill. I'd come this far, why not go a little farther? What if Erica really was there?

ELEVEN

From the trail, Brody and I climbed down into the hollow. Now that the leaves were gone, the cabin was more visible, but it looked as bad as it had the last time I'd seen it, maybe a little worse.

"Somebody's been here." Brody pointed at Dad's finds—broken stuff, old bottles, animal skulls, still lined up on the stone wall.

"My dad's a photographer. He was taking pictures of those things."

Brody stared at me as if I were even weirder than he'd thought. "You kidding me? Why would anybody take pictures of junk? You got all them beautiful mountains and you waste film on busted plates and broken bottles?"

"Dad's got a digital camera, so he's not wasting film," I said, "and besides, anybody can point a camera at a mountain. My dad's pictures are original. They tell stories."

"Well, let me tell you something. Nobody with any sense messes with Old Auntie's stuff. In fact, hardly anyone ever comes near this place."

"You're here."

"I ain't touched nothing of hers, and I ain't going inside. I'm just trying to help you, that's all."

Brody looked at the cabin's dark doorway. "You went in there, didn't you? That's why the door's open."

A cold wind riffled through the fallen leaves, sending them scurrying through the open door. I shivered, remembering the cabin's dark, damp, creepy atmosphere.

"I didn't stay inside long," I told Brody, "and Erica didn't go in at all. But Dad, well, he poked around, taking pictures, hauling stuff outside, and taking more pictures." I remembered how Erica and I had sat on the wall, barely speaking to each other. Her absence stabbed me with guilt.

Brody kicked at piles of dead leaves and watched then fly up into the air when the wind blew. "Harm's done, I reckon."

"What do you mean? What does all this have to do with my sister?"

He continued to kick at the leaves. "I ain't sure," he said, "but folks say Old Auntie takes a girl and keeps her fifty year—then lets her go and takes another one. It's been going on since folks first came to this place."

I wanted to hit him in his lying mouth. "That's the stupidest thing I've ever heard."

"All I know is, fifty years before Selene disappeared, a girl was took, and one was took fifty years before that."

I sat down on the wall where Erica and I had sat. Brody was an ignorant, superstitious idiot, and I didn't believe a word he said, but I wanted to find my sister, I wanted her to come home, and I wanted us all to go back to Connecticut, to the life we had before we came to this horrible place.

Brody shuffled through the leaves and sat beside me. "Here's what you should do," he said. "Come back here at night. Sneak up real quiet, and don't get too close. The cabin will be like it was two hundred years ago. Old Auntie will be in there, and your sister will be with her."

"How can I believe anything that crazy?"

"'Cause it's the truth." Brody was so close to me I could see his little gray teeth and the dirt rings in his neck. His pale eyes peered out from his tangled hair. "I swear."

The wind died down, as if it were waiting to blow my words across time and into Old Auntie's ears.

"Will you come with me?"

He shook his head and got to his feet. "Let's get out of here."

"Shouldn't we look inside before we go?"

He edged away from the ruins. "Not me," he said. "You go in there, she might take you, too."

"You're afraid," I said.

"So what if I am?" Brody's nose was running. He wiped it on his sleeve, leaving a slimy trail on the suede. "At least I ain't stupid."

"Won't you at least wait outside?"

"Nope." Brody turned away. "I told you what you need to know."

I watched him climb out of the hollow. For a while I heard him on the trail, and then it was just me and the wind and a pair of buzzards circling over-head.

I went to the door of the cabin. "Erica," I called softly. "Erica, are you in there?"

The ruins were silent. The only things moving were the dead vines blowing in the wind and three or four crows cawing to one another from the trees.

I should go home, I thought. *But why?* Everyone except Mom was out searching for my sister.

"Erica," I whispered. "Where are you?"

I heard a muffled noise, as if someone were moving around inside the cabin. What if Erica was trapped there? Not by Old Auntie but by a fallen rafter or something. I walked slowly through the cabin door. *Please please please, let it be my sister, let her be all right.*

It took my eyes a few moments to adjust to the dark. "Erica? Are you in here?"

More noise, frantic sounds, as if someone were trying to hide or run away. "Who's here?" I hoped my voice didn't give away my fear.

Scrabbling sounds. An animal, I thought, a fox or a raccoon.

I started backing toward the door when I saw a flash of green in a shadowy corner, red hair, a blue scarf.

"Erica!" I climbed over a rafter, ducked under a tree that had fallen through the roof, and stumbled across the uneven floor. "Erica, wait! Don't run. It's me, Daniel!"

But she was climbing up a pile of rubble and trying to squeeze through the splintered remains of a window. Frantically, I grabbed her foot and tugged.

"What's wrong with you?" I shouted. "I've come to take you home!"

Suddenly she fell back toward me, and I saw her face. She was not my sister. Sickly and pale, her skin grimy with dirt, she had the look of a wild creature.

I gripped her skinny wrists tightly. "Who are you? How did you get my sister's clothes? Where is she?"

"Let me go, let me go." The girl twisted and turned. She was so thin I was afraid of breaking her bones, but I couldn't let her go, not until she told me where she'd gotten Erica's things.

"That's my sister's jacket, her scarf, her jeans and

sweater, her shoes." I shook her. "Where did you get them?"

"She give 'em to me. Told me they was my clothes, I could keep them."

"Erica gave you her clothes?"

"I don't know nothing about Erica."

"Who gave the clothes to you, then?" I was frantic now. And scared.

"Auntie, she told me to wear 'em home. But I'm scairt to leave the cabin. I don't remember none other home."

She looked around. "Thing is, I don't know what's happened to it. There must have been a fearsome storm to make it look like this."

The girl was beginning to scare me. "What's your name?"

"Let me go." She began to struggle again, but she was weaker now and easier to hold on to.

"Look," I said. "You don't need to be scared. I'm not going to hurt you. Just tell me your name."

"Auntie calls me Girl."

"Girl isn't a name. It's what you are."

"Ain't that what a name is? What you are?"

"No, a name is *who* you are."

"I can't see no difference. Besides, Girl is all the name I got."

She couldn't be who I thought she was. No matter what that liar Brody said, it was impossible — Selene would be almost sixty years old now. Still, I asked anyway. "Does the name Selene Estes mean anything to you?"

"No, no it don't." She struggled to get away. Her wrist bones moved under her skin. "Let me go, please. I didn't do nothing, only what Auntie told me."

Holding her tightly, I pulled her toward the door. "You're coming with me."

"No. No!" She fought me with all her strength, but she was puny and probably underfed.

With one free hand, she grabbed the doorpost and held on. "Let me get the pretty dolly. Auntie give her to me. She said I was to take good care of her."

Keeping her close, I let her go back to the corner where she'd been hiding. There, in a pile of rags, was Little Erica.

Seeing the doll gave me shivers all over. "That's my sister's doll," I said. "She left her in the woods, and someone stole her. Either you or Auntie —"

"I never stole nothing. Auntie found her." The girl picked up the doll by one arm and cuddled her close. "She's the prettiest thing I ever seen. I love her to death."

Little Erica stared at the girl with her blank blue eyes. The small smile still curved the corners of her mouth, but her clothing was soiled, her hair tangled, and her face dirty.

"It's a special doll made to look like my sister," I told the girl.

"Your sister must be real pretty," the girl said.

"Are you sure you haven't seen her? She's been missing since yesterday. Please, you must know something. You have her clothes, her doll."

"I never see anyone but Auntie." The girl looked around, as if she hoped to find Auntie hiding in the shadows. She was as desperate as I was.

"Where is Auntie now?" I asked.

"Gone. She don't want me no more because I can't do the work she needs done. She says she's got someone new to help her."

The girl's eyes filled with tears. I watched them run down her dirty face, leaving little trails in the grime. She was the most pitiful creature I'd ever seen. "Come home with me." I tugged her wrist hard. "You can't stay here all by yourself."

I expected her to fight me, but she followed me outside as if she'd lost all her strength. One hand held Little Erica, the other held mine. Maybe she was as tired of struggling as I was.

She looked back at the cabin so often, she stumbled on roots and stones and almost fell. When she could no longer see the ruin, not even the chimney, she whimpered like a frightened puppy.

"Are you afraid?" I asked her.

"Yes," she whispered. "I'm scairt of leaving the cabin."

"How long have you lived with Auntie?"

"A long, long, long time."

"Were you a baby when you came here?"

"No. I always been just like I am now."

"Then you can't have been with her very long. You'd be older."

The girl looked far off into the trees and the mountains beyond them and up at the sky. "It seems like a long time."

"You know the story about Selene, don't you?"

She shook her head. "I told you and told you, I don't know nothing about Selene."

"Everybody who lives here knows the story!" I yelled at her. "You're just play-acting, aren't you? Did Brody put you up to this?"

"Stop yelling at me. I don't know Brody, and I ain't play-acting."

I studied her pale face, the dark circles under her eyes, the tangled wildness of her red hair. She seemed older than she was—exhausted, malnourished, neglected.

What if Brody was right and this strange girl was Selene? And Old Auntie had swapped her for Erica?

No, I told myself, *no*. Old Auntie was a legend, a folktale, not a real live person. She wasn't out here in the woods, roaming the hills and valleys with Bloody Bones, snatching girls to be her helpers every fifty years. How could anyone believe such nonsense?

Not my parents and not me, either. I held the girl's wrist tighter and made her walk faster. Sooner or later, someone would get the truth out of her.

In Auntie's Cabin

The old woman watches the boy lead Selene away. She chuckles to herself. She can see Selene, but Selene can't see her no more. The boy will take her down the hill to the farm. They'll keep her there until she dies, which won't be long, a few days, a week maybe. It's what happens when they go back to their time. Makes no difference to Auntie. She's got herself a new girl now.

Trouble is, the girl ain't quite up to the work. You'd think she'd never tended a fire or swept a floor or cooked a meal or scrubbed a pot. She acts like she never seen a washtub. She don't know how to make soap or candles or sew a seam. Out in the garden she pulls up more vegetables than weeds. She can't tell an onion from a beet.

She's scairt of spiders and anything else that crawls on floors or scurries across walls or hides in the firewood.

What can Auntie do with such a stupid, lazy girl but scold her and beat her and shut her up in the hidey-hole under the cabin floor.

When she can't stand it no longer, Auntie brings in Bloody Bones and tells the girl he eats bad children like her. The girl cries and shakes with fear at the sight of Auntie's dear boy. He rears up over her, taller than most men. Why, his head bumps the ceiling.

He clacks his teeth and rattles his bones. He makes the girl look into the dark eyeholes in his skull, which is like looking into a bottomless hole, blacker than the blackest night. The girl curls up into a ball like a baby that don't want to be birthed.

After Auntie sends her dear boy outside, the girl tells the old woman she's doing her best, but that ain't good enough, is it? She cries and promises to do better. But she keeps on dropping things and spilling things and breaking things like that's all she's good for.

What Auntie needs is a servant who does everything she's told and never gets tired or needs to be fed. She'd give just about anything to have herself one of them.

She reminds herself she's had the girl for only a few days. Maybe she'll catch on if Auntie beats her harder and locks her up in the hidey-hole more often and threatens to give her to Bloody Bones for his supper.

In the meantime, she better not catch that boy snooping around the cabin again. Or that pitiful Selene either.

TWELVE

When we came in sight of the house, the girl stopped for a moment and stared at it.

"Does it look familiar?" I asked. "Have you ever seen it?"

She shook her head. "I never seen a house that big before. Rich people must live there."

"It's where I live," I told her. "But we're not rich."

She pointed at the junk in the field, which was easier to see now that cold weather had stripped the leaves away. "Look at all the stuff your people threw away. Only rich people would throw out so many good things."

As we drew near the house, the back door flew open and Mom ran toward us. "Erica," she cried. "Thank God you're home! Where have you—"

She stopped a foot away and dropped her outstretched arms. "Who are you?" she said. "Where did you get my daughter's clothes? And her doll?"

Lunging at the girl, Mom grabbed Little Erica out of her arms and clasped the doll to her chest. She looked as if she was about to collapse from disappointment.

The girl reached for Little Erica. "She's mine. Auntie give her to me."

Ignoring the girl, Mom turned to me. "What's the meaning of this? Why have you brought her here? How did she get your sister's things?" Her voice rose with every question, as if she thought I'd played a cruel trick on her.

"She was hiding in the old cabin where Dad took pictures last month," I told Mom. "She says her aunt gave her the clothes and the doll and told her to leave, she was finished with her."

"Oh, no, no, no." Still hugging the doll, Mom sank down on the porch steps. "Erica," she cried. "Erica." She put her head on her knees and sobbed.

"Please." I held the girl's cold little hands. "If you know anything, please tell me."

She darted an ugly look at my mother. "She's got to give my dolly back. Auntie give her to me. She's mine."

Just then the kitchen door opened and a woman stuck her head out. A stranger. "Oh, thank goodness," she said. "You found her."

Mom ran past the woman and disappeared inside, holding the doll and crying. I heard her pound up the back stairs to her room.

The woman stood in the doorway, puzzled. "That's not Erica?" she asked.

I shook my head. "I found her hiding in the old cabin up the trail. She's wearing Erica's clothes, but—"

The woman came down the steps and looked closely at the girl. "What's your name, honey? Where do you live?"

"I'm Girl. I live up yonder with Auntie." She pointed toward the trail that led to the cabin. "Only she don't need me no more. She said so herself. She give me these clothes and told me to go home, but the onliest home I got is with Auntie." She began to cry again, washing more streaks of dirt down her face.

The woman knelt in front of the girl and cupped her face in her hands. "It can't be," she whispered. "God's love, it can't be."

"What can't be, ma'am?" Girl peered at the woman, her face creased in worry.

"Never you mind. It's just my mind wandering." The woman got to her feet and said to me, "You must be Daniel. I'm Mrs. O'Neill. I believe you've already met my husband."

Taking the girl's hand, Mrs. O'Neill said, "Let's take this poor child inside and give her something nice to eat. Hot soup, maybe? She looks cold and hungry."

Mrs. O'Neill led the girl into the kitchen and settled her at the table. While she opened a can of chicken soup with rice and poured it into a pot, the girl looked around.

"My goodness," she said. "You told me you ain't rich, but look at the things you got. Nothing's broken or busted either. It's all clean and new and shiny."

"Well—" How could I tell her that Mom complained about the old-fashioned gas stove she had to light with a match and the refrigerator she had to de-frost and the ugly white metal cabinets she hated and the dripping faucets and the black and white squares of cracked linoleum covering the floor?

Mrs. O'Neill made toast and poured two bowls of soup—one for the girl and one for me. Then she sat down with us and studied the girl. The girl's manners were terrible. She slurped and slopped the soup, holding the bowl with one hand, as if she thought I might take it from her. She stuffed the toast into her mouth and almost choked. It was like eating at the table with your dog or something.

When the girl was finished, she wiped her mouth with the back of her hand and blew her nose on the napkin.

Mrs. O'Neill stroked her tangled hair. "How would you like a nice hot bath?"

The girl frowned. "I don't much care for baths."

"Let's go upstairs. When you see the tub, you might change your mind." Mrs. O'Neill led the amaz-ingly docile girl up the back stairs. I waited to hear yelling and screaming and thuds and thumps and doors slamming, but instead, the water ran into the tub and all was quiet.

I fixed a cup of hot chocolate and stood at the kitchen window. The wind was blowing harder now and the short day was running out of light. The second night without Erica was almost here.

After a while Mrs. O'Neill came downstairs carrying the girl. She'd changed her from a scary little wild creature into an almost normal kid. Her hair had been washed and combed, her face and hands were clean, and she was wearing one of Dad's old plaid flannel shirts, last seen hanging on a hook in the bathroom. It fit her like a long nightgown.

"She needs to rest," Mrs. O'Neill said. "I don't want to put her in your sister's room. Can she sleep in your bed for a while?"

I hesitated, but where else was the girl to sleep? At least she was clean now. Reluctantly, I led the way to my room.

By the time Mrs. O'Neill laid her down, the girl was asleep. Covering her with a quilt, she looked at her in the dim light. "You poor child," she whispered. "Where have you been all this time? What's happened to you?"

"Do you think she's Selene?"

"Let her sleep. We'll talk downstairs." Mrs.

O'Neill led me into the hall and closed my bedroom door. Glancing at Mom's closed door, she said, "Don't wake your mother. She's exhausted."

I followed her down the back stairs to the kitchen. Now that it was dark, the wind blew harder. It tugged at the corners of the house and wailed, as if it wanted to come inside. The sound made me cold all over.

"Help me lay out the food," Mrs. O'Neill said. "The men will be back soon, cold and hungry."

Women from town had sent casseroles, sandwich platters, cakes, and pies. It surprised me that they'd cared enough about us, the outsiders, to help. Except for the O'Neills, no one had made any effort to welcome us until now.

While we set out dishes, Mrs. O'Neill said, "We knew Selene Estes, John and I."

"He told me that Selene was best friends with your daughter." I looked at her. "But she'd be almost sixty years old now. And that girl upstairs appears to be my sister's age. How can she be Selene?"

Mrs. O'Neill shook her head. "When I first saw her, I was struck by her resemblance to Selene. It wasn't until I bathed her that I began to think she really is Selene—not only the same hair and the same eyes, but even the same birthmark on her shoulder."

"Maybe she's faking it," I suggested. "Play-acting a story everybody knows."

"That doesn't explain the birthmark." Mrs. O'Neill paused to set out ladles for the macaroni and the baked beans.

"The trouble is," she went on, "I can't think of any other explanation for your sister's disappearance and this child's appearance."

Maybe I was as crazy as everyone else in this valley, but the more Mrs. O'Neill talked, the more I began to think the girl upstairs might actually be Selene Estes. In this valley, anything could be true, even a conjure woman walking the hills with her pet hog and stealing a girl every fifty years.

"It's happened before, you know," Mrs. O'Neill said. "When Selene disappeared, the search party found a little girl in the woods. Nobody knew who she was, and she couldn't tell them."

"What happened to her?"

Mrs. O'Neill sighed. "They put her in an orphanage. She wouldn't eat or drink. In less than a month, she died without ever saying who she was or where she came from. But somebody remembered that a child had disappeared fifty years previously. So it seemed the old stories were true after all."

I was about to ask more questions, but the sharp sound of barking dogs scattered my thoughts. I ran to the window. The day had ended and flashlight beams sliced the darkness, illuminating a tree here, a man there. The search party was coming back.

The back door banged open, and Dad led a group of men into the kitchen, big men in work clothes, stomping their feet, red-faced from the cold, talking in low voices.

"Where's your mother?" Dad asked me.

Before I could answer, Mom came stumbling down the back stairs, still half asleep, from the look of her. "Have you found Erica?" She gazed around the room wildly, her eyes flitting from one person to the next. "Where is she?"

The searchers drew together, holding sandwiches but too polite to eat them.

Dad drew Mom close. "I'm so sorry, Martha."

Mom beat her fists against his chest. "You didn't look long enough. You must have missed something, you, you—" She collapsed against him.

He held her up, kept her from falling, stroked her hair, tried to comfort her.

"Believe me, ma'am," Mr. O'Neill told Mom, "we searched every inch of these woods. We didn't find a trace of her. Neither did the dogs."

Mom turned to me. "Where's that girl you brought home? The one with Erica's doll, the one wearing her clothes? Ask *her* where my daughter is. Make her tell you!"

Everyone in the room seemed to stop breathing. No one moved. No one spoke. The only sound was the *tick-tock-tick* of the kitchen clock and the wind rattling the windowpanes.

"What girl?" Dad asked, looking from Mom to me. "What's she talking about, Daniel?"

Before I could answer, Mrs. O'Neill said, "She's talking about Selene. Daniel found her. She's upstairs sleeping."

The group of searchers huddled together, half-finished plates of food in their hands, and mumbled to one another. I heard Selene's name once or twice, but their voices dropped even lower into whispers. Men shook their heads. They looked worried. Frightened, even. A couple of them made excuses and left the house. I heard a car start, saw its headlights, watched its taillights as it sped away.

"What's wrong?" Dad asked Mr. O'Neill. "Why are they leaving?"

"It's the girl," he said slowly, as if answering the question embarrassed him. "They're saying that Old Auntie's got your daughter, and there's no use looking for her."

While Dad stood there, flabbergasted, the last three men thanked us for the food and drink and edged out the back door. In the yard, engines revved, headlights lit the field, and in a couple of minutes the search party was gone.

Mr. O'Neill turned to his wife. "Maybe you should get the girl, bring her down, let Ted see for himself."

Mrs. O'Neill started up the back stairs, and I followed her. Stopping at my closed door, she tapped gently. "So as not to startle her," she whispered.

When no one answered, she opened the door and peeked inside. The window was wide open, and the curtains blew like streamers in the cold air.

Mrs. O'Neill ran to the window and looked out into the night. All that moved were the shadows of trees tossed by the wind.

"She must have gone back to the cabin," I said. "Someone should go after her."

Mrs. O'Neill shook her head. "There's not a man from these parts who'll go near that cabin at night."

"Not even the police?"

"Every one of them grew up here. They've heard stories all their lives about Old Auntie. Most of them swear they've seen her and Bloody Bones in the woods or alongside a dark road."

I watched Mrs. O'Neill hurry down the back stairs, and then I took a quick look around my room. A sweater and pair of jeans I'd left on a chair were gone, and so were my old running shoes. I tiptoed across the hall and checked Mom's room. Little Erica was gone too.

I went to the top of the back stairs and listened. Mom was crying, and Dad was calling the state troopers. "Surely they don't believe in this superstitious nonsense," I heard him say.

Mr. and Mrs. O'Neill were talking in low voices. It sounded as if they were cleaning up the kitchen.

Taking care to make no noise, I crept down the front stairs, grabbed my parka and hat from the coat-rack by the door, and slipped quietly outside. For a second, I hesitated. What if I got lost? I needed someone to come with me, someone who knew the way.

Brody had refused to go near the cabin in broad daylight, but maybe I could talk him into going to the top of the trail with me—it was a long shot, but who else could I ask?

THIRTEEN

By the time I was in sight of Brody's ramshackle old house, I heard a dog bark, then another. In the dim light of the half-moon I saw three or four of them coming down the driveway toward me. What should I do? If I ran, they'd chase me. Maybe if I stood still, they'd just sniff me and leave me alone. They looked like hounds of some kind, not very big, hopefully not very fierce, either.

They stopped about two feet away and kept barking. A light on the front porch came on, and the front door opened.

"Brody!" I yelled. "It's me, Daniel! Call off the dogs."

A gruff male voice called, "You the boy from the Estes farm?"

"Yes, sir." The dogs surrounded me, sniffing and muttering to one another in dog language.

The man whistled, and the dogs ran up the drive toward the house. "Come on," he called to me. "They won't hurt you."

Keeping an eye on the dogs just in case he was wrong, I climbed the porch steps.

"I saw you at the house," he said. "I was in the search party. I'm sorry we didn't find your little sister. We done our best, but—" Shaking his head, he called Brody. "The boy from the Estes farm is here. He wants to see you."

Brody came to the door. "What you want?"

"Can I talk to you about something?" I shot a quick look at his dad, hoping Brody would get the message that this was just between him and me.

"If it's about your sister, I already told you what I think."

"Well, it's actually about Selene."

"Selene?" Mr. Mason leaned closer. I smelled beer and cigarette smoke on his breath. "It's really her, then?"

"The O'Neills think so."

"Where's she now?" Brody asked.

I gave up on trying to keep things between him and me. "I don't know. She ran away."

"Went back to the cabin, I reckon," Mr. Mason said.

"That's what I think." I looked at Brody. "Maybe Erica's there, too. Will you go up there with me?"

Mr. Mason put a hand on my shoulder. "You go on home, boy. Ain't a soul in this valley will go there with you. Certainly not my boy."

"She's my sister," I said. "I have to get her back."

Brody shook his head. "How you think you'll do that? Just knock on the door and say, 'Please, Miss Auntie, give me my sister'?"

Mr. Mason sighed. "Do like I said, boy. Go home. There's nothing you nor me nor anyone else can do for your sister."

"But—"

Mr. Mason stopped me. "Go home. Before you freeze to death."

I left them standing on the porch, watching me, as if to make sure I went home. I walked off in the right direction, but once I reached the end of their driveway, I headed into the woods.

I hadn't gone far when I heard a noise behind me, as if something was following me. I glanced over my shoulder and saw nothing. If I ran, whatever it was would chase me. So I kept walking and hoped it was a fox.

"Wait up, Daniel." Brody ran toward me. He had one of the dogs with him. "You're going up there, ain't you?"

"Are you coming with me?"

"Not me, but I brought Bella. Don't know if she'll protect you, but if you get lost, she'll bring you home." He held out the dog's leash, and I took it.

"She's a good old dog." Brody bent down to scratch behind Bella's ears. "Part beagle, part fox hound, part something bigger—just a mutt, really, but smart as all get-out. You tell her 'home' and she'll lead you there."

"Thanks." I patted Bella, and she wagged her tail. She had a pointed nose, a sharp face, and perked-up ears. Her fur was white with dark patches, and her legs were long. She was sleek and slim, and I could tell by her eyes that she was smart, like Brody said.

"You be careful." Brody stepped back, and I didn't know if he was talking to the dog or to me. "I got to get back before Dad misses me or Bella. He says you're crazy to even think about going near Old Auntie's cabin, but being you're a stranger here, he reckons you're just plain ignorant."

Brody backed away into the woods. "Good luck." With that, he was gone into the night as quickly as he'd come.

Bella looked after him and whined, but she seemed to know she was supposed to stay with me. "Come on, girl," I said, and she darted ahead, as if to lead the way.

I watched her prance along and wished she were mine. It comforted me to think of coming home with Erica and then getting into bed with Bella curled up beside me.

But Bella wasn't mine, and I wasn't sure I'd bring Erica home or even come home myself.

I followed the dog up the trail. Every now and then an owl hooted, sometimes close by, sometimes far away. Once in a while Bella stopped and looked into the woods, as if she saw things invisible to me. She growled or whined, glanced back at me, then went on. She never tugged at the leash but kept a steady pace. She'd been on this path before, I thought, probably hunting raccoons or something.

As the trail grew steeper, Bella paused more often, her body tense. She walked slower, dropping back until she was almost by my side. The wind blew harder up there, and the moon slid in and out from the clouds, sometimes lighting the path, sometimes casting it into darkness. I shivered; my teeth chattered—not just because I was cold, which I was, but also because we'd reached the drop-off.

Bella pressed against my side, and I felt her body tremble. "Careful, girl," I whispered. "We're right on the edge of the trail."

From where I stood, I looked down, way down into the valley, which was awash with moonlight. One misstep, and you'd be over the side of the hill, falling, falling, falling to certain death on the rocks below.

Staying as far away from the edge as possible, I forced myself to keep climbing. Finally we reached the top. The hollow lay in shadows, darker than anywhere else, as black as an underground cavern.

Suddenly Bella stiffened and moved forward, ears erect, body tense, growling softly. Something moved in the hollow below us.

Bella's growl turned to a whine, and she pressed against me as if she were frightened.

For a second, I hoped I'd found Erica, but instead Selene stepped out of the cabin's shadow, more woebegone than ever.

Bella whined and looked up at me. "It's okay," I whispered to the dog.

Selene stayed where she was. "Will that dog bite me?"

I shook my head. "She's a good dog. Her name's Bella."

As Selene came closer, Bella made no effort to greet her. If anything, she pressed closer to me. She was still trembling.

Selene looked at the dog. "She don't like me," she said sadly.

I wasn't interested in how Bella felt about Selene. All I wanted was to find my sister. "You said the cabin would look like it did when you lived here."

"It does," Selene said. "Can't you see the light in the window?"

I peered into the blackness. "There's nothing there," I said.

She pointed. "Right there. And smoke's coming from the chimney. Your sister's in there. I seen her through the window, but I can't get in."

I stared into the darkness until my eyeballs ached, but I couldn't see anything. "Are you telling the truth or play-acting?"

"I'm telling you the honest-to-God truth. She's setting by the fire, stirring the pot like I used to. Only she's not doing it right, and Auntie will give her a walloping when she comes home."

"She'll beat my sister?"

"That's what she does if you don't do things right—she wallops you. I used to get bruises all over me till I learned."

Nobody was going to hurt my sister. If she was in that cabin, I'd break the door down and rescue her. With Bella and Selene behind me, I plunged downhill into the hollow, scrambling and slipping on loose stones. But all I saw were the same ruins I'd always seen.

Bella hung back, as if she knew something was in the ruins, but Selene ran to one of the few standing walls and looked through a broken window.

"There she be, your sister, just like I said. I don't see my auntie, though. She must be out in the woods."

I watched Selene struggle to open the sagging door. "Let me in, girl!" She pounded on the wood with her fists. "Let me in!"

I pulled her away. "There's nothing here. You're imagining it."

Bella whined and danced around me, but I was too busy with Selene to pay any attention to the dog. Finally the dog grabbed my parka. Frantic with fear, she tugged and growled through her clenched teeth and did her best to drag me away from the cabin's ruins.

In the struggle, I lost my grip on Selene, and she ran into the woods, calling for Auntie.

Even with the girl gone, Bella wouldn't let go of my parka. She continued to whine and growl and pull me toward the trail.

Freeing myself from Bella, I chased Selene. The dog darted in front of me and blocked my way. I dodged and shouted Selene's name until I was hoarse. She was gone. I'd lost her, just as I'd lost Erica.

At least that's what I thought, until Bella cowered beside me. The woods were very still. The wind stopped. The moon hid behind the clouds.

Coming toward us was Selene. An old woman walked beside her. She leaned on a staff and carried a bundle. Her long skirt was the color of the winter sky on a starless night, her shawl as black as midnight. Long strands of white hair blew about her head. Shadows hid her face.

I wanted to run, but I couldn't move. Neither could Bella. We were frozen, paralyzed, under a spell. We could do nothing but watch the two of them approach. Old Auntie shoved Selene toward me. "I brung her back. She ain't mine no more. Take her home and keep her there, boy. She's your sister now. The girl in the cabin is my girl. Look for her in fifty years if you want her back."

"No, Auntie," Selene cried. "Ain't I worked hard all my life for you? Give her back and let me stay with you. I'll work hard, I'll do better, I promise you."

Selene tried to embrace Old Auntie, but the old

woman pushed her away. The girl sprawled on the ground at my feet. Bella sniffed her and whimpered.

"Now, you go on and get out of here," Old Auntie told her. "Don't let me see you no more. Don't come looking for me. Stay away from my cabin. You hear me?"

Selene lay on the ground, a pathetic little creature. Her body shook with sobs.

"If you come begging at my door again, I'll send my boy after you." Old Auntie spit on the ground. "You know what he can do, Girl. He'll make you sorry. And that's the truth."

Selene shuddered and peered into the darkness. "Is he close by?" she whispered.

"Bloody Bones can be here or he can be far, but I reckon he's close enough to come if I whistle." She leaned down to peer into Selene's face. "You want me to fetch him?"

"No, no, Auntie, don't whistle for him," Selene begged. "I'll go away and I won't come back no more." While she spoke, she stared about wild-eyed, searching the darkest shadows, as if Bloody Bones might be hiding behind a tree or a bush or a rock.

The moon came out then and shone full on

Auntie's face. Her eyes were sunk deep in their sockets, her skin stretched tight across her skull. A few yellow teeth sat crooked in her lipless mouth and her nose was no more than sharp bone. She looked like she should be in her grave, not here in the woods.

She screeched with laughter and stuck her face so close to mine that I could smell her breath, rotten with decay. "Why, boy, I believe you ain't never seen the likes of me afore."

I backed away, stumbled over Bella, and fell flat. The dog whined and cowered beside me. Behind the old conjure woman, I saw something move in the woods, snapping branches under its feet, snuffling, rooting in the dead leaves.

Auntie laughed again, a wild whoop this time that echoed from tree to tree and bounced off rocks. "He's here," she hissed to Selene. "Old Bloody Bones hisself. Get yourselves away from here afore I send him after you both — and the dog, too."

In a swirl of skirt and shawl, Auntie turned her back and strode away. The wind picked up, the woods stirred. She was gone.

But instead of following her, Bloody Bones stepped out of the woods and into the moonlight.

His head was a hog's skull, the rest of him bones. Taller than my father, he walked toward us on two feet. His ragged overalls fluttered about him as he raised his arms to show us the bear claws. Then he grinned to show us the panther's teeth. As he moved slowly toward us, a whistle sounded in the trees. His head swung toward the sound, and he snorted.

"Come to me, dear boy," Old Auntie called from somewhere in the woods. "Let them go for now, but if they come back, eat them."

With a grunt of disappointment, Bloody Bones turned away and lumbered into the dark.

Bella threw back her head and howled, the eeriest sound I'd ever heard a dog make. Turning to Selene, who still lay on the ground sobbing, the dog sniffed her cautiously, going over every inch of her, as if reading the fine print in a contract. Then, looking up at me, she licked the girl's cheek.

My heart pounded and my knees shook with fear, but I leaned over Selene. "You heard what she said," I told her. "We have to get out of here."

With Bella leading the way, Selene stumbled silently beside me, keeping a tight grip on the doll. When we got to the hollow, she looked at me. "I can't see the cabin no more," she said. "The lights are out and the chimney smoke's gone."

She ran to the broken window and peered inside. She seemed to see what I saw—a ruined cabin rotting away in the woods, full of shadows, dark and abandoned.

"Come on." I held out my hand. "There's nothing here for you or me now."

In Auntie's Cabin Again

The old woman comes into the cabin and slams the door behind her. Her shadow rises up and rolls across the room before her. She's so angry, she slaps the girl across the face, hard enough to knock her out of the chair where she's been sleeping.

The girl cringes on the floor, covering her face with her hands. "Don't hit me no more, Auntie," she begs. "I ain't been sleeping long."

But the old woman picks up her stick and whacks the girl on the back. "Look there—you done let the fire go out! Cain't I trust you to do nothing right?"

The girl scrambles to her feet and tries to light the

fire, but she's fumble-fingered with fear. Any minute Auntie will hit her again.

"Get out of my way." The old woman shoves the girl aside and squats to light the fire. She hears Selene crying outside, hears the boy dragging her away.

"Your brother come here to get you," she tells the girl. "But me and my dear boy chased him off. Don't make no difference. He's got hisself another sister now."

The girl stares at her, blank eyed. She doesn't have a brother. She's Auntie's girl. She's been here all her life. Just her and Auntie. Nobody else. Nobody except—except—her eyes go to the window. The pale face of Auntie's dear boy peers in at her. He grins and shows her his sharp teeth. But he's not her brother. Or is he? She doesn't know. She doesn't know anything.

The old woman sinks into her rocking chair and laughs at the girl's mystified face. "You ain't got no idea what I'm talking about, do you?" She feels like hitting her again. Or kicking her. Or throwing something at her. But she's tired from walking in the woods.

She leans toward the girl, baring her yellow teeth in a smile as hideous as the dear boy's wicked grin. "Your brother won't be back," she says. "My dear boy has scairt him off. But if'n he does come back, you won't go with him 'cause you love your old auntie and you know she loves you."

She reaches out and pinches the girl's cheek. "Say you love me. Tell me, let me hear you."

Tears of pain fill the girl's eyes. "I love you so much, Auntie, more than anything." She wants to pull away from those fingers and their sharp nails, but if she does, Auntie will pinch harder.

"Tell me I'm good to you. Tell me I give you what you deserve."

"You're good to me, Auntie," she whispers. "You give me what I deserve."

The old woman releases her grip on the girl's cheek and settles back in her rocking chair. The fire flickers and casts dancing shadows on the walls and across the ceiling.

The girl crouches by the hearth. Over her head, three bats hang upside down, sleeping the winter away. Bundles of dry herbs dangle from the rafters. The girl hates their smell. The whole cabin reeks of deadly nightshade, henbane, hemlock, and foxglove – poisons, every one of them. Auntie makes potions from them, things that harm and hurt and sometimes kill.

She tells the girl about them and cackles. "I got me a bunch of names on a list, both the living and the dead. One by one I gets my revenge on them who done wrong to me."

In dark corners, black widows and other poisonous spiders lurk. The girl is afraid to sweep away their webs. She's also afraid of the scuttling noises the rats make. Sometimes she glimpses them darting across the floor from one corner to another. They're bigger than cats, and their teeth are long and sharp.

But most of all she's afraid of Bloody Bones. If she dared, she'd give him one of those little bottles of poison and kill him dead. That's how much she hates Auntie's dear boy.

But she doesn't hate Auntie. Oh, no. She loves Auntie. Auntie is all she has to keep her safe from Bloody Bones.

FOURTEEN

Bella led us eagerly down the path, never faltering, steering us deftly around rocks and roots and fallen branches. I'd lost the flashlight in the confusion and was grateful for the dog's sure footing.

All the way down Brewster's Hill, neither Selene nor I said one word. We didn't look behind us, for fear of what might be following us. Every noise made my heart pound. I thought I heard Bloody Bones snuffle, heard his hooves on the stones, smelled his hot, bloody breath, thought he was getting closer, closer. Soon he'd have us both, and Bella, too.

But when we came out of the woods at the bottom of Brewster's Hill, Bloody Bones was not behind us after all. Or if he had been, he wasn't there then. I paused and took a deep breath. Here on the edge of the field, with the house in sight, I felt almost safe. Bella licked my hand and wagged her tail. I watched her trot off toward Brody's house, sad to see her leave.

Selene's cold hand touched mine. She'd been crying silently. "I got no one now," she whispered. Her voice was like a song you hear in the dark just before you fall asleep.

I squeezed her hand and felt its tiny bones shift in my grip. People were so fragile, so easily broken, so hard to put back together. "Mr. and Mrs. O'Neill will take care of you," I told her.

Selene said nothing, but she let me lead her across the field toward the farmhouse.

The back porch light lit the yard like a spotlight. Before I opened the door, Dad threw it wide. "Where have you been?" he shouted. "Aren't we worried enough without your going off somewhere without a word to anybody?"

His eyes lit on Selene. "Is this the girl your mother was talking about?"

I nodded and squeezed Selene's cold hand. "She ran away, and I went to find her."

Mom came into the kitchen, followed by the O'Neills. Looking at Selene with hostility, Mom said, "She took the doll with her. And she's wearing your clothes, Daniel."

"Now, Martha." Mrs. O'Neill patted Mom's shoulder in an effort to calm her. "What have I been telling you?"

"Nothing I believe." Mom never took her eyes off Selene. "What's your name?"

"Girl." Selene lowered her head. She was so pale and so little and so skinny—how could Mom be so mean to her?

Mom scowled down at Selene. "Your real name. Tell me your *real* name. Tell me who you are."

"I'm his sister now."

Mom seemed too stunned to speak, but Dad said, "You are not my son's sister!"

"That's what Auntie said," Selene whispered. "I'm to be his sister now. To take the place of the other."

Before Mom or Dad could say more, Mr. O'Neill knelt beside Selene and studied her face. "I knew you a long time ago, Selene. You lived right here in this house. You were friends with my daughter Eleanor. I knew your parents, too. Do you remember my wife and me?"

"I never lived here," Selene told Mr. O'Neill, obviously confused. "I don't have no mama or daddy. No friends, either. I've lived my whole life long with Auntie. But she don't want me anymore."

Pointing at me, she added, "Auntie says I'm to be *his* sister now. And I'll be hurt bad if I come back to the cabin looking to be with her again."

"I can't take this anymore." Mom left the kitchen and clattered up the back stairs. We all heard her bedroom door slam shut. It was just like before, only this time she didn't take the doll.

"Will you please tell me what's going on, Daniel?" Dad asked.

I did my best to explain it, but I knew I was losing him. He kept interrupting and saying, "This is ridiculous. Do you expect me to believe you?"

Mr. O'Neill sighed. "I tried to tell you, Ted."

Dad turned his back and followed Mom upstairs. The O'Neills, Selene, and I were left in the kitchen. I had no idea what to say or do.

Mrs. O'Neill sat down and lifted Selene into her lap. The girl leaned against Mrs. O'Neill and pressed her face against the woman's body. Little Erica stared over her shoulder, her blank blue eyes focused on nothing.

"Do you remember anything about this house?" Mrs. O'Neill asked Selene. "Your mama or your daddy?"

Selene shook her head. "I been tellin' you and tellin' you. I'm Auntie's girl."

"But not anymore," Mrs. O'Neill said.

Selene didn't say anything.

"She's almost asleep, poor thing," Mr. O'Neill murmured.

"How about we take her to our house?" Mrs. O'Neill asked me, as if she expected me to make the decision. "The very sight of her upsets your mother and angers your father."

"Maybe that would be best," I said.

I found a spare blanket and gave it to Mr. O'Neill. He wrapped it around Selene and carried her out to the car.

I stood on the back porch, shivering in the cold.

"Just make sure she doesn't run off," I called. "She'd freeze to death in those woods."

"Don't worry," Mr. O'Neill said. "We'll keep her safe."

"Come by and see us tomorrow," Mrs. O'Neill added. "I've got things to talk about with you."

I watched the car turn and head down the driveway. When its taillights disappeared around a curve, I went back inside. I was so tired—so, so tired. So sad. My head ached, as if my brain were about to explode from trying to understand what I'd seen in the woods. It couldn't be true. It was true. It couldn't be. It was.

The next morning, I woke up early, ate breakfast, and left a note telling Mom and Dad I was at the O'Neills' house. It was cold, and the sky was a solid light gray, so heavy with clouds that the sun couldn't break through. It felt as if snow was coming. Maybe it was better to think of Erica being with Old Auntie than to imagine her wandering in the woods, lost and cold and hungry.

I saw Brody at the end of our driveway. He was

wearing his suede jacket and a pair of filthy pink tennis shoes with holes in the toes.

Bella was with him, trotting along the edge of the road and sniffing in the weeds. When she saw me, she ran up and wagged her tail.

"Did you go to the cabin?" Brody asked. "Was Selene there?"

I looked up from petting Bella and nodded. "She swore Erica was inside, but all I saw were ruins, looking just like they always have."

"Did you see Old Auntie?"

"I was never so scared in my whole life. She's, she's—" I couldn't say any more for fear of somehow bringing her to me.

Wiping his nose on the sleeve of his jacket, Brody stared at me. "What did she do? What did she say?"

"She told me to take Selene home. She said she's my sister now."

"That girl don't want to be your sister." Brody spat on the ground.

"She wants to be with Auntie, but Auntie says that if Selene comes near the cabin, she'll sic Bloody Bones on her."

Brody's eyes widened. "Did you see him?"

I stared off into the woods and tried not to think about what I'd seen. "He's horrible, just like you said."

"Did he chase you?"

"No. He stood there and looked at us, and then Old Auntie whistled for him."

Brody sucked in his cheeks and let his breath out in a puff of air. "You must be really brave or really stupid, I'm not sure which, but I'm glad you brung my dog home safe."

With Bella between us, we stood on the edge of the road for a while, staring at the trees, as if we expected to see Bloody Bones or Old Auntie. A red-tailed hawk soared overhead, dark against the pale sky, and the wind picked up. It looked more like snow than ever. You could practically smell it in the wind.

"Is Selene at your house?" Brody asked.

I shook my head. "The O'Neills took her home with them last night. That's where I'm going."

"Can I come with you? I want to see that girl."

He and I and the dog walked on down the road. Snow began falling. Bella snapped at the flakes, and Brody opened his mouth like a kid and caught snow on his tongue. Even though I was half crazy with worry about my sister, I did the same. I've always loved the way snow feels on my tongue.

When we got to the O'Neills' house, the snow was at least half an inch deep, falling fast and thick now, making it hard to see. Trees blurred, fields blended in with the sky, and the house was no more than a faint outline against the smudge of woods behind it.

Mrs. O'Neill opened the door wide and let us all in, even Bella, who immediately made herself at home in front of the fire. "You must be freezing," she said.

Brody stopped in the living room doorway and stared at Selene, who was sitting on a couch beside Mr. O'Neill. A photo album lay open in his lap, but she seemed more interested in combing Little Erica's hair than in looking at the pictures. She didn't appear to notice the dog, Brody, or me.

"Get those wet shoes off, boys, and dry your feet by the fire," Mr. O'Neill said. "How's your father doing, Brody?"

"'Bout the same." Brody busied himself taking off his shoes and laying them carefully on the hearth.

He'd already shed his jacket and hung it on the back of a wooden chair in the corner. "He ain't found a job yet."

I put my hiking boots beside his worn-out tennis shoes. It always makes me feel guilty to have better stuff than other people. Something's wrong with a world that lets me have waterproof boots and someone else have tennis shoes with holes in the toes.

I looked at Selene, but she kept her eyes on the doll. Mr. O'Neill nudged her. "Aren't you going to say hello to Daniel? You haven't met Brody before—he lives on the other side of your old home, just over the bridge."

Without looking at either one of us, she shook her head. She wore a gray plaid dress and a dark green sweater. Her hair had been combed until it was free of tangles. If you didn't look too closely, you'd think Selene was a perfectly normal girl. Maybe a little shy, but nothing out of the ordinary.

When she finally raised her head and stared at us with those pale green eyes, you could see right away that she was different, not normal after all, a wild child with wild ways.

Brody actually took a step back when he saw Selene's pale, pointed face and her fierce eyes. For a moment I thought he was going to grab his jacket and shoes and leave, but he stayed where he was, wiping his nose and staring at the girl.

Ignoring Brody's reaction to Selene, Mr. O'Neill motioned to us to join him. "I'm showing Selene some pictures. Maybe you'd like to see them too."

I sat beside him, on the opposite side from Selene. Brody perched next to me on the arm of the sofa, ready to head for home if he needed to. He was a little wild himself, but nothing like Selene.

"This is my daughter's first-grade class picture." Mr. O'Neill pointed at a tall dark-haired girl in the back row of a faded black-and-white print. "That's Eleanor." Glancing at Selene, he moved his finger slowly to a child sitting in the middle of the front row. "And this is Selene."

Selene faced the camera, a big grin on her face. Like the other girls, she wore a dress with a round collar, very much like the one she was wearing now. Her curly red hair touched her shoulders.

Brody leaned past me to see. "It's her all right."

We both looked at Selene. With her face turned away from the photo album, she continued to comb Little Erica's hair.

"Selene disappeared not long after that picture was taken," Mr. O'Neill went on. "I've been showing her photos taken here at our house."

I looked at a page of snapshots of Selene and Eleanor. It was hard to believe that the frightened, unhappy kid sitting with us on the sofa had once hung upside down by her knees from a tree limb, ridden a bike, splashed in a swimming pool, and made silly faces.

"This is Selene's mother." Mr. O'Neill pointed to a pretty woman pulling both girls on a sled on a snowy day and smiling at the camera. "And her father. See? That's Selene on her dad's shoulders. She must have been two or three."

Mrs. O'Neill joined us then. "Don't you want to look at the pictures, Selene?" she asked gently. "It might help you remember your family—and who you are."

Keeping her head down, Selene said, "I know who I am."

"These were taken at Eleanor's seventh birthday party." Mr. O'Neill turned the page and moved the album closer to Selene, but she slid off the sofa and sat in a rocking chair by the fire.

Mrs. O'Neill smiled. "It was November, but unseasonably warm, so the children played outside. Look, here's Selene. I still remember that pretty blue dress—she was so adorable. And so happy." She paused a moment and turned to Brody. "Look at this—it's your uncle Silas."

Brody leaned closer to stare at the skinny boy in the photo. "Whew, he sure don't look like that now—bald and fat. Got a scruffy old beard and spends most of his time down at the tavern on State Street."

"Here's your dad. See? Right there beside Silas."

Brody squinted at the slightly blurry face of a five-year-old. "Now, he ain't changed so much, except for his hair, which is mostly gone. He's still skinny as a fence post."

Mrs. O'Neill's eyes returned to Selene in her blue dress. She was backlit by the sun, and her hair glowed in its light. "A week after the party, Selene disappeared," she told us. "Eleanor cried for weeks.

She's never forgotten Selene or gotten over her disappearance."

We all looked at the girl across the room. Humming to herself, she rocked the doll. She might as well have been alone, for all the attention she paid us.

Mr. O'Neill closed the album and laid it gently on the table. "I was hoping," he said wearily, "that seeing the pictures might make her remember, but I guess not."

He excused himself, saying he had work to do in his shop. "I'm building a dollhouse for my granddaughter—still hoping to finish it in time for her birthday. Maybe I'll build the next one for Selene."

Mrs. O'Neill beckoned to Brody and me. "You boys, come along with me."

We followed her down a narrow hall to the kitchen. It was big and modern, the kind of place Mom wanted so badly. I looked through a sliding glass door to an outside deck. The snow was about an inch and a half deep on the railing and still falling. The mountains had vanished behind a white curtain, and the woods were hard to see. Erica was out there somewhere.

"I told you last night I wanted to talk to you, Daniel," Mrs. O'Neill said. "You, too, Brody."

She sat on a stool at the counter, and we perched on either side of her. "First of all," she said, "I've called Eleanor and told her the news. If the snow doesn't keep her from coming, she'll be here one day this week. Maybe, just maybe, she'll find a way to communicate with Selene."

"But what about Erica?" I asked. "Now that we know where she is, can we get her back?"

Turning to Brody, Mrs. O'Neill asked him what he knew about an old woman who lived down at the end of Railroad Avenue.

"Miss Perkins?" Brody hunched his shoulders. "She's crazy, that's what. Nobody has nothing to do with her unless it's something secret, like, like—well, I don't exactly know what—except every cat and dog that goes missing ends up in her stew pot. And maybe other things, too."

"Yes, I've heard plenty of stories myself." Mrs. O'Neill paused. "But I've also heard she's a descendant of Old Auntie and knows a thing or two about conjuring herself."

Brody folded his arms across his skinny chest, hiding the puppy face that was knitted into the moth-eaten sweater he wore. "Not to be rude or nothing, but I ain't going near that old lady. And you shouldn't either."

Mrs. O'Neill turned to me. "How about you, Daniel?"

What choice did I have? If I refused, it would be like saying I didn't care what happened to my sister. "As long as somebody comes with me," I said. "I'll go."

I heard a whisper of sound behind me and turned to see Selene standing in the doorway. "Can I come too?"

"Oh, no, Selene," Mrs. O'Neill said. "This woman—"

"I heard you say she's kin to Auntie. Maybe she can change me for that other girl, the new one she got to help her. Then everybody'd be happy. They all want the new one back, and no one wants me."

Mrs. O'Neill studied the girl's pale face. "Oh, Selene, that's not true. Of course we want Erica back, but we don't want to lose you."

"You got to take me to see her, you got to!" Selene cried. "She's my onliest chance to see Auntie again."

"Maybe you should be there," Mrs. O'Neill said slowly. "Maybe Miss Perkins should see you."

Selene leaned against the doorframe. Holding the doll tightly, she hummed to herself. It was the same tune I'd heard Erica hum, a strange, sad song, like an old ballad, but without words.

I turned away from the girl's sad face. Sometimes I couldn't bear to look at her. What if my sister came back in fifty years, looking just like Selene?

"When should we go see Miss Perkins?" I asked Mrs. O'Neill.

She went to the sliding doors and peered out. "The snow's letting up," she said. "If the roads are plowed tonight, we can go to Woodville tomorrow."

She was right. I could see the mountains again, as soft against the sky as clouds resting on earth. The trunks of trees in the woods were smudged charcoal lines on white paper.

"I ain't going with you," Brody said, "so don't bother to ask."

Nobody argued with him. It was bad enough that Selene was coming. We didn't need Brody, too.

He joined Mrs. O'Neill at the door and pressed his nose against the glass, making a big smear. "Bella and me should get on home soon." He didn't make a move to get his jacket or the dog, but stood watching the snow.

"Let me give you lunch first. How about grilled cheese sandwiches and hot chocolate?"

While Mrs. O'Neill fixed the sandwiches, Selene stood at the window, her back to us. From the way she held Little Erica up to the glass, I guessed she was showing her the snow.

Mrs. O'Neill set sandwiches and hot chocolate on the counter and called Selene.

"I don't want to eat with them boys." She didn't turn around, but stayed at the window, her back to the room.

"Well, how about if I seat you at the breakfast table over by the window?"

Selene agreed to that, but made sure her chair faced the window, not us.

After we'd eaten, Brody thanked Mrs. O'Neill

for lunch. "I really ought to go home before my daddy starts in to worrying about me."

I said goodbye to the O'Neills and followed Brody outside. There must have been six inches of snow on the ground, and it was still falling. Bella leaped and danced ahead of us, barking as if the snow were the best thing she'd ever seen. My father always said it didn't take much to make a dog happy. Bella was certainly proof of that.

FIFTEEN

I let myself into the house quietly. No fire in the living room, no smell of cooking, but I heard low voices in the kitchen. Mom and Dad were sitting at the table, their breakfast dishes pushed to one side. Last night's pots and pans and dishes filled the sink.

Caught by surprise, they looked at me as if I were a stranger. "Daniel," Dad said. "We thought you'd stay overnight with the O'Neills. The snow and all—" He waved a hand vaguely at the window.

"It's almost stopped."

Mom turned her attention from me to her coffee. I'd never seen her look so bad. Her hair was limp and uncombed, her face shadowed with grief. She wore an old UMass sweatshirt and baggy corduroy pants, the same clothes she'd worn since Erica disappeared.

Dad hadn't shaved, and gray stubble covered his cheeks. His eyes were puffy and red rimmed. He wore a navy sweatshirt and sweatpants, an outfit he usually reserved for watching TV after dinner.

There was an empty wine bottle on the table and an ashtray full of cigarette butts and ashes.

"What's going on?" I asked, fearful that something bad had happened—they'd found Erica dead in the snow or frozen in the woods or, or . . .

"Nothing," Dad said. "Nothing is going on. Nothing has changed. She's still missing, and no one wants to look for her in this snow."

"They don't want to look for her at all," Mom said. "Even the state police say it's hopeless." She lit a cigarette and inhaled so deeply that she coughed.

"Please don't smoke," Dad said. "You know I hate it."

"I'll smoke if I want to." She gave him a nasty look. "It calms my nerves."

Dad shoved his chair away from the table and started up the back stairs.

"Where are you going, Ted?" Mom called.

"To check my email. Just in case—"

"Just in case what?"

"Just in case . . ." He didn't finish the sentence.

"Face it, we'll never see her again." Mom started crying.

Dad went to his den and slammed the door.

My parents had lost their minds. Their marriage was collapsing. The only way to fix things was to find Erica and bring her home. And no one could do that except me.

The next day was gray and cloudy, and the snow was pockmarked with drops falling from trees. School wasn't closed, but Mom said she didn't want me going back yet. That was fine with me.

"The kids and the teachers will torment you with questions," she said. "I don't want them making you even more miserable. People are so insensitive at times like this."

"Is it okay if I go to Woodville with Mrs. O'Neill?

She knows someone who might be able to help Selene."

Mom shrugged. "Go ahead, do what you want, but please tell Mrs. O'Neill I want Erica's doll returned."

Her voice sounded mean and hard again. The mother I used to know had disappeared with Erica.

Mom went to the kitchen and stood at the window, smoking and watching the woods, as if she were waiting to see Erica run toward the house. Dad was working at his computer. He'd set up a website in hope of getting in touch with someone who'd seen Erica. He had lots of hits, all worthless. A man had seen her in a diner in Kentucky; a woman had seen her in a Walmart in Tennessee. Someone else saw her waving frantically from the rear window of a car on I-95 North. She was in Alaska, Italy, California. On buses, planes, trains. Those who hadn't seen her either prayed for her or accused my father of faking the disappearance. Maybe he'd murdered her. Maybe he wanted money. Yet Dad checked every one of them and alerted the police when he received a sighting.

With no one to talk to and nothing to do, I spent most of the day in my room, playing games on my iPad to keep from blaming myself over and over again for Erica's disappearance. Why hadn't I let her pick up the doll? Why? Why?

The phone rang around two. It was Mrs. O'Neill. She'd come by for me in half an hour, if that was okay with my parents. I told her it was fine. I didn't say they probably wouldn't even notice I was gone.

When Mrs. O'Neill arrived, she handed me the clothes Selene had helped herself to. I left them on the porch so I wouldn't have to go back inside, where my parents were arguing endlessly over whose fault it was.

I sat in the front seat, and Selene sat in the back. I guessed she was wearing clothes Eleanor had worn when she was little—a blue jacket with a belt and a fake fur collar, corduroy jeans, and a pair of yellow rubber boots. Selene didn't look at me, but kept her head bent over the doll. Nothing unusual about that.

Railroad Avenue was in the worst part of Woodville. We passed taverns, boarded-up stores, an abandoned gas station. A stray dog poked its nose into overflowing garbage cans that were half buried in snow. Newspapers blew down the icy sidewalks. A few people came in and out of a shabby market.

Mrs. O'Neill drove slowly, looking for the house number. "Forty-eight eleven," she said. "This is it."

She parked in front of a shabby little house that was badly in need of paint. The roof sagged under the weight of the snow. No one had shoveled the walk. No footprints led to the door.

"Do you think she's home?" I asked.

"Let's find out." Mrs. O'Neill picked up Selene and led the way to the porch through knee-deep snow.

Not a sound from inside. She pressed the bell, waited awhile, and tried again.

"Maybe it's broken," I said.

She nodded and knocked. Once, twice, several times. I shivered from cold and maybe a little fear. The house was rundown and dark. One window was covered with a sheet of plastic, another boarded up. The porch buckled under our feet. The walls were sprayed with gang tags and badly drawn pictures of witches and devils and monsters.

Just as we were about to give up, the door opened a crack and a woman peered out. She was not just old — she was ancient. Bent and bony, no bigger than Selene, her flyaway white hair floated around her head like dandelions gone to seed. She'd wrapped herself in a thick knitted shawl of every imaginable color woven into complex patterns—a sun here, a moon there, stars all over, rivers and trees and birds and animals. A person could look at it all day and still find something he hadn't noticed before.

"What do you want with me?" she croaked. Her eyes glittered in her shadowy face.

Mrs. O'Neill put Selene down and held out her hand. "I'm Irene O'Neill, and I've come to you for help." The old woman looked at her hand, but didn't take it.

"I don't help strangers." She was about to slam the door in our faces.

"Wait, don't be so hasty!" Mrs. O'Neill pushed Selene forward. "What if I told you this girl is Selene Estes? Would you help us then?"

Miss Perkins froze. Instead of slamming the door, she leaned out and peered down at Selene, studying her as if she were a book she needed to learn. She touched Selene's cheek, stared into her eyes, examined a strand of her hair. I think she even sniffed her. Shaking her head, she mumbled and muttered to herself and gazed over Selene's head at the darkening sky.

At last she spoke to Mrs. O'Neill. "I smell Auntie on this here girl. I feel her touch."

Selene tugged at Miss Perkins's arm. "Can you make her take me back, ma'am? I'm still strong. I can do the work."

"Go back to Auntie? Whatever for?"

"She told me to go live someplace else, she was done with me. But I ain't done with her."

When Selene began to sob, Mrs. O'Neill tried to comfort her, but the girl pulled away. "Leave me be," she cried. "I don't want nobody but Auntie!"

"I reckon you better come inside." Miss Perkins opened the door wide, and we followed her into a dark hallway. The house smelled of mildew and mold and cat pee. An old carpet, stained and worn through in spots, covered the floor. Bulging boxes and bundles stood in piles and stacks against the walls. It was a good thing Miss Perkins was a skinny little woman. A normal-size person would need to turn sideways to squeeze down that hall.

At the top of a flight of steps, several cats stared down at us. Others crouched on the stacks of boxes. A few more wound around our ankles, meowing.

To our left, raggedy velvet curtains framed a

doorway into a small room that was also filled with bundles and boxes, with just enough space left for a sagging couch and a rocking chair. The windows were covered with blinds. A small fire burned on the hearth, barely enough to light the room, even though it wasn't much past three o'clock.

"Set there on the sofa," Miss Perkins said as she took a seat in the rocking chair.

Displacing more cats, the three of us crowded onto the sofa, Selene on one side of Mrs. O'Neill and me on the other. Pressed close to her, I felt the tension in her body. I was tense too. Scared, even. The house reeked of dark secrets, of sorrow and misery. I understood why Brody had refused to come with us.

I glanced at Selene. She hadn't stopped staring at Miss Perkins. Maybe not even to blink. She and the doll had the same blank-eyed look on their faces.

"Now then," Miss Perkins said to Mrs. O'Neill. "Here's the way I see it. Auntie must have took the boy's sister when she let Selene go. She'll work his sister fifty years, and then, when she's worn-out like this one, she'll let her go and take another girl."

"I ain't worn-out. I can still do the work," Selene insisted.

Miss Perkins ignored Selene. Closing her eyes, she rocked in her chair for a few moments, nodding to herself, clasping and unclasping her hands. "You won't like it, but here's the truth of it," she said. "Auntie's been doing this for over two hundred years now. She's got no reason to quit, and I ain't got the power to stop her."

I peered into the old woman's face. Her eyes, hidden by drooping lids and wrinkles, were set way back in her skull, so I couldn't guess what she was thinking or even be sure where she was looking.

"Please," I whispered. "There must be something you can do to get Erica back. My parents are going crazy."

Firelight danced across her face, making her wrinkles stand out as if they'd been carved into her skin. "What on earth do you want me to do, boy?"

"Can't you trade Selene back?"

"Daniel!" Mrs. O'Neill turned to me, obviously shocked. "You can't mean that."

"It's what Selene wants," I told her, surprised at her disapproval of my idea. "She said so herself. She wants to be with Auntie."

Before Mrs. O'Neill could say a word, Miss

Perkins said, "Didn't I just tell you—that girl is worn-out, used up. She's no good to Auntie—which is why she took your sister."

"Just take me to her," Selene begged. "Give me a chance to show her I can still do the chores."

Miss Perkins shook her head. "I know it ain't easy, but you got to make the best of your life here."

The old woman sat back in the rocker, her face now hidden in shadows. She was quiet for so long that I thought she'd fallen asleep. I looked at Mrs. O'Neill and whispered, "Should we leave?"

Miss Perkins must have heard me. "I ain't sleeping. I'm pondering." With surprising energy, she pushed herself up and out of the rocking chair. "You all come back here tomorrow afternoon. By then I might have an idea or two."

She walked to the door with us and watched Mrs. O'Neill help Selene with zippers and mittens. "The poor child," Miss Perkins said softly. "She's under a spell, like that girl who come back fifty year ago and died in the orphanage. When Auntie lets them go, they ain't long for this world."

Mrs. O'Neill stared at the old woman. "Please don't talk like that in front of the child."

Selene didn't seem to have heard. She was standing with her back to us, watching the cats racing each other up and down the steps.

Miss Perkins sighed. "Ain't none of that girl's fault my auntie took her. Must be something I can do to stop that old woman, her and that hog of hers."

She opened the door and ushered us out. "I'll see you tomorrow."

With that, we were on the porch with the door shut behind us. It was dark now, and the sliver of moon high above us didn't do much to light our way down the icy sidewalk to the car.

"Well," Mrs. O'Neill said as she started the engine. "I don't know what to make of the old woman."

"Do you trust her?" I asked.

Mrs. O'Neill bit her lower lip and eased the car over the ruts in the icy road. In the headlights I saw a skinny dog running along the sidewalk. He had something in his mouth—a scrap he'd found in the garbage, I guessed.

"I'm truly hoping she can get your sister back. How, I don't know—just so it doesn't involve trading one child for another."

She paused as she turned right from Railroad

Avenue onto Main Street. It was only five o'clock, but not a single store was open. Except for the street-lights and a traffic light set on blinking red, the town was dark.

"I'm also hoping we can keep Selene with us for a long time," she said.

I looked over my shoulder at the back seat. Selene was staring out the window, watching the buildings and houses slip past. Her face was pale and sad. The doll lay beside her as if she didn't care about it anymore. I think she knew then that she'd never see Auntie again.

SIXTEEN

As Mrs. O'Neill pulled her car into my driveway, she asked me if I'd like to have dinner at her house. "My daughter Eleanor will be here," she said. "It should be interesting to see what happens between her and Selene."

While Mrs. O'Neill and Selene waited, I ran into the house to ask permission. Dad was sitting on the couch by himself, staring into the fire. The room was dark.

Barely acknowledging me, he nodded. "Sure, sure, go ahead. I don't think your mother plans on cooking anything tonight."

"Where is she?"

He shrugged. "Upstairs, taking a nap."

"At five thirty?"

"Go on, Daniel. Don't keep Mrs. O'Neill waiting." He poured himself a glass of wine and went back to staring into the fire.

On the way out, I glanced upstairs, wondering if I should check on Mom. I decided against it and ran from the house to the warm car. Was this how it was going to be from now on? Mom upstairs sleeping, Dad drinking wine in the dark? I had to get my sister back.

"Is everything okay?" Mrs. O'Neill asked.

"Fine." I kept my head turned so she wouldn't see my face. One sympathetic look and I'd break down and tell her everything.

At the O'Neills' house, lights shone from windows and woodsmoke rose from the chimney into the cold night. Mrs. O'Neill helped Selene out of the car and led us inside. From the sounds and smells, I figured that Mr. O'Neill was busy in the kitchen. A tall gray-haired woman waited in the hallway as we took off our coats and jackets, scarves and hats and mittens. While she hugged her mother, Eleanor stared at Selene. She was so pale, I thought she might faint dead away.

Selene didn't so much as glance at Eleanor. Turning her back on all of us, she went into the living room, sat down near the fire, and began whispering to Little Erica.

"My God, Mother," Eleanor whispered. "She's fifty-seven years old, but she looks like she did on the day she disappeared. How can that be?"

"I warned you," Mrs. O'Neill said.

Eleanor took her mother's arm. I could almost smell her fear and confusion. "Do you think she'll remember me?"

"Maybe you should go sit beside her and tell her who you are."

Eleanor looked so scared, you'd have thought Selene was a ghost—which in a way I guessed she was, a girl come back from the dead unchanged.

"What's the matter?" Mrs. O'Neill asked.

Eleanor bit her lip just the way her mother did when she was nervous. "It's a shock, Mom, seeing her again, looking exactly the same. I recognize her, but how can she possibly recognize me?" She glanced uneasily at the child in the living room. "I don't know what to say, what to do."

"Selene needs our help, Eleanor. She's so unhappy, I fear she'll fade away from us altogether if we don't reach her." Mrs. O'Neill patted her daughter's arm. "Why don't you talk to her awhile — win her trust, maybe."

I watched Eleanor cross the room slowly. Sitting on the floor beside Selene, she smiled at her. "I'm Mrs. O'Neill's daughter Eleanor," she told her. "What's your name?"

Without looking at Eleanor, Selene said, "I'm called Girl."

Eleanor sent her mother an anxious glance. "I had a friend when I was your age," she told Selene. "She looked just like you."

"It wasn't me, if that's what you're thinking."

"Her name was Selene, and she lived right up the road. We played together every day."

"Well, I ain't never played with nobody. I worked every day and half the night for Auntie."

Eleanor glanced at her mother again. Mrs. O'Neill joined the two of them in front of the fire.

"Try to remember, Selene," she said gently. "You spent the first seven years of your life playing with Eleanor—hopscotch and jump rope and—"

Selene jumped to her feet, her face flushed with anger. "I declare I'm sick to death of hearing about that girl! My name ain't Selene. How many times I got to tell you?"

Mrs. O'Neill reached out to pat Selene's shoulder, but the girl pulled away from her. "Leave me be!"

Jumping to her feet, Selene ran from the room and up the stairs. Overhead, a door slammed shut.

Mrs. O'Neill started to go after her, but Eleanor stopped her. "You heard her, Mom. She wants us to leave her alone."

Mrs. O'Neill looked upstairs. Even with the door shut, we could hear Selene crying. "She's so unhappy, so confused. She needs someone to help her remember who she is."

"I don't know who she is, but she's *not* Selene," Eleanor said. "She can't be—it's simply not possible."

I could tell that Eleanor's attitude disappointed her mother. "You grew up here," Mrs. O'Neill said. "You know about Old Auntie. She's turned Selene loose and taken Daniel's sister."

"I'm sorry, but I don't believe those old stories anymore. Maybe that girl was abandoned in the woods and raised by wild animals. That's no more far-fetched than your explanation. Call Social Services. They'll know what to do."

Mrs. O'Neill stared at her daughter as if she didn't know her. "And let the child die like the one before her?"

Eleanor gathered up her coat and her purse. "I'm going home. Call me when you come to your senses."

Mr. O'Neill came in from the kitchen, wearing his chef's apron. "What's going on?" he said. "Surely you're not leaving before we eat. I roasted a chicken and made your favorite dressing."

But Eleanor went on zipping her parka. Her face was determined. "I'm sorry, Dad, but I can't stay in the same house with that girl. It's too upsetting."

"We were hoping you could help her," he said.

"There's nothing I can do for her." Eleanor took her mother's hands in hers. "Please hand her over to the authorities."

Mrs. O'Neill shook her head. "I can't do that. I *won't* do that. Selene stays here."

Eleanor released her mother's hands. "All right,

do what you think is best, but don't ask me to be involved." She went to the kitchen door, but before she opened it, she looked at her parents. "I'm sorry, I really am, but there's something very wrong with that child, and it scares me."

As Eleanor stepped out into the cold, dark night, Mrs. O'Neill followed her to the door, as if she meant to call her back.

Mr. O'Neill stopped her. "Give her time," he said. "Let her think about this. For fifty years she's believed that Selene was dead. And now—put yourself in Eleanor's place."

Mrs. O'Neill sighed. "Well, dinner is ready for those who want to eat."

Mr. O'Neill went to the foot of the stairs and called Selene. Silence. He called again. And again. After three tries, he climbed the steps and knocked on a door.

"Selene, dinner's ready. Come down and join us."

"I ain't hungry," she answered.

"It's roast chicken and mashed potatoes and green beans."

"I said I ain't hungry."

"We'll save some for you," he said.

While we ate, I glanced at the empty places set for Eleanor and Selene. I wished Eleanor had stayed and tried harder, but maybe Mr. O'Neill was right and she'd change her mind. I wished that Selene was sitting at her place, eating her food, and behaving like a normal girl.

But most of all, I wished that Erica was sitting beside me.

After dinner, Mr. O'Neill offered to drive me home. When we were alone in the car, he asked me how my folks were doing.

"Okay, I guess."

He looked at me. "Okay, you guess? That doesn't sound good."

We were heading down the driveway toward our house, which stood out stark and gray against the snowy fields. One light shone in Mom and Dad's bedroom window. The clock on the dashboard said eight fifteen. Too early for them to be in bed.

Mr. O'Neill parked beside the back porch. To my surprise, he walked up the steps with me. The door wasn't locked—in case Erica came home, Mom said.

"Dad? Mom?" I called. "It's me."

Nobody answered. The kitchen was dark and cold.

Mr. O'Neill went to the foot of the back stairs and called, "Ted, you up there?"

A door opened, and light from Dad's study spilled down the steps. "John, is that you?"

"Yep, I brought your boy home."

Dad appeared at the top of the steps, backlit so we couldn't see his face. "Good of you," he said to Mr. O'Neill. "Thanks. I hope he wasn't a nuisance."

"Oh, no, not at all. Daniel's no trouble."

I turned on the kitchen light and watched Dad come downstairs. "Where's Mom?" I asked.

"In bed, reading." He went to the cupboard and pulled out a whiskey bottle. "Have a drink, John."

Mr. O'Neill sat at the table, and Dad filled a couple of glasses. I opened a can of soda and started to join them, but Dad told me to go up to bed. I started to protest, but changed my mind and did what he said. Maybe a talk with Mr. O'Neill would be good for him.

Before I went to my room, I knocked on Mom's

door. "It's me, Daniel," I called softly. "Are you awake?"

"Come in," she said.

"Are you all right?" I asked. She didn't look all right—hair still uncombed, bags under her eyes, dressed in an old bathrobe over her pajamas. Huddled under blankets and quilts, she had the look of an invalid.

"Of course I am. Why do you ask?"

I shrugged, embarrassed. "You don't usually go to bed this early."

"The house is so cold. I can't get warm anywhere but here." She looked around the room. "Why did we move here? Why did I let your father talk me into it?" She pulled the covers up around her shoulders and stared at the black night pressing against the windows.

"Mom," I said. "I—"

"Who's downstairs with your father?" she interrupted.

"Mr. O'Neill. He brought me home."

"Did you see that girl at their house?"

"Yes. She's staying with them."

"She belongs in an institution." Mom handed me an empty wineglass. "Make yourself useful, Daniel. Go fill this up for me. Red, not white. I hate white wine in the winter."

I backed away from her, but she was staring out the window again. "Do you think she's out there somewhere? Will she come back? Will we see her again?" She began to cry. "I can't stand this. I can't bear it. I want my daughter. I want Erica!"

"Mom—"

"Go to bed, Daniel. Let me alone, please, just go away."

"But what about—" I held up the wineglass.

"No. I changed my mind. I don't want it." She lay down and hid her face in her pillows.

"Well, good night," I said.

When she didn't answer, I left the room and closed the door. What was I supposed to do? Nothing was right in our house. Not even me.

SEVENTEEN

The next day, Mrs. O'Neill picked me up around three. Selene huddled in the back seat, hugging the doll, her face mournful. Snowflakes drifted in the gray air, floating up and down, swirling like tiny moths.

By the time we parked in front of Miss Perkins's house, an inch of fluffy snow coated the old snow, making it look fresh and new. We walked to the front door silently. No one had said much during the ride into Woodville. I think we were each locked in our own thoughts, wondering what Miss Perkins might tell us. Each of us hoping, hoping, hoping . . .

We waited on the cold porch for at least five minutes before the door opened and Miss Perkins stepped aside to let us enter. Three cats shot out of the house and two ran in.

Inside, it was as dark and cold and smelly as before. A small fire burned low on the hearth, but we didn't take off our coats.

For a while, no one spoke. It was as if we were waiting for Miss Perkins to tell us something and she was waiting for us to tell her something. A black cat crept into her lap, and two more emerged from the shadows to crouch at her feet. They watched us steadily, unblinking. I wondered how she told them apart.

The fire popped and crackled, and the wind did its best to squeeze in through every crack. Selene coughed. Mrs. O'Neill crossed and uncrossed her ankles. Somewhere in the back of the house, a cat yowled. *There must be dozens of them,* I thought, mostly black, gray, and dark tabbies.

"This is how it is," Miss Perkins said suddenly. "Selene, there's no way you can go back to my auntie. She don't want you no more. You must learn to live in the here and now—or die. Them's your choices. If I was you, I'd choose to live."

Tears ran down Selene's face, but she said nothing. She simply sat and stared as if she were a cat too, half wild, not one you dared to pet.

Miss Perkins turned her eyes to me. "She means to keep your sister for fifty years," she said, "just like she kept Selene and all the ones before her."

"There must be something you can do," I whispered. "My family is wrecked. My mother, my father—" I couldn't go on without losing my self-control and throwing myself at her feet, crying and begging for her help.

"I didn't say there's no way to get your sister back." Miss Perkins spoke so sharply, the cat on her lap raised its head, startled out of its nap.

"Have you actually spoken to her?" Mrs. O'Neill asked.

"Not exactly." Miss Perkins stroked the cat on her lap. "I got my ways of finding out things on the sly. Things folks don't want me to know. Things I don't want them to know I'm interested in."

Mrs. O'Neill nodded as if she understood, but

like me, I was sure she didn't quite see what the old woman meant. But she was a witch, and we weren't, so why should we expect to understand?

Miss Perkins stretched a hand toward Selene. "Bring me that dolly, dear."

Selene gripped the doll. "What do you want with her? She's mine."

The old woman leaned toward Selene and stared into her eyes. "The dolly," she said. "Give me the dolly."

The air seemed charged with electricity, and my skin tingled as if a thunderstorm were rolling through the house. I wanted to jump up and run from the dark room and the craziness of the old woman, but something kept me where I was.

Selene rose slowly and gave the doll to Miss Perkins. "Good girl," she said as Selene backed away and collapsed on the sofa. Mrs. O'Neill put her arm around her. For once, Selene did not pull away.

In the meantime, Miss Perkins turned the doll this way and that, studying her intently in the dim light of the fire. She caressed Little Erica, moved her arms and legs, and hummed to herself, as if she'd forgotten we were in the room. After a minute or so, she bent her head over the cat in her lap and seemed to listen. He made a strange sound, not a meow, not a growl, not a purr, but something like all three. She nodded her head slowly.

At last Miss Perkins looked up. Her eyes seemed unfocused, as if she weren't seeing us or the room, but was looking at something far away. Selene and I moved closer to Mrs. O'Neill. She held us both tightly.

Miss Perkins slowly came back to the room and the fire and the three of us. Her sharp eyes fixed themselves on me. "Come here, boy. Come close."

Even though I wanted to stay where I was, safe and warm beside Mrs. O'Neill, I did as she said. The old woman smelled of dried grass and herbs and flowers. A nice smell. I sniffed and breathed it in, feeling it spread through me like magic.

"How much do you want your sister back, boy?" she whispered. Her eyes probed mine.

"I'd do anything to get her away from Auntie."

"Will you go to Auntie's cabin tonight, all by yourself? No mammy, no pappy, nobody. All by yourself. Just you. Are you brave enough?"

I stared at her, almost speechless. "Tonight?"

"You said you want your sister back. You said you'll do anything. This is the onliest way to do it."

I glanced at Mrs. O'Neill to see what she thought. Her eyes were open but unfocused, as blank as Little Erica's eyes. She and Selene seemed to be in a trance.

Miss Perkins leaned toward me and studied my face. "You brave enough? 'Cause if you ain't, you'll never see your sister till fifty years from now. And that one there will be soon be dead." She nodded at Selene. "It's for both these girls you're doing it. You break the spell for your sister, you break it for Selene, too. Once the spell's broke, Auntie will be finished. The dark will take her."

I tried to stand tall and straight. Maybe if I acted brave, I'd be brave. "What do I have to do?" My voice came out in a squeak.

"You go to the door of the cabin at midnight — not one minute earlier, not one minute later. Knock three times. Auntie will call out, 'Who's that knock, knock, knocking at my door?' You'll say, 'A poor traveler lost in the cold.' She'll say, 'What you want with me?' You'll say, 'To sit by your fire a spell.'"

Miss Perkins stroked the cat's black fur and

crooned to him. Except for the wind and the fire, the room was as still as death.

"She'll ask you to tell her a riddle," she went on. "First you say, 'I brung you a cherry without a stone.'" Miss Perkins reached into her pocket and drew out a blossom. She laid it carefully on the table beside her. "A cherry don't have a stone when it's blooming."

"Second, say, 'I brung you a chicken without a bone.'" Miss Perkins took an egg from her pocket and laid it beside the blossom. "A chicken don't have bones while it's in the egg."

"They're old riddles," she said. "Everyone knows the answers, so she'll ask for something harder, a riddle she's never heard before."

The old woman coughed and sniffed and fidgeted with the doll. "Last of all, say, 'I brung you a servant that never tires and never grows old.'" She added Little Erica to the objects on the table.

"It ain't a riddle she'll have heard before. If she can't guess the answer in three tries, she's got to open the door and let you in."

My heart knocked about in my chest, hammering and pounding my ribs. "But when she sees me, she'll know who I am."

"Auntie ain't the onliest one that knows her way around the dark side of the moon. I got tricks of my own, boy. She won't know you. I'll see to that."

The cat interrupted her with an odd, questioning sort of noise. Miss Perkins stroked him till he purred loud enough to make my bones vibrate.

"Soon as you're through the door," she went on, "Auntie will ask you for the answer to the riddle. Open the sack and show her the servant that never tires and never grows old. Once she sees that dolly, she'll forget about your sister. At least for a while—"

"But—" I couldn't stop myself from interrupting the old woman again. "She *knows* the doll belongs to Erica. And how can a doll be a servant? She's plastic, she's not alive, she can't move or talk or—"

"Hush up and quit asking fool questions. You got to trust me, boy. Get your sister out of the cabin as fast as you can. She won't want to come. You'll have to drag her away. Run for home like you got wings on your heels or seven-league boots on your feet."

"But what if—"

"Don't vex me no more, boy. Do what I tell you, bring your sister home, and the spell will bust at sunrise—for both girls. They'll remember who they are in this world, but they won't remember nothing about Auntie's world." Miss Perkins scrunched her face into a tight fist, and the cat lashed his tail and hissed at me.

My brain whirled with questions, but my voice had dried up and my mouth felt numb, the way it does in the dentist's office when he gives you Novocain. I nodded, as if I understood, and hoped I'd be able to do all she asked.

Miss Perkins put my sister's doll into a burlap sack, tied it shut, and gave it to me. "No matter what, don't open this sack until you're inside the cabin, and don't be scairt of the dolly."

Before I could ask her why I'd be scared of a doll, she gave me a warning look, and I shut my mouth.

Miss Perkins nodded, took a deep breath, and let it out slowly. "Now go sit on that sofa and keep your mouth shut about everything I done told you."

I took my place next to Mrs. O'Neill, who continued to stare straight ahead at nothing I could see.

Miss Perkins murmured a few words to the cat. The moment he closed his eyes, Mrs. O'Neill and Selene came back from wherever they'd been. They stretched and yawned as if they'd been napping.

Selene looked bewildered, as if she wasn't quite sure where she was. Although I expected her to ask about the doll, she didn't say a word.

"Thank you for your time," Mrs. O'Neill said to Miss Perkins. "I'm sorry you can't do anything to help us. That poor child—fifty years is a long time."

"The years will go by in a flash." Miss Perkins picked up a ball of yarn and her knitting—a lumpy black scarf already long enough to wrap two or three times around her neck.

Gently helping Selene to her feet, Mrs. O'Neill turned to me. "Come along, Daniel. The snow's getting worse. Your parents must be worried."

"See yourselves out," Miss Perkins said. "I'm a mite weary tonight. When you're old as me, the cold settles in your bones and sets them to aching and scraping against each other."

"Good night, then," Mrs. O'Neill said. "Take care of yourself, Miss Perkins."

"You, too, dearie, and don't fret yourself about the snow. It'll stop soon enough."

We left Miss Perkins sitting by the fire, knitting and humming to herself while the cat dozed on her lap. Outside, the cold air froze the hairs in my nose, and my eyes watered, but I was glad to be away from the smoky smell of the house.

I kept the sack behind my back, but no one noticed it. Selene sat behind me with her nose pressed against the window and watched the empty streets of Woodville glide past. A flake or two of snow drifted past the windshield, but Miss Perkins was right—the moon was already breaking through the clouds.

As usual, our house looked dark and vacant. As it had the previous night, a lamp glimmered in Mom's bedroom window, but the downstairs windows were lit only by the headlights of the car.

Mrs. O'Neill stared at the house. "My goodness, Daniel, is anyone home?"

"They're upstairs," I said. "The light's on in the bedroom. Dad's office is in the back—that's where he is." Where he always is—lost in computer games and websites for missing children.

As I opened the car door, she asked, "Do you want me to come in with you?"

"No, it's okay. Everything's fine." What a good liar I was getting to be. "Thanks for taking me to see Miss Perkins again."

While we talked, I was aware of Selene watching

me through the window. I waved to her, but she turned away.

Mrs. O'Neill said goodbye and turned around slowly, her headlights washing over the unpainted sides of our house. I watched the taillights grow small as the car disappeared around the curve in the driveway.

The kitchen looked the way it always did. Sink full of dirty dishes. Trash can overflowing with pizza boxes, beer cans, and wine bottles. Table littered with newspapers, paper plates, coffee cups, forks and knives and spoons, an empty wine bottle, ashtrays heaped with cigarette butts.

"Dad? Mom?" I called.

"Up here," Dad answered.

I climbed the back stairs slowly, keeping the sack behind my back. It was the new normal—Dad playing a war game on the computer, Mom huddled in her room under a quilt, reading.

"We saved some pizza for you," Mom said. "It's in the fridge. Just heat it up in the microwave."

"Thanks." I stowed the sack under my bed and went down to the kitchen to warm up the pizza. The crust tasted like burned cardboard and the cheese had turned to something that resembled melted plastic and stuck to my teeth, but I ate it anyway. I was going to be out in the cold a long time. I needed something in my belly.

For a while I sat at the table and watched the clock. Seven p.m., eight p.m.—time crept past. Upstairs, my parents were silently engrossed in their books and games.

I said good night to them and went to my room. They barely acknowledged my presence. It was as if I'd disappeared too. If I failed tonight, if Bloody Bones killed and ate me, would they care? Would they send anyone to look for me? Or would they just sink deeper and deeper into the house, burrowing under blankets, eating bad pizza, drinking, smoking, not even noticing I was gone?

For at least an hour I stood at my window, trying to remember the way our family used to be, but only seeing myself teasing Erica and making her cry, forcing her to leave the doll in the woods. Why had I been so mean to her?

I shivered in the cold air that leaked through the

loose windowpanes and watched the wind blow the clouds away. The moon sailed into sight and shone on the snowy fields. In its bright light I saw the beginning of the path that led to Auntie's cabin.

I glanced at my clock. Ten thirty. It was time to go.

EIGHTEEN

I hauled the burlap sack out from under the bed, grabbed a flashlight, and tiptoed downstairs. Even though I'd heard Dad go to bed and I knew Mom was with him, the house felt empty, so dark and cold and silent I could hear my own breathing. I pulled one of Erica's old jackets off the coatrack, grabbed a pair of mittens, a hat, and her red boots, and stuffed everything into a backpack. Zipping my parka, I stepped into the darkness. The cold wind hit me like a fist, and the freezing air hurt my chest.

Crouched in the snow, I took a long look at the house. Then with my head down, I ran across the field and into the woods. No one but deer and small animals had walked on the path since it snowed, so I slipped and slid and sank to my knees over and over again, clambering out of one snowdrift and stumbling into another.

The burlap sack made everything worse. With every step I took, it grew heavier. I didn't understand how the doll could weigh so much. Maybe plowing through the snow was taking all my energy, leaving me tired and weak legged.

I was about to open the sack to make sure something else wasn't in there—a few boulders maybe—but I remembered what Miss Perkins had told me. If I wanted to rescue Erica, I had to do exactly what the old woman said.

By the time I reached the trail to the top of Brewster's Hill, I was exhausted. There was no protection from the wind. Snow blew in my face. Hard, icy pellets stung my skin and made my forehead ache. Every now and then I glimpsed shadowy shapes in the darkness—deer, I hoped.

There were noises, too—owls, foxes, and the low mutters of other things, growling and snarling, squealing and yelping in the woods. Brody told me there were wild hogs up here, razorbacks like Bloody Bones. I told myself it wasn't the monster hog I heard out there, but my knees shook with fear.

The sack grew so heavy I could barely drag it uphill. Gasping for breath, I thought it was like a backpack that never weighed much when I left home, but grew heavier after an hour or so of hiking. I felt like Atlas carrying the world on my shoulders.

Again I was tempted to open the sack and take out whatever was weighing it down, but when I started fumbling with the rope that held it closed, I swear I heard Miss Perkins's voice in the wind telling me not to do it. I sighed and began climbing again, dragging the sack behind me.

When I finally reached the top of the hill, it was almost midnight. Stunned, I stared at the scene before me. No longer in ruins, the cabin looked like something in a fairy tale. Snow covered its roof, icicles hung from its eves, smoke rose from its chimney, and candles glowed in its windows.

I crept closer, scared that Old Auntie would hear my footsteps. After hiding my backpack behind a rock near the cabin, I laid the sack down by the cabin door, glad to be relieved of its weight. Shadows cast by the windblown trees made the sack seem to be moving. Uneasily, I edged away from it. It wasn't a trick of the shadows. The sack had begun to move, as if something inside wanted to get out.

I heard Old Auntie walking around inside the cabin, berating someone in a harsh voice. "Lazy girl, stupid girl," she said. "You ain't worth a wooden nickel. The girl afore you done all I asked and more, but you act like you never scrubbed a pot in your life."

I heard a smack and a low cry. "Don't hit me, Auntie. I'm doing my best." *Erica,* I thought, *Erica's in there.* Yet I stood at the door like a statue, afraid to raise my hand and knock.

"Well, your best ain't good enough, is it?" Another slap. Another cry from my sister.

The moon cast my shadow on the door, making me seem much larger than I was. I forced myself to knock three times.

From inside, a shrill voice called, "Who's that knock, knock, knocking at my door?"

"A poor traveler lost in the cold." Fear made it hard to keep my voice steady.

"What do you want with me?"

"To sit by your fire a spell."

"Ask me a riddle, and maybe I'll let you in."

I took a deep breath. Hoping I remembered the words, I said, "I brung you a cherry without a stone."

"A cherry when it's blooming, it has no stone," Old Auntie answered. "Ask me another that ain't so easy."

"I brung you a chicken that has no bone."

"Hah, another easy one—a chicken when it's pipping, it has no bone." Old Auntie laughed. "Now you tell me one I ain't heard, laddie, and make it snappy."

"I brung you a servant that never tires and never grows old." At my feet, the sack lurched wildly, and a harsh voice cried, "Let me out!"

I backed away in horror, but inside the cabin, all was silence. Auntie must have been mulling over the riddle. "A servant that never tires and never grows old?"

"Yes, ma'am."

The sack heaved. "Let me out!"

"Is the answer *time*?" Auntie called.

"No, ma'am."

Another silence. "You sure it's not *time*?"

"Yes, ma'am."

"That's right. Time ain't nobody's servant," she muttered. "T'other way round, I reckon." Another moment of silence. "How about water? Is that the answer?"

"No, ma'am."

Again the sack twitched with life. Again the voice cried, "Let me out!"

"Is it fire, then?" Auntie asked through the door.

"No, none of them is right, ma'am." That was three wrong guesses. She had to let me in.

Sure enough, a key jiggled in a lock and the door slowly opened. The old woman who'd terrified me in the woods poked her head out.

Spotting the sack, she asked, "What's in that there gunnysack?"

"The answer to the riddle," I told her. "Let me in and you'll see."

She stepped back, and I dragged the sack inside.

It was all I could do to manage it. It humped up and swayed from side to side. Something in that sack was definitely alive.

Behind Old Auntie, my sister crouched by the fire. Although I'd told myself that Erica might not look like herself, I had no idea she'd be almost un-recognizable. Thin and pale, dirty and barefoot, her hair an uncombed thicket of tangles, she wore a col-orless, shapeless dress that hung loosely from her bony frame. More than anyone else, she looked like Selene—the same sullen expression on her face, the same fear, the same exhaustion. She could have been Selene's twin.

It was clear that she didn't know me, and judg-ing by the look in her eyes, she didn't trust me either. How was I to get her out of the cabin and drag her all the way home?

Auntie must have noticed me staring at Erica, because she said, "Don't pay her no mind. She ain't nobody. Just Girl. The worst servant I ever had. Don't know the meaning of work."

Hiding her face, Erica fed twigs into the fire. "I'm sorry, Auntie," she whispered. "I do my best."

"I told you your best ain't nearly good enough, Girl." Old Auntie started struggling with the rope that tied the sack closed. "There's something alive in here," she cried. "It wants out. Get away, laddie. Let's see what you brung me."

She shoved me aside. At the moment I was more scared of the doll than I was of Old Auntie.

"It's my servant, ain't it? The answer to that there riddle about never getting tired and never getting old."

She tore the sack open, and the doll jumped out. It was the size of Erica herself, but it looked nothing like Little Erica. Its hair was tangled and fell over its bony face like a thicket of brambles. Its arms were long and skinny, its sharp nails like claws. It wore tatters of clothing, stained and faded. The fabric was so thin I saw its ribs.

With a grin as wicked as death, the conjure woman laughed with delight and picked up the doll. "Why, ain't you the ugliest little critter I ever did see!"

"Let me down, Auntie, let me down!" As soon as its feet hit the floor, it grabbed a broom and began sweeping, running this way and that like a wind-up toy, lurching and bumping into things, knocking furniture over, breaking bowls, scattering Auntie's things like leaves in a winter storm.

"Auntie, Auntie," it cried, "catch me if you can!"

While Auntie chased it around the cabin, I grabbed Erica and hauled her toward the door. Just as I expected, she fought the way Selene had, kicking, scratching, biting. It was like holding a wild animal.

"Auntie!" she screamed. "Auntie!"

But the old woman was too busy to notice what was happening. Or maybe she didn't care about my sister now that she had a new servant. She caught the creature and slapped its face hard.

"Bad girl," she screamed, and shook it until its bones rattled and its head bobbed. "Look what you done!"

Once Erica and I were outside, I held her still, forced her arms into the jacket's sleeves, and zipped up the front. I jammed the hat on her head, but she kicked so hard I couldn't get the boots on her feet. Abandoning them, I snatched up my backpack and dragged my sister toward the trail.

"Auntie, Auntie!" she shrieked.

"What's wrong with you?" I shook her. "We've got to get away from here."

"Leave me be. I don't want to go anywhere!"

"I'm your brother. I've come to take you home."

"Liar! You ain't my brother. I don't have no brother. I got no one save for Auntie—no home but here!" Erica thrashed and flailed and kicked. "Let me go! Let me go!"

I held her tight and kept going, stumbling through the snow. Behind us, I heard a sort of grunting, squealing, growling sound. I looked back and saw Bloody Bones come out of the trees. The moon shone on his bald head and cast his shadow across the snow. His ragged clothes fluttered in the wind. I saw his bones and his claws and his sharp teeth.

Even though Erica slowed me down, I ran and jumped over the snow, going as fast as I could. Bloody Bones wasn't going to stop me from bringing my sister home and making things right again.

Behind us, the cabin door opened, and Old Auntie screamed, "Get them, dear boy, bring them back to me!"

"No, Auntie," Erica cried. "Don't sic him on me! I'll work hard, I'll do things right, I promise!"

Still struggling to keep hold of my sister, I slipped and slid down the trail, trying to keep us from falling. The wind blew us toward the edge of the drop-off, roots and stones rose up to trip us, but I kept going, forcing Erica to keep up with me.

Bloody Bones crashed through the snow behind us, gaining on us with every step. I imagined his breath as foul as death itself, his sharp claws squeezing around my throat, his eyeless skull looming over me in the moonlight.

"Don't let them get away!" Old Auntie's voice mingled with the wind shrieking through the trees. "Stop them—they'll bring us both to ruin."

Bloody Bones snuffled and snorted. His bones rattled. He was gaining on us. I felt him grab at my jacket and miss. I tried to run faster, but a stone turned under my foot, and I fell. I lost my grip on Erica and lay stunned.

Above me stood Bloody Bones. While I lay in the snow staring up at him, he threw back his head and snorted. Then he bent down and pulled me to my feet. His bear claws sank into my shoulders. His face was so close I could see his tusks and his panther fangs and his empty eye sockets. The stink of him made me gag.

His bones rattled as he lifted me above his head. He was going to throw me off the cliff.

Just as he tensed to hurl me into the valley, I heard the crack of something hard hit Bloody Bones. He staggered backward, away from the edge of the cliff, and lost his hold on me. One leg collapsed, and he fell with a clatter of bones.

As he struggled to stand, another rock hit him. This one broke his arm clean off. The shattered bones dropped into the snow. Howling with anger, Bloody Bones lunged toward me, his one arm outstretched to push me to my death, his right leg useless.

Without thinking of anything but surviving, I dodged away from him. Unable to stop in time, Bloody Bones plunged over the edge of the cliff, screaming as he bounced from rock to rock, his bones flying apart and scattering as he went. In seconds, he was gone, leaving only the echo of his scream.

Auntie hobbled down the trail toward us. "My

boy, my dear boy!" she screamed, her face and voice filled with rage and sorrow. "What have you done, you miserable, wicked creature?"

I backed away, but it wasn't me the conjure woman was speaking to. Erica stood behind me. Pale and trembling, she held a rock in each hand.

Old Auntie flung a string of strange words at both of us, but the wind turned them back on her. Raising her hands as if to fend off what she'd said, she began backing slowly up the trail.

"What will I do now without my dear boy?" she cried.

With each step she took, the wind blew harder and her shadow grew fainter, her body less solid. By the time she vanished into the woods, she was almost transparent.

"Auntie." Erica stretched her arms toward the old woman. "Auntie. I'm sorry. Don't leave me. I only meant to stop him from hurting the boy."

Seizing my sister's arm, I yanked her down the trail. She was still struggling when she looked back and screamed, "The cabin's on fire. It's burning! Put it out! Save her!"

I spun around. At the top of Brewster's Hill, flames leaped into the air, lighting the bare trees with an orange glow, sending sparks shooting toward the winter sky.

With a burst of strength, Erica broke away from me and ran up the trail. I ran after her, but this time she was too fast for me. I caught up with her at the cabin.

Or what was left of it. The old rotten wood had exploded in flames and burned so fast that the fire was already flickering over charred logs. Smoke blew sideways in the wind. Embers scattered. I kept a firm grip on Erica to keep her from running into the ruins to rescue Auntie.

"She's gone," I said. Dead and gone, I hoped. Burned to ashes. "You can't do anything for her now."

Erica collapsed against me, sobbing. "Now I got nobody. No home. Nothing."

The fight had gone out of her. I held her tight and wondered if I'd ever hugged her before. I couldn't remember, but I kind of doubted it. Right now, though, I wanted to hold her for a long time, never let her go, never let anything bad ever happen to her again.

"You have me," I told her, "and Mom and Dad."

She shook her head and snuffled. "I ain't got nobody," she insisted. "No brother, no sister, no mother, no father."

In tears, she pulled away from me and stumbled down the trail. She had nothing more to say, and neither did I.

As we came out of the woods, I pointed to our house, a dark box in the field, moonlight glinting off the glass in its windows

"That's where we live," I told her. "You and me and Mom and Dad."

"I never saw that house. I never lived there." Her voice was as dull and lifeless as Selene's, but she let me lead her into the kitchen.

"Mom, Dad!" I shouted. "Come down here."

Upstairs, a bed creaked, footsteps crossed the floor, a door opened. "Daniel," Dad called, "what are you shouting about? It's three a.m."

"Come see!" In a few seconds I'd be a hero, the boy who rescued his sister from the old conjure woman. They'd be so happy, so proud of me. I could hardly wait for them to see Erica.

Dad fumbled with the hall light and came slowly

downstairs, barely awake, from the sound of it. He stopped halfway and stared at Erica. "What's that girl doing here? I thought she was staying with the O'Neills. Your mother won't—"

I stared at him, shocked. "Dad, it's Erica. I found her!"

"Are you crazy?" Dad asked. "Have you completely lost your mind?"

Mom appeared behind him. "Why did you bring that creature here? I won't have her in this house!"

Erica scowled at me. "Didn't I tell you? I'm not your sister. They don't want me. They don't love me. It's just like Auntie said."

She pulled away from me and ran toward the back door, but I grabbed her before she opened it. Holding her tight, I made her face Mom and Dad.

"Please look at her," I told them. "She's been living with a crazy old woman up on Brewster's Hill, and she doesn't remember anything about us—just like Selene. But she's Erica."

"She can't be," Mom whispered. Dad shook his head. With his back to Erica and me, he stared out the kitchen window at the black night.

How could they not recognize their own daughter? Yes, she was dirty, her hair uncombed. She was thin and pale, obviously in the same state as Selene, but under it all, she was my sister and their daughter, the one they'd been mourning for almost a week.

Erica began to cry. "Let me go," she begged. "I don't belong here, I don't belong anywhere, I might as well be dead."

"Please don't talk like that." Slowly Mom reached out and touched Erica's shoulder. "I don't know who you are, but I can't bear to see a child so unhappy."

Erica collapsed against Mom's side. Her bare feet were blue with cold. Her face was bruised, and she was shaking hard enough to make her teeth chatter. "I'm so tired," she whispered. "Please can I sleep by your fire till morning? I promise I won't be no bother. If you got work for me to do, I'll do it. I'll sweep. I'll scrub floors. I'll chop wood."

"You'll do no such thing," Mom said. "You're in no condition to work for us or anyone else."

"And you certainly won't sleep by the fire," Dad said.

"Auntie says my place is on the hearth," Erica said, "by the fire. It's warm there, and I don't mind the hard floor no more."

"You poor child. I don't know who your aunt is, but she's not fit to take care of you." Dad bent down and picked Erica up. She lay as limp as a kitten in his arms, her eyes half closed. "She hardly weighs anything," he said.

I watched him carry her upstairs to her room. She was asleep before Mom covered her with her lavender checked comforter. Mom and Dad stood together, looking down at her, their eyes full of questions.

NINETEEN

At dawn, Erica's cries woke me with a jolt that nearly knocked me out of bed. "Mommy!" she screamed. "Mommy!"

I ran into the hall and followed Mom and Dad into Erica's bedroom. My sister flung herself at Mom, crying hysterically. Over her head, Mom stared at Dad, her eyes wide with shock. Both looked as if they were sleepwalking—groggy, unsteady, trembling.

"Erica, oh, Erica," Mom cried. "It's you. It really *is* you. Oh, darling, you've come home at last."

"We thought we'd lost you," Dad whispered.

"And then, when Daniel brought you home, we, we" — his voice broke for a second — "we didn't even recognize you."

I don't think Erica heard a word my parents said. She was still caught in the snares of her dream. "Hold me tight, Mommy. Don't let Auntie come for me. Keep her away."

Mom rocked Erica as if she were a baby, murmured to her, held her tight. "We won't let anyone take you away."

Gradually Erica stopped crying, but she shivered and shook and looked around fearfully, as if she expected to see Auntie's face at the window.

"You're safe now," Dad said. "Don't be afraid. It was just a dream."

It was then that Erica noticed her hands. "Why are my hands so dirty?" Pulling away from Mom, she stared at her reflection in the mirror over her bureau. A wild-eyed girl with tangled hair and a dirty, bruised face stared back at her. "What's happened to me?"

Mom looked at Dad as if she wasn't sure what to say.

"You've been missing for almost a week," Dad finally said.

"Daniel found you on Brewster's Hill last night," Mom added, "and brought you home."

"What were you doing up there in the cold?" Dad asked. "We've searched every square inch of the woods, the creeks, the lakes, and no one found a trace of you. And now you're here. It's a miracle."

Erica looked puzzled. "I was looking for my doll with Daniel. We couldn't find her—someone took her."

Pausing to catch her breath, Erica spread her fingers and studied her broken nails and the dirt ground into her skin. With a shudder, she flung herself back into Mom's arms. "And then someone took *me*."

Mom held Erica, hugging her and stroking her hair. "No, no," she murmured. "You were lost, but now you're home. We'll never let anyone take you from us."

We sat with Erica for a long time, soothing her, calming her. At last, just as morning light filled the room, she relaxed and fell asleep.

Mom told Dad and me to go to bed. "I'll stay

and watch over her," she whispered. "I don't want her to wake up frightened again."

Even though it was morning, I did what Mom said. I was warm and safe. I'd brought my sister home, and she was sleeping in her own bed. As soon as I pulled up the covers, I dropped into sleep like a stone falling into a well.

When I came downstairs, Dad was in the kitchen. While I'd been sleeping, he'd shaved, showered, and exchanged his sweatpants for jeans and his sweatshirt for a wool sweater. He'd washed the dishes and taken out the trash. He'd swept the floor and scrubbed the countertops. The smell of freshly made coffee filled the air.

"You must not have gone back to bed," I said.

"I couldn't sleep, so I cleaned up the place." He poured himself a cup of coffee and sat down at the table. "I apologize for not believing you, Daniel," he said, "but you have to admit your story sounded like something out of a fairy tale—old conjure women roaming the mountains, stealing children, keeping them for fifty years. I'm a practical man, a rational man. I've never believed in the supernatural."

He frowned and rubbed his chin. Except for the uncertainty in his eyes, he looked like himself. "I'd never have believed in Old Auntie when we lived in Connecticut, but here, well, crazy as it sounds, I can't come up with any other explanation."

I looked at him, surprised. "You *believe* me?"

"Like I said, what other explanation is there? Erica couldn't have survived on her own in this cold. There's no evidence that she was kidnapped by a passing stranger. Her dream fits in with what you've told me about that conjure woman or witch—or whatever she is or was."

He drank more coffee and stared past me at nothing in particular. "And then there's Selene," he added. "Surely the O'Neills are too sane to believe in old stories unless there's some truth to them."

Before I could say a word, someone began pounding on the back door. "Mama," a voice cried. "Daddy, it's me. Let me in, let me in!"

Dad was so startled, he almost spilled what was left of his coffee, but I jumped up and flung the door open. Selene stood on the porch, staring at me.

"Who are you?" she asked. "What are you doing

in my house? Where's my mother? Who's that man at the table?"

"Don't you remember me?"

"I've never seen you in my life." Pushing me aside, she headed toward the back stairs. "Mama, Daddy, it's me," she called. "Where are you?"

Before Selene was halfway up the steps, Mrs. O'Neill followed her into the kitchen. "Wait," she cried to the nearly hysterical girl. "I need to tell you something."

Selene ignored her. "Mama!" she screamed. "Mama!"

Her eyes darted around the kitchen. "What have you done with our table? Where are our chairs? And the clock on the wall and the calendar by the door and the curtains Mama made?"

Dodging Mrs. O'Neill, she ran into the hall. We heard her go from room to room, her feet clattering across the floor. "This isn't right. This isn't our couch, not our chairs—where's the wallpaper? Mama! Daddy!" Her voice rose with every word.

Mrs. O'Neill caught her at the foot of the front stairway. "Selene, Selene, I know everything seems wrong and you're scared, but you must be still and listen to me."

"What are you and those other people doing in my house?" Selene cried. "Why have you changed all the furniture? Where's my mother and my father and Nadine?"

"Please, please, Selene, let me explain."

Mrs. O'Neill managed to lead the girl into the living room. "Here," she said gently. "Sit with me, and I'll tell you the best I can."

Selene sat on the edge of the couch and stared at Mrs. O'Neill. Her face pale, her eyes huge, she asked, "Has something terrible happened to them? Is that it?"

"Oh, my dear child," Mrs. O'Neill said sadly. "I hardly know where to begin."

Silently I went back to the kitchen. Dad had made another pot of coffee. Upstairs, Mom was giving Erica a bath. In the living room, Mrs. O'Neill murmured to Selene. For now, at least, the house was quiet—the way it used it to be.

We sat together silently, Dad and I. Neither of us knew what to say. He drank his coffee and stared out the window, his face expressionless.

I'd had time to adjust to the reality of witchcraft and spells and hogs that walked on their hind legs, but just a few hours earlier Old Auntie had turned my parents' beliefs about the nature of reality upside down. Maybe they should visit Miss Perkins. She could explain the way things were in Woodville.

I heard footsteps on the stairs. Scrubbed clean, her hair washed, brushed, and combed, wearing clean clothes, Erica seemed to be exactly the same as before — until you saw the bruises on her face, until you looked into her eyes and saw the shadows there. She'd been somewhere only she and Selene knew about.

Mom had washed *her* hair, too, and finally changed her clothes. Like Erica, she seemed her old self, the mother I knew, except her face had wrinkles I hadn't noticed before and there were new gray streaks in her hair.

Erica sat beside me. "You look really nice," I told her.

She put her hands over her face to hide the bruises. "I look awful."

Mom opened a catalog and showed Erica a page.

"I know how much you loved your doll," she said. "We can order another one just like her."

With a look of horror, Erica shoved the catalog away so fast she knocked over the glass of orange juice Dad had set in front of her. "Get that picture away from me," she shouted. "I hate that doll. Throw the catalog away. Burn it up!"

"But Erica," Mom began.

"No!"

When Erica began to cry, Mom hugged her. "It's all right, honey. I just thought . . ." Her voice trailed away as she stroked Erica's hair.

I glanced at the catalog lying open on the floor. There she was, Little Erica, red hair and all. *Oh, Mom, I thought, if you only knew* . . . I picked up the catalog and carried it to the garbage can. No more Little Erica.

Once Erica calmed down, Dad asked, "Who wants pancakes for breakfast?" He seemed to be making a huge effort to act as if this were an ordinary morning.

Mrs. O'Neill appeared in the doorway. "Did we hear something about pancakes?"

Pale and quiet, Selene followed her into the kitchen. While Dad stirred the batter, Mrs. O'Neill urged Selene to join us at the table, but she shook her head and held back.

"Who's that?" Erica asked.

"Selene," Mom said. "She lives down the road with Mr. and Mrs. O'Neill."

"She's your age," I told Erica.

Erica slid out of her chair and crossed the room. Taking Selene's hand, she said, "Come sit beside me. We're going to be friends, you and me. I just know it."

Erica led Selene to the chair next to hers. "Do you like pancakes?"

Selene nodded. "With maple syrup."

"Coming right up." Dad set plates in front of Erica and Selene, and Mom passed them the syrup.

Before either girl picked up her fork, they studied each other for at least a minute. They didn't say a word, but I sensed something flowing back and forth between them. Slowly Erica put her hand on Selene's hand and smiled at her. Selene smiled back.

It was the first time I'd ever seen that girl look happy.

After breakfast, Erica took her new friend upstairs. I heard Selene say, "You sleep in my old room." Then the door closed behind them.

I looked around the quiet kitchen, which was neat and orderly again. Sunlight filled corners that once were dark. No whispers disturbed the silence.

Mrs. O'Neill took a sip of coffee. "I believe those girls will be good friends."

Mom smiled. "Erica needs a friend."

"So does Selene," Mrs. O'Neill said.

After a little silence Mrs. O'Neill added, "Thank goodness, they've both forgotten Auntie and all that happened to them in that cabin."

Except in dreams, I thought. *Except in dreams.*

TWENTY

A few days later, Brody showed up. It was the first time he'd been in our house, and he spent some time looking around and making comments like "Your roof's leaking, that's why that brown stain's on your ceiling" or "You better get your dad to put some putty in them window frames. You're letting cold air in and warm air out. That'll run your heat bill sky-high."

Of course, what he'd really come for was to see Erica, who was helping Mom clean the living room—

she'd been doing chores ever since she came back from Old Auntie's.

"She looks real good," he said in a low voice. "Lots better than Selene."

"Selene's fine now," I told him. "Miss Perkins was right about the spell. She said it would break when the sun came up, and it did. Just like that — Erica knew who she was, and so did Selene."

"Must've been mighty bad news for that poor girl — her parents being dead and all. Ain't no fun losing your mom, I can tell you that, brother."

"She's going to be all right. The O'Neills treat her like a granddaughter."

While we had a glass of milk and some cookies, I told Brody what he wanted to hear — all the details of Erica's rescue.

When I was done, Brody said, "I been telling the kids at school about you going to the cabin and seeing Old Auntie and her hog. Boy, was they surprised you done that. Didn't think you had the guts."

Brody helped himself to more cookies and grinned at me. "When I tell them what you done to get your sister back, they'll all want to be your friend."

I took a handful of cookies and grinned back at him. "You want to climb Brewster's Hill and take a look at what's left of the cabin?"

Brody swallowed a mouthful of cookies and thought about it. "You sure Old Auntie's really gone, both her and that hog?"

"I told you, Bloody Bones fell off the cliff and broke into bits, and Old Auntie died in the fire."

Brody dipped his last cookie into his milk and shrugged. "You mind if I whistle for Bella? She's good company."

So with Bella leading the way, Brody and I climbed the trail to the top of Brewster's Hill. The dog acted as if there was nothing to fear in the hollow. In fact, she ran over and peed on the charred wood just as if she were saying it was her place now.

While Bella sniffed in the ruins, Brody and I kicked at the logs and poked around in the ashes as if we were looking for something. I don't know what. Just something.

Brody wandered over to the chimney, which was still standing. "Daniel!" he yelled. "Come here!"

He was backing away from whatever it was, plainly scared. I ran to see what he'd found. Little Erica lay in the ashes, looking up at me with one eye, almost as if she were winking. The other eye had melted into its socket. Her hair was singed, and her face was black and wrinkled from the fire, but it was Little Erica all right.

Looking at the doll made me feel as if I were about to throw up the cookies I'd stuffed myself with before we'd left the house.

"It's my sister's doll," I told him.

"The one that started all the trouble?" He looked puzzled. "But she's little, like a plain old ordinary kid's doll. You told me she growed big and come to life."

"When the spell broke, I guess she changed back to what she really was—a lump of plastic, mostly melted now."

"You ain't going to give her back to your sister, are you?"

"Erica doesn't want anything to do with dolls anymore."

I couldn't take my eyes away from Little Erica.

She had a wicked look, like some kind of shrunken mummy—maybe because of the fire, maybe because of something else.

Bella ambled over to see what we were looking at. As soon as she saw the doll, she whined and backed away. She was shivering the way she had the night we'd visited the cabin and seen Old Auntie and Bloody Bones.

"You think it's okay to leave her here?" Brody asked. He was worried about the doll, too. I could tell by his voice.

I shook my head. Little Erica didn't seem like a lump of plastic anymore, and I didn't want someone to find her. What if a bit of Old Auntie was in that doll?

"Let's bury her," Brody said.

Using boards from the cabin, the two of us dug a hole by the fireplace, making it as deep as we could. The ground there was soft despite the cold, probably because of the fire.

Neither of us wanted to touch the doll, so we scooped her out of the ashes with one of the boards we used to dig with. We dumped dirt on her, stamping it down with our feet so it was as hard as we could make it. Then we pulled and tugged and pushed stones from the old wall and piled them on top of the grave.

"There," Brody said. "She won't never get out now."

Wiping our hands on our jeans, we whistled for Bella and hiked down the trail toward home.

Summer, Two Years Later

An old woman stands on the hilltop, just on the edge of the green woods, smiling down on the farmhouse below. What she sees pleases her. The house has a new roof and a fresh coat of pale blue paint. The junk in the yard is gone. The barn has been cleaned out and repaired. The woman who lives in the house uses it for a workroom. She's in there now, weaving a rug on a loom. The old woman hears the music she plays – folk songs, ballads, with fiddles and dulcimers, tunes she's known all her life.

A man mows the grass in the front yard. He's riding one of those little tractor things they use now. Flowers bloom along a picket fence – daisies, black-eyed Susans, coneflowers, bright colors, bees swarming. A vegetable garden behind the house grows strong and healthy, just as it ought to. They'll have tomatoes, squash, beans, lettuce, spinach, even some corn. More than they can eat, but they've built a stand at the end of the driveway where they sell the extra.

The old woman watches Daniel play catch with Brody, the boy who lives down the road. She watches Erica and Selene take turns swinging on a tire hung from a high branch. She hears them laugh, all four of them.

She sees the woman come out of the barn and cross the yard, shooing chickens out of her way. A few minutes later she calls the children to come into the house and cool off with lemonade.

"Well, Auntie," the old woman says to someone she can't see, someone who once roamed these woods and watched the farmhouse with dark intent. "You been took yourself, and I aim to make sure you stay took. These children don't recollect a thing about you, except sometimes when they dream. But we all got nightmares, don't we? Then morning comes and sweeps them away like cobwebs."

Walking slowly and carefully, the old woman climbs the trail to the top of Brewster's Hill. Vines and weeds have grown over the charred wood. Wildflowers sway in the breeze. A mockingbird sings in a nearby tree.

With her walking staff, the old woman pokes at the ashes, as if she's making sure the fire's out and Auntie and Bloody Bones are still took. She pays close attention to the stones piled up near what's left of the chimney. A tall clump of Queen Anne's lace almost hides the burial place. All is as it should be. Calm. Peaceful.

The old woman sits down on the stone wall to rest. She watches a butterfly flit among the flowers. Bees hum in the wild clover.

One of her cats has followed her, solid black except for a little white spot on its chest.

"Cat, come set a spell." She pats her lap, and the cat curls up on the old woman's bony knees.

"You and me and that boy, we done good work that snowy night." She strokes the cat until its whole body vibrates with a rumbly purr. "We made us our own tale, didn't we—a tale like the tellers told back and back and back to the first tellers sitting around their fires, keeping the dark away with their words."

The old woman yawns. Before she stands up, the cat jumps off her lap and the two of them disappear into the green woods.

MARY DOWNING HAHN

The Ghost of Crutchfield Hall

a ghost story

ONE

❦

"**T**AKE GOOD CARE OF THIS GIRL,"
Miss Beatty told the coachman. "She's
an orphan, you know, and never set foot
out of London. Make sure she gets where she's going safely."

After turning to me, Miss Beatty smoothed my
hair and checked the note she'd pinned to my coat:
"Mistress Florence Crutchfield," it read. "Bound for
Crutchfield Hall, near Lower Bolton."

"Now, you behave yourself," she warned me.
"Don't talk to strangers, no matter how nice they
seem, sit still, and don't daydream. Keep your mind
on what you're doing and where you're going." She
paused and dabbed her eyes with her handkerchief.

1

"And when you get to your uncle's house . . ." She sniffed and went on, "Be a good girl. Do as you're bid. None of your mischief, or he'll be sending you back here."

Unable to restrain myself, I threw my arms around her. "I'll miss you."

Miss Beatty stiffened a moment, as if unaccustomed to being embraced. Certainly I'd never had the nerve to do so before.

"Now, now—no tears." She gave me a quick hug, then stepped back as if she'd done something wrong. Affection of any sort was not encouraged at Miss Medleycoate's Home for Orphan Girls. "Remember your manners, Florence. Always say please and thank you, and don't slurp your soup."

"Is that girl coming with us or not?" the coachman asked.

"Go along then, Florence." Miss Beatty gave me a gentle push toward the coach. As a passenger held out his hand to assist me, she said softly, "I pray you'll be happy in your new home."

Once inside the coach, I looked out the window just in time to glimpse Miss Beatty's broad back vanish into the crowd in the coach yard. The last I saw of her was the big yellow flower on her hat. She was the only grownup at Miss Medleycoate's Home for Orphan Girls who'd treated me—or any of us—with kindness.

On his rooftop seat, the coachman cracked his whip, and away we went, bouncing over cobbled streets and rattling through parts of London I'd never seen. I glimpsed the Tower, the dome of St. Paul's Cathedral, and mazes of twisting alleyways. Then we hurtled across Tower Bridge and into the narrow streets of Southwark, crowded with coaches, wagons, and people, all doing their best to move onward at the expense of everyone else.

In the crowded coach, I was squashed between a large redheaded woman and an even larger gentleman with a beard that threatened to scratch my cheek if I was jostled too close to him.

Directly opposite me sat a narrow-faced young man with a mustache and a wispy beard, attempting to read his Bible. Next to him a rough-looking fellow frowned and scowled at all of us. Making herself as small as possible, a timid lady with gray hair and spectacles pressed herself against the side of the coach.

Before five minutes had passed, the gentleman beside me fell asleep and commenced to snore loudly. On my other side, the stout woman fussed to herself and even went so far as to reach across me and poke the sleeper with her umbrella. She failed to rouse him.

Across from me, the rough fellow began a conversation with the Bible reader, which soon turned into an argument about Mr. Darwin's theory of evolution—the Bible reader for and the rough fellow against. The old lady closed her eyes and either fell asleep or feigned to.

The woman beside me opined that she was not descended from apes, no matter what Mr. Darwin had thought. She did not, however, voice her opinion loudly enough to be heard by the Bible reader and the rough fellow.

While all this went on about me, I mused upon the sudden change in my circumstances. My parents had drowned in a boating accident when I was five years old. When no relative stepped forward to claim me, I was sent to Miss Medleycoate's, where I spent seven wretched years learning to sew and read and write from a series of strict teachers who had little patience with girls who could not stitch a neat row or learn their arithmetic. We were cold in the winter, hot in the summer, and hungry all year round. If we dared to complain, we were beaten and locked in the punishment closet.

4

Then one day, just a week ago, a solicitor appeared at the orphanage and informed Miss Medleycoate that I was the great-niece of Thomas Crutchfield, my father's uncle. My uncle had searched for me a long time and had finally learned my whereabouts. As soon as proper arrangements were made, Mr. Graybeale said, I was to live at Crutchfield Hall with my uncle, his spinster sister, Eugenie, and my cousin James, the orphaned son of my father's only brother.

Glancing around the dreary sitting room, Mr. Graybeale had told me I was a fortunate girl.

"She certainly is." Miss Medleycoate fixed me with a sharp eye. "I am certain Florence will show her gratitude as she has been taught."

I knew full well how fortunate I was to escape Miss Medleycoate's establishment, but I merely bowed my head to avoid her stare. Now was not the time to express my feelings.

"What sort of boy is my cousin James?" I asked Mr. Graybeale. "Is he my age? Is he—"

"I've never met the child," Mr. Graybeale said, "but I hear he's rather delicate."

I stared at the solicitor, wondering what he meant. "Is he sickly?"

"Florence," Miss Medleycoate interrupted. "Do

not pester the gentleman with trivial questions. Your curiosity does not become you."

"It's all right," Mr. Graybeale told Miss Medleycoate. Turning to me, he said, "The boy has suffered much in his short life. His mother died soon after he was born, and his father succumbed to a fever a few years later. Not long after James and his older sister, Sophia, arrived at Crutchfield Hall, the girl was killed in a tragic accident. So much loss has been difficult for James to bear."

I stared at Mr. Graybeale. "I'm so sorry," I whispered. Perhaps I should not have asked about James's health, but if I had not, how would I have known about my cousin's tragic past and Sophia's death? Disturbing as these events were, I needed to be aware of them, if only to avoid asking my aunt and uncle inappropriate questions.

With a rustle of silk, Miss Medleycoate rose to her feet. "I believe Mr. Graybeale has satisfied your unseemly curiosity, Florence. You may return to your lessons while I sign the necessary papers."

Now, as the coach bounced and swayed over rough roads, I thought about Sophia. If only she hadn't died, if only she were waiting for me at Crutchfield

Hall, the friend I'd always wanted, the sister I'd never had.

I imagined us whispering and giggling together, sharing books and games and dolls, telling each other secrets. We'd sleep in the same room and talk to each other in the dark. We'd go for long walks in the country. She'd show me her favorite things—a creek that swirled over white pebbles, lily pads in a pond, a bird's nest, butterflies, a tree with branches low enough to sit on and read. Maybe we'd have a dog or a pony.

Suddenly the coach hit a bump with enough force to hurl me against the man beside me. He drew away and scowled, as if offended by my proximity. Brought back to the stuffy confines of reality, I let go of my daydream. Sophia would not be waiting for me at Crutchfield Hall. I would have no sister. Just James, delicate James, a brother who might not be well enough to play.

With a sigh, I reminded myself that I was a fortunate girl. With every turn of the coach's wheels, I was leaving Miss Medleycoate's Home for Orphan Girls farther and farther behind. Surely I'd be happier at Crutchfield Hall than I'd been with Miss Medleycoate.

Two

∞

AS THE CITY SLOWLY FADED away behind us, I caught fleeting glimpses of open countryside, green meadows rolling away toward distant hills, red-roofed villages marked by church steeples, cows and sheep under a cloudy sky much higher and wider than it looked in London. I felt very small, rather like an ant riding in a coach the size of a walnut shell.

After an hour or so, the sky darkened and the wind rose. Rain pelted the coach and streamed down the windows, making it impossible to see out.

We stopped several times to let passengers off and take more on. The rough fellow was replaced by a farmer who had nothing to say to anyone. The old lady was replaced by a young woman who blushed whenever anyone looked at her.

The coach grew stuffy, and the voices around me blended into a sort of soothing music. The jolts and bumps and lurches changed to a rocking motion, and I soon fell asleep.

I was startled awake by the large woman beside me. "Stir yourself, child. This is where you get off."

"Crutchfield Hall," the coachman bellowed from his seat above us. "Ain't there someone what wants to get out here?"

I scrambled to my feet and stepped outside. Wind and rain struck me with a force that almost knocked me down. Groggy with sleep, I gazed at empty fields bordered by a forest, bare and bleak on this dark January afternoon. In the distance, I saw a line of hills, their tops hidden by rain, but no house. Not even a barn or a shed.

Bewildered, I peered up at the coachman through the rain. "Where is the house, sir?"

Gesturing with his whip, he pointed to an ornate iron gate topped with fancy curlicues. "Follow the drive till you come to the house," he said. "It's one or two mile, I reckon. A big old place with chimneys. Pity there's no one to meet you."

With that, he handed me the small wooden box that held all my belongings. "Be sure and latch the gate behind you," he said. "They won't like it left open."

Before I could say another word, he cracked his whip. In seconds, the coach vanished into the rain.

With a sigh, I lowered my head and pushed open the heavy gate, then latched it behind me. The rain came down harder. The wind sent volleys of leaves flying against my face, as sharp edged as small knives.

Frightened by the creaking and groaning of tree limbs over my head, I walked faster, almost losing my shoes in the mud. They were thin soled, meant for city streets, not country lanes. I supposed I was meant for city streets as well, for I did not like the vast sky above me. The endless fields and the distant hills made me feel as if I were the only living person in this desolate place.

I was tempted to turn around and walk back to the road. Perhaps another coach would come along, warm and crowded with passengers, and take me back to London's familiar streets.

But I kept going, fearing Miss Medleycoate would not accept me. Had she not been happy to see me leave? I did not want to end my days begging in the street.

Finally, ankle deep in mud and soaked by the rain, I came to the top of a hill. Below me was a gloomy stone house, grim and unwelcoming, its windows dark and lifeless. Except for a dense grove of fir trees, the gardens and lawn were brown and bare.

A writer like Miss Emily Brontë would have been entranced by its Gothic appearance, but I hung back again, suddenly apprehensive of what might await me behind those towering walls.

It was the rising wind and icy rain that drove me forward. Exhausted and cold, I made my way carefully downhill to the house. In the shelter of a stone arch, I lifted an iron ring and let it thud against the door. Shivering in my wet coat and sodden shoes, I waited for someone to come.

Just as I was about to knock again, I heard footsteps approaching. The door slowly opened. A tall, thin woman dressed in black looked down at me. Her face was pale and narrow, her eyes were set deep under her brows, and her gray hair was pulled tightly into a bun at the back of her head. With a gasp, she pressed one bony hand to her heart. "It cannot be," she whispered. "It cannot be."

Fearing she was about to faint, I took her cold

hand. "I-I'm Florence Crutchfield," I stammered. "From London. I believe you're expecting me."

She snatched her hand away and looked at me more closely. "For a moment I mistook you for someone else," she murmured, her voice still weak. "But now I see you bear no resemblance to her. None at all."

Without inviting me in, the woman said, "We were told you'd arrive tomorrow."

"I beg your pardon, but Miss Medleycoate said I was to come today." Panic made my heart beat faster. "She said I was to come today," I repeated. "*Today.*"

At that moment, an old gentleman appeared in the shadowy hallway. The very opposite of the woman, he was short and round, and his cheeks were rosy with good humor. In one hand he held a pipe and in the other a thick book. "Come in," he said to me, "come in. You're wet and cold."

To the woman he said, "This poor child must be our great-niece Florence. Why have you allowed her to stand on the doorstep, shivering like a half-drowned kitten?"

"You know my feelings about her coming here." Without another word, she turned stiffly and vanished into the house's gloomy interior.

Puzzled by my aunt's unfriendly manner, I followed my uncle down the hall. What had I done to cause Aunt to dislike me almost on sight?

"As you must have guessed," my uncle said, "I'm your Great-Uncle Thomas, and that was my sister, your Great-Aunt Eugenie. I apologize for her brusqueness. I'm sure she didn't mean to be rude. She, er, she . . ."

Uncle paused as if searching for the right words to describe his sister. "Well," he went on, "once she becomes accustomed to you, she'll be friendlier. Yes, yes, you'll see. She just has to get used to you."

I didn't dare ask how long it would take Aunt to get used to me. Or how long it would take *me* to get used to *her*. Indeed, I felt I had escaped Miss Medleycoate only to encounter her double. Which was neither what I'd hoped for nor what I'd expected.

"And then of course," Uncle went on, "we really did expect you to arrive tomorrow. I'd have sent Spratt to meet you if I'd known you'd arrive today. A misunderstanding on someone's part, but, well, what's done is done. I am very happy to see you."

Uncle led me into a large room lit by flickering firelight and oil lamps. Rain beat against its small windows, and the wind crept through every crack around the glass panes, but I felt cheered by the fire's glow and my uncle's smile.

"Here, let me have a look at you." Uncle grasped my shoulders and peered into my face. "Goodness, Eugenie, have you noticed how much she favors the Crutchfields? Blue eyes, dark hair—she could be Sophia's sister."

My aunt frowned at me from a chair by the hearth. "Don't be absurd. This girl is quite plain. And her hair is a sight."

Busying myself with my coat buttons, I pretended not to have heard Aunt. I didn't know what Sophia looked like, but I was quite ready to believe she was much prettier than I. Aunt was right. I was plain. And my hair was tangled by the wind and wet with rain and no doubt a sight.

Uncle took my sodden coat and settled me near the fire. "You must be tired and cold," he said. "You've had a long, muddy walk from the road." He picked up a bell and rang it.

A girl not much older than I popped into the room as if she'd been waiting by the door. She was so thin, she'd wrapped her apron strings twice around her waist, but the apron still flapped around her like a windless sail.

"Nellie," my uncle said, "this is Florence, the niece we expected to arrive tomorrow. Please bring tea for us all and something especially nice for Florence. Then build up the fire in her room."

Darting a quick look in my direction, Nellie nodded. "Yes, sir, I will, sir."

As she scurried away, Uncle turned back to me. "First of all, permit me to say how sorry I was to learn of your father's and mother's death. To think they died on the same day. So tragic. So unexpected."

"Sensible people do not go out in boats," Aunt said, and then, with a quick glance at me, added, "Death is usually unexpected. That is why we must endeavor to live righteously. When we are summoned, we will be ready. As Sophia was, poor child."

Ignoring his sister, Uncle patted my hand. "We'll do our best to make up for the years you spent with Miss Medleycoate. You'll have a happy life here at Crutchfield Hall, I promise you."

I did not say it, but the prospect of a happy life with Aunt seemed uncertain at best.

As Uncle drew in his breath to say more, he was

interrupted by the arrival of Nellie, who carried a heavy tray. In its center was a steaming teapot, which was surrounded by an array of sliced bread, cheese, and fruit, as well as milk and sugar for the tea and jam for the bread. Somehow she managed to set it down on a low table by the fire without rattling a teacup in its saucer.

I hadn't eaten since breakfast, and my empty stomach mortified me by rumbling at the sight of so much food, more than I'd ever seen at the orphanage. At that establishment, we received one cup of tea served lukewarm and weak, a slice of stale bread, and a dab of jelly.

Nellie's eyes met mine again, but she didn't linger. With a nod, she left the room, her feet scarcely making a sound.

Uncle offered me the bread and jam. "Don't be shy," he said. "Take as much as you want. Walking in the cold sharpens one's appetite."

While we ate, I looked around the room. Despite its darkness, I saw it was well furnished with chairs and sofas and shelves of books. Oil paintings covered the walls. Some were portraits of long-ago men and women, their faces grave in the firelight. Others were landscapes of forested hills and grassy meadows. A marble statue of a Greek god stood in the corner behind Aunt's chair, peering over her shoulder as if hoping for a biscuit.

"And now, my dear," Uncle said, "tell us about yourself. Do you play an instrument? Sing? Draw? What sort of books do you enjoy?"

"I'm sorry to say I don't play a musical instrument," I told him. "Neither do I sing. Indeed, my talents in music resemble those of Mary Bennet in *Pride and*—"

"How unfortunate," Aunt cut in. "Your cousin Sophia played the piano *and* the violin. She sang like an angel. Such talent she had, such grace." Her voice trailed away, and she sniffed into her handkerchief.

"You were about to say something more," Uncle prompted me.

Embarrassed by my inferiority to Sophia, I murmured, "I was just going to say that I draw a little. Not very well, I'm afraid."

With a worried look at Aunt, I hesitated. "As for books," I went on nervously, "I love Mr. Dickens's novels, and also those of Wilkie Collins. I've read all of Jane Austen's books, but my favorite is *Pride and Prejudice*, which I've read five times now. I adore *Wuthering Heights* and—"

"Do you read nothing but frivolous novels?" Aunt cut in. "I have read the Bible at least a dozen times, but I have not read *Pride and Prejudice* even once. Nor do I intend to. As for Mr. Dickens—I believe him to be most vulgar. Wilkie Collins is beneath contempt. And the Brontë novel is quite the worst of the lot, not fit for a decent young girl to read."

Her tone of voice and stern face silenced me. I fancied even the clock on the mantel had ceased ticking.

Aunt peered at me over the top of her spectacles. "If the Bible is too difficult for you," she added, "I recommend *Pilgrim's Progress*. It should prove most instructive. Your cousin Sophia told me it was her favorite book." Then, without saying farewell or making an excuse for her departure, she left the room.

When the door closed behind her, Uncle sighed. "Your aunt is very set in her ways, I fear," he said. "You may read what you wish. I for one see nothing wrong with your taste in literature. Dickens is my own personal favorite. *Martin Chuzzlewit*, *Bleak House*, *Our Mutual Friend*—ah, what untold hours of pleasure his books have given me."

I tried to return his smile, but I feared I'd made a poor beginning with Aunt. "I didn't mean to offend my aunt."

"Don't worry. She'll come round." He set his teacup down. "She was very fond of Sophia, you know. Absolutely doted on the girl. Still wears nothing but black."

"Sophia must have been perfection itself," I said sadly.

"No one is perfect, my dear. Certainly not Sophia." He picked up his tea as if to end the conversation.

I sat quietly, sipping my tea and listening to the incessant sound of the wind and the rain. The journey had exhausted me, and I tried without success to stifle a yawn.

Uncle looked at me and smiled. "Perhaps you'd like to rest and refresh yourself before supper."

"Will James join us?" I asked. "I was hoping he'd be here for tea. I can scarcely wait to meet him."

Uncle sighed again. "James is quite ill, my dear. He never leaves his room."

Before I could say another word, Uncle summoned Nellie. "Please show Florence to her room," he said. "She's tired from her long day of travel."

Almost too weary to walk, I followed Nellie up a wide flight of stairs to the second floor. She opened a door at the end of a hall and led me into a room almost as large as the dormitory where I'd slept with eleven girls. A coal fire glowed on the hearth, filling the room with warmth.

As Nellie busied herself lighting an oil lamp, I contemplated my new surroundings. A tall four-poster bed wide enough to hold three girls my size. Bookcases, chests, bureaus, a tall wardrobe, all made of dark wood, massive, designed for giants. I felt like Alice after she drank the shrinking potion.

Under a curtained window was a writing table and a chair, a perfect place to read and draw.

Lamp lit, Nellie looked at me shyly. "Supper will be served at seven, miss."

After the girl left, I took off my wet shoes and stockings and lay for a while on my bed, staring up at the canopy above. Finally, too restless to sleep, I went to the window and pulled the curtains aside. Night had fallen while we'd had tea, and darkness and rain prevented me from seeing anything except a few bare trees close to the house. There were no lights in sight. To one accustomed to the busy streets of London, it was a bleak and lonely view.

Chilled by the draft creeping in around the window frames, I closed the curtains and retreated to the warmth of the fire.

Shortly before seven, I pulled on a pair of dry stockings and forced my feet back into my damp shoes, the only ones I owned. I wished I had a nicer dress, but I was wearing my best, a simple frock meant for church. My only other was the orphanage uniform made of coarse material, and a bit small for me. I did what I could with my hair, a wild mass of dark, curly tangles, and left my room.

At the top of the stairs, I had the strangest sensation that someone was watching me. I looked behind me. The hall was dark, and even though I saw no one, the sensation persisted. A chill raced up and down my spine, and my scalp prickled. "Is someone there?" I whispered fearfully.

I heard a faint sound like muffled laughter.

"Nellie, is that you?"

The laughter faded. The watcher was gone and I was alone.

Almost tripping over my own feet, I ran downstairs as if I were being chased.

THREE

BY THE TIME I REACHED THE dining room, my heart had slowed to its normal speed. I told myself sternly that no one had been watching me. No one had laughed. I'd been a silly child scared of my own shadow.

Uncle rose from his seat at the table and greeted me warmly. "It will be just the two of us tonight," he said. "Eugenie is indisposed and will not join us."

"Oh, dear, I'm sorry to hear that," I said as graciously as I could. "I hope it's not my fault."

"No, indeed," Uncle assured me. "It's merely a spot of dyspepsia. Nervous stomach, Dr. Fielding says. She's high strung, you know. Nervy."

I nodded sympathetically, but even though I knew it was uncharitable, I hoped Aunt's condition would cause her to miss many meals.

The two of us sat across from each other at the end of a long table covered with a spotless white cloth and set with fine china, crystal, and silver. A blazing candelabra illuminated the table, but the rest of the room lay deep in shadow.

I'd never eaten in such surroundings, and I was suddenly nervous about my manners. Which fork to use first? Which spoon? There were so many utensils to choose from.

Nellie brought our meal. Giving me her usual quick, curious look, she served us each a plate of roast chicken, potatoes, and carrots. With a nod to Uncle, she left the room.

Watching my uncle closely, I chose the same utensils he did and tried my best to demonstrate I knew proper etiquette.

While we ate, Uncle told me about Crutchfield Hall. "It was built in the early 1700s by my great-grandfather, not so old or so big as some country houses, but more than ample for our needs at the present."

He paused to eat a forkful of potatoes and then

23

went on. "Not many servants now either. Mrs. Dawson does the cooking, and Samuel Spratt tends the grounds. Nellie is the maid—a jack-of-all-trades, you could call her. Once a week Mrs. Barnes comes in from the village to do the heavy cleaning. We used to have a larger staff, but we get along fine without them."

As Uncle helped himself to more chicken, I summoned the courage to ask what I really wanted to know. "When will I meet James?"

"I can't really say. Your aunt doesn't think he's well enough for you to visit him. It would tire him, she claims." While he spoke, Uncle rolled his silver napkin holder back and forth on the tablecloth.

"What sort of illness does he have?" I asked. "Will he always be an invalid?"

Uncle shook his head. "Dr. Fielding is as puzzled as I am. It's as if the boy wants to be sick. He told me once that it suits him to lie in bed all day."

"How sad." I wished I could think of something else to say, but I couldn't imagine why any child would prefer sickness to health. I hated staying in bed. I detested fevers and aches and pains and upset stomachs. I abhorred coughing and sneezing and blowing my nose.

"Yes, it is indeed sad." Without looking at me, Uncle continued to roll his napkin holder back and forth, as if it were a little wheel engaged in an important task. "After his sister's death, the boy went into a long decline. Sometimes I think he blames himself . . ." Unable to go on, he pulled a handkerchief out of his pocket and blew his nose.

Embarrassed by his obvious distress, I lowered my head. Despite my earlier promise to myself, I'd asked the wrong questions, upset my uncle, and had no idea what to say to make amends.

For the rest of our meal, we ate quietly. Uncle did not mention James again, nor did he speak of Sophia.

After supper, we sat by the sitting room fire and read. Uncle's book was thick and heavy. I made out the name Thomas Carlyle on the spine. I'd never read him, but I had a feeling his writings might be a bit tedious.

Hoping to find something more interesting, I searched the shelves until I found *Great Expectations*. I'd read it three times already, but I was happy to be reunited with my old friend Pip, especially here, so far from my playmates at the orphanage.

When the clock struck nine, I said good night to Uncle and went up to bed. I did not linger at the top of the steps but went quickly to my room and closed the door firmly.

Used to sleeping in a roomful of girls, I lay alone in the dark and tried to accustom myself to the silence. No one breathed or sighed or sniffled. No one turned and tossed. No one coughed. No one sobbed into her pillow.

I watched the coals smolder in the grate. Little blue flames flickered here and there but did not cast much light. The wind rose and made an eerie sound at the window. Drafts of cold air stirred the curtains and crept under my covers.

Unable to sleep, I gave up and went to my window. The wind had swept away the rain, and a full moon floated high in the sky, dodging clouds. How vast and empty the land was. Fields and hills, turned silver and black by the moon's light, rolled away into the hills beyond. Beautiful as it was, the solitude frightened me. I longed for lighted windows and chimneys, for voices and the clippety-clop of horses in the street.

Pressing my face against the glass, I turned from the fields and stared down at a terrace directly below me. In the moon's fitful light, I saw something move in the shadows—a child, I thought, but I couldn't be sure. For a better look, I opened the casement and leaned out. As I did so, a cloud covered the moon and threw the terrace into darkness.

When the moon emerged, I saw a cat mincing daintily along the garden wall. Not a child. Just a cat out for a ramble in the dark.

Too cold to stay at the window, I closed the casement and returned to bed.

I woke to a room full of sunshine. Nellie knelt by the hearth, feeding coal to the fire.

Nellie glanced over her shoulder and caught me staring at her. "Beg pardon, miss," she murmured. "I didn't mean to wake ye."

"The sun woke me," I told her, "not you."

She nodded and began gathering her things—a coal scuttle, a scrub brush, and a pail of water.

"You needn't rush off," I said. "Stay awhile."

"Oh, miss, I can't do no such thing. Miss Crutchfield would be cross, very cross indeed. She thinks I'm too slow as it is." By now Nellie was on her feet, headed toward the door. She struggled to manage the bucket and the coal scuttle.

I jumped out of bed and grabbed the bucket just before it slipped from her hand. "You poor thing," I said. "This bucket is much too heavy for you."

"I can manage, miss." Nellie held out her hand for the bucket, but I hid it behind my back.

"First you must tell me about James. What's wrong with him? Is he as sick as Aunt says?"

Nellie busied herself sweeping up soot and a few stray chunks of coal. "Well, miss," she said at last, "there be no doubt Master James is poorly. Ashy white he is, and thin as a bone, fretful as a baby with a bellyache. He sleeps with a light, for the dark scares him. He has fearful bad dreams and wakes up screaming. Dawson don't know what to make of him. It ain't natural, she says, for a boy to carry on like that."

It was the most I'd ever heard Nellie say. Seemingly worn out from talking, she sat down on the hearth stool.

"What was he like before he got sick?" I asked.

"He were sick when I come to the hall. I only been here a few months." She held out her hand. "Can I have me bucket now, miss?"

"Where are you going?"

"To Master James's room, miss."

"Wait." After handing her the bucket, I flung on my robe, stepped into my slippers, and followed her down the hall.

"Please, miss." Nellie turned to face me, her eyes filling with tears. "Miss Crutchfield don't allow no one to enter Master James's room without her say-so. She'll have me sacked."

"I just want to see him," I said. "He won't even know I'm there."

Nellie shrugged. "I reckon there be no stopping ye." She turned back, her thin shoulders bent under the weight of the pail and the coal scuttle, and made her way down the hall and past the stairs. On tiptoe, I followed her.

Nellie stopped in front of a closed door and set down her bucket. As she began to turn the knob, the door suddenly swung open. Aunt stood on the threshold, frowning down at poor Nellie, who dropped her brush in fright.

"How often must I tell you to knock before entering a room?" Aunt said to Nellie. "You don't have the sense you were born with—that is, if you were born with any sense at all."

Nellie scurried into James's room before the woman could say any more, and Aunt closed the door.

I made a move to return to my room without being seen, but Aunt spied me. Striding toward me, she grasped my arm. "In proper households, young ladies do not go about in their robes and nightgowns."

"You're hurting me," I protested.

Aunt released me so abruptly, I almost lost my balance. "Dress yourself." With that, she hurried downstairs, her back as straight as a broomstick, her black dress rustling like dry leaves.

Rubbing my arm, I stared at the closed door at the end of the hall. At least I knew where James was.

FOUR

ऌ

BREAKFAST WAITED AT MY place. A pot of tea, two slices of toast, a jar of jam, a soft-boiled egg in a cup, and two pieces of bacon. A book lay beside my plate—*Pilgrim's Progress* by John Bunyan.

I knew who'd put it there. I also knew that I had no intention of opening it. Once in a desperate search for something to read, I'd tried to interest myself in Pilgrim's journey, but I'd found him an unpleasant hero who'd left his wife and children behind to search for his own salvation. I'd gotten as far as the slough of despond and tossed the book aside, thoroughly bored with both Pilgrim and his progress.

Turning to my meal, I found that my egg was cold, my toast was cold, my tea was cold, and my bacon was more fat than meat. I glanced at the clock ticking solemnly on the sideboard and realized that I was an hour late. Small wonder my food wasn't hot.

After eating what I could, I grabbed my coat and ran outdoors, eager to escape the gloomy house. The wind nipped my cheeks and ears and nose and tangled my hair, but the rain had stopped and the air was fresh and cold. Cloud shadows raced across the fields. Ravens hopped about the terrace and chattered to one another like schoolchildren on holiday.

The cat I'd seen last night was grooming itself in a sunny spot. I did my best to entice it to play, but every time I got within touching distance it would run off again.

I heard someone laugh and wheeled around to see an old man watching me. He wore a tweed jacket, faded corduroy pants patched at the knees, and a red wool scarf knotted round his neck. Despite his bristly beard and pointed nose, he had a kindly look.

"If that don't be a cat fer ye," he said. "Only lets ye pet him if it suits 'im."

"Does he have a name?"

"He be called Cat like all the others afore him. No sense us naming 'em. They got their own names, secret from us'n." He chuckled. "I have a name, though. It be Spratt. Mr. Samuel Spratt. I be gardener, groundskeeper, driver. Whatever Mr. Crutchfield needs me to do, I do."

By now, Cat was perched several feet away on the head of a statue. Tail twitching, he regarded me with disdain.

"Ye'd be better off with a dog," Spratt said. "A dog cares about ye. Might even save yer life. Which no cat would do."

"I've never had a dog," I said. "Or a cat, for that matter."

"Master James had a dog name of Nero. A terrier. Good ratters they be, but not Nero. He were spoiled. Wouldn't dirty his little white paws digging up a rat tunnel."

"What happened to Nero?"

"He were run over by a farm wagon. It near broke Master James's heart. He were right fond of that little dog." Spratt gazed into the distance. Without looking at me, he said, "It were her fault, ye know. Her throwed a ball right in front of that wagon and

Nero gone after it. I swear she done it a-purpose. A spiteful thing, she were."

I stared at the old man, horrified. Surely he couldn't be speaking of Sophia. A girl from the village, maybe. A servant. But not the perfect Sophia. "You must be mistaken," I said. "It was an accident, surely."

Spratt came back to the present with a jolt. "Lord, I be getting old and addled. Don't know what I were talking about, thinking of somewhat else altogether. Happens when ye get old like me. Things run together—time past, time present. Time future, for all's I know."

Taking a moment to gather his wits, he touched the brim of his cap and said, "Ye must be Miss Florence." He smiled at me. "What do a young lady all the way from London think of the country?"

"It's beautiful," I said, still unnerved by his account of Nero's death. "But it's very quiet."

"Most city folks comes here for the quiet," he said.

"I suppose when you're old it must be very calming."

He laughed as if I amused him. Encouraged, I followed him deeper into the garden. While he pruned shrubbery, I told him about the orphanage and my friends there and how big and noisy London was and how long the coach ride had been. He had little to say, so I talked until I ran out of things to tell him. "I think I'll explore the garden now," I finally announced.

Spratt laughed. "Me ears do be in need of a rest, miss." He gave me a clumsy pat on the shoulder, a bit like a trained bear might. "Be careful how ye go. Stay on the path and don't step on nothing. Yer aunt don't like folks in the garden, but I don't see no harm in it."

I set off with some excitement. Heretofore, my jaunts had been limited to outings in Kew Gardens with the other orphans. We'd never been allowed to put one foot off the path. Hand in hand with our partners, we'd strolled slowly behind Miss Medleycoate. No pausing to watch a squirrel or a bird. No flower picking. No talking or laughing.

Forgetting Spratt's warning, I ran and hopped and skipped, turning down one path and then another. I watched two squirrels chase each other up and down and round a tree. When they saw me, they chattered as if they were scolding me for spying on them.

After about half an hour, I thought I heard some-one following me. I looked this way and that but saw no one. The wind sighed in the bare branches of a tall oak. Birds hopped about in the bushes. A rabbit darted across my path and vanished into the shrub-bery. Was that what I'd heard? Ordinary outdoor noises?

I walked a little farther. My skin prickled again. Someone was nearby, I was sure of it this time—someone watching me from the hedges and shrubs.

I turned quickly and began running back the way I'd come, but instead of reaching the house, I found myself beside a pool I didn't remember passing. In its center was a fountain topped with a statue of a boy and a girl holding a swan. Tiers of thick icicles dripped from the swan's beak.

An inscription had been carved into the foun-tain's stone rim. I bent down to make out the time-worn words.

Here and There and Everywhere.

"Here and there and everywhere," I whispered. "Here and there and everywhere."

Certain it was a riddle, I touched each letter, tracing the curves and angles, but I couldn't come up with the answer.

Surrounded by a dense growth of tall yews, the clearing was a forbidding place. Dark clouds blew across the sun, and I shivered, suddenly cold. I was hungry, too. Time to go back to the house, I thought. But where was it?

Four paths led away from the pool, laid out like spokes in a wheel. I looked behind me at the way I'd come, then at the other paths, but I didn't know which one to choose. I'd run this way and that through the garden, paying no mind to directions.

Finally I chose a path at random and began walking quickly, then running. After ten minutes, I found myself at the pool again. Breathless with fright, I chose another path with the same result. Desperate, I tried the last path and once more found myself staring at the fountain. It seemed I couldn't escape from those two stone children and their captive swan.

Suddenly laughter broke out again, loud and shrill, a child's laugh.

I spun around, expecting to see Nellie. I saw no one, but the shrubbery shook as if someone hid there. "You can't scare me," I cried, more angry now than frightened. "Come out and face me, Nellie!"

The shrubbery rustled. "Hide and seek," a voice called. "You're it!"

Pushing aside a yew's heavy branches, I ran after the voice. The trees' needles whipped against my face, caught my hair, snagged my coat. I tripped on knotted roots and fell more than once. Sometimes the laughter was ahead of me, sometimes behind, but each time I thought I was close, my tormentor eluded me, laughing all the while.

In tears, I burst out of the yews and saw the house at last. "No more games, Nellie," I called. "Where are you?"

"Come and find me," the voice cried from somewhere in the yews. "If you dare!"

"You can't fool me, Nellie! Come out at once!"

Nellie didn't answer. Nor did she appear. The yews swayed softly in the wind, but nothing else moved.

"I'm not leaving until you come out!" I waited on the terrace until my feet hurt from the cold, but Nellie stayed hidden. At last I gave up and ran inside.

Mrs. Dawson looked up from the pot she was stirring. "Miss Florence," she said. "Where have you been? It's almost time for tea."

Before I had a chance to answer, she looked at me closely. "Your face is scratched—you're bleeding."

"It's Nellie's fault," I said. "I got lost chasing her in the garden, but I never did find her."

Mrs. Dawson stared at me as if I'd spoken in Chinese. "Nellie's got no time for games. She's been inside working the whole time you've been outside."

I stared at Mrs. Dawson. "If it wasn't Nellie, who was it?"

"I have no idea what you're talking about." Mrs. Dawson examined my cuts and scratches. "These need tending to before they get infected."

Suddenly tired, I sank down in a chair and let Mrs. Dawson wash my face. She worked deftly and gently and took time to comb the tangles from my hair.

"Let me tell you something," she said. "Neither your uncle nor your aunt wants to hear stories about children you may or may not have seen in the garden."

"But—"

Mrs. Dawson took my chin in her hand and looked me in the eye. "You heard me, miss. Keep that talk to yourself."

I watched her cross the room and open the oven door. Out came the smell of fresh-baked bread. "Would you like some?" she asked.

"Oh, yes, please."

Mrs. Dawson sliced off the end of a loaf, spread it with butter, and handed it to me. "No more stories."

I bit into the bread, the best I'd ever tasted. "I don't understand—"

"That's just it, miss. You're new to this place. There's much you don't know and even more you don't understand. So listen to them that's been here longer than you, and hush."

"But—"

"Finish that bread and go find someone else to pester." Cross now, Mrs. Dawson began chopping onions with a knife that could have cut off my head.

Frustrated and confused, I ate my bread in silence. Someone had teased me in the garden. If Mrs. Dawson was right, it could not have been Nellie.

I hesitated in the doorway. Mrs. Dawson glanced at me. "Well, what is it now?" she asked, still cross.

"Do children from the village ever play in the garden?"

Mrs. Dawson mulled that over. "Of course," she said. "That's what you heard. One of those naughty rascals was teasing you." She smiled then, her anger forgotten. "Don't tell anyone you saw them. Miss Crutchfield would order Spratt to chase them away."

I went to my room, glad the mystery was solved. If I heard the children again, I'd find them this time, and become their friend.

FIVE

HE NEXT DAY, IT RAINED. THE day after that, it rained again. By the fourth day of unrelenting rain, I was tired of reading, tired of sketching, and tired of myself. I missed the girls at the orphanage and devoted hours to writing to each of them, describing in detail my tedious life at Crutchfield Hall.

I wrote to Miss Beatty, as well, but not to Miss Medleycoate, who would most likely answer with a long letter reprimanding me for being an ungrateful girl who complained when fortune smiled upon her.

It occurred to me that I was indeed ungrateful. Compared to what I'd endured at Miss Medleycoate's establishment, I had nothing to complain of.

I had no chores, I had books to read, I never went to bed hungry. A little boredom was nothing to complain about.

Thrusting my letters into the fire, I watched them burn. Later I'd try writing again to my former companions, but feared it might be a difficult task. If I didn't complain, they might think I was bragging. If I complained, they might think I had forgotten what I'd escaped by leaving the orphanage.

I'd finished *Great Expectations* the night before, so I decided to go downstairs and look for something else to read.

After some thought, I selected *Vanity Fair* from the shelves in the sitting room. I'd heard Becky Sharp was a wicked girl, and I thought I'd enjoy reading about someone worse than myself.

On my way to the stairs, I passed my uncle's study. The door was open, and I decided to have a look. His books were dull, having to do with law and history and collections of essays by men such as Carlyle and Macaulay. His papers consisted of deeds and other legal matters, some of them quite old and brittle and written in Latin.

Uncle had a large globe on a stand. I spun it round and round and stopped it with my finger. I pretended to be in the place my finger landed. First I was lost at sea in the Pacific Ocean, a female Robinson Crusoe in search of a desert island. Then it was on to Africa, where I explored jungles and escaped from lions. In America, I traveled in a stage-coach pursued by Indians. At the North Pole, I nearly perished in the cold but was rescued by Eskimos.

Tiring of that, I made up stories about the portraits hanging on the walls—long-nosed ladies with small chins and close-set eyes, red-faced gentlemen with round cheeks and bushy whiskers, handsome young men with curly hair and dimples in their chins, pretty girls with rosy lips and cheeks. I imagined them riding horses and dancing at balls, falling in love, marrying, living to be old or dying tragically young.

I had no idea who the subjects actually were or what had become of them, or even if they were my ancestors or someone else's. All I knew was that they'd been painted long ago.

When I'd run out of stories, I examined the things on my uncle's desk. I nearly cut myself on a fancy letter opener. I spun a revolving stand filled with pipes of many shapes and sizes. I examined the pictures on tobacco tins. And then I spotted an oval photograph of a boy and a girl.

Judging by the style of their clothes, the children could have been photographed yesterday. The girl was about my age and very pretty. Her hair was long and dark and curly like mine, tied back with a ribbon the same way I wore mine. The boy was several years younger, about nine, I guessed. His hair was a mop of dark curls, but his face was rounder than the girl's and his expression sweeter. Sophia and James, I thought. They had to be.

To get a better look, I took the picture to the window. Sophia had my straight nose and oval face, but she had Aunt's narrow-lipped mouth, and the expression on her face was sulky. She stood stiffly, as if she didn't want to be closer than necessary to her brother.

My musing was interrupted by Aunt's voice. "What are you doing in here? You have no business touching the things on your uncle's desk. Put that down!"

I was so startled, I dropped the photograph. The glass in the frame broke with a sharp snap. As I stooped to pick it up, I pricked my finger on a sliver. Horrified, I watched a drop of my blood fall on Sophia's face.

Aunt snatched the picture. "Look what you've done! The photograph is ruined."

"I'm sorry, Aunt." As I spoke, I wrapped my handkerchief around my finger to stop the bleeding. "I didn't mean—"

With an angry look, she interrupted me. "Your uncle will be quite upset when he sees this. I will speak to him as soon as he returns from town." Photograph in hand, my aunt wheeled about to leave the study.

I hurried after her. "Please, Aunt," I cried. "I'm sorry, truly sorry."

"Go to your room," she said. "And do not come down for supper. Nellie will bring your meals."

"But, Aunt—"

She turned a cold and angry face to me. "Go to your room immediately—or I shall see that you stay there until I find a suitable boarding school for you."

Left alone in the room, I listened to my aunt's footsteps fade away. I'd wanted to ask her if the girl was Sophia, if the boy was James, but she'd given me no opportunity. As usual, I'd offended her.

Worse yet, she'd threatened to send me to boarding school. Despite my aunt's unkindness, I did not want to leave Crutchfield Hall. Boarding school might be no better than Miss Medleycoate's establishment.

Evening was coming on fast. In the silence, the room grew colder and darker. A draft stirred the air around me, and for a moment I felt something like the touch of a cold hand on my cheek. Certain that I was being watched, I moved closer to the fire.

When Nellie brought my supper, I was still huddled by the hearth, brooding on Aunt's conduct toward me.

"I'm sorry Miss Crutchfield were so angry with you," Nellie said. "She have a wicked temper. I sees it meself when I do wrong."

"It's not just her temper, Nellie. She hates me."

Nellie fidgeted with her apron. She seemed to want to tell me something but wasn't sure she should. Finally she said, "Ye mustn't ever tell Dawson this, but her says it's account of Miss Sophia that yer aunt hates ye so. Yer aunt thinks Mr. Crutchfield brung ye here to take Miss Sophia's place. And her don't want ye, her wants Miss Sophia. Nobody else. Just her."

"But Nellie, how can that be? Sophia is dead. Aunt can't bring her back."

"Dawson says Miss Crutchfield be daft." Nellie tapped the side of her head.

I didn't know what to say. I was so accustomed to Miss Medleycoate's behavior, I'd assumed Aunt was of a similar disposition. Mean spirited and cross, but not crazy.

"It's on account of Miss Sophia that there be so few servants," Nellie went on. "Folk from the village are scared to work here. Some even say Crutchfield Hall be haunted." Here Nellie's eyes widened, and her voice dropped. "Do ye ever feel someone a-watching ye?"

"Sometimes." The room was quiet, hushed.

"They say it be Miss Sophia," Nellie whispered. "They say her won't lie quiet in her grave."

Suddenly Nellie hid her head under her apron like a child hiding under the blankets. "Oh, lord, I be a-scaring meself," she cried. "I can't bear thinking on spirits, miss. It's only the wicked what comes back. The good stays in the ground and waits for the Lord's call on Judgment Day."

Equally scared, I patted Nellie's shaking shoulders. I'd never given much thought to ghosts before.

Just getting through each day at the orphanage had taken all my energy. But now, in this dark house, with time to spare, the spirit world seemed very real. Maybe even dangerous.

At last, Nellie emerged from her apron, her face blotchy with tears. "Oh, miss, I pray there be no ghosts here." With that, she jumped up and headed for the door. "Dawson must be a-wondering where I'm at. There be work to do afore I goes to bed."

No longer hungry for my supper, I went upstairs to my room. There I undressed quickly and climbed into bed. With the covers snug around me, I felt warmer and safer. I planned to read *Vanity Fair* until I was too sleepy to make sense of the story, and then I'd go to sleep.

Just as I'd gotten comfortable, I heard a knock on my door. It was Uncle, come to say good night.

"I hear my sister was quite cross with you this afternoon," he said.

"Yes." I bit my thumbnail and looked at him sadly. "I'm very sorry I broke the glass on the frame, Uncle. I hope I didn't ruin the photograph."

"Don't worry, Florence. The picture is fine. All it needs is a new piece of glass." He reached for my hand and looked at my finger. "Did you wash the cut?"

"Yes, Uncle. It was just a nick."

He hesitated, taking a moment to smooth my blankets and adjust the lamp's wick, before he crossed the room to the fireplace. "The picture was taken almost a year ago, shortly before Sophia died."

I sat up straight and stared at Uncle. "How did she die?"

He stirred the fire with a poker. The blue flames leapt a little higher and made shadows dance on the wall. "Sophia had a bad fall," he said in a low voice. "She and James were playing together when it happened."

Giving the fire another poke, Uncle said, "Sometimes I fear the boy wants nothing more than to die himself. It's as if he believes his death will atone for hers."

We sat together and watched the fire. The wind tugged and pried at the windows, making the curtains sway.

After a while, Uncle got to his feet. As he leaned down to kiss me good night, I found the nerve to ask him one last question. "What was Sophia like?"

"Sophia." Uncle spoke her name as if it were a long, soft sigh, a winter wind in the treetops, a drift of snow, a wash of water over stones. "It's hard to say what Sophia was like. She was a difficult child, quick to anger and long to sulk. She was quiet and secretive, not always truthful, and often unkind to James."

I looked at Uncle, puzzled. "But Aunt adored her."

"Yes, she spoiled her with pretty dresses and dolls. Never scolded her, never found fault, never made her behave. Unfortunately, Sophia did not return her aunt's affection. Indeed, she took advantage of my sister."

I seized Uncle's hand. "Do you believe in ghosts?"

"No, indeed." He chuckled. "Why do you ask?"

"People in the village think Crutchfield Hall is haunted. Did you know that?"

Uncle laughed. "The villagers are a superstitious lot. Pay their stories no heed, Florence." He looked at me closely. "You're not frightened, are you?"

"Sometimes I think Sophia is still here," I said quietly. "I feel her following me, watching me, listening to me. Wherever I go, she's nearby."

Uncle looked at me earnestly, his kind face filled with concern. "Oh, my dear, foolish child, that's quite impossible. When we die, we leave this world and do not return. Be a sensible girl." He handed me

Vanity Fair. "Read your Thackeray. You'll find no ghosts in his stories, just ordinary people like you and me and a thousand others going about the world as we must."

Uncle sat with me for a while, trying to calm me. I was too imaginative, I was too sensitive, I was alone too much, he said. Because I wanted to please him, I did my best to dismiss my fears as silly and childish.

After he left, I listened to his footsteps until I heard them no more. Let Uncle believe what he liked, but I knew Sophia was here in this house. I hadn't imagined the laughter and the voice in the garden, or that cold hand on my cheek. Sophia was watching me, and I didn't know if I should fear her or try to befriend her.

SIX

THE NEXT DAY I WOKE ONCE more to the sound of rain driven hard against my window. I dressed and went down to breakfast, deliberately arriving too late to join Aunt or Uncle. I was not in a happy mood. I'd slept poorly, waking from one bad dream after another. Sophia traipsed through each one, taunting me, chasing me, frightening me. Sometimes she looked like a living girl, but in the worst dreams, her face was a skull and her bony hands stretched toward me like claws.

When I'd eaten all I could, which wasn't very much, I wandered through the house aimlessly, drifting from room to room, lonely, sad, and scared. Uncle had gone to Lewes on business, and Aunt had gone with him. James was shut up in his room, too sick to be a companion. Nellie was hard at work somewhere in the house, and Mrs. Dawson was busy in the kitchen. Neither had time for me.

But I wasn't alone. No matter where I was, no matter whether it was day or night, Sophia hovered in the shadows, watching and listening, daring me to find her.

I climbed the stairs to the second floor, but instead of going to my room, I went to James's room and stood at his door. All was quiet within. What did he do all day? How long could books interest him if he did nothing but read? I was tempted to turn the knob and confront him.

But I didn't do it. Aunt would find out. She'd already threatened to send me away to boarding school. If I flagrantly disobeyed her, she'd make sure I went as soon as possible.

I backed away from James's room. What else was there to do? I was tired of reading, tired of drawing, tired of being trapped inside by the rain and the wind.

At the bottom of the stairs to the third floor, I paused. Aunt had told me there was nothing up there but empty rooms where the servants used to live. Maybe she was right, but exploring those rooms would give me something new to do.

At the top, I was confronted by a narrow hall lined with closed doors. I opened one after another. Except for dust, spider webs, and more dust, the small rooms were all empty. Curtainless windows looked out on bare fields under dark clouds and pouring rain.

I found a dead bird in one room, most likely trapped inside last summer. I touched its brittle feathers lightly, then drew back. Its dark, dull eyes frightened me.

At the end of the hall, I stopped in front of the last closed door. I struggled to turn the knob, but it wouldn't move. To get a better grip, I wrapped my skirt around the knob and used all my strength. At last it yielded, and I shoved the door open. In front of me, a narrow flight of stairs led up to the dark attic.

Over my head, the wind rumbled. Rain beat against the roof. I heard creaking sounds and rustlings. I thought of Jane Eyre's climb to the tower where Mr. Rochester kept his insane wife. Things worse than a dead bird could be up there.

As I hesitated, I heard the cleaning woman's voice on the floor below. I'd forgotten it was her day to come. My fear of being discovered was greater than my fear of the attic's secrets. As quietly as possible, I closed the door behind me, plunging myself into a cold darkness given voice by the wind and the rain.

Cautiously, I climbed the creaking steps, listening for odd sounds and watching for signs of danger.

Dim light leaked in through a row of small windows under the eaves. Gradually furniture emerged from the shadows—bureaus, chairs, mirrors, boxes and chests, heaps of old, mildewed books. I opened drawers and cabinets crammed with faded silks, ancient linens, and yellowing documents written in Latin. I peered into boxes and found tarnished silverware, chipped bowls, cracked plates, and dainty cups without handles.

In hope of finding something more interesting, I looked around and spied a large trunk. Lifting its curved lid, I was amazed to find myself staring into the faces of half a dozen dolls. They had long curly hair and rosy cheeks. Their hands and feet were delicate. Their dresses were silk. They looked brand new, untouched, sleeping as if nothing would ever wake them.

Gently, I lifted one out. Her hair was dark and curly, and her eyes were the same blue as her dress. Her lips were parted in a smile revealing tiny white teeth and the tip of a pink tongue. She wore white stockings and button-top shoes.

In the orphanage, we used to daydream about dolls like these. We saw them in shops when we went out for walks with Miss Beatty. While she waited patiently, we pressed our noses against the window and chose our favorites, the ones we'd buy if we were rich. I always called mine Clara Annette, a beautiful name, I thought.

This doll, I thought, would be my Clara Annette. I had no idea who she belonged to or why she was in the attic. I did not care. I'd found her and I planned to keep her. In the daytime, I'd hide her in my wardrobe under the spare blankets and quilts. In the nighttime, she'd sleep with me.

Laying Clara Annette gently on a nearby chair, I moved the other dolls aside to see what else was in the trunk. Wrapped in tissue paper were dresses and slips, nightgowns and robes, coats and hats, shoes and stockings and underwear. I held up a blue silk dress and stared at myself in an age specked mirror. It had been made for a girl about my size. Like the doll's dress, the dress matched my eyes.

As I turned this way and that, admiring my reflection, I felt a familiar shiver run up my spine. Clasping the dress to my chest, I stared about me. "Is that you, Sophia?" I whispered to the shadows.

Rain pounded on the roof and gales of winter wind moaned in the eaves. But no one answered.

"Why do you hide from me?" I called.

I heard a rustling sound, followed by a giggle. "It's a game," Sophia whispered. "I found you—now you must find me."

Dropping the dress, I ran toward Sophia's voice. "Where are you?"

"Here, there, everywhere," she whispered, repeating the fountain's riddle. "Here, there, everywhere."

I whirled in circles, trying to locate her, but I couldn't. She truly was here, there, and everywhere. Suddenly frightened, I said, "Go away. Leave me alone."

"Don't you want me to be your friend?" She came closer, so close I could feel her cold breath on my cheek. "Aren't you lonely, Florence?"

"How can you be my friend? I can't see you, I don't know where you are."

"You're afraid of me," Sophia said scornfully.

"Yes," I cried, "yes, I am. I'm afraid of you! You, you—"

"Why don't you say it?" Sophia mocked me. "I'm dead. That's why you're afraid."

The cold air came closer, circled me once or twice, and then backed away. "How can I harm you? I have no substance. No strength."

With a whisper of silk, the dress I'd dropped slid across the floor toward me as if blown by the wind. I jumped back when it touched my shoes.

"Take it," Sophia whispered. "You need a new dress. That drab rag is dreadful. It's the sort of thing a pauper orphan would wear to scrub the floor."

I looked at the silk dress, fearful of it yet wanting it.

"If Aunt loved you as she loved me, she'd lavish expensive gowns on you as she did me." Sophia sighed. "Judging by what I've seen, I'm certain she doesn't even like you. Indeed, I believe she despises you."

Head down, I gazed at the dress. I couldn't argue with the truth.

"She hates you because you're not me," Sophia added.

I remained silent.

"Aunt gave me everything in that trunk," Sophia said. "After I died, I watched her pack my dresses and dolls as if she thought I'd come back for them someday." She laughed. "Poor old Aunt. She wept as if her heart were broken."

As Sophia spoke, Clara Annette floated across the attic and dropped softly into my arms. Without intending to, I hugged the doll. She was too beautiful to leave in the attic.

"I can't take your things," I whispered, holding the doll even tighter.

"Of course you can," Sophia said. "I want you to have them as a token of our friendship. Besides, I have no need for dresses or dolls now."

"Aunt will not want me to have them."

"Tut," Sophia said with a laugh. "Aunt needn't know."

I stared into the shadows and tried to see her. But no matter how hard I looked, I saw nothing. "Please, Sophia," I begged. "Please let me see you."

"Someday." With that promise, a cold breeze whirled away, taking Sophia with it.

Scooping up the dress and the doll, I ran down the attic steps, mindless now of how much noise I made. Behind me, the door to the attic slammed shut.

In my room, safe behind my own door, I dropped the dress on my bed. With Clara Annette in my arms, I warmed myself in front of the fire. Why had I accepted Sophia's gifts? I didn't want the belongings of a dead girl. Yet I'd been unable to refuse them. Because they were beautiful, I supposed. Because I'd never owned anything like them. Because I was afraid of angering Sophia.

A soft rap on my door startled me. Clutching the doll even tighter, I cried, "Who's there?"

"It's Nellie, miss, come to tidy your room." The door opened a crack and Nellie peered in. Never was I so happy to see her ordinary freckled face.

Nellie stared at the dress on the bed and the doll in my arms. "Oh, miss," she whispered, entering the room, "they be ever so pretty. Did your uncle give you them?" As she spoke, she touched the silk gently.

I shook my head. It was then that Nellie noticed my state. "Why, miss, what be wrong?"

"No one gave them to me. I found them in the attic."

"Ye went to the attic?" The sympathy on Nellie's

face changed to shock. "Nobody goes there. The floor be rotten. Even a body small as me could fall through."

From the corner behind me I heard a soft sound. The rustling of a dress maybe. A sigh, a laugh so low, I wasn't sure I really heard it. Sophia was there, watching me, assessing me, scorning me, scorning Nellie.

Despite myself, I was beginning to feel cross. "Do you always do what people tell you to do, Nellie? Don't you have any curiosity?"

"I knows my place, miss," Nellie said in an annoyingly humble voice.

I was horrified to find myself wanting to slap her face or pull her hair. It was what Sophia would have done.

"I know it ain't right for me to tell ye what to do, but don't go up there again," Nellie begged. "And don't keep them pretty things. They ain't yers."

While Nellie talked, Sophia whispered, "Don't listen to her. She's an ignorant servant. Keep the doll, keep the dress. She's jealous because I gave them to you instead of to her."

"No," I heard myself say to Nellie, "it's not right for a stupid girl like you to tell *me* what to do. Go back to the kitchen where you belong. I'm tired of your foolish chatter."

"Oh, miss." Nellie gave me a horrified look and ran from my room.

As soon as she was gone, I wanted to call her back. What was wrong with me? I'd never spoken to anyone like that, and I was ashamed of myself. I'd been cruel, thoughtlessly and needlessly cruel.

At the same time, I was aware of Sophia watching me from the shadows. Had she put those words into my mouth? Was it she who made me speak so cruelly to poor little Nellie?

I knew that Sophia would scorn me if I ran after Nellie. No one apologized to a servant. It simply wasn't done.

So I stayed where I was and stroked Clara Annette's dark ringlets. "Such a pretty doll," I whispered. "Do you miss your old owner?"

"Of course she misses me," Sophia said. "Everybody misses me. I was the favorite—until James came along and ruined everything."

On noiseless feet, a shadowy shape crept toward me. The closer it came, the colder I was. It was as if winter had taken a form and entered my warm room.

At first, Sophia was no more distinct than a figure glimpsed through fog or mist, but as she came nearer, her wavering outline slowly solidified. She wore a stained white silk dress, and her dainty slippers were muddy. What was left of her dark hair was dull and sparse. Her face was narrow and pale, her skin stretched tightly over her skull. Dark shadows ringed her eyes. Her teeth were brown. She smelled of earth and mold.

In abhorrence, I closed my eyes and tried to tell her to leave, but my mouth shook so badly, I couldn't speak. Never had I seen such a dreadful sight.

"Look at me," Sophia said.

Unwillingly, I opened my eyes. "What do you want with me?" I whispered.

"I'm so cold and so lonely." Sophia nestled into the rocking chair beside me, as weightless as a puff of cold air. "I need a friend, and so do you. We could be like sisters, sharing secrets."

I studied her white face, her stained teeth, her unruly hair, her dull eyes. "I don't want to be your friend. Or your sister. I won't, I can't." To my shame, I began to cry.

Sophia gave me a narrow-lipped smile, just the

sort I'd expect to see on my aunt's face. "I tell you, you *will* be my friend, whether you wish to be or not. I always get my way. It's useless to fight me."

With that, she slipped out of the chair and disappeared as quickly as she'd come. For a moment the coal fire flared up; then it died down to embers.

In shock, I gazed at the place where Sophia had first materialized. She'd stood right there beside the bed. She'd squeezed into the chair beside me, close enough for me to smell her. She'd spoken to me.

Uncle said the dead did not return. He was wrong.

Unable to stop shaking, I stared at Clara Annette's china face. Sophia's doll, I reminded myself. Not mine.

Filled with revulsion, I threw the doll across the room. Her head hit the edge of the mantel and she landed on the floor. Like a child fatally injured in a bad fall, she sprawled on her back, arms flung out, head broken.

Stricken to see such a pretty thing ruined, I picked her up and hid her in the back of a drawer full of extra linens. It wouldn't do for Aunt to see her gift to Sophia so badly treated.

Stricken to see such a pretty thing ruined, I picked her up and hid her in the back of a drawer full of extra linens. It wouldn't do for Aunt to see her gift to Sophia so badly treated.

Not daring to leave the dress on the bed, I scooped it up and stuffed it into the wardrobe, behind my best dress and my coat.

Once dress and doll were hidden, I ran downstairs. I did not want to remain alone in my room for fear Sophia might return.

SEVEN

⚯

UNCLE AND AUNT HAD NOT come back from their trip to town, so I joined Mrs. Dawson in the kitchen. To my relief, Nellie wasn't there. After speaking to her so rudely, I couldn't face her.

"You look poorly," Mrs. Dawson said. "Are you coming down with something?"

I shook my head. "I'm just tired."

"Drink your tea. It should perk you up."

I poured milk into my cup, added sugar, and filled it with tea. Steam rose around my face, comforting me. I breathed in the sweet smell of Earl Grey, my favorite blend, rich with bergamot.

Mrs. Dawson sliced bread and passed it over to me, along with a serving of shepherd's pie. Its mashed-potato crust was baked golden, and the vegetables and beef inside filled the kitchen with an aroma that made me hungry in spite of myself.

Mrs. Dawson watched me eat. "You may not be ailing," she said, "but something's eating at you."

Looking Mrs. Dawson in the eye, I said, "Do you believe in ghosts?"

Mrs. Dawson must have heard the fear in my voice. Studying me closely, she said, "Has something frightened you, Florence?"

Surrendering to my need for comfort, I flung my arms around her and pressed my face against her soft body. "Sophia," I sobbed. "I saw her today. She was hideous, horrible, monstrous."

Mrs. Dawson rocked me gently. "No, no, Florence. Sophia is dead and gone."

"But I tell you, I saw her," I insisted. "She *spoke* to me."

Mrs. Dawson took me by my shoulders and held me at arm's length. "And I tell you, you dreamed it." Her eyes implored me to agree with her. "You're lonely here, you want a friend, and you've made yourself believe in Sophia."

I shook my head. "Surely Aunt has seen her—"

"No more, no more. I'll hear no more." Mrs. Dawson's voice quivered as if I was scaring her. "The poor child's soul rests in peace now. Father Browne saw to it. He blessed her proper."

Making a shooing motion, she said, "Go on now. Find a book to read. Forget the dream. Forget Sophia. Say nothing about her to Nellie or anyone else. You'll only bring grief on yourself."

Defeated, I gave up and left Mrs. Dawson to her work. As I walked away, I heard laughter in the shadows. A cold finger brushed my cheek. Footsteps pattered behind me. I did not look back. I knew who it was.

At the top of the steps, Sophia appeared beside me, her face tinged blue, her eyes circled with dark smudges like bruises. "Why don't you visit James?" she whispered. "I know you want to."

I drew back, repulsed by the smell of damp earth that clung to her. "Aunt and Uncle forbid it."

"I never let others stop *me* from doing what I want." Keeping her hand on my arm, she floated into my room as if no more than air, but I could not break away from her.

My wardrobe opened, and Sophia pulled out the

blue silk dress. "Wear this. You must be presentable if you are to visit James."

Even though I knew it was futile to argue, I said, "I am not going to visit James." But as I spoke, I found myself taking off my own drab brown dress and slipping into the blue silk. The fabric touched my skin, as delicate as butterfly wings.

Sophia picked up my brush and comb and began brushing my hair. When it shone as brown and glossy as hers once did, she tied it back with a blue velvet ribbon. "There," she said. "You're not nearly as pretty as I am, but I suppose you'll do."

I wanted to tell her she was not pretty now, but instead I stood silently before the mirror and admired my reflection. Instead of a wretched orphan, I saw a well-dressed girl, the sort I'd admired on the streets of London.

Behind me, I noticed Sophia kept her back to the mirror. "Why don't you stand beside me and look at yourself? Then you can see who's prettier—you or me." It was a terrible thing to say, and I was ashamed of myself for speaking the words out loud.

Ignoring my question, Sophia seized my hand and led me away from the mirror and out of my room. As we walked down the hall, the blue silk rustled like autumn leaves. My hair was a soft, sweet weight on my shoulders and neck. I walked lightly, gracefully. I forgot to be afraid, forgot to worry. At last I was going to meet my cousin James.

Sophia stopped in front of James's door. First she pressed her ear to the wood and listened. Then she bent to peek through the keyhole.

Straightening, she favored me with her thin-lipped smile. "He's all alone, sitting in bed, reading. Don't bother to knock. Just walk in and stand quietly until he notices you. He loves surprises."

"Aren't you coming with me?" I asked.

But I was speaking to empty air. Sophia was gone, leaving an echo of her laughter behind.

For a moment, I hesitated. Perhaps it was unwise to enter without knocking. Suppose I frightened James? What if Sophia was tricking me into doing something I shouldn't? Could I trust her to be truthful?

But I simply could not resist visiting my cousin. Quietly I turned the knob and slowly opened the door. The curtains were closed tightly, and the fire burned low. An oil lamp beside the bed gave enough light for me to see James. Propped up on pillows, he was deeply engrossed in a book.

Like Sophia, he bore little resemblance to the child in the photograph. His round cheeks were gone, leaving his face narrow and solemn. His skin was pale, and the hair tumbling over his eyes was long and curly. Even from this distance, I could see he was thin and frail. Sickly.

Cautiously I took a few steps forward, unsure whether I should approach him or tiptoe out of his room. What I was doing seemed intrusive, rather as if I'd entered a sanctuary without permission.

I must have made a sound, for suddenly he turned and saw me. His reaction horrified me.

"No," he screamed, "you can't cross my threshold. It's forbidden! Get out! Get out!" He was on his knees now, hurling a book at me. Then another and another.

The heavy volumes hit the wall over my head, and I ducked this way and that to avoid being struck. He was definitely stronger than he looked.

When he ran out of books to throw, James fell back against his pillow, shrieking and crying. "Don't come near me!"

I ran to him and seized his hands. "Don't be afraid. I'm Florence, your cousin. Hasn't Uncle told you about me?"

"You can't trick me," James cried. "I know who you are—I know what you want!"

"No, no, James, please listen. I'm Florence Crutchfield. My father was your father's brother. I'm an orphan, just as you are. We're both wards of our uncle, Thomas Crutchfield."

Gradually, James's struggles lessened, and I released his hands. Although he still trembled, he breathed more naturally and his body began to relax.

He studied my face. "You're not Sophia," he whispered, "but you're wearing her dress and your hair is like hers. When I saw you in the shadows by the door, I was certain . . ."

He lay back against the pillows, his face as white as the sheets tumbled about him. "You frightened me."

"I'm so very, very sorry. I didn't mean to, but Sophia—"

"Do you see her too?" he interrupted, his eyes wide with surprise. "I thought I was the only one."

"She made me wear her dress, she fixed my hair, she sent me here . . ." I clenched my fists in vexation. "Please forgive me, James. She, she . . ."

I looked warily around the room. Was Sophia hiding in the corner by the wardrobe? Was she watching from behind the curtains?

James looked at me. "You're afraid of her too."

"She terrifies me. She could be here, she could be there, she could be anywhere."

James took my hands in his small ones. "Not here. We're safe in my room," he said. "She can't cross the threshold."

"Everywhere I go, she goes. The house, the garden. I can't get away from her." I shuddered and continued to search the corners for signs of Sophia.

James shook his head. "Spratt made a charm and hid it over my door. As long as it's there, she can't come in."

"Spratt made a charm?" I stared at my cousin, thinking I'd misunderstood him. "What sort of a charm?"

"Since you come from London," James said, "I doubt you believe in potions and charms and such, but Spratt's mother was a healer. And so was her mother and her mother before her and so on, back and back in time. She taught Spratt all she knew, including the making of charms to ward off evil."

Not sure what I believed, I looked at him, huddled under blankets and propped up on pillows, trusting in a charm to protect him from his own sister. His dead sister.

I moved nearer to him, fearful of the shadows around us. "What can Sophia actually do to harm you? We *see* her, we *hear* her, but she doesn't have a real body."

Fixing me with the same blue eyes we all had, James sat up straight and leaned closer to me. "Sophia doesn't need to be flesh and blood. Haven't you felt the cold touch of her hand? Hasn't she influenced you?" He paused and added, "Was it your idea to come to my room? Did you want to do it, or did she make you?"

My silence answered for me.

James lay back against his pillow, but he kept his eyes on me. "My sister has no body. She's never hungry. She's never tired. She's never sick. She's free to concentrate all her energy on one thing and one thing only. It's all she wants, and she's determined to have it."

He closed his eyes for a moment as if talking about Sophia's strength had exhausted his own. The room was so silent, the very air seemed to hold its breath.

"What does she want?" I whispered.

James looked at me then, his face as pale as the pillow. "She wants me to die." His voice was flat and dull, his eyes almost as lifeless as Sophia's.

"She can't hate you that much. It's unnatural, it's wicked, it's—"

"You don't understand." James's voice rose until he was almost shouting. "It's my fault she's dead. I killed her. I didn't mean to, but I did. And now she wants to kill me."

"How could you have killed her?" I asked. "You're younger and smaller than she is. You—"

"I don't want to talk any more," James cried. "I'm tired and need to rest—you've overexcited me. Go away!"

Confused by the change in his behavior, I reached out to comfort him, but he swung at me, striking me with his fists, not caring whether he hurt me or not. "Go away, I tell you," he shrieked. "Go away!"

Afraid of making him truly ill, I shrank back from the bed. At that moment, the door opened and Aunt entered the room.

At the sight of me, her face lit with joy. Holding out her arms to embrace me, she cried, "You've come back to me! I knew you would. I've saved all your things. I've waited and prayed for your return."

When I recoiled from her touch, Aunt realized her mistake. Immediately her happiness turned to rage. Seizing my shoulders, she shook me so hard, my head bobbled on my neck like a rag doll's. "Where did you get that dress? It's Sophia's, not yours. You have no right to help yourself to her things."

James cowered in his bed, his anger at me forgotten. "Stop, Aunt—you're upsetting me. Do you want me to die too?"

Pushing me aside, Aunt ran to him. "My poor lamb. What has Florence done to you?"

She reached for his hands, but he pushed her away. "Leave me alone! Florence has done nothing to me."

Aunt drew back, rigid with anger. "How dare you speak to me like that! After all I've done for you! Have you no gratitude?"

"Can't you ever leave me alone?" James cried. "I hate you! You wish I'd died instead of her. I heard you say so when you thought I was sleeping."

Unable to bear any more, I ran out of the room. The things I'd imagined in my days at Miss Medleycoate's mocked me. Sisters and brothers were jealous and hateful; they didn't love one another as I'd thought. Aunt was mean and spiteful. Sophia had despised her little brother. James claimed he'd killed his own sister.

After locking myself in my room, I stripped off the blue silk dress, ripping a sleeve in my haste. Buttons popped off and rolled across the floor. Without pausing to think about what I was doing, I stuffed Sophia's dress into the fire.

It smoldered for a moment and then burst into flame. Fire shot up the chimney. Seizing a poker, I did my best to keep it contained. As unhappy as I was, I had no desire to burn Crutchfield Hall to the ground.

With relief, I watched the fire subside. The smoke made my eyes water, and the room reeked of burnt silk. Wearing only a thin slip, I ran to the window and let in a torrent of cold fresh air.

As the casement swung outward, I saw that the constant rain had turned to snow. Trees and shrubbery, roofs and walkways, everything blended together in a sparkling white. Sharp lines disappeared, square shapes softened, hills and flat land merged.

If I'd been in a happier frame of mind, I might have thrilled to the snow's beauty. I'd certainly never witnessed its like in London's crowded, dirty streets.

But today I stared at the snow without really seeing it, too angry and scared by the morning's twists and turns to appreciate it. I'd reached a point so low that I almost wished to return to Miss Medleycoate's establishment. Perhaps the food was worse and the beds less warm and comfortable, but no ghosts roamed the orphanage's halls. I had Miss Beatty to comfort me and friends to laugh and talk with. I was often sad but never lonely or frightened. Here I was all three.

EIGHT

INALLY THE COLD DROVE ME to close the window and put on my own dress, rough and brown and scratchy against my skin. Afraid to stay in my room alone, I took my book and ran down to the sitting room and made myself comfortable in the big leather chair by the wood fire, much warmer than my coal fire.

I was so deeply immersed in *Vanity Fair* that I didn't notice Sophia until she exhaled her cold breath on my cheek. Startled, I dropped my book. "Go away," I begged. "I've had enough of you."

"But I haven't had enough of you, dear Florence." She perched on the arm of the chair and studied me with her dull eyes. "I see you've changed your clothes. Did you not like my dress?"

"I hate your dress!" I told her. "When James saw me wearing it, he thought I was you."

"Much more flattering to you than to me. Even dead, I'm far prettier than you are." She laughed her spooky little laugh and ran her bony fingers through her tufts of hair. Looking at me closely, she touched my nose. "Consider that bump in your nose: it's especially unattractive and bound to get worse as you age."

She jumped off the chair and did a few turns about the room, as graceful as a sylph in a ballet. Perhaps more so, for a living ballerina could not have floated as lightly as Sophia did.

"I must say, I enjoyed hearing Aunt's response to the sight of you in my dress," she said. "Poor old thing to mistake you for me—her eyesight must be failing."

She twirled around the room again, her ragged skirt floating around her. "I still have Aunt wrapped around my little finger, but she positively *detests* you."

"Why don't you haunt her and leave me alone?" I asked. "She'd be happy to see you."

"Aunt is a boring old bat. She was useful when I was alive, but now . . ." Sophia shrugged. "I have no need of pretty things or sweets. Indeed, it's a relief not to make a pretense of loving her. Why should I continue the charade by appearing to her?"

"You are the most wicked creature I've ever met," I whispered. Despite my own feelings toward Aunt, I was glad she hadn't known Sophia's true nature.

Sophia smiled as if I'd complimented her. Twirling back to the chair, she settled next to me, numbing me with cold. "Poor James is so afraid of me," she giggled. "Did he scream and cry and throw a tantrum at the sight of you?"

I tried to move away from her, but she kept me close to her. "He told me you want him to die," I said.

Sophia twirled a strand of hair around her finger and curled it into a ringlet. "I was cheated," she said. "James was meant to die, not me."

"How can you believe such a thing?" I asked. "No one knows who is meant to die and who is meant to live."

Clenching her fists in anger, Sophia jumped to her feet. "It's not fair! It's not fair! It's not fair!" she screamed like a small child. "Why should he be allowed to make me miserable even after I'm dead? Didn't he make me miserable enough while I was alive?"

Frightened by her anger, I cowered in the chair. "I cannot believe James ever caused you pain," I whispered.

"He was *born*, wasn't he? Isn't that enough?" Giving me a look of pure hatred, Sophia ran from the sitting room. Behind her, the fire died down, nearly extinguished by the draft of cold air she created.

As soon as she was gone, the flames on the hearth leapt up, snapping and crackling, but it took a long time for them to warm the icy air.

When I was certain I was alone, I drew my knees to my chest and curled up in the chair like a cat. I tried to lose myself in my novel, but instead of reading Thackeray's words, I heard Sophia's voice in my head, taunting me. What did she want with me? Could I really resist her? Or was James right about her being too strong for me to fight?

Just before the clock struck seven, Nellie appeared in the doorway. "Miss," she said almost fearfully, "I come to say dinner be ready and they be a-waiting on ye."

"Nellie." I ran to her side and took her arm. To

my dismay, she flinched as if she expected me to hit her. "Oh, Nellie, I am so sorry I spoke harshly to you. I don't know where those words came from. Please accept my apologies."

Nellie studied my face, her eyes troubled. "Ye scairt me, miss. I thought I'd done summat wrong to make ye so mad."

"No, you did nothing wrong." I gave her a quick hug. "I promise never to speak to you like that again."

Nellie nodded and darted out of the room as if I'd embarrassed her.

Behind me, I heard a mocking laugh. "You have the mind of a servant," Sophia whispered. "Soon you'll be helping that detestable girl with her chores."

A draft swept out of the room ahead of me and vanished into the shadows.

In the dining room, Uncle sat at the end of the table and Aunt sat at his right. They looked at me but neither smiled. Their faces were solemn. Indeed, Aunt's was grim.

"Sit down, Florence," Uncle said.

I sank into my chair across from Aunt. It was clear she'd told Uncle about my disobedience. Lowering my head, I toyed with my spoon, moving it to the right and back to the left. I had no appetite for the steaming soup in front of me.

"You know that James needs peace and quiet," Uncle said. "He must not be upset or disturbed in any way. Yet you entered his room without permission and frightened him."

"I'm very sorry, Uncle." My face burned with shame. Unable to meet his eyes, I kept my head down. "I never meant to harm James—I just wanted to meet him. I didn't think—"

"You are a thoughtless, selfish, disobedient girl," Aunt interrupted. "Excuses cannot change what you did. It is unforgivable."

"Now, Eugenie—" Uncle began.

"The girl is a troublemaker. I sensed it from the first." She took a deep breath and added, "If you need to be convinced, listen to what else Florence has done. She went to the attic and removed things from Sophia's trunk."

To my mortification, Aunt pulled Clara Annette from her lap and brandished the doll as if it were evidence in a criminal trial. "I found this hidden in a drawer in her bureau."

For a moment, we all stared at the doll as if we expected it to speak.

"The head is broken beyond repair," Aunt went on, nearly in tears. "It was Sophia's favorite, very expensive. I brought it home from Paris. A Madame Jumeau doll with a little trunk of clothing, made to order to match Sophia's wardrobe. And look at it. Look at it!" She shook the doll in Uncle's face.

Uncle tried to say something, but Aunt wasn't finished. "There's more. When I caught her in James's room, she was wearing Sophia's best dress. Then do you know what she did with it? Thrust it into the coal fire in her bedroom. She could have burned down the house!"

"That was very foolish." Uncle turned to me, clearly puzzled. "I don't understand your reason for burning the dress."

"I had to get rid of it," I wept. "I had to!"

"You see?" Aunt leaned toward her brother. "The girl doesn't have good sense. Who knows what she'll do next?"

Uncle shook his head sadly. "I do not understand," he repeated. "Your thoughtless act endangered us all."

"I recommend locking up the kitchen knives," Aunt said, her lips pursed so tightly, she could barely speak. "Next she might take it into her head to murder us in our beds."

"Now, now, Eugenie," Uncle said calmly, "you are on the verge of hysteria."

"I'm sorry." I wrung my hands in dread and remorse. "I'm truly, truly sorry, Uncle. If you wish to send me back to Miss Medleycoate, I'll go."

"Send you back to Miss Medleycoate?" Uncle stared at me. "Whatever gave you such an idea? You're my flesh and blood, Florence. I have no intention of sending you away."

"Except to boarding school," Aunt said primly. "We have agreed to that, brother. At Saint Ursula's Academy, Florence will be taught etiquette and deportment. She will cease reading novels and apply her mind to serious moral works."

Uncle Thomas winced at his sister's rising voice. "Perhaps we should discuss these issues at some other time," he said, "when we are all calmer. It's obvious that Florence is sorry she behaved thoughtlessly."

"*Thoughtlessly.*" Aunt looked heavenward as if seeking patience. "Her behavior is more than *thoughtless*, Thomas. In my opinion, it borders on malice."

Malice. I stared at my aunt. If she knew Sophia as well as she thought she did, she'd have a better idea of the difference between malice and thoughtlessness.

"She is clearly jealous of her cousin Sophia," Aunt went on. "Why else would she destroy her things and upset her brother? Poor, blameless Sophia, struck down in her youth and beauty by a cruel accident. How can anyone be jealous of a dead girl?"

"I am *not* jealous of Sophia," I said. "She—"

"Sophia was your superior in every way," Aunt interrupted, before I could tell her the truth about her precious Sophia. "Beauty, intelligence, grace, and rectitude," she went on. "Perfect manners, too."

Uncle frowned at his sister. "Sophia had her faults, Eugenie. We are all flawed. You as well as I."

"Speak for yourself, Thomas!"

Ignoring his sister, Uncle began to carve the roast. "Let us eat while the food is still hot." So saying, he passed a plate to me. "Please help yourself to potatoes and carrots, my dear."

Suddenly Aunt leaned across the table and tapped my hand sharply with a bony finger. "Have you begun reading *Pilgrim's Progress*?"

"No, I have not." I looked her in the eye as I spoke. "I do not care for it."

"You do not *care* for it." She shook her head. "I suppose you do not care for the state of your immortal soul either?"

"Eugenie, please." Uncle patted his sister's hand. "Allow the child to enjoy her dinner."

"As you wish, Thomas." Aunt rose from the table. "Please tell Nellie to bring my dinner to my room."

In the silence that followed her departure, the air settled around us comfortably.

"I'm sorry, Uncle," I said. "It seems I can do nothing to please Aunt."

"Don't blame yourself, Florence. Eugenie is not an easy person to please." He smiled at me. "Now stop fretting and eat your dinner. You don't want to disappoint Mrs. Dawson."

Pushing my cold soup aside, I picked at the food on my plate. What little I ate, I did not enjoy.

When Nellie came to clear the table, Uncle and I retreated to the sitting room and settled by the fire to read, he with a thick book of essays by Thomas Carlyle and I with *Vanity Fair*.

"Uncle," I said, "am I really to go to boarding school?"

He looked up from his book, his face rosy in the

firelight. "You need a proper education, Florence. You're obviously a highly intelligent girl."

"Couldn't you teach me here?"

"Me?" He chuckled. "I wouldn't have the slightest idea of where to begin. My mathematics are quite rusty, and my scientific knowledge is limited to the ancient Greeks."

"Aunt teaches James."

"Not very well, I fear." He looked at me closely. "I don't think you'd enjoy her methods."

"No, probably not." I snuggled deeper into my chair and watched the fire dance upon the logs, slowly consuming them.

"I've been considering hiring a governess for James," Uncle continued. "Eugenie is opposed to the idea, but she hasn't the skill to teach the boy more than the rudiments—which he has already mastered, as have you."

Remembering my cousin's hysterical behavior, I touched my uncle's hand. "Is James well enough to have a governess?"

"Yes, I think it will do him good." Uncle smiled at me. "She could give lessons to both of you. I can't think of anything better for him. Or for you."

Suddenly worried, I looked at Uncle anxiously. "Will James want to see me again?"

"I talked to him before dinner. He wants you to know he's sorry for his outburst."

"I'm relieved to hear that, Uncle. I would enjoy taking lessons with James." I paused a moment before asking an important question. "But will Aunt agree to my staying here? She seems determined to be rid of me."

Uncle contemplated the fire as if the words he needed might be found in its flames. "My sister often wants things she doesn't get," he said softly. "She hasn't had a happy life."

With an attempt at a cheerful smile, he turned to me. "I prefer to keep you here with James. So here you will stay. Tomorrow I shall begin my search for a suitable governess."

With that, he reopened his book and I reopened mine. For some time we read in silent harmony. It didn't matter that Sophia joined us. It didn't matter that she crept close and whispered, "Aunt might not get everything she wants, but I do." It didn't matter that she drew some of the warmth from the fire. With uncle beside me, I felt safe.

Going up to bed after supper was a different matter. Buried under a heap of quilts, I shivered as if I'd never be warm. Although I didn't see or hear her, I knew Sophia could be anywhere, visible or invisible, hiding in dark corners, watching and planning, mocking me, scaring me, a presence following me as closely as my own shadow.

NINE

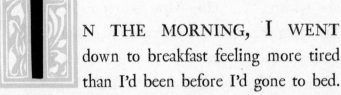

IN THE MORNING, I WENT down to breakfast feeling more tired than I'd been before I'd gone to bed. Sophia had chased me through dream after dream all night long. She wanted me to do something, she said I had to, and I knew I mustn't obey her. She was wicked, and the thing she wanted done was wicked too. I had to escape, but we were in the garden and she was here and there and everywhere. I couldn't get away from her. Or the thing she wanted me to do.

"You're up early," Mrs. Dawson said.

Yawning a great yawn, I reached for my teacup. "I had bad dreams."

"Never tell a dream before breakfast." Mrs. Dawson handed me a plate of bread, butter, and jam. "It's the surest way to make it come true."

I shuddered. "That's the last thing I want," I told Mrs. Dawson.

As I was finishing my oatmeal, I saw Nellie hesitating in the doorway as if she weren't sure of her welcome. I raised my hand and beckoned to her.

Like a mouse, she scurried across the room and slid into a place beside me. "I been thinking, miss," she whispered, eyeing Mrs. Dawson's broad back. Deciding the cook was intent on her chores, Nellie continued in a voice so low, I could barely hear her. "Maybe it were *her* that made ye speak so mean." As she spoke, her eyes darted around the room. "Her ain't here now, is her?"

I looked around uneasily. "No, not now."

"But her can come anytime her wants." Nellie laid a cold hand on mine. "I been feeling her meself. Like a shadow her be, dark and cold and hateful."

"Can you see her, Nellie?"

"Almost." Her body tense, Nellie peered about just as I had, checking dark doorways and corners. "Her scares me something terrible, miss."

"How long have you known about her, Nellie?"

"Her been comin' upon me slowly." Flustered, Nellie knocked a spoon off the table and onto the floor.

Surprised by the noise, Mrs. Dawson looked over her shoulder. "Are you finished with your chores, Nellie?"

"No'm. I come to fill me bucket." With that, Nellie scooted to the sink and pumped water into her scrub bucket. Giving me a small, scared smile, she hurried out of the kitchen.

Left on my own, I took my book to the sitting room and sat down to read. Before long, Sophia waltzed across the room, dipping and turning as if she actually had a partner.

"I don't believe you could dance a waltz," she said, "as untrained and clumsy as you are."

It was true. I'd never taken a dancing lesson. Miss Medleycoate had never encouraged any of us to imagine we might someday spin around a ballroom with a handsome suitor.

"I could play the piano with a precocity that amazed both Aunt and Uncle," Sophia went on. "I sang, too, but I am now sadly out of practice."

I looked at her with both pity and loathing. Pity because she was most certainly dead and not about to go dancing with anyone. Loathing because she was mean and spiteful and obviously had not bene-fitted morally from dying.

Pulling the drapes aside, Sophia peered at the snow. "Quick, put on your coat. I have a mind to build a snowman."

Although I was comfortable where I was, I found myself running to my room. When I returned with my coat, scarf, hat, and mittens, Sophia wrinkled her nose.

"If you were as I am now, you wouldn't need those cumbersome garments," she said. "You'd never be hot, never be cold, never be hungry or tired or afraid."

"I'd never be anything," I murmured.

Although I hadn't meant her to hear me, Sophia gave me a hateful look. "If justice prevails," she said, "I will soon be as you are." Under her breath, she added, "And James will be as I am."

"What do you mean?" I asked, but she merely laughed.

"Come along," she called. "I'm eager to build my snowman."

Nellie looked up as we ran through the scullery. She opened her mouth to speak but stopped, her face puzzled, then frightened. "Miss," she cried. "Miss!" But she didn't follow me.

Outside, Sophia darted across the snow and disappeared into the garden. She left no tracks, but I found her easily enough, waiting for me by the fountain. The stone children and their captive swan wore hats and coats of snow, and the words on the rim were hidden.

"This has always been my favorite place." Sophia brushed the snow off the fountain's rim and read the inscription. "Here and there and everywhere—it's a riddle," she said. "Do you know the answer?"

I shook my head, and she smiled. "Just as I thought. You're not nearly as clever as I am."

Leaning close to me, she chilled my cheek with her wintry breath. "Uncle says the answer is time, though he thinks it could also be the wind. But *I* know the true answer."

Sophia's eyes held mine. I couldn't turn away. "It's *Death*," she whispered. "Death is here and there and everywhere."

Sophia looked at the house, its dark stone almost black against the whiteness, its roof and tall chimneys blending into the sky. "You cannot escape death," she said softly. "You'll find out for yourself someday. Perhaps when you least expect it, he will come for you."

I drew away from her, burrowing my face into the warmth of my scarf. It was true. There was no escaping something you couldn't see, even if you knew where to look.

"I've scared you, haven't I?" Sophia's laugh was as brittle as the sound of ice breaking. "Start rolling a ball for the snowman. I want it to be as tall as the chimney tops."

She kept me working until my toes and fingers were numb from cold. Slowly the snowman took shape. Three balls of snow balanced one atop the other, not nearly as tall as the chimney tops, but lofty enough to see eye to eye with the stone children on their pedestal.

Sophia studied the snowman. "He needs a carrot for his nose and lumps of coal for his eyes and mouth. Run to the kitchen and come right back. Promise."

Obediently I darted through the snow and into the warmth of the kitchen. Stuffing a handful of coal into my pocket, I grabbed a carrot from the table.

"Here," Mrs. Dawson said. "Where are you

going with that carrot? I just pared it for to-night's stew."

"It's for the snowman we're building in the garden."

"'We'?" Mrs. Dawson looked at me in surprise. "You and who else? If Nellie is out there playing, you tell her to get herself inside. She has work to do."

A bit rattled by my slip, I shook my head. Mrs. Dawson would not want to hear about Sophia, waiting impatiently for me. "I'm building it. Just me. I don't know why I said 'we.'"

Mrs. Dawson held out an unpeeled carrot and I returned the one she'd pared. "Your lips are blue with cold, child. Stay inside a bit and warm up. The snowman can wait for his nose."

"No, I promised I'd be right back."

"Promised who?"

Without answering, I slipped out the door and ran to the garden. I didn't dare keep Sophia waiting.

"You took your time," Sophia said.

She watched me add the snowman's eyes, mouth, and nose. "No, no," she said crossly. "He mustn't smile."

Snatching the lumps of coal, Sophia rearranged them and stood back, with a grin. She'd transformed my creation. With frowning brows and a grim, down-turned mouth, he stared at me. He was fearsome, almost as frightening as Sophia herself.

"Perfect." She smiled and stepped back to admire her creature. "It will give everyone a start to see him standing here exactly where I built mine."

Suddenly she tensed as a cat does when it hears something no one else does. "Hide," she cried. "He's coming!"

Frightened, I followed Sophia into the yew trees around the fountain and huddled under the snowy branches. "Who's coming?" I whispered.

There was no answer. Sophia had vanished.

"Who be here?" Spratt called. "Come out and show yerself."

With some embarrassment, I crawled out from the yew tree. In doing so, I brushed against a branch that then dumped its load of snow on my head.

"Well, it be hard to say which be the girl and which be the snowman," Spratt said with a chuckle.

I brushed the snow off. My nose felt like the carrot in the snowman's face, frozen hard as diamonds.

While I stamped my feet to warm them, Spratt studied the snowman. "This be a right good job," he said, "but there's summat familiar about him." He put his hand on my shoulder. "Could it be ye had some help a-building it?"

When I didn't answer immediately, he went on, "I sees onliest one set of footprints. I reckon they be yers. *Her* don't leave no footprints."

"Sophia," I whispered. "*She* made his face."

"Hush, don't be saying her name. That's like inviting her to come." Spratt leaned on the shovel he'd been using to clear snow from the garden walk, and peered into my eyes. "Ye see her, do ye?"

I nodded. "First I felt her, then I heard her, and now I see her. She comes to my room, she follows me upstairs and down. No matter where I go, I can't escape her."

Spratt sighed and shook his head. "It be a shame for a child to be so wicked as that 'un. Wish I knowed a way to make her lie peaceful in her grave like most folk do."

"You gave James a charm to protect him. Can you make one for me?" My voice rose. "She wants him dead—she wants me dead too. She hates me. I tell you, she hates me!"

"No, no. Her just be toying with ye. It's always been her way to taunt and tease and hurt." He paused and stared at the snowman, its tall shape white against the darkening sky. "It be Master James her wants to harm, not ye. But we won't let her get to him, will we? We'll keep a close watch, ye and me."

My teeth chattered so hard that I couldn't speak. Sophia was the cat and James and I were the mice. When she was tired of playing with us, she'd bite off our heads and eat us.

"Poor lass, ye be just about froze." Spratt took my hand. "Let me take ye back to the house. Be dark soon. Mr. Crutchfield will be a-looking for ye."

In the dusky light of a winter afternoon, the land rolled away toward the distant hills, its whiteness shading into a bluish gray. The snow creaked under our feet, but ahead, the hall's windows glowed with warmth. Hot tea would be waiting by the fire in the sitting room, along with bread and butter and jam.

Behind us, Sophia hid in the snow-laden garden, watching me, smiling that spiteful smile. She would come inside when she wished, but she'd drink no tea, she'd eat no bread and jam. All the fires in the house could not warm her bones. Alone, she'd twirl through the house like a cold draft, thinking of nothing but ways to make James pay for her death.

TEN

LL NIGHT LONG, THE WIND blew and Sophia pursued me into my dreams as she had the night before. Awake or asleep, I could not escape her.

Exhausted, I dragged myself down to breakfast and sank into my seat at the kitchen table.

Mrs. Dawson looked at me sharply. "Bad dreams again?"

I nodded and she clucked her tongue. "Poor child. You'll be needing a good dose of my special tonic."

Nellie slid in beside me. "Don't take none of that," she said. "It be poison for certain."

"Hmm," Mrs. Dawson said. "Looks like you could use some yourself, Nellie dear."

"It's me dreams," Nellie said. "Lately they be a-wearing me out."

She looked out the window at the snow-blanketed garden. "It were on account of that snowman you made, miss. I seen it afore I went to bed, a-standing in the garden, looking like the devil hisself. Why'd ye make him so big and scarifying?"

Mrs. Dawson joined Nellie at the window. "It's strange, but Sophia built a snowman just like that on the day before she died. She told James the snowman would come to life at night and steal him from his bed. He'd bury James deep in the snow. No one would ever see him again. She terrified the poor—"

"Stop, mistress, stop!" Nellie cowered at the table, her hands pressed to her ears. "That be just what I dreamed, only it were me the snowman took."

Wide awake now, I stared at Nellie and then turned to Mrs. Dawson. "I dreamed the same thing," I whispered. "The snowman dragged me to the churchyard and laid me in a grave and heaped snow over me."

By now, Nellie had her apron over her head and was sobbing. "Yes, yes, he took me to the churchyard too, and he buried me under the snow, and I couldn't dig me way out or move or cry for help. I wanted to come home so bad."

Mrs. Dawson's face lost its ruddy color. "The day Sophia was buried it snowed again. They'd no sooner shoveled the dirt onto her grave than the snow covered her. I couldn't help thinking how cold she must be." Her hands shook, and tea slopped over the rim of her cup.

She moved closer to the fire. "Poor child." Mrs. Dawson crossed herself. "Poor, cold child." She glanced at a calendar hanging on the wall and crossed herself again. "It was on this very day she died. Twelve months ago, a whole year now."

As she spoke, I felt Sophia creep up behind me. Her cold breath lifted the hair on my neck. No one saw her, not even me, but she was there in the kitchen, making the fire on the hearth flicker and flare.

Mrs. Dawson shivered. "There's a draft in here today, worse than usual. Makes my old bones ache."

"Sophia were a wicked 'un," Nellie whispered.

The air quivered, and a heavy stoneware pitcher fell from a shelf. Just missing Nellie's head, it shattered harmlessly on the stone floor.

"See what happens when you speak ill of the dead?" Mrs. Dawson bent to clean up the shards of china. "Show me a perfect child, Nellie, before you criticize Sophia."

For a moment, Nellie sat still and stared at Mrs. Dawson and the broken pitcher. Then she and I looked at each other. We both knew the pitcher had not fallen by accident.

Mrs. Dawson dumped the remains of the pitcher into the trash bin. "You have work to do, Nellie. Master wants his boots polished, and the floors need sweeping and the fires must be tended."

Nellie ran off, glad to leave the kitchen where Sophia lingered unseen. "If I was you," Mrs. Dawson said to me, "I'd busy myself with needlework or knitting, maybe even read the Bible and say some prayers. Remember, Satan casts his nets far and wide. And you aren't as smart as you think you are."

Behind me, Sophia chilled my neck with her breath again. Mrs. Dawson drew her shawl more tightly around her shoulders and rose to put more wood on the fire. "I've never known this kitchen to be so cold."

I excused myself to fetch a wrap, but as soon as I left the kitchen, Sophia stepped in front of me. "I have a mind to show you something."

Even though I struggled to resist her, Sophia

seized my hand and dragged me outside. Snow had begun to fall again, and a strong wind made a din in the treetops. I tried to hang back, but my cousin dragged me away from the house. "Where are we going?" I cried. "I need my coat, my hat."

Sophia did not answer. Clad only in her thin silk dress, she struck out across the snow, pulling me with her. From time to time, the wind lifted her off her feet and threatened to carry her away, but it never succeeded. Somehow she stayed on, or close to, the ground. Perhaps my weight held her down—I did not know, could not tell.

Faster she ran and faster still, dragging me behind her. The wind bit my face, and sprays of flying snow blinded me. "Please," I cried, "go slower. I cannot keep up with you."

With a laugh, Sophia glanced over her shoulder, her face stark white. "The living are not as light on their feet as the dead."

On we went, across fields, up hills and down, skirting a pond, ducking under tree limbs heavy with snow. Using the last of my strength, I followed Sophia to a hilltop where the wind blew so savagely, I thought it might carry us across the sea to America. Just below us lay a small huddle of houses, a couple of shops, an inn, and a church. The scene reminded me of a Christmas village I'd seen once in a shop window.

"Lower Bolton," Sophia said.

I said nothing, but I was cheered by the thought that living people were nearby. Fires and hot tea and warm food. Comfort. If only I could escape Sophia and seek a kindly person to help me.

Tightening her grip on my wrist, Sophia glided downhill toward the village, slowed only by my stumbling gait. When we reached the churchyard, I was prepared to collapse and freeze to death in a snowbank.

Sophia smirked. "That's the price you pay for dragging your cumbersome body everywhere you go."

Too weary to speak, I followed her through the gate. We wound our way through a city of tombstones, some taller than I was, some in danger of falling, some already fallen. The inscriptions on many were too weathered to read, and the stones were black against the white snow. It was a desolate place on a winter day.

Sophia stopped beside a stone about her height, capped with snow. With a dramatic gesture, she pointed to the inscription, its letters crisply cut and recently done:

Here Lies
Sophia Mary Crutchfield
Only Daughter of William and Susannah
15 September 1871 to 27 January 1883
Our Loss, Heaven's Gain

"Aunt's doing," Sophia said. "She's one of the few who believed I'd go to Heaven. Poor old thing—she was so easily duped."

"Someone left flowers." I pointed to a half-dozen roses as red as blood against the white snow.

"Aunt again." Sophia picked up a rose and watched it turn black in her fingers. "As Dawson remarked, today's my death-day. Twenty-seven January. Exactly one year ago."

She glanced at me slyly. "Odd, isn't it? You know when your birthday is, but not your death-day, even though you pass the date year after year, never suspecting that someday . . ." She smiled and left the thought unfinished.

I'd pondered the same thing myself many times.

Indeed, I supposed most people wondered what date would mark their life's end.

"I don't suppose you like to think of the period at the end of the sentence," Sophia said.

I shrugged and pulled the collar of my dress tightly around my neck. No matter what I did, I could not keep out the wind. Its busy fingers squeezed between my buttons and pushed their way up my sleeves and funneled down my neck.

"Should we celebrate my death-day? With gifts and cake and song?"

I shook my head and said nothing. I wanted my coat, my scarf, my hat. I wanted to be home, safe and warm by the fire, reading my book.

"No, I suppose one does not celebrate one's death-day." For a moment Sophia seemed to sink into sorrow, but then she brightened. "Here's something I'm certain you do not know. The dead are strongest on their death-days, just as the living are weakest on their birthdays."

"Nonsense. I'm no weaker on my birthday than any other day."

Sophia looked at me sharply. "Don't you feel strangely vulnerable on your birthday? As if the force that birthed you can take you back on the same day?"

"Sometimes," I admitted, "but I don't understand why it should be so."

"There's much you don't understand," Sophia said. "This part I will tell you. I've watched and I've waited for this day, feeling myself strengthen as the months passed. At first I could not crawl out of my coffin, just as a baby cannot crawl out of its cot. It took me a month to climb from my grave, but at first I could do no more than creep around the graveyard like a loathsome worm. By June, I was standing and soon walking. In July, exactly six months after my death-day, I made my way home and began to terrify James. Spratt set me back when he made that charm, but at least I'd made certain James was not enjoying the life he stole from me."

She paused and smiled, revealing the rotten little stumps of her teeth. "Then you arrived, dear cousin," she said, "and I knew if I waited until my death-day I'd be strong enough to make you do whatever I wished."

"No." I shook my head. "No, no." But I heard the weakness in my voice, and so did Sophia.

Turning back to her grave, Sophia said, "Just

imagine, if you will, that the inscription reads 'Here Lies James Ernest Crutchfield, Only Son of William and Susannah, 20 July 1873 to 27 January 1883—Our Loss, Heaven's Gain.'"

She paused a moment to allow me time to imagine. "And then," she said, "imagine I stand here beside you, a living girl, telling you the sad story of my brother's untimely death."

I wrapped my arms tightly across my chest, unwilling to picture James dead and Sophia alive. "That's not the way it happened," I whispered.

She glared at me. "I tell you, it is the way it *should* have happened!"

"No—"

"Yes!" She held my wrist so tightly, I felt the sharpness of her bones dig into my flesh. "Think of your body buried deep in the earth, lying there in the cold and the dark, day in and day out, for a whole year. Spring, summer, fall, and winter again. Stars wheeling overhead, the moon and the sun rising and setting, grass growing and dying, and the snow returning. Would you not want to be free of the grave? To live again? No matter who paid the cost?"

I gazed at the grave, knowing I would not want to lie where Sophia's body lay, knowing I wanted to live as long as I could. Pitying her, pitying me, pitying all of us, I hugged my living self as tightly as I could.

Sophia stared at me from her dull dark eyes. "How can you blame me for wanting what everyone wants?"

I shook my head, unable to answer.

"Why should James live and I die? Is he better than I am? Is he more valuable than I am?" Sophia grabbed my arms and forced me to look at her. "I tell you, he does not deserve to live! He took everything from me—he owes me his life."

Fed by her own fury, Sophia began to run once more, towing me behind her again. Headstones spun away from us, the churchyard gate flew open, homes and shops blurred as we ran past them, away from the church, away from the village, up the road toward Crutchfield Hall.

ELEVEN

~

THE SNOWY GROUND SLID AWAY beneath my feet as if I were ice skating, faster and faster until I was sure we'd left the ground altogether and were flying on the wind. When I inhaled, the cold air burned my lungs and drew tears from my eyes. My forehead ached as if it were packed in ice.

At last Crutchfield Hall came into view, its dark stone walls a welcome sight. Down one last hill, across the lawn and the terrace, and through the door we went, Sophia leading, me following.

When Sophia released her grip on me, my legs were as weak as a baby's and my knees shook. I slid to the floor and leaned against the wall, certain I'd never stand or walk again.

"I thought you'd enjoy a fast trip home," Sophia said, "but I see your body is simply not up to it."

"Please, I want to go to my room now," I whispered. "I need to lie down and rest and recover my senses."

"Not yet." Seizing my hand again, Sophia pulled me to my feet and led me upstairs and down the hall to James's room.

"Why are we stopping here?" I asked.

"So you may enter the room and remove the charm over the door, the one Samuel Spratt put there. Be very quiet. My brother must not see you."

"No, I won't do it." My voice shook and my limbs trembled. I had to force myself to defy her. "The charm is there to protect James from you."

"You must not oppose me on my death-day." With a smirk, Sophia added, "I wish to see my brother—whether he wants to see me or not."

Although I did not intend to obey her, I found myself turning the knob slowly and quietly. I knew I shouldn't open the door, I knew I was endangering

James, I knew I couldn't trust Sophia, but I could not resist her. It was her death-day. She stood behind me, a force I lacked the strength to resist.

The room was dim. James was curled on his side, his back to the door, apparently sleeping. I turned my eyes from him. I couldn't bear to see him lying there, trusting in a charm to keep him safe.

Slowly I reached above the door and fumbled in the dust and cobwebs for the charm. It was no more than a bundle of twigs, moss, and dried flowers tied together with a green ribbon, so little a thing to keep Sophia away. Holding it tightly, I stepped back into the hall and closed the door behind me.

When Sophia saw what I had, she took a step backwards. "Get rid of it," she hissed. "It reeks of comfrey and hyssop and other vile things."

"What should I do with it?"

"Throw it out the window at the end of the corridor," Sophia ordered. "Be quick!"

With an aching heart, I went to the window, opened the casement, and flung the little bundle as far as I could. I watched it fall into the snow and vanish. "Wrong," I whispered. What I'd just done was wrong. Why hadn't I stopped myself?

Turning back, I saw Sophia slip into James's room. Filled with dread, I hurried after her.

She stood beside the bed looking down at the sleeping boy. "He's grown taller," she whispered, "but he's frail and thin and almost as insubstantial as I am." Her voice was scornful.

"He's ill," I reminded her.

Sophia studied her brother's face. "First he killed our mother and shortly thereafter our father. Then he killed me. I tell you, he deserves to die."

"Your mother died in childbirth, and your father died of fever," I reminded her. "James isn't responsible for either. If he had anything to do with *your* death, it was accidental."

James stirred and slowly opened his eyes. He saw me first. "Florence," he murmured, "I was sleeping."

"Have you nothing to say to me?" Sophia leaned over her brother, her face inches from his.

"Sophia!" James looked at her with horror. "You cannot come here. The charm—"

Sophia smiled. "Our sweet cousin did my bidding and removed Spratt's silly old contrivance."

James stared at me. "How could you have done so?"

I shook my head, too ashamed to answer or even to look at him.

"I *made* her do it," Sophia said. "Everyone does what I say. You know that."

"I'm sorry," I whispered to James. "Truly, I am."

"Enough jibber-jabber," Sophia said. "Do you know what today is, James?"

"Today?" He thought a moment, his forehead as creased as an old man's. "It's January twenty-seventh," he said in a low voice.

"Does that date have any significance for you?"

He plucked the edge of his blanket with nervous fingers. "It's the day you died," he whispered.

Sophia made him repeat himself three times until she was satisfied he'd spoken loudly enough. "Now answer this. Who is stronger today, you or I?"

James slid deeper into his bed until he was almost totally covered by blankets. "You are" came the muffled reply.

Sophia pulled back the covers, revealing her brother's shaking body. "I didn't hear you," she said. "Answer me again. Who is stronger today—you or I?"

"You are," James sobbed. "You are."

I touched her arm. "Please, Sophia," I begged. "Don't torment him. You'll make him sicker."

She shrugged me off. "I do not care how sick he is. He has not long to live." Turning to James, she said, "Get out of bed and dress yourself."

"I can't," he whimpered.

"Do as I say. Now!"

"No, Sophia." I tried to thrust myself between them, but she shoved me aside as if I were made of paper.

Dragging James from his bed, she said, "We're going somewhere, you and I. We have things to settle."

Shoving me out of her way, she opened the door and looked up and down the corridor. Seeing no one, she took James's hand and ran with him the way she'd run with me, fairly flying down the hall and up the stairs to the third floor.

TWELVE

FOLLOWED THEM AS FAST AS I could, but when I reached the top step, they had vanished. Breathing hard, I listened to my heart pound.

"Sophia," I called. "James. Where are you?"

As I waited for an answer, I heard creaking sounds over my head. Footsteps, I thought. In the attic.

I ran to the door and climbed the stairs so quickly, I tripped on the top step. Sprawled on the attic floor, I saw one pair of footprints in the dust, small and shoeless. I scrambled to my feet and followed them to an open window. When I poked my head out, I saw my cousins on the roof.

Frightened nearly to death, I climbed through the window and crept upward, slowly and cautiously. The wind had blown the snow off the slates, a good thing, but it tugged at my clothing and my hair. Worse yet, it billowed under my dress, threatening to lift me into the air like a balloon.

"Well, well." Sophia eyed me from her perch on the roof's highest point. "Here comes Cousin Florence. I thought you'd be afraid to follow us."

James huddled a few inches away from his sister, weeping. "Go back, Florence," he sobbed. "Go back."

"Oh, stay, cousin, stay," Sophia said. "And bear witness to an amazing feat. They say the past cannot be changed, what's done is done, but I mean to prove them wrong. Yes, that's what I mean to do."

Steadying myself against the side of a tall chimney, I stared at Sophia. "I don't understand," I said.

"Let me tell you our history at Crutchfield Hall," my cousin said. "We came here when I was ten and James was eight. Aunt was fond of me, but Uncle preferred James. He doted on him and took his side when we quarreled. Whatever James wanted, he was given—a book, a top, a ball, a dog, anything at all."

Sophia shot a venomous look at her brother,

whose face was as white as the fields stretching out to the horizon.

"You killed my dog," he whispered.

"Tut. I threw a ball. Is it my fault the dog was stupid enough to run in front of that cart?"

"You did it on purpose. You saw the cart and you threw the ball."

"You're a stupid little boy. Ask Aunt. She'll tell you it was an accident."

"Aunt wasn't there. It was just you and I." James's voice was getting stronger. Despite the wind and the flying snow, he faced his sister. "Spratt knew the truth. So did Uncle, even if he wouldn't dare say it."

"James, James, James," Sophia chanted, giving his name a nasty sound in the cold air. "*Everyone* adored James. Spratt, Uncle, the servants, the vicar, the village shopkeepers, the blacksmith. When James and I were together, no one noticed me. I was invisible."

"If you'd smiled more," James said tentatively, "if you hadn't been so sullen, then maybe people would have—"

"What did *I* have to smile about?" Sophia turned on James angrily. "My dear darling mother died giving birth to *you!* A brother I neither asked for nor wanted. And what a fuss they all made about the poor, motherless babe, without a thought for me, the poor, motherless girl. Father forgot about me—he paid me no mind at all. He cared only for you. Believe me: I had nothing to smile about and great reason to be sullen."

James had nothing more to say. Frightened, he stared at his sister. His lips shaped the word "please." But he did not say it. We both knew "please" meant nothing to Sophia.

Against my will, I looked down at the ground. Covered in new-fallen snow, the terrace lay far below. Spratt and his helper, a boy about my age, were no bigger than dolls as they went about their business. Dizzy with vertigo, I turned back to Sophia.

"Why have you chosen the roof to settle your quarrel?" I asked her.

She looked at James with contempt. "On this very day, I dared the little ninny to walk the ridge of the roof at its highest point, from this chimney to that one."

She pointed to a chimney about fifteen feet from the one James clung to. "He said he'd do it if I did it first." With a fierce scowl, she turned to her brother. "Didn't you say that? Didn't you?"

James nodded. He'd begun to cry again. His nose ran.

"You *promised.*"

"Yes," he whispered, "yes, I did. I promised to do it if you did it first."

"So I did—just like this." Sophia walked along the roof to the other chimney, touched it, and came back. The wind made her waver as if she were a paper doll, but she didn't fall. "You see? I did it then and I can do it now."

I supposed if one didn't look down, it wouldn't be too difficult to walk along the roof line. But how could one not think about the height of the roof and the certainty of death if one fell? I could never do such a foolish thing, no matter who dared me.

Sophia sneered at James. "Now it's your turn. Let's see if you can keep your promise this time."

"No," James sobbed. "I couldn't do it then and I cannot do it now. Please, Sophia, please, I'm sorry. It's my fault, all my fault. Blame it on me. Say I killed you. Say I deserve to suffer, but don't make me walk to the chimney. I cannot do it!"

Sophia was implacable. "I'm giving you a second chance, James. Not everyone is that fortunate."

"No, no—I cannot!"

Sophia tried to force him to stand. "Hold my hand. We'll do it together."

But James resisted. "I won't. You can't make me."

"You must do what you promised." She tugged at his hands as if to break his grip on the chimney.

"Please, stop," I begged. "Do you want to kill him?"

Sophia turned to me. Never had I seen a more malevolent expression on anyone's face. "Haven't I told you that already? Did you not believe me? Of course I want him to die," she said, "as he should have last year. I was stronger than he was—I was more agile. I had the grace and daring he lacked. What happened was a twist of fate, and I plan to correct it."

"You cannot correct anything," I said.

"You're wrong, cousin." Sophia gave me a scornful smile. "If James falls from the roof and dies today, I shall live. I know I shall. I must!"

I looked up at her wavering on the roof line, a small figure against a turbulent winter sky.

"If James falls, he will be dead," I cried, "and so will you. You can go on fighting for all eternity, but neither of you will ever return to life."

"You'll see." Sophia managed to pull James to his feet.

I watched my cousins struggle. The wind tugged at them almost as if it wanted them both to fall. James teetered, Sophia swayed. He leaned one way, she the other.

"Stop," I cried. "Stop!"

But they paid me no heed. Indeed, I don't think they heard me. Or remembered I was there.

Suddenly James pulled free of Sophia's grasp and tried to retreat. Hands outstretched, she came after him. Terrified, he pushed her away.

Sophia stumbled, her feet slipped on the slates, and she slid down the roof. With a scream, she shot off the edge and disappeared.

"It's just like before," James cried. "I pushed her and she fell. I killed her—I killed my sister!" Sobbing, he pressed his face against the chimney.

Cautiously, I peered over the edge of the roof. Sophia did not lie on the terrace below. She was gone.

With my heart pounding, I inched my way up the slates, struggling to find finger and toe holds. My fingers were so numb with cold, I expected to fall as Sophia had, but somehow I managed to join James by the chimney.

Putting my arms around him, I said, "You didn't mean for Sophia to fall. You were protecting yourself. It was an accident."

With a sob, James pulled away from me. "I must do as I promised. Perhaps I should have died and Sophia should have lived. I have to find out."

Ignoring my cries of protest, he began walking toward the other chimney. Step by step, slowly putting one foot just in front of the other, arms spread for balance, he teetered and tottered along the roof's ridge. The wind tugged at his nightgown, and his hair streamed behind him.

"No, James," I shouted. "Come back! You'll fall!"

He didn't answer; nor did he obey. He kept going with agonizing slowness, swaying as if he might lose his balance at any moment. Somehow he stayed upright. Unable to watch any longer, I covered my eyes and braced myself for his scream.

"Open your eyes and look," James cried. "Look at me!"

With great relief, I saw him touch the other chimney. Now all he had to do was return to me safely. Holding my breath, I watched him begin to make his slow and careful way back. Despite the wind, he kept his footing. Above him, clouds heavy with snow rolled across the sky. Below, crows as black as coal cawed in the trees.

At last, James's fingers touched the chimney. "I did it," he whispered. "I kept my promise, and I didn't fall." Exhausted, he sank down beside me.

"You were very brave." I hugged him, loving the warmth and solid feel of him, the life in his small body. *My brother*, I thought. *He's my brother now. I'll take better care of him than his real sister did.*

"But you were very foolish, too," I added in a whisper.

"Don't you see?" he asked. "I had to prove *I* wasn't meant to die. It was the only way to free myself from her."

I shivered in a blast of cold wind. "Do you think she's gone now?"

James looked at me, a long look that required no words. We both knew we weren't done with Sophia and she wasn't done with us. Her fall hadn't killed her. No one can die twice. She would return.

THIRTEEN

T THAT MOMENT, SPRATT looked up and saw us. "Stay where ye be," he yelled. "Don't take one step. I be sending the boy with a ladder."

While James and I huddled together, Spratt and his helper ran up to the attic. They managed to lay a ladder across the slates from the window to the roof's ridge. The boy climbed out on the slates and crawled up the ladder until he reached our perch. First he helped James climb down the ladder to the attic window. Once my cousin was safely inside, the boy returned for me. Spratt held my hands and guided me inside.

Uncle and Aunt were waiting in the attic. At the

sight of us, Uncle ran to embrace both James and me, but Aunt stood aside, her face tight with anger.

Pulling me away from Uncle, she shook me. "How could you do such a thing? And on this day, the very day Sophia died!"

"It's not Florence's fault," James cried. "It was Sophia. She made us do it."

Hearing this, both Aunt and Uncle forgot me and turned to James in consternation. "James, James," Uncle cried. "Your sister cannot make you do anything now. She's dead and gone. Please don't say such things."

"The boy is in a state of shock, and no one to blame but her." Aunt pointed at me. "I don't know what she's up to, but I tell you she's the devil's own."

Uncle ignored his sister. "You," he said to Spratt, "hurry to the village and fetch Dr. Fielding. I fear my nephew will have a seizure."

Spratt scowled at Aunt. "The boy be telling the truth. It were her, all right."

"You daft old man," Aunt cried. "Be quiet and fetch the doctor."

Spratt stood his ground, his brows lowered, his face flushed. "I tell ye, that girl be here yet, a-lurkin' and a-sneakin' and tryin' to do mischief to the little lad. Jealousy be stronger than death, as any fool knows."

"I'll not listen to this." Aunt turned away, her hands clasped. "It's a torment to be reminded of my darling's death."

Uncle took Spratt's arm. "Samuel," he said. "Get the doctor!"

"Yes, sir." Spratt hurried past Aunt and ran down the attic steps. Carrying James, Uncle followed close at his heels.

"Florence," he called, "find Nellie and tell her to build up a good fire for Master James. He'll need hot tea, too."

Eager to escape Aunt's baleful eye, I ran to fetch Nellie and Mrs. Dawson.

Halfway down the steps, Sophia stopped me with a cold hand on my shoulder.

"Now do you see how I suffered?" she whispered. "Nobody showed concern for me, just as nobody shows concern for *you*. Did anyone ask if you were cold or hurt? Oh, no. It was go fetch tea for *James*, Florence. Make sure the fire is warm enough for *James*, Florence. *James*, *James*, *James*. Always and forever, *James*, *James*, *James*."

I wheeled and faced Sophia. "Of course Uncle is worried about James. He's been in bed so long, it's a wonder he has any strength. He needs a doctor. I don't. Why shouldn't he come first?"

Sophia stared at me, her features twisted with anger. "You're on my brother's side, too. When will anyone ever be on my side?"

"Aunt is on your side."

"But I do not care for Aunt. She's such a tiresome old thing. Manners, deportment, etiquette, never a smile or a laugh or even a hug. How dreary it was to sit and play the piano for her. So much effort on my part simply to win a doll or a dress or a pair of fancy slippers. It wasn't what I wanted!"

Sophia withdrew further into the shadows, weeping now. It seemed to me she was dissolving like a paper doll in the rain, blurring, wavering. I could barely see her. But I could hear her.

"I wanted someone to love me the way they loved James," she sobbed. "That's all! If he hadn't been here, maybe someone would have loved me. But no, he took everyone's love and left me nothing. Nothing, nothing at all!"

With a wail of sorrow, Sophia vanished and I was

alone on the stairs. All that was left of her was an aching emptiness, a loneliness that hung in the air where she had disappeared.

"The tea," Aunt called to me from the top of the stairs. "You were to tell Nellie to bring tea and stoke the fire! Why are you still lingering on the stairs? Have you no sense? Do you not care what happens to James?"

Without answering, I ran to the kitchen and found Nellie scrubbing the kitchen floor. "Quick," I said. "Fix a good, hot fire in James's room, and bring hot tea for him."

Nellie wiped her small red hands on her apron. "What's happened, miss?"

"Never you mind," Mrs. Dawson said. "Fetch the coal."

"Yes'm." Nellie ran to the scullery.

Mrs. Dawson looked at me. "I knew there'd be trouble today. It was her, wasn't it? Causing mischief like she used to."

Before I could answer, she said, "No, don't tell me. I don't want to know." Grabbing a tray, she added, "Run along. I'll bring the tea."

I left Mrs. Dawson in the kitchen and slowly climbed the stairs. Poor Sophia. Poor pitiful, sad

Sophia. Had she gone uncomforted to her grave? I thought of her tombstone, already tilting over her grave, her name, her birth and death dates. What a short life. What an unhappy life.

Anxious to escape my thoughts, I went to James's room. Uncle had gotten him into bed and heaped blankets over him. "More coal on the fire," he barked at Nellie. "Build it up and drive away the chill."

As I approached the bed, Aunt took my arm. "What are you doing here? Your presence is not required."

As she began to usher me to the door, James stopped her with a cry. "Please let Florence stay," he begged. "Please."

"Hasn't she caused enough mischief already?" Aunt asked.

Pushing Uncle's hands away, James sat up in bed. "I tell you, this is Sophia's fault. *She* made Florence and me go to the roof. *She* wanted—"

"Nonsense!" Aunt exclaimed. "Sophia rests in peace as do all the dead. No one returns from the grave. It is heresy to think so."

Uncle gazed at his sister, his face solemn. "You heard what Samuel Spratt said, Eugenie. Perhaps there is some truth in this talk."

"Are you mad, brother?" Aunt tightened her grip on my arm. "The boy is ill, the girl is a liar, and Samuel Spratt is a superstitious, ignorant old man."

"Please, Aunt," I said. "You're hurting me."

"Release Florence," Uncle said. "James wishes her to stay."

"Then *I* shall depart!" With that, Aunt left the room in such haste that she almost bumped into Mrs. Dawson, who had chosen that moment to appear with the tea tray.

Mrs. Dawson set the tray down and beckoned to Nellie. "Come—you left the kitchen floor half scrubbed."

Touching Uncle's hand as she passed, Nellie whispered, "I ain't seen her, master, but she be here a-watching us all."

Uncle nodded. "Yes, my dear," he said softly. "I'm beginning to believe my niece haunts this house. There have been times when I . . ." His voice trailed off and he gazed into the fire. "Even Mr. Dickens believed in ghosts, I daresay. And Shakespeare, too. Who is to say what is real and what is not?"

Nellie glanced about fearfully. "Don't be saying too much about spirits, sir. Some folks say talking of the dead brings them out of their graves and into a house. They wants a warm place, too, I expect. The burial ground be powerful cold."

"That's quite enough, Nellie." Mrs. Dawson took the girl's arm and led her toward the door. "Beg your pardon, sir. We're all a bit unsettled."

"It's perfectly all right, Dawson." His face thoughtful, Uncle leaned back in his chair and watched Nellie follow Mrs. Dawson out of the room.

For a while we all sat in silence, drinking our tea and staring into the fire.

At last Uncle spoke. "Did not Mr. Shakespeare say 'There are more things in heaven and earth than are dreamt of in your philosophy, Horatio'—or something to that effect?"

"In *Hamlet*," I said. "After the ghost of Hamlet's father came to say he was murdered."

Uncle looked at me, pleased. "You've read Shakespeare, have you?"

"A few plays," I said. "I didn't completely understand them, so I plan to read them again when I'm older and know more about life."

Uncle chuckled. "What fun a governess will have with you and James."

James frowned as if he did not like the change of subject. "What we told you is true, Uncle. Sophia forced me to go to the roof."

"She thought she could change the past," I said. "She wanted James to fall and die so she could live."

"But it happened exactly the same way it did before," James said. "Sophia fell and I didn't."

"She's jealous of James," I said, "and she always has been. She thinks no one loved her." I paused and stared into the darkness beyond the firelight, wondering if Sophia was there now, listening. Overcome with pity, I dropped my voice to a whisper. "Sophia's very lonely. And very sad."

Uncle sighed. "I hope our loneliness and sorrow does not follow us to the grave and torment us there as it did in life. I've always thought of death as a release from mortal cares, but if what you say is true, my dear Florence, my philosophy, like Horatio's, must be reexamined."

Our conversation was interrupted by a knock on the door, followed by the entrance of Dr. Fielding. His face was ruddy from the cold, and the fresh smell of a winter evening clung to him.

"Well, well, young man," he said to James. "I understand you've been so foolish as to venture onto the roof again."

"It wasn't my idea," James began, but stopped when Uncle shook his head and frowned at him.

"Not your idea?" Dr. Fielding looked at him inquisitively.

James interested himself in the loose thread in his blanket, plucking at it to avoid looking at the doctor.

"It was my idea," I said quickly. "I wanted to see the place where Sophia fell, but I didn't expect James to climb up on the roof. I thought he would point from the window."

Dr. Fielding looked at me as if he'd noticed me for the first time. "So you followed him in case he needed rescuing?"

"Yes, sir." My cheeks burned with shame at telling a lie.

Turning to Uncle, Dr. Fielding said, "The girl bears an amazing resemblance to Sophia."

"Physically, yes," Uncle said. "But she is of an entirely different temperament."

A look passed between the two men, and Dr. Fielding took a seat on the edge of the bed. Taking

James's wrist, he felt his pulse. "Quite normal," he said. "How do you feel?"

"I feel surprisingly well, sir, though a bit tired from so much exertion."

Dr. Fielding listened to James's chest with his stethoscope, examined his throat, and finally leaned back with a smile and pronounced him much improved.

"Although I do not recommend doing it again, I must say, climbing the roof seems to have been good for you."

"I have no intention of doing it again, sir," said James.

"I am very glad to hear it," Uncle said.

Dr. Fielding nodded in agreement. "I suggest a day of rest tomorrow. Your aunt and uncle should watch for signs of a chill or some other adverse reaction to today's activities."

"Would it be possible for me to rest downstairs in the sitting room?" James asked. "I've grown weary of my bedroom."

"That's a splendid suggestion," said Uncle. "Do you give your permission, Fielding?"

"Wholeheartedly. James has spent entirely too much time in bed. Hopefully he'll soon be outside playing in the garden with Florence." Dr. Fielding patted James on the head. "But stay warm."

Uncle kissed James and left the room with Dr. Fielding. Alone, James and I sat on the bed and gazed at the fire. Outside, the wind blew harder. The snow seemed to have turned to ice from the noise it made striking the windows.

James yawned and snuggled under his covers. "I'm so tired," he whispered.

Curling up beside him, I peered into the corners where the shadows were darkest. Nothing stirred there. Nothing spoke. The fire murmured, and the sleet rattled the windowpanes. For a moment, I imagined I saw Sophia making her way through the night, her thin form battered by the wind. Slowly she walked, her head down. She paused at the churchyard gate, rimmed in ice now, and looked back as if she could see me from where she stood. Never had I witnessed such unhappiness, such loneliness, such despair.

Gradually Sophia faded out of sight among the crooked rows of tombstones. Moving close to James, I put one arm around him and fell into a deep sleep.

FOURTEEN

AWAKENED BY A RAPPING ON the door, I sat up and stared about me, surprised to find myself in James's room. He lay beside me with eyes closed, breathing peacefully, his face pink with health.

"Miss, are you in there?" Nellie called. "Mrs. Dawson has sent me to fetch you for supper."

James opened his eyes. "Where is Sophia?" he asked, still groggy from sleep.

"Gone," I whispered, remembering my vision of her vanishing among the tombstones in the church-yard, defeated forever, I hoped.

"Truly gone?" James looked doubtful.

"She's not here now, I'm certain of it."

Nellie knocked and called again.

"Who's knocking?" he asked, suddenly fearful.

"It's just Nellie," I told him.

James rubbed the sleep from his eyes. "You're certain it's not—"

I put my hand gently over his mouth. "Don't say her name."

"Tell Nellie to come in," he mumbled.

The girl entered, carrying a coal scuttle as usual. "Beg your pardon, but the fire needs tending," she said to James. To me, she said, "Be ye coming to supper, miss?"

"I am." I turned to James. "How about you? Do you feel well enough to join us?"

"If Uncle would be kind enough to carry me down. My legs are a bit shaky still."

Nellie gave him a shy smile. "It'll be a rare sight to see you at table," she told James. "Never have ye been out of yer bed since I come here."

James sat up straighter, a grin on his face. "I hope to be out and about every day, Nellie. I've stayed in this room much too long. There's more to do than lie in bed and read and sleep."

Nellie turned her attention to the fire. When she'd added coal and stirred it with a poker, she asked

James if she should ask Mr. Crutchfield to bring him down to the dining room.

James nodded. "Yes, please, Nellie."

Cheeks flushed with pleasure, Nellie darted away.

Soon Uncle appeared, a bit breathless from running up the stairs.

"Nellie tells me you wish to dine with us," he said. "Dr. Fielding advised you to rest, but if you feel strong enough, you jolly well shall join us!"

With a smile, Uncle wrapped James in a blanket and carried him downstairs. As he settled him in a comfortable chair, Aunt shot her brother a disapproving look but said nothing. Without speaking to any of us, she sat quietly, cutting her mutton into small bites, chewing slowly, and pausing now and then for a sip of water.

All around her, Uncle, James, and I talked and laughed and discussed the days that lay ahead. We did not mention the roof. We did not speak Sophia's name.

When Mrs. Dawson came to clear the table, she was humming an old song about wild mountain thyme and blooming heather. She gave us all a cheerful smile and patted James on his head.

"It's right glad I am to see you here, my boy," she said, "eating your dinner and enjoying yourself. It's as if a dark cloud has lifted and the days ahead will be bright and sunny and you'll play like the lamb you are."

James ducked his head and looked embarrassed, but I had a feeling he was glad of the happiness in Mrs. Dawson's voice. Glad to be at the table instead of in his lonely room. Glad his sister was gone.

From that night on, James's health improved quickly. Although Dr. Fielding was delighted, he couldn't explain it medically. But he was happy to attribute it to his skill.

Unfortunately, Aunt continued to compare me unfavorably to Sophia, refusing to listen to anyone else's opinion of her niece. She also considered me a bad influence on James.

"He was no trouble while he was sick," she pointed out with a frequency that quickly became monotonous. "A perfect little angel, he was, before that girl took an interest in him."

Early that spring, Aunt took it into her head to move to Eastbourne, where she shared a residence with a cousin even more disagreeable than she was—or so Mrs. Dawson claimed. No one missed her. Indeed, we were all glad she was gone.

As he'd promised, Uncle hired a governess for James and me. Miss Amelia was young and pretty and good natured. She made our lessons entertaining, and I found myself enjoying subjects I'd previously disliked. Even mathematics lost its terror.

As winter waned and the days grew longer and warmer, Miss Amelia encouraged James and me to spend more time out-of-doors. Impressed with our drawing skills, she urged us to try what she called *plein air* exercises.

"Find a tree, a building, a view," she told us, "and sit outside and sketch."

At first we were satisfied to draw the garden, the terrace, the fine old oaks lining the drive, and the distant hills. There seemed no end of interesting views to capture. Old stone walls, outbuildings, Spratt at work with hoe or shovel, Cat sleeping in the sun.

One afternoon, I was hard at work drawing the cat's ears, a very difficult thing to get right. Suddenly James sighed in exasperation and threw his pencil down.

"I'm tired of drawing that cat," he said.

"Draw something else then," I suggested. I was vexed with the cat myself. He kept changing his position, which meant everything I'd drawn before was wrong, including his dratted ears.

James looked around and frowned. "I don't see anything I want to draw."

"We could go for a walk," I said. "Maybe we'll find something new."

Gathering our pencils and sketchpads, we headed for the fields beyond the stone wall. A narrow public walkway led over a hill.

"I've been this way before," I told James.

"When?"

"I walked up the drive the day I came to Crutchfield Hall, so it couldn't have been then." I looked around, beginning to remember. "There was snow on the ground, and I was cold. The wind blew in my face. I was running."

"Were you alone?" James asked, suddenly serious.

I shook my head, remembering everything. "I was with Sophia. She took me to the churchyard to see her headstone. It was the day she made you climb out on the roof. Her death-day."

"Poor Sophia," James whispered. "She's been gone all this time, and we haven't visited her grave once."

"Do you think we should?" Truthfully, I wasn't at all certain I wanted to be that near Sophia. Suppose we disturbed her somehow? Suppose she came back?

He looked at me. "She's all alone there."

Reluctantly, I followed James up the hill, through the gate, and down the road to the village. It was a weekday, so not many people were about. A woman hung laundry in her yard. A small child pulled an even smaller child in a wagon. A horse trotted by hauling a carriage at a good clip. I glimpsed a bonneted head inside. A dog sleeping in the middle of the road got up and moved slowly out of the horse's way.

Under an almost cloudless sky, the old stone church dozed in the shade of trees. How different it had looked on that snowy day last winter, the stones dark and imposing, the trees bare, the wind howling. Now the headstones rose from freshly cut grass, tilting this way and that, some mossy with age, others newer. A flock of crows strutted among the stones, pecking in the grass. From the church roof, a line of wood pigeons watched us. Their melancholy voices blended well with the setting.

Hand in hand, James and I walked along gravel paths looking for Sophia's grave. Then we saw it. Her tilted stone cast a shadow across the grass.

In a low voice, James read his sister's inscription aloud. When he spoke her name, I braced myself, fearing she might rise up before us.

She did not appear. The wood pigeons cooed, a crow called and another answered, a breeze rustled the leaves over our heads, but Sophia remained silent.

"Do you know what today is?" James asked.

I thought for a moment. "It's the twenty-seventh of July," I whispered. "Half a year since we last saw her."

James held my hand tighter. "Do you think she'll come back again?"

"I hope not," I said, but I couldn't hide the uncertainty in my voice.

"Perhaps her spirit isn't here anymore," James said. "Perhaps she's with Mama and Papa." He looked at me as if for confirmation.

I nodded, hoping it was true.

"Maybe she's not angry now," James said softly. "Maybe she's not jealous. Maybe she knows now that she can't change her fate."

I nodded again, still hoping it was true, still not sure. Sophia was not the sort who would accept what could not be changed.

"I miss her sometimes," James said. "She wasn't always mean, you know. She could be quite nice when she wanted to be."

"I'm glad to hear that." I stared at the gravestone, warmed by the afternoon sun. It was almost impossible to picture Sophia lying peacefully six feet below us, tucked into her grave as snugly as a child is tucked into bed. All that anger, all that energy— where had it gone?

For a moment, the grass over Sophia moved as if something deep down below stirred in its sleep. With a flash of terror, I remembered what she'd told me about crawling from her grave six months after her death. I backed away, almost tripping on a tree root. *Six months*, I thought. *Six months today.*

Unaware of my distress, James contemplated Sophia's headstone. "Can we sit here for a while?" he asked. "I have a mind to draw a picture of my sister's grave."

I wanted to say no. I did not like graveyards, especially this one, but he'd already sat down and spread his art supplies on the grass.

While James sketched, I resisted the urge to seize his arm and pull him away. Perhaps I was being overly cautious, but I did not dare risk disturbing Sophia. Anything might rouse her—the scritch-scratch of James's pencil, the sad calls of the pigeons, the wind in the grass, even the soft sound of my breath or the solemn beat of my heart.

"James," I whispered. "We should go home. Uncle will wonder where we've gone."

He looked at me and smiled. "All right. I've finished my drawing."

As James gathered his things, I glanced at his picture. He'd drawn not only the tombstone, but his sister as well, standing in its shadow, blending in with the trees behind her. I couldn't be sure if she was smiling or frowning.

"Why is Sophia in the picture?" I asked him.

"She's not," he said.

I held the picture up and pointed to the indistinct image. "Who's this, then?"

James stared at what he'd drawn and shook his head. "I didn't put her there—I swear I didn't." He began to cry. "I was just sketching the trees. That's all. How did she get in my picture? Who drew her?"

I put my arms around him and stared over his head at Sophia's grave. Once again the grass stirred. A wind rose and rustled the leaves. For a moment, I thought I heard someone laughing at us.

Dropping the picture, I took James's hand. He looked at me, his face pale with fear. "Is she coming back?" he whispered.

I stared at the shadowy place under the tree, not sure whether she was there or not. "Even if she does come back," I said, "she can't hurt us. What's done is done. No matter how often she tries to change her fate, she will fail."

James tightened his grip on my hand. "It's very sad," he whispered. "I feel sorry for her."

"Better to feel sorry than frightened." Turning back to the shadowy place under the tree, I said loudly, "We are stronger than you are, Sophia. You cannot harm us, you cannot frighten us, you cannot make us obey you anymore."

"Leave us alone!" James cried. "Please, please, Sophia, rest in peace."

The wind rustled the leaves and blew through the grass on Sophia's grave. Its sound was as low and sad as the pigeons calling to one another on the church roof.

Wordlessly, James and I left the churchyard. Over our heads, the sky was a clear blue dome, and the road lay before us, dappled with sunshine and shadow. When we got home, Mrs. Dawson would have tea and cake ready for us. Later, we'd take our books outside and read in the garden or play croquet with Miss Amelia.

I looked over my shoulder. The old church spire rose above the trees. I could no longer see the graves, but I knew they were there, dozing in the sunlight, tilting this way and that, some cradled in tree roots, some almost hidden in tangles of weeds and wild-flowers. I hoped Sophia had heard what we'd said and would remain where we'd left her, at peace among the dead.

MARY DOWNING HAHN

THE GIRL IN THE LOCKED ROOM

A Ghost Story

The Girl

The girl is alone in the locked room. At first, she writes the day of the week, the month, and the year on a wall. She means to keep a record of her time in the room, but after a while she begins skipping a day or several days. Soon, days, months, and years become a meaningless jumble. She forgets her birthday. And then her name.

But what does it matter? No one comes to visit, no one asks her name, no one asks how old she is.

At first, the room seems large, but soon it shrinks — or seems to. It becomes a prison. The key disappeared long ago. No matter — she's afraid to leave. They're waiting for her to open the door. She feels their presence, faint in the daytime but solid and loud at night. Their boots storm up the steps. They hammer on the door. They yell for her to come out.

But how can she? The door is locked from the outside. Even if she wanted to, she could not obey their commands. She huddles in the shadows, her eyes closed, her fingers in her ears, and waits for them to leave.

The trouble is, they always come back. Not every night, but often enough that she always waits to hear their horses gallop toward the house, to hear their boots on the stairs, to hear their fists on her door.

She used to know who they were and why they came, but now she knows only that they are bad men who will hurt her if they find her. They say they won't, but she doesn't believe them.

So she huddles in the wardrobe, under a pile of old dresses, and doesn't move until she hears their horses gallop away.

Every morning, the girl looks at a date written on the wall—June 1, 1889. She doesn't remember why she wrote the date or what happened that day. Indeed, she isn't even sure she wrote it. Maybe someone else, some other girl, was here once. Maybe that girl wrote the date.

Someone, perhaps that other girl, certainly not herself, drew pictures on the wall. They tell a story, a terrible story. The story frightens her. It makes her cry sometimes.

In a strange way, she knows the story is true, the story is about her. Not the girl she is now, but perhaps the girl she used to be before they locked her in this room.

But who was that girl? A girl should remember her own name, if nothing else. Why is her brain so fuzzy?

Near the end of the picture story, men on horses gallop to the house. They must be the ones who come to her door at night. Did they draw the pictures to scare her?

There are other paintings in the room, real paintings, beautiful paintings. A few hang on the walls, but most lean against the wall. The same people are in most of them. A pretty woman, a little girl with yellow hair, a bearded man—a family. She pretends she's the little girl. The woman is her mother. The man is her father.

She must have had a mother and a father once. Doesn't everyone?

She talks to them, and she talks for them. They have long, made-up conversations that she never remembers for more than a day.

If only she could bring them to life. They look so real. Why can't they step out of the paintings and keep her company?

✦

Years pass. The girl stops looking at the drawings on the wall. She wearies of the people in the paintings. What good are they to her? They're just faces on canvas. Flat. They cannot see her or hear her. They cannot talk to her. They cannot help her. They are useless.

She turns their faces to the wall. She forgets they are there.

✦

Seasons follow each other round and round like clockwork figures. Leaves fall, snow falls, rain falls. Flowers bloom, flowers wilt, flowers die. Snow falls again. And again. And again.

Birds nest under the eaves and sometimes find their way into the room. Trees grow taller. Their branches spread. Young trees surround the house. They push against its walls. In the summer, their leaves press against the only window and block the sunlight. The room is a dim green cave.

Brambles and vines climb the stone walls. Their roots burrow into cracks and crevices, and they cling tight. Tendrils manage to find their way inside. Every year, their leaves fall on the floor of her room.

Gradually the house blends into the woods, and people forget it's there.

The girl stays in the locked room and waits. She no longer knows who or what she is waiting for. Something, someone . . .

She is lonelier than you can imagine.

2

The Girl

One morning, the girl hears loud noises from somewhere outside. It sounds as if an army has invaded the woods, bent on attacking and destroying everything in its path.

Confused and frightened, the girl hides in her nest. Buried completely under the rags of dresses, she hears sounds she can't identify, louder even than thunder. They come closer. The trees surrounding the house crash to the ground. Sunlight pours through the window. She squints and shields her eyes with her hand.

Outside, near the house, men shout. Who are they? Where have they come from? Why are they here? Have they come for her?

She smells smoke. They must be burning something.

Suppose the fire spreads to the house? She trembles. She'll have no place to hide.

Men enter the house. They tramp about downstairs. They speak in loud voices. They come to the second floor and then the third. Their footsteps stop at her door. The doorknob turns, but without the key, the men can't come in.

The girl burrows deeper into the rags. She doesn't think they're the ones who come on horseback at night. They don't pound on the door or shout at her, but she doesn't want them to know she's here — just in case. So she remains absolutely still.

Just outside her door, she hears a man say, "This is the only room in the house that's locked. Should we bust it open and take a look?"

The girl cringes in her hiding place. She's sure the men will find her.

"Nah," says another. "Nothing in there but trash and broken stuff."

The men shuffle past the door and go downstairs, laughing about something as they go.

When she's sure they won't come back, she tiptoes to the window and looks out. A huge yellow machine with long, jointed arms lifts and lowers, lifts and lowers, scooping up things from one place and dumping them somewhere else. Its jaws have sharp teeth.

Not far from the yellow machine are red machines with scrapers attached to their fronts. They push mounds of grassy earth into piles of red clay. Other machines have rollers that flatten everything, even hills.

She's never seen anything like these contraptions. They're bigger than steam locomotives and much scarier. Trains stay on tracks; they can't hurt you if you stay off the tracks. But these machines can go anywhere. Nothing is safe from them.

While they work, the machines roar and snort and make beeping sounds. They puff clouds of smoke into the air. The girl covers her ears, but she can still hear the noise they make.

A flash of movement catches her eye. A rabbit runs across the muddy ground. She holds her breath and prays the machines won't kill him. He disappears behind a pile of tree stumps, and she lets out her breath in a long sigh.

But where will the rabbit live? The fields have been destroyed, the woods chopped down. The men and their machines are everywhere. She wishes she could go outside and bring the rabbit to her room.

✦

Day after day, the girl watches the wreckage spread. The men and their machines cut down more trees and destroy barns and sheds. They haul furniture from the house. Sofas and chairs, their velvet upholstery stained, faded, and torn. Stuffing hangs out of holes. She sees a bed missing a leg, a bureau without drawers, a large broken mirror, fancy tables with cracked marble tops.

Did she once sit on that sofa, curl up in those chairs, sleep in that bed, look at herself in that mirror? Now everything is ruined. It's of no use to her or anyone else.

The men pile up the broken furniture and set fire to it. The smoke drifts up to her window and stings her eyes. She feels as if she's watching her life turn to ashes along with the sofas and chairs.

The men don't stop with the furniture. They burn tree stumps, carts, wagons, fences, and stacks of boards. The fire smolders for days. After dark, the embers glow and the night wind teases flickers of flames from charred wood. The smell of smoke poisons the air.

When nothing's left to burn, the men turn the fields to mud and plow roads through them. On the flat land below her window, they dig deep square holes. Their nightmare machines destroy everything in their way. Her world disappears before her eyes.

Then comes a quiet time. Machines still shake the ground, but they're down on the flat land now, hard at work building houses. The girl's home is empty again. Peaceful. She spends most of her time at the window, watching and listening, enjoying the summer breeze and the smell of honeysuckle.

She keeps her eyes focused on the distant mountains, blue and serene against the sky. She doesn't look at the fields and meadows destroyed by the machines.

One afternoon she dreams of a picnic by a stream. She's sitting under a tree with a man and a woman. She's had this dream many times. But it always ends before she's ready. She wakes up reaching for the man and woman, but it's too late. They're gone, and she's alone in the locked room.

3

Jules

It was August, hot and humid. The air conditioner in the truck wasn't working. My T-shirt stuck to my back, and Mom's hair had changed from smooth and sleek in the morning to frizzy and curly in the afternoon. The three of us sat elbow to elbow in the front bench seat, Dad driving, Mom beside him, and me next to the open window.

After spending most of the day on the Interstate, we were now on a narrow country road that twisted and turned, uphill and down, passing house trailers tucked away in the woods, tumbledown barns in weedy fields, cows grazing in pastures, and farmhouses at the end of long lanes.

I'd gotten tired of asking if we were almost there, so I closed my eyes and concentrated on not getting carsick. The bumping and swaying were definitely affecting my stomach. Why had I drunk that disgusting milk shake?

At last Dad said, "We're here."

I opened my eyes and saw a sign welcoming us to Oak Hill — "A future community of luxury homes designed and built by Stonybrook."

Ahead of us, a bumpy dirt road looped around the foundations of future luxury homes. On top of a hill above the construction site stood an old stone house. The land around it had been scraped down to raw red clay, rutted with tire tracks filled with muddy water. Waist-high weeds had sprung up everywhere. Piles of uprooted stumps, tree trunks, branches, and rocks waited to be hauled away.

I stared at the old house in dismay. Three stories tall and built of stone, it loomed above us, dark and empty against a cloudy sky. Sheets of weathered plywood hid its windows. A blue plastic tarp covered the roof. Its edges lifted when the wind blew, making an eerie flapping sound.

Dad specialized in restoring historic houses like this one, so for as long as I could remember, we'd lived like nomads, moving from place to place, staying in each one long enough for him to complete the job. Some of them had been scary. Their steps creaked at night, footsteps crossed their floors, their doors opened and shut without cause, but not one of them had been as frightening as Oak Hill.

Even from a distance, I knew something bad had happened in that house. Maybe it was the crows perched in a line on the roof, maybe it was the utter desolation of the scene, but the word *foreboding* came to mind, along with *haunted, misery, and sorrow.* It was the perfect setting for a ghost story.

"You weren't exaggerating," Mom said to Dad. "The house is practically in ruins. Are you sure it's worth fixing up?"

"Stonybrook has big plans for it," Dad said. "When the restoration's done, the house will be an inn. I'm told it's to be the jewel in the crown of the Oak Hill community. The perfect place for guests and potential buyers to stay."

I looked at Dad. "Please tell me we are not *living* in that house."

Dad laughed. "Of course not, Jules. The corporation built an addition on the back of the house for us. Modern kitchen, family room, two bedrooms, two bathrooms. New heating system, air conditioning, Internet, satellite TV—all the necessities."

"Oh, Ron," Mom said. "I thought we were staying in Oak Hill. I've always wanted to live in a haunted house."

I didn't know whether she was serious or joking. With Mom, it was hard to tell, but if she meant what she'd said,

I had even more reason to be scared. I shuddered. "Do you really think it's haunted?" I asked her.

"No, of course not." She laughed. "I was just being silly."

"Ha-hah, some joke," I said, only slightly relieved.

Dad patted my shoulder as we got out of the truck. "Don't worry, Jules. The only thing wrong with Oak Hill is dry rot, termite damage, leaks in the roof, mold, and mildew—the plagues of every old building I've ever worked on. No ghosts, I promise."

I felt a little better, but not much. It would take more than Dad's promise to convince me the house wasn't haunted.

"Can we go inside?" Mom asked.

Dad smiled. "I'll give you the grand tour."

Mom and I followed him up the sagging front steps, she eagerly, I reluctantly. Dad pulled an old-fashioned iron key from his pocket and struggled to unlock the door.

"Maybe it's the wrong key," I said, hoping the door wouldn't open.

Ignoring me, Dad continued to jiggle the key. After some pushing, pulling, and a little swearing, he finally got the door open. "Keys like this are works of art," he said, "but not easy to use."

The darkness inside the house exhaled dampness, old

cellars, and decay, but Dad ushered us inside as if he were leading us into a king's palace. "Try to picture this place as it was a couple of hundred years ago," he said. "Polished floors. a curving staircase, sunlight falling through tall windows. I can't wait to bring it back to life, to reveal its beauty."

While Dad raved, I stopped on the threshold, over-whelmed by a sense that something hid in the shadows, listening, watching, waiting. I'd often had feelings like this, but nothing had ever come of them. I'd seen no ghosts, and as the days passed, I'd stopped looking for them. This time, my fear was more intense than usual.

"What's wrong, Jules?" Mom looked at me with concern. "Is your stomach still upset?"

"I'm kind of queasy from that strawberry milk shake." I made a face. "Maybe some fresh air . . ." I backed out of the doorway, into the warmth of the sun.

Mom seized my hand and stopped me. "We'll just take a quick look. Then you can lie down for a while before dinner."

"Come on, Jules," Dad said. "This house is magnificent. I want you to see it as it is now so you can appreciate my work when I'm finished. It's probably the best project I've ever had."

Light from the open door illuminated crumbling walls

streaked with stains and mold. In one corner a huge wasp nest clung to the ceiling. Bird poop splattered the floor, along with a scattering of feathers, tiny bones, and dead insects. A heavy tree limb had crashed through the roof and landed on the steps to the second floor. Its branches had smashed the banister, and the entire staircase tilted to one side.

"Just look at those marble fireplaces," Mom said. "Can't you picture velvet drapes, crystal chandeliers, polished tables, carpets, paintings on the walls. . . . I can just imagine the people who lived here, women in long dresses, bearded gentlemen."

"Maybe you could use the house as a setting for your next book," Dad said.

"What a great idea. I've always wanted to write a historical novel. Maybe a ghost story or a gothic mystery." Her voice trailed off, as if she were thinking about the possibilities.

"You need to finish the one you're working on now," Dad reminded her.

Mom sighed. "I'm so tired of coming up with new mysteries for Inspector Turner to solve."

She took a step, and the floor groaned under her feet.

"Careful." Dad rocked on his heels and bounced. The boards creaked under his weight but held firm. "The floor's fairly solid here, but it's caved in elsewhere." He glanced at me. "It's strictly off-limits to you, Jules. Don't get any ideas about exploring."

I looked at Dad in wonder. Did he actually think I'd set foot in this terrifying place by myself?

"How old is Oak Hill?" Mom asked.

"When I looked at the property last month, I visited the county courthouse and did some research—land records, wills, census returns," Dad said. "I like to get a feeling for a house—when it was built, who lived there, that sort of thing. A man named Pettifer built Oak Hill in 1786."

"When was it abandoned?" I asked.

"Sometime after the 1880 census was taken," Dad said. "Henry Bennett and his family lived here then. That's the last reference I found."

"Where did they go?" I asked. "What happened to them?"

"I doubt anyone living today could answer that question."

Mom sneezed three times in a row. "The dust and mildew are getting to me," she said. "Let's go see our living quarters."

Dad led us into a room that once must have been a kitchen. A stained and rusty sink lay on the floor as if it had simply fallen off the wall. Rusty pots and pans had been swept into a corner along with broken china and odds and ends of rubble. Vines crept through cracks in the plywood covering the windows. The bones of a small animal lay in another corner.

Unlocking a new door with a modern key, Dad ushered us into a sunny kitchen. A sliding glass door led to a deck overlooking a field and the woods beyond. Light spilled from skylights in the family room ceiling. In one corner was a big fireplace made of stone.

"Oh, Ron," Mom said, "it's beautiful. I love it!"

It was definitely better than the old house, but it shared a wall with it—which meant it was too close to those dark, empty rooms for me. Sometimes we lived in an apartment in town while Dad worked on a house. I liked that arrangement better.

Our furniture was already in place, moved here by Stonybrook. All we had to do was unload the truck and bring in our suitcases and boxes of personal things that Mom hadn't trusted to a moving company.

My bedroom was across the hall from Mom and Dad's. Light poured through a floor-to-ceiling window and a skylight, something I'd wanted all my life. I moved one of my twin beds under it so I could look up at the stars and the moon before I fell asleep.

Thanks to Dad's job, we'd moved in and out of many houses, so I was a pro when it came to organizing my things. In less than an hour, I'd put my clothes away, unpacked my books, and charged my iPad.

Last of all, I made my bed and lay down, tired from the long drive from Ohio to Virginia.

From where I lay, I could see the back of the old house from my window. My eyes moved from one boarded-up window to the next, first floor to second floor to third floor, where the windows were smaller.

Oddly, one window hadn't been boarded up. Its small panes caught the afternoon light.

Something moved behind the glass but disappeared so quickly, I wasn't sure what I'd seen. I blinked and looked again. Nothing moved.

I told myself it must have been a trick of the light, a reflection, my imagination, but I wasn't convinced. I'd seen something at that window, just as I'd sensed something listening when Dad showed us the house. We weren't alone in Oak Hill.

Suddenly I didn't want to be alone in my room, scaring

myself with silly thoughts. Turning my back on the house and its secrets, I went looking for Mom and Dad.

Mom was in the kitchen, putting the finishing touches on a salad, and Dad was carving the roasted chicken we'd bought before we turned off the highway.

"You're just in time," Dad said. "We're having dinner outside on the deck." He gestured at the sliding glass doors, open to the fresh evening air. "Our first meal at Oak Hill."

"Maybe tomorrow we'll find a good place for a picnic," Mom said. "What do you two think?"

"Definitely a picnic," I said, "in a meadow by a stream."

"A meadow by a stream." Dad smiled. "How do you know we'll find a place like that?"

I shrugged. "It just popped into my head."

While we ate, I pictured us sitting under a willow tree, listening to water running over pebbles and stones. We'd watch minnows and those funny long-legged water bugs. Gerridae, my sixth-grade science teacher called them. I saw the scene so vividly it seemed like a memory of something I'd done.

"Well, what do you think of our accommodations, Jules?" Dad asked. "A lot better than that dingy apartment in Cleveland, right?"

"Not to mention the Chicago third-floor walkup," said Mom, "or the house with the leaky roof in Indiana."

"It's nice," I said, "but if you want to know the truth, I'd rather live in town."

"What do you mean, honey? This is a great place," Dad said. "And it's provided at no cost by the corporation. We don't often get free housing."

Mom waved her arm at the woods behind the house. Tall trees hid the shopping centers strung along the highway and muffled the traffic's roar. "Just look at that view. Why on earth would you want to live in town?"

"In town, there's stuff to do—a swimming pool, a library, movie theaters, kids my age. I'll never make any friends out here. When school starts, I won't know a single soul!"

"It's only a fifteen-minute drive into Hillsborough," Mom said. "We can go anytime you want."

"But that's not all. Oak Hill is right outside my bedroom window. It's ugly and dark and scary, and I hate it."

Dad leaned across the table and patted my hand. "It's only temporary, Jules. In another year or so, we'll be living somewhere else."

"But Dad, that's just the point. I've told you over and

over again how sick I am of changing schools and losing friends and getting behind on stuff. It's not fair, Dad. I want to live like ordinary people, not like some kind of nomad." I glared at him. It was the angriest I'd ever been with him. "This house is just the last straw!"

Dad started to say something, but I wasn't finished. "Cleveland, St. Louis, Detroit, Chicago, Philadelphia, St. Paul, Baltimore—" I said. "They all run together in my head. I can't remember how many houses we've lived in or all the schools I've gone to."

I fought to keep myself from crying. Why couldn't they understand what it was like for me? Always the new girl, always trying to fit in, wearing the wrong clothes, making friends just to leave them behind and start all over again somewhere else.

Mom looked at Dad. "Maybe we should think about what Jules is saying. She's almost thirteen, Ron. It's hard for her to change schools every year. She needs to settle down and make friends."

Dad sighed and took a few swallows of iced tea. "When I was your age, Jules, I couldn't wait to grow up and get out of Plainsville. The day I left for college . . ."

Long before Dad stopped talking, I stopped listening. I'd heard it all before. His boring hometown, his father's boring job running a furniture store, his mother's boring bridge club, his aunts and his uncles, his neighbors, all stuck in the same boring routines year after year. Most of them had never been more than a hundred miles from home. In their eyes, Plainsville had everything any human being needed. The outside world was a dangerous place.

That life hadn't been for Dad. He'd seen most of the world by the time he was twenty-five. You'd think by now he'd be ready to settle down, but oh, no, he was still on the road.

Mom interrupted him. "But Ron, couldn't you at least consider—"

"I go where the work is, you know that." He poured himself another glass of iced tea. "Restoring old buildings is my passion. When I have a chance to renovate a grand house like this one, how can I say no?"

Too annoyed to say another word, I watched the moon rise over the darkening field. The clouds had blown away, and a nearly full moon hung just above the treetops. The sky was studded with stars, more than I'd ever seen.

I pictured the mysterious Bennett family looking at the same stars and the same moon. They'd heard the chorus of cicadas in the trees, they'd seen the flash of lightning bugs in the woods, they'd felt the evening breeze cool their skin. Just like I did now.

I imagined the Bennetts strolling across the field—a man, a woman, and maybe a daughter, a family like mine, enjoying a summer night. They seemed to step from my imagination into the real world. The man said something, and the little girl laughed. I stared at them, entranced, convinced now that they were real people, out for an evening walk.

Just as I was about to beckon them to join us, Dad yawned loudly. The family immediately disappeared into the woods.

Perplexed, I turned to Mom. "Did you see those people?"

"Where?" She peered at the field. "I don't see anyone out there."

"They're gone now, but they were just there." I pointed to the spot. "A man, a woman, and a little girl."

Dad shook his head. "No one lives within miles of this place, Jules."

"But I'm sure—"

"Your eyes were tricked by shadows," Mom said. "You saw a bush, a small tree, that's all."

Maybe that was it. I was tired, and it was hard to focus without much light. But still—they seemed real when I saw them. And I'd heard the girl laugh.

I looked again at the edge of the field. The family must

have taken a path into the woods. If they'd really been there, that is. Dad was right. No one lived near Oak Hill. Where had they come from? Like Mom said, my eyes must have been tricked by the darkness.

Dad swatted a mosquito. "It's a long drive from Ohio to Virginia." He yawned again. "I don't know about you two, but I'm ready for bed."

Mom gathered up the paper plates and cups, and Dad and I helped her carry everything inside. We dumped the remains of dinner into the trash. No dishes to wash tonight.

Dad yawned again. "The crew arrives at eight a.m. tomorrow to start work," Dad reminded us. "Better be up, dressed, and ready."

Mom groaned and followed him into their bedroom.

Too tired even to open a book, I undressed quickly, fell into bed, closed my eyes, and went to sleep.

Long before daylight, a loud noise woke me. Thunder, I thought at first, but no, that wasn't it. As the noise grew louder, I realized it was the sound of horses galloping toward the house. On they came, two or three of them, running fast and hard though the dark. A man shouted in anger, a woman called out in fear.

Frightened, I sat up and peered out my window. The moon threw shadows everywhere, slicing the night into a confusing pattern of blacks and whites. I saw no horses, no riders. I heard nothing but the wind in the trees and the *bang bang bang* of a loose shutter striking the side of the old house. If horses and riders had come this way, the darkness had swallowed them up.

I slid under the covers and shivered, not just from the cool night air but also from fear. What was going on? I hadn't been at Oak Hill for twenty-four hours, and I'd already seen something move at a window on the third floor, watched a family crossing a field at twilight, and heard the steady beat of horses' hooves pounding toward the old house.

The night was silent now. Nothing moved. Yet a presence lingered in the stillness. I wanted to run across the hall to my parents' room and tell them what I'd seen, but I knew they'd say I was dreaming.

Maybe they were right. Maybe not. Either way, they'd be annoyed if I woke them up in the middle of the night.

Maybe tomorrow I'd talk to Mom and Dad. Maybe they'd heard the horses too. Maybe they'd believe me. . . . Maybe they wouldn't.

Finally, too exhausted to worry about what Mom and Dad would or would not believe, I curled up like a child, shut my eyes, and fell asleep.

The Girl

The girl stands at the window and peers down at the addition. A light goes on. She draws back, frightened. The light isn't soft, like the glow from a candle or a kerosene lamp, but harsh and more brilliant than any she's ever seen.

A girl, a big girl, walks past the window. She has long dark hair, and she's tall.

Once, she thinks, long ago, she might have had friends like that dark-haired girl. She can't recall their faces or names or what they said, but she thinks that sometimes they laughed together. It's been a long time since she's had anything to laugh about.

Maybe they were never real, those friends. It's hard to be sure of anything except this room and what she sees from the window.

But the dark-haired girl in the addition is definitely real. She watches her move around her room, then change her clothes and get into bed.

Once, the girl in the locked room must have slept, but not now. She's tired all the time, but never sleepy. Just sad and scared and lonely.

The light in the room goes out; the girl is alone again.

She watches the dark-haired girl's window long after the light goes out. The moonlight is bright on the wall of the addition, but it casts dark shadows on the grass beneath her window.

Suddenly she steps back into the shadows. Now is the time of night when they come, she thinks, and sure enough, no sooner has she thought it than she hears the horses. Their hooves pound the earth. A man yells. A woman cries out in fear.

She senses that the dark-haired girl is awake and frightened. She wishes she could tell her that the men are not after her. It is the girl in the locked room the men want.

They're at the kitchen door now. Soon they'll come upstairs. She scurries to the wardrobe and hides in her nest.

While the men shout, while the woman waits in the yard, she comforts herself by thinking about the dark-haired girl. Perhaps she'll see her in the morning. She'll watch her and learn about her. Perhaps the girl is the one she waits for. Perhaps she will rescue her. Perhaps she will free her from this room.

5

Jules

The foreman of Dad's crew and two of his assistants arrived just after breakfast. They spread out plans on the kitchen table and began talking about the morning's work.

Dad looked at Mom. "Why don't you and Jules go for a walk? Maybe you'll find that stream and we'll have a picnic there."

Mom turned to me with a smile, and we left Dad to pore over his plans with his crew.

Not sure where we wanted to go, we wandered across a field and found a narrow path that led downhill through a field of wildflowers.

At the bottom of the hill, Mom stopped. "Listen. I hear water running, a creek or a stream. Let's find it."

We ran through the weeds and ducked under the

branches of a willow tree. A shallow stream, almost wide enough to be a river, ran past.

Mom kicked off her sandals and splashed into the water near the bank. The water was so clear I could have counted the stones on the sandy bottom.

Mom held her hand out to me. "Come on, Jules. The water's a little cold, but it's only ankle-deep here."

When I hesitated, she laughed and kicked water at me.

"Stop it." I drew back. "Come out of there."

"Look." She pointed at a school of minnows swimming past. "And water striders."

"Their official name is Gerridae," I told her.

"Where on earth did you learn that?"

"Last year, from my sixth-grade science teacher."

Mom laughed. "Well, I'm going to call them water striders. It suits them better." She leaned over and watched the insects move across the stream's smooth surface. "Gerridae indeed."

Suddenly she grabbed my hands and pulled me into the water.

"Mom!" I shouted. "I still have my shoes on!"

"They're rubber flip-flops. It won't hurt them to get wet, and it won't hurt you either."

"The stones are slippery. I'm going to fall."

"Goodness, Jules, don't be such a scaredy-cat." Mom took my hand and led me deeper into the water. It wasn't as bad as I'd feared. Sunlight splashed down through the willow leaves. Minnows darted around us, their silver bellies flashing as they turned, and the Gerridae walked in circles on the still water near the shore. If I slipped and fell, I'd get wet, but I wouldn't drown. The day was so hot, it might even feel nice.

Mom smiled. "It's fun, right?"

I laughed and splashed her. She splashed me. I splashed back. By the time we hauled ourselves out of the stream, our jeans were soaked to our hips and we were laughing so hard we could hardly walk.

"Let's bring Dad next time," Mom said. "It's the perfect spot for a picnic."

It was perfect, almost too perfect. I'd imagined a place like this, and here it was—exactly as I'd pictured it. The stream, the willow tree, the field. I felt as if I'd waded in the stream before, watched the Gerridae and the minnows, seen the sun shine through the willow's leaves. When a rabbit hopped into sight, I knew he'd disappear into a thicket of honeysuckle.

I'd had this feeling often. I'd ride my bike past a house and think I'd seen it before, even though I'd never been on that road. Sometimes I'd be talking to someone and know what she'd say next.

I asked Mom about it once, and she told me the experience is called *déjà vu*—French for *already seen*. She had it too; almost everyone did.

But this time the sensation was strong enough to make me uneasy. Turning to Mom, I asked, "Does this place seem familiar to you?"

She looked around, taking in the willow tree, the stream, the fields rolling away toward the mountains. "It reminds me of a park in Ohio where we picnicked. The field, the stream, the trees—very similar. No mountains, though." She laughed. "It was definitely a different place. We've never been here before."

I looked around and shook my head. "I don't remember any picnics in Ohio."

"Well, you were only two or three years old, too little to remember, but it's probably imprinted in your memory."

Mom flopped down on her back and patted the ground beside her. "Let's lie here for a while and let the sun dry our clothes."

I lay down and watched clouds float across the sky like a flock of sheep wandering across a wide blue field. Birds sang, leaves blew in the breeze. I let my mind drift with the clouds.

While I lay there, I had a strange feeling that someone had joined Mom and me. Turning my head, I saw a little girl sitting near me, her face hidden by long yellow hair. She wore an old-fashioned dress, and a doll with a china head lay beside her. The girl was weaving a chain of clover blossoms, her fingers quick and deft as she tied the stems together. She sang too softly for me to hear the words, but the tune was familiar.

Suddenly she turned her head and looked at me. She opened her mouth as if to speak, but a woman called, "Come along, darling. It's time to go home."

The girl turned toward her mother, held up the clover chain, and laughed. "Look what I've made for you, Mama! A crown!"

Before I had a chance to ask who she was, the girl vanished, just like that. She was here, and then she wasn't.

I jumped up to see where she'd gone. I saw no tree close enough for her to hide behind. Not a ripple in the grass betrayed her hiding place.

"Where are you?" I called. "Come back."

Mom opened her eyes and sat up. "Who are you talking to, Jules?" She looked around at the empty field. "Is someone here?"

"A girl was sitting right there." I pointed to the spot a

few feet away from me. "She was making a clover chain. I thought she was about to tell me something, but her mother called her and she disappeared."

Mom shook her head. "You must have been dreaming, Jules."

"She was *right there!*" I pointed again, just in case Mom had looked for the girl in the wrong place.

"Where is she now?" Mom asked. "People don't just disappear into thin air."

"I know, I know, but Mom, listen to me. I *saw* her. I even heard her tell her mother she made the clover chain for her." I stared at the place where the girl had sat. I hadn't been sleeping, I hadn't been dreaming; she'd been there and I'd seen her.

Mom held my face close to hers and stared into my eyes. "Jules, you've always had vivid dreams," Mom said. "I remember one particularly, a nightmare. You claimed it really happened."

"What are you talking about?"

Mom leaned back on her hands and smiled. "You must have been four or five. We were living in Vermont at the time—your father had been hired to turn a barn into a house and studio for an artist, and we were staying in an old farmhouse on the property. Almost every single night you'd climb into bed with Dad and me, crying, shivering, scared. There was an old woman in your room, you'd claim, sitting in the rocking chair by your bed. The moon shone through the window and lit her white hair but hid her face in shadows. She was knitting a sweater.

"You heard her needles click and clack. You heard the chair creak. 'As soon as this sweater is finished,' she told you, 'I'm going to put it on you and take you away with me.' 'No,' you'd cry, 'no.' She'd cackle, and you'd jump out of bed and run to our room, crying and screaming."

I stared at Mom. "I don't remember that."

Mom laughed. "Well, I do. You woke us up night after night. The sweater was getting bigger, you said. Soon it would fit you, and she'd take you away. We told you it was a dream, but you said she was a real live witch. Your dad and I took you to your room and showed you the empty rocking chair, but you said she was in the corner, hiding in the shadows, or under your bed, or in the closet. We turned on the lights. No one was there. But you still insisted she was real."

While Mom talked, the image of an old woman popped into my head. She sat by my bed knitting a sweater. The moon lit her hair, but not her face. Every night the sweater was bigger.

"Aha," Mom said, "you *do* remember!"

I nodded slowly. "She was going to take me away. I'd never see you again. I was so scared."

"But now," Mom said, "you know the old woman was a dream. She wasn't real—just like the girl in the field."

No, I thought, *not* like the girl in the field. When I saw the girl, I was wide-awake, and I wasn't scared.

"You were a fearful child with a big imagination," Mom went on. "It's no wonder you had bad dreams."

I didn't want to spoil the day arguing with Mom, but no matter what she said, the girl hadn't been a dream. Certainly not a bad dream.

"Perhaps it's the house," Mom mused. "I know it scares you. Maybe it unsettles your mind—the people you saw last night, the girl today. Maybe they're manifestations of your anxiety."

I ignored Mom. She loved probing her characters' fictional minds to uncover their motives for doing things. Well, I was real, not fictional, and I didn't like her attempts to analyze me.

While she talked, I watched a summer breeze race across the field, rippling the weeds. Trees bent to and fro. Leaves sighed and rustled. For a moment I glimpsed the flutter of a white dress in the woods, but it was gone too quickly for me to be sure it was the girl.

Mom got to her feet. "Let's go home. It must be lunchtime."

I walked behind her, dragging my feet, unsure what to believe. Mom was right about one thing—the girl had vanished too quickly to be real.

What if the people I'd seen were ghosts? The thought stopped me in the middle of the path. I'd come to the edge of the woods, and I shivered in the shade.

But how could that be true? Ghosts don't appear in the daytime. They come at night, moaning and wailing, maybe even rattling chains. They might walk across a field at dusk, but they don't sit in a sunny field making clover chains. At least not in the stories I'd read.

Ghosts are transparent, you can see through them, they can walk through walls, but both the family and the girl were so solid, I'd thought they were real people.

I folded my arms tightly across my chest and shivered again. I hadn't been scared when I saw the girl, but I was scared now. I'd read enough ghost stories to know that the dead sometimes linger to seek help from the living or atone for a crime.

She'd seemed like an ordinary little girl, but she'd

probably been dead for a long time — which meant she was far from ordinary, and possibly dangerous.

But no. I'd looked into her face and seen nothing to fear. Surely she'd committed no crime. That left help — is help what she wanted from me? How was I to help a ghost?

6

The Girl

The girl is at the window again. Earlier, she'd watched the dark-haired girl and her mother walk down a path that led away from the house. She'd heard them laughing and talking, but soon the trees swallowed them up and they were gone.

She thinks they went to a field where a willow grows. If she closes her eyes, she sees the dark-haired girl sitting in the grass, but it must be a dream. She hasn't left this room, not once in—oh, ever so much time, oceans of time. But her dream is so vivid. She's sitting in the grass near the girl. She's making something. A clover chain. Yes, that's what it is. She remembers the limp stems and the fading blossoms and the way she knotted them together.

But who is the chain for? Not the dark-haired girl or her mother, who is fast asleep. It's for someone else.

The dark-haired girl looks at her. That girl is about to speak when someone calls her. The dream ends, and the girl is at the window again.

She sighs. Even though it was a dream, she feels as if she really left the room and sat outside in the sunlight. She remembers its warmth and the sound of bees buzzing in the clover. She'd like to visit the field again and see the other girl. Maybe this time the dream will last longer. She thinks she needs to tell that girl something. If only she could remember what it is — or why she should tell her.

Now she waits for the girl and her mother to return. She's not sure how long they've been gone. Hours, days, and years blend together in the most confusing way, a flow of light and dark, light and dark.

When the sun is high above the house, she hears them coming. Mother first, the dark-haired girl following behind. The girl is very quiet. She looks worried. She doesn't look up at the window. Her head down, she follows her mother into the addition.

Below her, out of sight, a door opens and closes. Once more, the girl in the locked room is alone at her window.

7

Jules

After lunch, Mom opened her laptop and got to work on book four of a mystery series set in Maine. I knew better than to interrupt her when she was writing.

I grabbed a book and sat outside in the shade cast by the picnic table's big green umbrella. In the old house, the crew ripped plywood off windows and tore up floorboards. Drills, hammers, saws—the noise made it hard to concentrate on reading.

I laid the book aside and decided to take a walk. Maybe I'd go back to the stream and sit in the shade of the willow tree. It was cooler there. And a lot quieter.

I hadn't gotten out of sight of the house when I noticed a broken wood chair poking up from the weeds. Looking closer, I saw a few window frames and a heap of warped boards. The cleanup crew must have forgotten to haul the stuff away. Maybe they hadn't even seen it.

In one of my history classes, I'd learned about middens, the name for places where people threw their trash in olden days. Archaeologists discover a lot about the past from what they find in middens, our teacher said.

Suppose I'd found the place where the Bennetts threw their trash?

I squatted down and poked in the weeds. This would be my dig. If I dug deep enough, I'd unearth older, more interesting stuff, things the Bennetts had owned. Like an archaeologist, I'd learn about the family from what they'd thrown away.

I found a large bent spoon and used it to dig in the muddy ground. At first, all I found were broken china, misshapen forks and spoons, fragments of wood, scraps of cloth — odds and ends that told me nothing about the Bennetts or what had happened to them.

With a sigh, I turned back to the midden. I was hot and sweaty now, and a cloud of gnats had discovered me. Just as I was about to quit, I saw a small hand sticking out of the muddy ground. I drew back, startled, but almost immediately realized it was the hand not of a baby, but of a doll.

Carefully I dug around it and eased it gently out of the ground. The doll's hollow china head was bald, she had no eyes, and her face was cracked and chipped. Her leather body was stained, and her arms and legs dangled loosely from it. One hand was missing altogether, and the other had no fingers.

Although the doll looked more like a dead body than a toy, I laid her carefully on the grass with the other broken things. Perhaps she belonged to the girl I'd seen in the field. She'd had a doll with her. It had been beautiful, not hideous, but the doll from the midden might have looked like that once.

I studied the doll's damaged face. Yes — with eyes that opened and shut, rosy cheeks, a wig of long curls, and a pretty dress, she'd look just like the one lying beside the girl. Maybe Mom would know of a place that repaired antique dolls.

Turning back to my dig, I probed the earth gently, the way I thought an archaeologist would, hoping to discover other things the girl once owned. I dug up a noseless china shepherd, an armless shepherdess, and several tailless dogs, most of them lacking a leg or two as well.

My favorite discovery was a set of seven small china

dolls. The two largest were about five inches tall, but the others were much smaller, just two or three inches. Each was molded in one piece, so neither their arms nor their legs moved. Their hair was painted on, and their painted faces were almost worn away.

I laid them beside the ugly bald doll and lined them up from biggest to smallest. I pictured the girl playing with them in a dollhouse built by her father. I saw her kneeling on the floor, her hair hiding her face, and moving the dolls on their tiny feet from room to room, *click click click*.

Then I heard a tiny, scratchy voice begin to speak. *"I'm scared,"* the littlest doll said.

"Hush," said the biggest one. *"Go upstairs and lock yourself in your room before the bad men get you."*

Frightened, I dropped the dolls and spun around to see who'd spoken. No one was behind me, but when I looked up at the window on the third floor, I saw something that might have been a small figure almost hidden in shadows.

I jumped to my feet. "Who said that? Where are you?"

Whoever had been at the window was gone. At my feet, the little dolls lay silently in the weeds where I'd dropped them. Beside them was an old key, about six inches long, coated with rust and mud. How had I missed seeing it?

I picked the key up and examined its scrollwork and fancy details. It weighed heavy in my hand—a serious key, an important key, a powerful key. A key to what?

The sun was lower now, and the long shadow of the house lay like a dark hand over the midden and the things I'd found. Suddenly I didn't want any of them—the bent silverware or the broken china, the ugly bald doll or the little china figurines. They were the possessions of dead people, contaminated somehow. I dumped them into the hole I'd dug and shoved dirt on top. This time, they'd stay buried.

Without looking at the third floor, I walked away quickly, but I couldn't escape the sensation of being watched. The little girl was in that room. I was convinced of it.

Was she afraid of me? Was I afraid of her? Should she be? Should I be?

The Girl

The girl in the locked room looks down from her window and sees the dark-haired girl from the addition digging in the kitchen midden, of all places. It's the first time she's gotten a good look at her. If it weren't for her long hair, the girl would mistake her for a boy. She's wearing short pants. Her shirt is shapeless. Something the girl can't read is written on its front. Her feet are bare. And dirty.

She doesn't know what to make of the girl's appearance.

Not even the poorest of girls wears clothes like that. And children don't go barefoot unless they cannot afford shoes.

Everything in the midden is trash, yet the dark-haired girl has picked bits of porcelain, medicine bottles, tarnished silver, and broken dishes from the rubbish as if they were valuable. She's even dug up a broken doll, which seems vaguely familiar.

Perhaps the doll once belonged to her. Yes, it must have. But surely it was prettier then, not broken and bald as it is now. It distresses her to look at the doll. She turns away.

Later she returns to the window. The dark-haired girl is still there. If she expects to find treasure buried along with the trash, she'll be sorely disappointed. Indeed, she already looks disappointed. She swats at gnats, she pushes her hair out of her face, she's hot and impatient.

But she keeps digging. She finds a group of tiny dolls and lays them beside the ugly doll.

The girl's fingers remember how those dolls feel, cool and smooth and hard. They're dirty and chipped now, but she remembers making them talk. What should they say now?

Perhaps the littlest one says, *"I'm scared."*

And the big one says, *"Hush. Go upstairs and lock yourself in your room before the bad men get you."*

Suddenly the dark-haired girl drops the dolls and looks around. Something seems to have frightened her. Did she hear what the dolls said?

Fearful of being seen, the girl in the locked room ducks below the window but slowly raises her head to see what the dark-haired girl does next.

She's throwing all the things she found into the hole she dug. Even the little dolls. She's finally realized it's trash, nothing but trash.

Then the dark-haired girl looks down and sees a key. She picks it up and turns it slowly, as if she's examining it.

The girl crosses her fingers and whispers, "Don't throw it away. Keep it. Find the lock it fits."

The dark-haired girl can't possibly know which lock the key fits, but what if she tries the key in every door? She'll come closer and closer — from the first floor to the second, from the second floor to the third. She can almost hear the girl's footsteps, rather like a story she heard once long ago about a teeny-tiny woman who stole a teeny-tiny bone. . . .

She imagines the girl stopping at her door and poking the key into the lock. She'll jiggle it back and forth, take it out, and poke it in again. *Jiggle, jiggle, jiggle.* Finally, the door will open and the dark-haired girl will enter the room. It will be the first time someone has come through that door since the girl was locked in.

Everything will change. She doesn't know how she knows this. Nor does she know how things will change. Maybe for good, maybe for bad.

But how can anything be worse than it already is?

She paces around the room. Her feet leave no tracks

in the dust. Perhaps she's waited here long enough. Perhaps no one will come for her except the men. Night after night, they'll come, and she'll hide in the wardrobe. Day after day she'll stand at the window and watch the seasons change. Years will pass. Centuries. And nothing will change. Is this what she wants?

The girl tiptoes to the window. Taking care to hide in the shadows, she whispers, "Keep the key. Find the right door. Find me. Let me out."

Below her, almost as if she doesn't notice what she's doing, the girl from the addition drops the key into her pocket and walks out of sight.

The girl in the locked room claps her hands soundlessly. Soon the door will open and she will be free.

Free to do what?

"Oh, mercy," she whispers. She has no idea what she'll do when she's free.

Jules

Mom was where I'd left her, working on her novel. Without even looking at me, she said, "Not now, Jules, I'm busy."

I had nothing to do, nowhere to go. So I went to my room and opened my iPad. Using a drawing app, I made silly sketches of cats and dogs and horses. They weren't very good, so I deleted them, then checked my e-mail. As usual, I had no messages.

My thoughts wandered to the girl in the field. Out of curiosity, I typed in "1880 U.S. census" and hit Search. Maybe I'd spot something Dad had missed.

Most of the websites charged for accessing the census, but I finally found a free one. I entered "Bennett" for the surname as well as "married" for status and "Virginia" for residence. One hundred and fourteen Bennetts came up.

Dad had mentioned a first name. What was it?

Harry came to mind. No one with that name turned up, but the search engine coughed up several Harriet Bennetts, one Harold Bennett, and three Henry Bennetts.

Henry sounded possible, so I looked at all three Henrys. The most likely choice was thirty-two years old. His occupation was "artist." His wife was named Laura, and their daughter, Lily, was one year old.

Also in the household was a tenant farmer, his wife, and a hired man. Sure that they were of no importance, I ignored them.

I stared at my iPad, almost as mystified as before. The girl in the field must have been Lily Bennett, but I still had no idea what happened to her or why I'd seen her — or what she wanted.

I went to my window and squinted at the window on the third floor. The sun lit the glass so brightly I could see nothing behind it.

"Lily," I whispered. "Lily, tell me what to do."

No one answered. No face appeared at the window. But she was there, I knew she was.

I wished I had someone to talk to, someone who'd believe me.

"Jules," Mom called from the kitchen, "please set the table."

As I arranged plates, glasses, and cutlery, I felt a weight in my pocket and pulled out the key. I was sure I'd reburied it with the other stuff, but here it was. I'd dropped it into my pocket without noticing.

For a moment I stood still and studied the old key. "What door do you unlock?"

The answer came like a whisper of air. *Lily's door. Of course.*

Dropping the key into my pocket, I finished setting the table. My mind spun with ideas. I'd go to the third floor, I'd unlock the door, I'd free Lily. But I couldn't go there in the daylight. I'd have to wait until late at night when Dad and Mom were asleep. Was I brave enough to do that? Just thinking about it made my hands shake so badly I dropped a spoon on the floor.

I said little during dinner, but Mom and Dad were too interested in their own conversation to notice. Dad described the progress he'd made with the walls and ceiling. Mom told him about her idea to add a character to her novel—a child whose recurrent nightmares hold clues to the mystery.

"I wonder where you got that idea," I muttered, but kept my voice too low for her or Dad to hear me.

That night, I hid the key in a little wooden box where I kept special things—seashells from a Rhode Island beach, stones from a creek in Ohio, a tiny silver bracelet Grandmother had given me when I was born, a plastic palm tree pin from Florida, a broken whistle, a couple of marbles, childhood treasures worthless to everyone but me.

Before I got into bed, I looked up at the third-story window. Its glass reflected the moon, but no one stood in the darkness, staring down at me.

"Lily, Lily," I whispered, "what do you want? Why are you here?"

✦

For the next two days, it rained, a cold, hard rain. Mom and I were trapped inside, with no escape from the pounding of hammers, the whine of drills, and the roaring of power saws. Heavy feet tramped around in the old house. Men shouted over the noise of their tools. They laughed and swore.

I finished my book. With nothing else to read, I played some games on my iPad, stared out the kitchen door at the rain puddling on the deck, and watched a few movies on demand—*The Black Stallion, National Velvet, The Secret Garden*. I'd seen them all before, but they were like comfort food for my mind. Knowing how they ended made me feel safe and happy. . . .

On the third day of rain I begged Mom to take me to Hillsborough. "There must be a library or a bookstore in town. I don't have anything to read, and Dad's crew is driving me crazy."

"A break's a great idea." Mom pressed Save and shut down her laptop. "The noise is giving me a headache."

She picked up her purse, grabbed her rain jacket, and tossed mine to me. She found the truck keys and headed for the door to tell Dad where we were going.

Reluctantly, I followed her into the house. Now that the plywood was off the windows, a gray, rainy light spilled into the rooms. The crew had pulled up the rotten flooring and put down a solid subfloor. They'd gotten rid of the tree limb and replaced the old stairs to the second floor. They'd swept up dead leaves, fallen plaster, and other trash.

The house smelled like new wood and sawdust. No more musty odor, no mold, no dark, scary corners.

I looked up the stairs toward the third floor. Dad's crew hadn't done any work there, and it was still dark, even in daylight. I sensed Lily hiding behind her locked door, waiting for me to climb the steps, unlock the door, and help her escape from whatever held her there.

If only I had someone who believed in Lily, a friend to climb those stairs with me and save a frightened child.

10

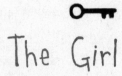

The Girl

The girl in the locked room stands at the window. She spends most of her days here now, watching for the dark-haired girl, who hasn't come outside since the rain began. The things that the girl dug up are lying in a hole filled with muddy water. She can make out the head of the bald doll. One of the doll's arms reaches out of the water, as if she were drowning.

Below her window, the dark-haired girl and her mother hurry through the rain to their tin machine. Their outfits are even more peculiar than usual. The dark-haired girl is wearing a coat so yellow it's blinding. It reminds her of pictures of sea captains steering their boats through stormy weather. She's even wearing the right sort of hat. Oilskins, that's what they're called.

Where on earth does that girl buy her clothing? Surely not in Browne's Emporium.

The mother is dressed in a shiny black belted coat, which looks less strange, but, like the daughter, she's wearing long blue pants. Why do they both dress like boys?

The mother calls, "Jules, watch out for that puddle. It's really deep."

She watches the dark-haired girl hop nimbly over the puddle. *Jules*—is that her name? It's an odd name for a girl, more like a French name for a boy. The world must have changed a great deal since the girl last saw it. Maybe boys wear skirts and play with dolls now. Maybe children take their grandparents for rides in baby buggies.

How silly. She giggles at the very idea.

Even if she dared to leave the room, where would she go in a world so strange? She understands the way things were, not the way they are now.

Jules and her mother get into the tin machine. The engine makes its usual loud noises before they disappear from sight.

The girl prefers a horse and carriage, but perhaps they are no longer in style.

She wonders where Jules and her mother are going.

Perhaps to town.

Town. The girl frowns. What gave her that idea? Has she been to town herself? Maybe. She pictures a narrow, dusty road, with rows of shops and houses on either side. There's a church with a steeple at the end of the street. Horses pull carts and carriages. Other horses are tied to railings. People are laughing and talking.

She holds a man's hand, but she can't see his face, only his dark jacket and trousers. A woman takes her other hand. Her dress is long, and tiny blue flowers dot the cloth.

She looks down at herself and sees a blue dress. On her feet are high-top shoes with buttons.

The girl clings to the hands holding hers. She feels safe with the man on one side and the woman on the other. She doesn't know who they are, but she'd like to stay with them.

The woman says something to her, but her voice is faint and far away, and the girl can't make out the words. She tries to smile, but her lips won't move.

Suddenly the man and woman vanish, and the girl is once more standing alone at the window. The rain still falls. It drums on the roof and gurgles in the gutters and splashes in the puddles.

She looks down at herself and smooths her white nightgown, but it isn't white anymore—it's yellowed and worn so thin it's beginning to fall apart.

Where did her blue dress go? Where did her shoes go? What happened to the man and woman? Where are they?

She goes to the mirror on the wardrobe door. Once, she talked to her reflection as if it were a dear friend, a kindred soul. But as the years passed, cobwebs draped the mirror. Its surface tarnished. Her image slowly faded. Now she sees nothing but a shadowy shape, too vague for her to be sure it's her reflection.

Perhaps she doesn't need to hide. Perhaps no one can see her.

Jules

In less than half an hour we were in Hillsborough. Even in the rain it looked like a nice place to live. Picket fences, flowers in gardens and window boxes, brick sidewalks, well-kept old houses with big yards, tree-lined streets.

We passed restaurants and coffee places, small clothing stores, a toy shop, a bookstore, a post office, a couple of banks, and a library. Just about everything a person could want or need was right here.

Mom parked in the municipal lot near the courthouse, and we walked toward the library. She paused to sniff a dense green hedge. "Boxwood," she said. "One of my absolutely favorite smells."

I sniffed too. The leaves had a sort of woody, old-fashioned fragrance. If we ever had a house of our own, I'd make sure Dad planted boxwood.

"I'd love to live in a town like this," Mom said. "It reminds me of where I grew up."

"Has Dad said any more about staying in one place for a while?"

"I've talked to him, but you know how difficult it is to pin him down. Always moving, always looking for something new."

I sighed. Dad would never agree to stay in Hillsborough. Or anywhere else. In another year or so, this town would be another memory.

Mom squeezed my hand. "Don't give up, Jules. I think he's open to the idea this time. I'll keep trying to persuade him. You try too. Together we'll wear him down."

Although I wasn't as hopeful as Mom, I let myself imagine living in one of the big old houses we'd driven past. I pictured a boxwood hedge, a tree tall enough for a swing, my bedroom with big windows and a view of the mountains in the distance. I'd make friends. I'd go to the same school every year. Maybe I'd have a dog or a cat, maybe both—why not? It was just a daydream, after all.

At the library, Mom headed for the history collection, and I went to the area set aside for teens.

I found the science fiction and fantasy shelves and started searching for a book I hadn't read. A girl about my age joined me. She had short brown curly hair and a friendly face.

Peering at me through eyeglasses with large round lenses, she said, "I haven't seen you before. Are you new here?"

Surprised by her friendliness, I nodded.

"My name's Maisie," she said. "Maisie Sullivan. What's yours?"

"Jules Aldridge." I fingered the paperbacks and struggled to carry on the conversation. "Do you read a lot of fantasy?"

"I *devour* fantasy. My favorite author is Diana Wynne Jones. Have you read the Chronicles of Chrestomanci?"

When I shook my head, she pulled three books off the shelf and thrust them at me. "Read them in order. *Witch Week* is my absolute favorite. You'll love them. I've probably read the whole series at least three times."

I studied the covers. "They look good."

"I guarantee you'll read all of them after you finish the first one. Try *The Magicians of Caprona* when you're done with these three."

"What are they about?"

"Enchanters and magic and alternate worlds."

"Alternate worlds—like space travel? And life on other planets?"

"No. It's more like there are lots of different worlds. The Almost Anywheres, they're called. In each one, something happens that didn't happen in the other worlds."

I had no idea what she was talking about. "Like what?"

"Well, suppose the Confederates won the Civil War. That world would split off from our world, and its history from then on would be different from ours."

"So there could be a world where the British won the Revolutionary War or a world where the Nazis won World War Two or —" I stopped and stared at Maisie. "Wait — how many alternate worlds are there?"

"Too many to count." She laughed. "Maybe there's a world where you didn't come to the library today and you never met me."

I leaned against the bookcase. "Stop. You're making me dizzy."

Maisie's face grew serious. "You know what? According to my dad, lots of people, scientists even, believe there really are alternate worlds."

"So it could be true that different versions of you and me, and everyone else, lead different lives in other worlds that are kind of like this one, only different?"

"Apparently — if you believe the theory."

"Do you?"

"Sort of, yes, pretty much. It's like ghosts and unicorns and magic. You can't prove they exist, but you can't prove they *don't* exist either. So why not believe in the Almost Anywheres? It makes life more interesting, I think."

I hugged the books to my chest and said, "I can't wait to read these."

Maisie grinned. "You sound like someone who loves books as much as I do."

"I get teased all the time about being a bookworm. Do you?"

"Just about every day," Maisie said. "Even my own father tells me, 'Get your nose out of that book and help your mother set the table.'"

"We should start a bookworm club."

"We'll call ourselves Worms R Us!" Maisie slapped her palm against mine, and I dropped my armload of books.

While we gathered them up, I hoped I'd found a friend for as long as I stayed in Virginia — which I hoped would be a long, long time. More likely, of course, it would be a year or two at the most. And then goodbye Maisie, goodbye Hillsborough, hello somewhere new.

Maisie sat down at a table, and I took a seat opposite her. "Do you live here in town?" she asked.

"Just outside," I told her. "My dad's fixing up an old house for a big corporation."

Maisie's eyes widened in interest. "Whoa. Is your dad the guy who's restoring Oak Hill?"

"Yes, that's his job. He —"

Maisie interrupted. "Do you actually live in the house?"

"No. In an addition behind it. My dad and his crew are working on the inside of the house now. It will be a long time before it's fit to live in."

Maisie leaned across the table toward me. "Do you know what happened at Oak Hill?"

I fidgeted with my stack of books. It was obvious Maisie knew something I didn't know, something bad, and I wasn't sure I wanted to hear it. Somehow I knew it would be scary, and Oak Hill was scary enough already.

"It was abandoned a long time ago," I said. "Woods grew up around it, and people forgot it was there. Then Stonybrook discovered it and hired Dad. That's all I know."

"Ha. What does some big company like Stonybrook know? Talk to the people who live here. Nobody ever forgot that Oak Hill was there," Maisie said. "It's been our haunted house story for years. Even in my grandma's day, people were scared to go there."

She pulled a pack of gum out of her pocket and offered me a stick. I took the gum, but all I wanted was to hear what Maisie knew about Oak Hill.

"People say," Maisie went on, "that robbers broke into Oak Hill and murdered the family who lived there. A man, his wife, and his daughter. They say the killers were never caught and the bodies were never found, but the family has haunted the house ever since. Lots of kids have seen their ghosts, my brother included—he says if you go inside the house, you never come out. He's heard stories about a hiker who went in there. All they ever found was his hiking boot. Just one. With *blood* on it. You can hear him screaming sometimes when the wind is right. He also says—"

I grabbed Maisie's arm. "Stop it. Just stop it. I knew something bad happened in that house. From the minute I saw it, I *knew*." I was shivering, and my teeth were chattering, and I thought I might throw up.

"What do you mean?"

"I get these feelings. And I see stuff no one else sees."

Maisie's eyes seemed to widen behind her glasses. "What do you mean? Like ghosts or something?"

I hesitated. What if Maisie didn't believe me? What if she thought I was lying? Maybe she wouldn't be my friend, after all.

She leaned closer. "Did you see a *ghost*, Jules?"

A teenager pushing a library cart stopped next to us to shelve some of the books on his cart. I dropped my voice so low Maisie had to lean farther across the table to hear me. "I saw *Lily*."

"Lily? Who's Lily?"

Maisie spoke so loudly the teenager looked at us. "Stop shouting, Maisie," he said. "You want Miss Hopkins to throw you out again?"

"Get lost, Blake," Maisie said.

"*You* get lost." Blake shoved another book into place and moved on. The sound of the cart's squeaky wheels faded as he disappeared between two rows of tall shelves.

"So who's Lily?" Maisie asked.

"The little girl who haunts Oak Hill."

Maisie stared at me, awestruck. "Where did you see her? Were you scared?"

"Mom and I were in the field behind the house. Mom was asleep, but I was awake. All of a sudden I saw this little girl sitting near me, making a clover chain. I didn't realize she was a ghost at first. She looked like a real girl. There wasn't anything scary about her."

"Did your mother see her?"

"No. She was asleep. When she woke up, she said I

dreamed the whole thing. Maybe I did, I don't know for sure, but—"

Maisie interrupted me. "What do adults know? Lily was *real*, Jules. I feel it in my bones." We were almost nose to nose now. "Have you seen anything else?"

"The first night we were here, I saw the Bennett family in the field behind the house. Nobody believed that either."

"*I* believe you," Maisie said.

Encouraged, I told her about the horses and the midden and the dolls and my feeling that Lily was watching me. "I looked up at a window on the third floor—I think it's her room. I swear I saw her, just a glimpse, but definitely her. Then I looked down. There was a key lying in the grass. I think it opens her door."

With a sigh, Maisie sat back in her chair. "Oh, Jules, I am so jealous. I've always, always, always wanted to see a ghost."

"Come to Oak Hill," I said. "And you just might get your wish."

It was a daring thing to say to someone I'd just met. What if she said no, she had lots of friends and she was busy with them most of the time.

But Maisie looked as if she wanted to hug me. "Oh, Jules, I'd absolutely love to see Oak Hill—and Lily. Just say when, and I'll be there!"

Before we could set a date, Mom appeared. "There you are, Jules."

"This is Maisie," I told her. "We've been talking about books."

Mom smiled. "I'm glad to meet you, Maisie." Glancing at the stack of Chrestomanci books, she said, "Oh, my goodness—Diana Wynne Jones. She was my favorite writer when I was your age. I read every one of her books at least twice."

"Maisie recommended them to me," I told Mom.

"You have great taste, Maisie."

"I've read them over and over again," Maisie said. "I adore them."

Mom smiled at Maisie. "Jules and I are about to have lunch at that little café around the corner. Would you like to join us?"

"Oh, yes, that would be great," Maisie said. "They have the best tuna melts in town."

We grabbed our rain gear, checked out our books, and headed for Mandy's Café and Tea Room. All three of us ordered tuna melts. They were just as delicious as Maisie had said they'd be.

While we ate, Maisie told Mom she'd always wanted to see Oak Hill. "My brother and his friends have been there lots of times, but they never took me. That was before

Stonybrook bought the land and found the house and started fixing it up. I guess it's really changed since Joe explored it."

Mom smiled. "Why don't you come over one day next week? My husband will be happy to take you on a tour, and you and Jules can continue your book discussion."

"Maybe she can stay for dinner and sleep over," I suggested.

Maisie gave me a big grin, and I knew I'd said the right thing. We decided that Tuesday of next week would be a good time for Maisie's visit. "We'll pick you up," Mom said. "The roads are a mess from all this rain. You need four-wheel drive to get through the ruts and puddles at Oak Hill."

We drove Maisie home to a big brick house on Third Street. A tabby cat sat on the porch, and a boy's bike lay on the sidewalk. A swing hung from a big tree in the side yard. The house looked friendly, not fancy, but just right. If Dad bought a house for us in the same neighborhood, Maisie and I could walk to school together.

Maisie thanked Mom for lunch and the ride. To me, she said, "I can't wait to see you next week!"

She waved and ran up the sidewalk, mindless of the rain puddles.

"Well," Mom said, "Maisie is delightful. I'm so glad you two got together."

"Me too." I leaned back against the seat. I had a friend. For once, I'd know someone when I started a new school in the fall. I'd ask Maisie what kind of clothes to wear and how to do my hair. I'd fit in right from the first day.

On the way to Oak Hill, I told Mom what Maisie's brother had said. "I told you something terrible happened in that house," I said. "Do you believe me now?"

Mom glanced at me and shook her head. "That's a good example of an urban legend. Every deserted, spooky old house has a story just like it. It's a cliché, Jules."

"But Mom, I've heard things, seen things—"

Mom frowned. "Oak Hill is simply an old, abandoned house. I admit it's creepy, but nobody was murdered there, nobody is buried there, and the Bennetts are not haunting it."

"You have to believe me! The girl I saw in the field, the one you said was a dream—it was Lily Bennett. She's in the house, she—"

Mom braked and pulled to the side of the road. "Stop it, Jules, right now. That sort of talk is irrational. You're just scaring yourself."

"What do you mean? Do you think I'm crazy?"

"No, of course not. Just calm down, think, use your common sense."

"Fine. Believe what you want to believe." I slumped in my seat and turned my face away.

Mom sat behind the wheel as if she'd forgotten how to drive. At last she sighed and started the car. For the rest of the way, we rode in silence.

The Girl

That evening, the girl stands at her window and looks down at Jules's window. The room is empty.

She longs to see Jules. There's a place she needs to go, a safe place where people will love and protect her. She thinks Jules might help her find it.

The moon rises slowly behind the mountains. So many moons, she thinks, so many years. So much waiting.

The sky darkens. Colors fade. Stars pop out, just as they always do, just as they always will.

A light goes on in Jules's room. The girl watches her pass the window and get into bed with a book. The girl thinks that she once had a book. Someone read it to her. The person had a deep voice. She sat on his lap and rested her head on his chest, just under his chin. She was safe then.

"When will you unlock my door?" she whispers to Jules. "When will you free me?"

After Jules turns out her light, the girl curls up in her nest in the wardrobe. She strokes the silken rags. She's so tired, but she cannot sleep. How long will she lie here?

13

Jules

That night, I dreamed of the horses again and woke to hear their hooves pounding the ground. On they came, louder and closer than ever before. The men cursed and pounded on the door of the old house. The woman cried out in fear.

Where was Lily? Where were her parents? Why didn't the hired help come to their aid?

Then, as quickly as the riders arrived, they vanished into the dark. Who were they? Why did they come? What did they want?

✦

In the morning, the sun shone and everything sparkled as if it were brand-new. Water drops shone on spiderwebs and blades of grass. Mud puddles reflected the cloudless sky.

To celebrate Dad's day off, we took a slow drive down the Blue Ridge Parkway to Roanoke and ate lunch at a little restaurant in the old part of town. It was too hot for walking, so Dad suggested going to the Taubman Museum of Art to cool off in air-conditioned comfort.

In the American Art section, all three of us stopped in front of a large oil painting. Even though Oak Hill looked very different now, the painting was definitely Oak Hill as it must have been many years ago.

Dad leaned down to read a small plaque on the wall beside it: HENRY BENNETT. OAK HILL, CIRCA 1883. OIL ON CANVAS.

"Isn't that the artist you found on the census?" I asked. "The man who lived at Oak Hill?"

"That's right, Jules." Dad studied the painting. "He was an amazing artist. So much detail, yet not stiff or overdone. His brushwork is especially nice."

"Oak Hill was beautiful then," Mom said. "The house, the trees, the stone walls ... And those flower gardens. Take a picture of the painting, Ron. Maybe Stonybrook can hire a landscaper to recreate the grounds as they once were."

While Dad got busy with his camera, I studied the painting. A little girl sat in a swing that hung from a tall oak tree. Her hair was blond and her dress was blue. A woman stood behind her, ready to push the swing.

The little girl was definitely Lily, but the woman was too old to be her mother. Maybe she was her grandmother or her aunt. In the background, a younger woman watered the flower garden. Lily's mother, I guessed. Every detail was so perfect, I felt as though—if I tried hard enough—I could step into the picture and visit Lily's world as it was before the robbers came.

I thought of the Chrestomanci books and the Almost Anywheres. What if alternate worlds really existed? Maisie's father said they might. Suppose there was a world where the robbers don't kill the Bennetts, a world where Lily grows up and lives a happy life. Suppose Maisie and I discovered a way to send Lily to that world?

Mom interrupted my thoughts. "Henry Bennett was so talented. It's a shame he's not better known. I wonder what happened to him, why he stopped painting."

Because he was murdered, I wanted to say, *just like I told you yesterday. But you didn't believe me then and you won't believe me now. So what's the use of saying it again?*

We walked around the room, looking for more of Henry Bennett's paintings, and found a few small landscapes of the Blue Ridge Mountains. While Dad and Mom admired the detail and brushwork, I discovered a picture of Lily making a clover chain. She sat in the field, her doll beside her, just as I'd seen her on the day Mom insisted I'd been dreaming.

Mom paused beside me to look at the painting. She glanced at me, and I hoped she'd say, *Oh, Jules, you really did see Lily.* But no. She frowned and turned her attention to a watercolor of an old barn.

I was disappointed, but I didn't say a word. If the painting didn't convince Mom, she'd never believe I'd actually seen Lily.

✦

On Sunday afternoon, Mom suggested that we have a picnic dinner by the stream. She put me in charge of carrying a chocolate cake she'd gotten from the bakery. Dad was responsible for a heavy picnic basket filled with food and drinks, and Mom carried an old quilt and a bowl of potato salad.

Dad gazed across fields of tall grass and wildflowers rolling off toward the mountains. Here and there, old stone walls and hedges divided the land. "Just look at that view," he said. "I haven't seen anything except that house since we arrived. We should do this every Sunday."

Mom took a deep breath. "The air's so fresh. All I smell is grass and honeysuckle."

Dad grinned. "I could live in a place like this."

I almost dropped the cake. "Dad, do you mean that? We'd stay here and not move anymore? Live like normal people? No more new schools?" In my excitement, my words tumbled over each other.

Dad looked at me. "Well, no, not now, Jules. I was thinking ahead to when I retire."

"Oh." I actually felt my heart drop like a stone.

I looked away, and Mom realized I was upset. Putting an arm around my shoulders, she said, "It would mean so much to Jules, Ron. This area is full of old houses in need of work. Surely you could find enough projects to keep you busy."

Dad turned from the view to look at me. "I'm not promising anything, but I'll take some time to drive around and see what's what." He shrugged. "Maybe it's time to settle down."

I put the cake down and hugged him. "Please, Dad, please."

"Okay, okay, Jules. Like I said, I'll do some reconnaissance."

"Let's not forget what we came here for," Mom said. "We have some serious eating to do."

From the look she gave Dad, I guessed they also had some serious talking to do.

"Please, please, please," I chanted to myself. "Settle down, buy a house, plant boxwood."

We spread the quilt in the willow's shade, and Mom opened the picnic basket. After we'd eaten all we could—which was just about everything—Dad wandered off with his camera, and Mom and I lounged on the quilt, too full to wade in the stream or do anything but lie still and listen to our insides rumble.

I'd brought *The Lives of Christopher Chant* with me, and Mom insisted on reading aloud from it. In the scene she chose, Christopher was in another world, one of many Almost Anywheres. I closed my eyes and surrendered to the magic of the second Chrestomanci book. No matter how old I was, I still loved to listen to Mom read out loud. It freed my mind somehow.

Gradually I realized that Mom's voice had been replaced by a voice softened with a southern accent. The book she read aloud had changed to *Little Women*.

In my drowsy state, the change didn't bother me. I

relaxed and let myself sink into the grass, into the story, into the warmth of the summer day.

A fly buzzed around my face, and I opened my eyes to swat it. A few feet away, a woman sat on a quilt, reading aloud from *Little Women*. Lily lay beside her, the doll nearby. Not far from them, a man stood behind an easel, painting the scene.

Doing my best to ignore the fly, I lay still and listened to Mrs. Bennett read about Beth's death. Mesmerized, I hung on every word of the story, as if I'd never read it.

Lily sat up. Tears ran down her face. "Mama, please stop reading. I don't want Beth to die. It frightens me to think about it." As her mother turned to lay the book aside, Lily looked at me. She saw me just as clearly as I saw her. "Lily," I whispered. "Lily."

She said something that sounded like *Help,* but her voice was low and indistinct, a whisper in a keyhole, a sigh under a closed door, a rustle in the leaves.

I leaned closer to hear better, but the moment I moved, Lily and her mother and father wavered like a reflection in a pond and vanished.

I looked at Mom, hoping she'd seen Lily at last, but she lay on the quilt, sound asleep, the Chrestomanci book face-down on her stomach. Dad slept nearby, snoring softly, a smear of chocolate icing on his upper lip.

The place where I'd seen the Bennetts was empty, the grass undisturbed. But Lily was still here, trapped in the house, waiting for me.

I walked to the stream and sat on the bank. Below my feet, the Gerridae skated in circles, and the minnows flashed beneath them, just as they had when Lily was alive. When Maisie came, we'd find a way to rescue her.

14

🔑

The Girl

The girl sits on the floor watching a bird fly around her room. Birds have come in before. Usually they flap about frantically, seeking a way out.

This bird is different. Instead of being in a hurry to leave, it hops around, investigating things. Perhaps it hopes to find a juicy bug to eat. She would like to help him, but even if there were a bug in her room, lately she's been having trouble picking things up. She's not very strong, perhaps because she hasn't been outside in the fresh air for a very long time. She can't remember when she last ate. She's never hungry, but maybe not eating has weakened her.

She stretches out her arms and looks at them. How thin she's become. Why, she can scarcely see her arms. The sun seems to shine through them, and they cast no shadow.

The girl contemplates the bird. "I wish you'd stay with

me and be my pet," she says. Her voice is low and raspy. Maybe she should talk more. But what's the point of that? She has no one to talk to.

Suddenly the bird spreads its wings and flies out the window. The girl watches it dip and soar, dip and soar, and finally disappear into the woods. If only she could spread her arms and fly after him.

After the bird leaves, she's lonelier than ever. The day before, Jules and her father and mother had gotten into their ugly tin thing and driven away. They were gone all day. She was afraid they might be gone forever, but late at night, she saw the lights of their tin thing. She was glad they'd returned.

Today the three of them left the house again, on foot this time. Jules carried a cake. Cake—she remembers cake. It's soft and sweet; it melts in your mouth. Once, in some other time, she ate cake. Chocolate cake. Outside in a field —a picnic, that's what it's called. There was a stream, a tree, wildflowers, butterflies. She ate until she thought her stomach would burst. Eating like that now might put some flesh on her bones.

Maybe Jules and her parents are having a picnic by that stream with the tree and the wildflowers and the butterflies. She hopes so. It's a happy place. She wishes she could go there herself.

The girl drifts into a dream. She's outside near the stream and the tree, lying on a quilt in soft grass. Someone is reading to her. It's a voice the girl knows and loves. She lies still and listens to a story about four sisters. She's heard it before, but she can't remember what happens to the sisters. She thinks one dies. She remembers crying. She's not sad now. She can't remember what dying is.

In her dream, she senses someone watching her. She turns her head. Jules is there, close enough to touch. She calls her Lily. The girl doesn't know who Lily is. Once, she knew, but it was so long ago, so long ago.

"Help me," the girl hears herself say. "Help me."

Jules doesn't understand her. When Jules moves, she vanishes, the way a reflection vanishes when you toss a pebble into water.

The girl comes to herself by the window. She sees Jules walk out of the woods with her parents. Just there, just below her. She hopes Jules will look up and see her, but she hurries into the house with her mother. She's not thinking about the girl.

The girl sighs and backs away into the shadows. Jules can't help her. No one can.

JULES

We came home from the picnic after dark. The shadows made me uneasy. Something screamed in the woods, and I grabbed Dad's hand.

"It's an owl hooting," he said. "A barn owl—the one with the pretty, heart-shaped face and the horrible screech."

I clung to his hand. Owl or not, the cry chilled me through and through. I became intensely aware of every sound—the snapping of a twig, a rustle in the bushes, the wind sighing in the branches. Even the man in the moon looked anxious.

"It's lovely to walk in the night with a full moon to light our way home," Mom said. "It makes me think of Byron's poem—'She walks in beauty, like the night . . .'"

The night didn't make me think of anything but galloping horses and angry shouts. What if the men came upon us here? Would I be the only one to see them? Would my parents believe me if I said we were in danger?

I walked faster, tripping over roots and stones. Mom and Dad urged me to slow down and watch my step, but I walked even faster. And so did they.

When we came out of the woods, I was actually glad to see the dark bulk of the house ahead of us.

It was nine thirty by the kitchen clock. I was too tired to keep my eyes open, so I went to bed. Instead of falling asleep, I lay there thinking of Lily. When I'd called her name, she'd looked right at me. Had she really asked me to help her?

✦

The next morning, after Dad left, I asked Mom if he'd said any more about finding permanent work in Hillsborough.

"We talked last night after you went to bed, but he's still unsure."

"Please make Dad understand how much I want to stay here."

"Your father seems stubborn to you, maybe even insensitive, but I'm sure I can convince him that it's in your best interest."

"Thanks, Mom." I gave her a hug. "I love you so much."

"I love you, too, sweetie." She raised her coffee cup in a salute. "Here's to our permanent home in Hillsborough!"

I clinked my juice glass against it. "To Hillsborough!"

Mom opened her laptop. "I promise I won't give up until your father says yes."

While Mom worked on her novel, I washed the breakfast dishes. The sink was under a window that had a view of the field behind the addition. With my hands in warm soapy water, I watched a doe and a pair of speckled fawns move leisurely through the weeds and vanish into the woods. A pheasant flew up from the underbrush, and three or four vultures circled above the treetops.

Vultures. High in the sky, soaring in circles, they were beautiful. But on the ground, up close, they were downright ugly. Scrawny red necks, black feathers, long, wicked beaks, they hunched by roadsides and gathered around dead animals, ripping them to pieces.

Dad said vultures keep the world clean, but most people saw them as I did—bad omens.

Just as I set the last plate in the dish drainer, a group of men appeared at the edge of the woods. Their clothing was old-fashioned—dark pants, white shirts, black suspenders. They wore wide-brimmed hats. They seemed to be looking for something. The vultures hovered over their heads and watched.

A man shouted to the others. "Oh, Lord, come quickly. I've found them."

"Are they all right?" one called.

"Dead," he cried. "Murdered."

The others rushed to his side and took off their hats. They looked down silently. One of the men groaned. "It's Henry and Laura."

Another said, "But where's their daughter? Where's Lily?"

No one answered. As the vultures circled above them, the men stood silently with their heads bowed.

A second later they were gone. Men and vultures both. I stared at the dark shadows between the trees and twisted a dishcloth in my hands. My legs trembled, and I leaned against the sink to steady myself. What was wrong with me? Was I hallucinating—or was I seeing ghosts from the past?

I backed away from the sink and bumped into a chair. Mom looked up from her laptop. "What's wrong, Jules?"

"Nothing. I just tripped over the chair." To hide my shaking hands, I crammed them into my pockets.

"But you look so pale." She got to her feet and peered at me. "Are you sure you're not coming down with some-thing?"

"I'm fine. Really."

"I was about to fix coffee. Shall I make a cup of tea for you? It'll only take a moment."

"That would be nice." I sat at the table. My legs were still shaking, and my heart was beating too fast. I was surrounded by the ghosts of Oak Hill, and I wanted to know why.

A few minutes later Mom set a teacup in front of me. "I put honey in it."

"Thank you." I picked up the cup and smelled bergamot. Earl Grey, my favorite.

Mom sat beside me. Her laptop was closed. "Something's bothering you, Jules. It's more than the old house, isn't it?"

I stared into my cup. The tea was so clear I saw the flowers on the cup's bottom. "I'm fine, Mom, really."

Mom turned her cup as if it had to be in a certain spot, its handle facing just the right way. Touching it lightly with her fingertips, she said, "Are you still worrying about the Bennett family?"

"Don't you want to know what happened to them?"

Mom sipped her coffee and then set her cup down carefully. "Not really. Some things are best left unknown."

"But what if you could change the past, so what happened in this world didn't happen in another world?"

"Like the Chrestomanci books?"

"Well, yes. What if it's true? What if —"

"Oh, Jules, I love those books as much as you do, but the Almost Anywheres don't exist."

"Maisie's father told her that some people believe in alternate universes. They think —"

"And some people believe the earth is flat." Mom opened her laptop. "Now, I really need to hit the keys. I promised my agent I'd have the manuscript ready last week, and it's still far from finished."

I lingered at the table, wishing Mom had more time to talk, but she was already engrossed in her novel. She wouldn't have believed me anyway.

I walked outside and sat on the deck. Inside, Mom typed away on her laptop. In the old house, Dad and his crew hammered and sawed.

A wind came up. The trees swayed and the sky darkened with heavy clouds. It looked as if it might rain again.

I thought of Lily in her room on the third floor. Was she at her window watching the same stormy sky?

I walked around the house and looked up at her window. Hoping Lily was there, I waved. I glimpsed movement behind the glass. It might have been a response. It might have been a reflection. I waited for a while, but when I saw nothing else, I went back inside and wrote an e-mail to Maisie.

"So much has happened," I told her. "I saw paintings of the Bennetts in a Roanoke museum, then we had a picnic by the stream, and I saw the Bennetts again, all three of them this time. They were having a picnic too, and Lily looked at me and she saw me and said something, but I couldn't understand what—maybe *help*. And then there were these men on the edge of the woods behind the house and they were looking for the Bennetts and they found their bodies, but Lily wasn't with them. Why do I keep seeing these things from the past? I wish you'd been there, Maisie."

16

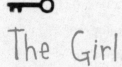

The Girl

The girl sees Jules wave. In a reckless moment, she waves back. Frightened by what she's done, she ducks away into the shadows. She still isn't sure she wants Jules to see her.

After a while, she crosses the room and looks at the paintings. She's been avoiding them. They make her both sad and angry, a strange mix, she thinks.

Slowly, she turns the ones facing the wall around so she can see the man and the woman. She stares into their painted eyes. They want to speak to her. They have something to tell her. Something important.

She waits patiently for them to open their mouths. She's used to waiting, she's used to being patient. But they remain silent.

She touches their faces. "I'm sorry I don't remember who you are."

They do not answer.

Next she notices a portrait of a yellow-haired girl wearing a pale blue dress. She's sitting in the shade of a tree that has long, drooping branches. Her bare feet dangle over a stream. She holds a doll in her lap. She knows that she has been in that exact place, but she can't remember when.

She stares into the yellow-haired girl's painted eyes. That girl also has something to tell her, but like the man and the woman, she doesn't speak.

"I knew you once," she tells the painted girl, "a long time ago, before . . ." She hesitates. Before what?

She continues to walk around the room, looking at the paintings. Many show the same three people. Some are portraits, and others show the woman and the girl with yellow hair going about their daily life.

She finds several pictures of a house. It might be the one in which she's trapped. Summer, fall, winter, and spring, flowers and gardens and a swing in a tree, snow and bare trees, trees with leaves of gold and red. The artist must have lived in this house once. Why else had he painted it so often?

The girl studies the landscapes. She counts the cows

and the sheep in the pictures. Dim memories stir—the smell of hay in the barn, the large brown eyes of the cows, milk spurting into a pail. The scenes comfort her.

Last of all, she turns to the drawings scribbled on the wall. They're poorly done, childish and clumsy. They tell a story she knew once but doesn't want to know now. They do not comfort her.

She turns away. Her mind is a jumble of half-formed images and memories. Fear hides in the shadows. She wishes she could escape into dreamless slumber.

Jules

At last it was Tuesday. I got into the truck with Mom, and we drove to Maisie's house. Mrs. Sullivan met us at the door and welcomed us inside. She was tall and plump, and her hair had turned gray already. It was wild and bushy, untamed. I liked her right away.

"I'm so glad to meet you, Jules." Maisie's mother gave me a hug. "Maisie tells me you love to read. I hope you enjoy those Chrestomanci books as much as she does. Otherwise you'll be sick to death of them long before you've read them all."

"I love them," I assured her. "After I read the last one, I plan to read them all over again."

At that moment Maisie came clattering downstairs, followed by a little girl—her sister, I guessed, because she looked just like Maisie. Maisie was carrying a suitcase and a pillow.

With a huff and a puff she dropped them on the floor. "Hey, Jules, I'm so glad you're here!"

"Are you planning to move in with the Aldridges?" her mother asked.

"Why?"

Mrs. Sullivan laughed. "You've packed so much. That suitcase holds two weeks' worth of stuff."

Maisie looked embarrassed. "Well, a person has to be prepared," she said.

By now the little sister was walking around me, studying me in great detail. "What's your name?" I asked.

"Ellie." She smiled, revealing a big gap where her front teeth used to be. "They both came out at once," she told me. "I tripped over our stupid cat and landed on my face and swallowed them. Not the cat—I didn't swallow her, just my teeth. But the tooth fairy came anyway, which was pretty nice of her, don't you think?"

"Now, Ellie," Mrs. Sullivan said, "don't talk Jules's ear off."

"Could that really happen? Could I talk someone's ear off? Wow. That would be amazing."

Maisie gave her sister a not-too-gentle push. "Get lost, Ellie. We're leaving now."

Ellie laughed. "Don't let the ghosts get you!"

"We'll send them to get *you*," Maisie said.

"I'm not scared of ghosts. If I see one, I'll hit him on the nose and tell him to scram!"

After a round of hugs and a flurry of goodbyes, we got into the truck and left for Oak Hill.

As soon as Mom parked outside the addition, Maisie jumped out and looked at the old house. She must have taken in every detail—the scaffolding the workmen had erected, the sagging roof, the shutterless windows, the weeds growing wild.

Turning to me, she said, "This is so cool. It's like something from a horror movie. I love it."

We followed Mom into the addition, and I led Maisie to my room. She plopped her pillow down on one twin bed and dropped her suitcase on the floor. "Which window is Lily's?"

I pointed. "The little one on the top floor."

Maisie stared so hard I expected the glass to break. "Can you see her? Is she there?"

I joined her at the window. We pressed our faces against

the glass and willed Lily to appear. We even tried chanting her name softly.

Maisie sighed. "I've heard that ghosts only appear to people who don't want to see them."

"That could be true. When we first moved here, I was terrified of ghosts. And then Lily came."

"And you didn't even know she was a ghost at first."

"And when I figured it out, I wasn't scared of her."

Maisie smiled. "Just think, we'll see her together to-night."

We high-fived each other just as Mom called us for lunch, saying, "Dad's made his special grilled cheese sandwiches in Maisie's honor."

After one bite, Maisie told him they were just as good as the tuna melts at Mandy's Café. "Maybe even better!"

"That's a huge compliment," Mom told him.

"Well, the next time I'm in town, I'll be sure to try one," Dad said.

After we'd eaten, Dad asked if we were ready for our tour. Maisie jumped up so fast, she knocked over her glass of cola.

Mom told her not to worry. "Go on," she said. "I'll clean up."

Dad unlocked the door and ushered us into the old

house. The crew was sitting on the parlor floor, eating lunch. Except for their voices, the building was quiet.

As Dad took us from room to room, Maisie stared at the unfinished walls and the roughed-in stairs. She practically sniffed the air for traces of ghosts. The only things I smelled were sawdust and fresh-cut wood.

Dad stopped at the bottom of the stairs. "We have more work to do on the second story, but come on up and take a look. The holes in the floor have been patched, so there's no danger of falling through."

Upstairs, I walked carefully around several stepladders, but Maisie walked under them, as if daring bad luck to find her. We both took care not to trip over tools scattered on the floor and tangles of extension cords snaking everywhere. In the corners, piles of trash waited to be swept up. The crew had left water bottles and soda cans all over the place.

Dad took us through six large bedrooms. Each one had its own fireplace and several big windows, with views of fields and mountains. Even with the walls stripped of plaster, it was easy to imagine how nice the rooms would be when Dad's work was done.

Maisie pointed at a dimly lit, narrow stairway. "What's up there?" she asked.

The hall at the top was dark. I pictured Lily hiding somewhere, her ear pressed to a door, listening to us. Was she afraid of us? Or eager to see us?

Dad shrugged. "Nothing that I know of. We've been hard at work on the first and second floors. A few of the workmen have gone up to take a look. They didn't find anything interesting—just more dirt and rotten floors and spiderwebs."

"Can we see it?" Maisie's foot was already on the first step.

Dad shook his head. "It's not safe, girls. We haven't stabilized the stairs, and the floor's weak."

Maisie and I looked at each other. Tonight we'd see the third floor for ourselves.

Once we were back in my room, I showed Maisie the key I'd found in the midden. She examined it with attention to every detail.

"It's magic," she whispered. "I can feel it. Like something from a fairy tale."

"Not 'Bluebeard,' I hope."

Maisie shuddered, and so did I. Neither of us wanted to find a room full of Bluebeard's dead wives.

"Tonight we'll see if it fits Lily's door," I said.

Maisie looked around my room. "Where are those little dolls you told me about? I'd love to see them."

"I left them in the midden," I confessed. "They scared me."

"How can dolls be scary?"

I put the key back in my box. "Wait till you see the bald one," I said.

18

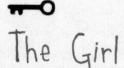

The Girl

The girl hears Jules's voice. She goes to her window and sees her walking on the grass below. Another girl is with her. Or at least she thinks it's a girl. Her hair is cut shorter than a boy's. Like Jules, she wears boys' short pants and a baggy shirt. A pair of spectacles bigger than Grandfather's perches on her freckled nose.

They stop at the midden. Once more, the girl wonders why Jules is so interested in trash and broken things.

Jules's friend picks up a stick and pokes at the ground. The first thing she finds is the ugly bald doll. "Look at this."

Jules makes a face. "Put her down, Maisie," she says. "That doll scares me."

So the friend is named Maisie. That means she's a girl. Unless boys have girls' names and girls have boys' names. Jules, for instance.

"Not me." Maisie examines the doll. "She must have come from the house. We should keep her."

"You keep her," Jules says. "I don't want her."

The girl watches Maisie lay the doll gently down in the weeds. Why does she want it? It's ugly and ruined. Its eyes are gone, its hair is gone, its body is stained, and its legs and arms are falling off. Jules is right. The doll is scary.

The girl can't bear to look at it. She is sure she doesn't want that doll. It's dead.

Jules sits in the weeds and watches Maisie dig in the dirt. She doesn't help her.

"Oh, look." Maisie scoops up the little china dolls.

The girl's fingers itch to hold them. She has an idea that they're all named Charlotte, but she doesn't know why they share the same name. Such odd notions she has.

She considers making the dolls talk again, but she doesn't want to scare Jules, so she keeps quiet and watches Jules and Maisie divide the little figures between them. The girl wishes they'd share them with her. One for her, that's all. Just one.

Maisie says, "It's hot. Did you say there's a creek where we can cool off?"

The girl watches them disappear into the woods. If only she could go with them. There's something at the end of that path she longs to see. The trouble is, she cannot leave the locked room. She promised not to.

Who made her promise? And why can't she remember?

She looks at the little dolls on the grass, their faces turned up to the sky, their bodies stiff and hard. The bald doll sprawls beside them. A few tufts of hair still cling to her head, and her empty eye sockets are dark holes in her cracked face.

The girl turns away from the window. If she could, she'd run outside and gather all the little dolls and bring them back to her room. She'd play with them. She'd make them talk.

The dead doll can stay where it is. If the girl had a shovel, she'd bury it so deep, no one would ever dig it up again.

Jules

Sometime around midnight, when I was sure Mom and
Dad were asleep, I led Maisie to the door that opened
into the old house. We paused on the threshold and switched
on our flashlights. For a moment we stood still and listened.

The house was dark and silent. Nothing moved. Dim
light fell through the windows in the parlor.

Maisie took my hand, and we stepped into the shadows. In the darkness, the past reclaimed the house. No matter what Mom believed, I knew people had been murdered
in these rooms. Blood had stained its floor. Silent screams
hung in its air.

Staying close to Maisie, I forced myself to take one
small step and then another. Each step led me farther from
the addition and deeper into the old house. No matter how
light we were on our feet, the floor creaked under us.

"Are you scared?" Maisie asked.

I shook my head. Actually, I wasn't as scared as I thought I'd be. Maisie made me braver — she wasn't afraid, so I wouldn't be afraid either.

Maisie swept the darkness with her flashlight. Its beam of light made the shadows jump and move. Drafts of night air crept across the floor and chilled my ankles. A shadowy shape scurried across the floor and disappeared into a hole. A mouse? A rat?

I shivered and edged closer to Maisie. Upstairs, Lily was waiting. Perhaps she heard us tiptoeing through the house and knew we were coming to rescue her. For good luck, I touched the key in my pocket.

We climbed the stairs to the second floor, stopping every time a step creaked under our feet. No one heard us, no one called out from the shadows. I tried to breathe slowly and evenly, but I couldn't control the loud thumping of my heart. I'm not afraid, I told myself. I'm brave like Maisie. Lily is waiting. She needs us.

At the bottom of the stairs to the third floor, Maisie touched my arm. Her fingers were so cold I jumped.

"Your hand's like ice," I said.

"It's freezing in here." She put her foot on the first step.

The stairs tilted to one side and the hand railing was loose, so we climbed even more slowly than before. The steps groaned and wobbled, but we kept going.

At the top, I leaned against a wall to catch my breath. Beside me, Maisie breathed hard. "I don't like this place," she whispered.

"I don't either." I looked behind me into the darkness below. Cold sweat ran down my spine. My legs felt so weak I was afraid I'd lose my balance and fall down the stairs.

Maisie turned as if to go back down. "This was a bad idea."

I grabbed her arm to stop her. "We can't leave now. Lily needs us."

Maisie pulled away from me. "You can stay if you like, but I'm getting out of here."

I stared at her in disbelief.

"Come on, Jules, let's go!"

"This was your idea, Maisie. You said nothing scared you."

"Well, I was wrong." Maisie looked as if she were about to cry. "I'm sorry, Jules, but I can't do this."

Just as I was about to follow her back to the addition, the sound I'd been dreading stopped me. "It's the horses," I whispered. "I hear them. They're coming."

"What should we do?" Maisie grabbed my hand and held it tightly.

"If we lock ourselves in Lily's room, the men can't get us."

"Are you sure?"

"It's always the same. The men go into the house, they come back out, and then they ride away. If they could get into her room, they'd take Lily and they wouldn't come back."

Somewhere in the night, very close by, a horse whinnied and a man yelled.

"There's not much time, Maisie, come on!"

We ran to the closed door at the end of the hall. My fingers shook so badly, I dropped the key. Maisie picked it up and handed it to me. She aimed the flashlight at the door while I poked the key at the keyhole. No matter which way I turned it, I couldn't fit it into the lock. My heart banged like a demented thing and my breath came in gulps. It didn't help that Maisie's hands shook so hard she couldn't hold the flashlight steady.

"Hurry up," Maisie begged. "They're coming—give me the key. Get out of the way, let me try."

As Maisie tried to push me aside, the key turned with a loud, grating sound. I grabbed the knob, but my hands were so sweaty and shaky I couldn't get a good grip on it.

"Hurry up, open the door!" Maisie cried. "They're in the yard!"

"Help me. It's stuck."

Together we pushed against the door. It opened so quickly we tumbled into the room and sprawled on the floor.

As soon as I'd locked the door behind us, the men came running up the stairs. "Let us in!" they shouted. "We know you're in there!"

Shaking with fear, Maisie and I cowered together, our arms around each other. The men had scared me when they were outside and I was safe in my bed, but to be this close to them reduced me to absolute terror. The wood groaned under their blows. The door shook in its frame. They'd break it down at any moment and find us.

From outside, a woman cried, "Leave the girl be, come away, come away. You've got what you came for."

The men kicked the door, they cursed and swore, but the woman called again and again.

"Fool of a woman," one muttered. "Just wait till I get my hands on her. She'll shut her mouth or I'll shut it for her."

"We'll be back," the other yelled at the door. "You ain't seen the last of us."

With that, they ran downstairs and out the back door. A few moments later they mounted their horses and rode away. Gradually their shouts faded into the dark, and the night was silent.

Maisie and I huddled together and gasped for breath. We were both crying.

Maisie clutched at me with shaking hands. "Are they gone?"

"Yes."

"Are you sure?"

"I told you, Maisie, they won't come back until tomorrow night."

Maisie wiped her nose with the back of her hand. "I'm scared to stay here. Let's go back to your room."

"We don't need to be scared now. Nothing's here but Lily, just Lily."

Maisie took several deep breaths and peered into the darkness. The only light came from the moon. The rest of the room was hidden in shadows. She didn't say anything, but at least she'd stayed with me.

I groped in the dark and found the flashlight she'd dropped. Its beam lit an easel in the center of the room. Beside the easel was a table covered with art supplies — a palette encrusted with dried paint, jars of brushes and pencils, bottles of turpentine, varnish, and ink, tubes of oil paint, sticks of charcoal, and stacks of drawing paper.

If it hadn't been for the thick gray fur of dust coating everything, I would have expected Mr. Bennett to return at any moment and finish the painting on the easel.

"Jules!" Maisie gasped and grabbed my arm. "There's someone over there, looking right at us."

I swung the flashlight and saw a man's face peering at us from the shadows. I staggered back in fright and bumped into something that fell over with a clatter. A lot of other things followed it, hitting the floor like a row of dominoes.

"It's a painting," Maisie cried in relief. "They're all paintings."

Laughing like loud, silly kids, we saw dozens of paintings leaning against the walls. Several more lay on the floor where they'd fallen after I'd knocked over the first one.

It was like being in an art gallery. Landscapes, animals, portraits. Dad was going to be so excited to know they were here, hidden in this house for over a hundred years, but still as beautiful as the day Henry Bennett painted them.

"My mother does watercolors of flowers," Maisie said, "but this is real art."

We stopped in front of a large painting of a girl sitting

on a tree limb, her bare feet dangling over a stream. The sun backlit her hair and illuminated each strand so it haloed her face. Her father had caught the life in her eyes and dotted her nose with freckles. She was so alive, I almost expected her to speak to us.

"This must be Lily," Maisie whispered.

"Yes," I said, and I leaned closer. "Lily Bennett is sitting exactly where I've sat. Isn't that amazing?"

"Look at the doll she's holding, Jules. It must be the one we found in the midden. I told you it belonged to Lily."

"It looked a lot better when it was new," I said.

"Are these her parents?" Maisie pointed at the portraits on either side of Lily. On the right was a woman, her face slightly turned toward a window. She wore a long lavender dress, and her dark hair was swept back into a loose twist.

On the left was a man sitting behind an easel, peering around the back of a canvas, as if he were looking into a mirror and painting his reflection. He held a brush in one hand. His palette lay on the table beside him.

"It's Henry and Laura Bennett," I said. "Without a doubt."

Behind us, I heard a faint rustling, as if we'd frightened a mouse. I looked at the wardrobe in the corner. The sound had come from there, I was sure of it.

I glanced at Maisie to see if she'd heard anything, but she was still looking at the painting of Lily sitting on the tree limb.

"Oh, Lily," she whispered, "please don't hide. Come out and talk to us."

20

Lily

The men are gone, but Jules and Maisie are in the studio. The girl wanted them to come, and here they are, but she's afraid to let them see her. Her nightgown is tattered and yellow with age. Her hair is long and tangled. She has no shoes.

The girl peeks through a crack in the wardrobe's door. Jules and Maisie have stopped in front of a picture of the yellow-haired girl, the very picture she herself looked at just the other day. If only she knew who that yellow-haired girl is. Her name is on the tip of the girl's tongue. That's something people say when they forget things. She remembers an old woman saying, "Oh it's on the tip of my tongue. Drat. Why am I so forgetful?"

Who was that old woman?

The girl returns her attention to the two friends. Maisie says something to Jules in a low voice.

In a louder voice, Jules says, "Yes." She leans closer to the painting. "Lily is sitting exactly where I've sat. Isn't that amazing?"

The girl trembles when she hears Jules say *Lily*. The name lingers in the air, it echoes in the girl's head, sparks fly up — *Lily, Lily, Lily*. Could it be *her* name? Could she be Lily?

"Yes," she whispers, "yes." Jules has given her something she lost a long time ago. Her name. Lily.

She hugs her name close to her heart and says it over and over. She mustn't forget it again. A dam has broken, and her memories are pouring over it, filling her head with so many forgotten things. She is Lily. She's six years old. She lives in Oak Hill. The doll in the painting is the one Jules dug up in the midden. The doll was new then, a birthday present from Grandmother Pettifer, the old lady who forgot things.

How did her favorite doll end up in the midden? Who threw it there? Surely not Lily herself.

And what happened to the doll to make her so ugly, so dead?

Lily shivers. There's something she knows but doesn't want to know. It hides in the shadows with her, dark and dangerous. She keeps her back to it. She will not face it. But it reaches for her, it whispers. She plugs her ears with her fingers and keeps her mind focused on the girls. She will not listen to the story the darkness whispers.

Jules tells her friend that the man and woman in the other paintings are Lily's parents, Laura and Henry Bennett.

More memories flood back. Mama's and Papa's faces float before her in the darkness, and Papa looks out from the portrait he painted of himself.

At the sight of them, Lily feels a fierce stab of pain. She retreats to the back of the wardrobe and burrows into the rags of her mother's dresses. She's a mouse, tiny and helpless and all alone. She's been abandoned. Left behind. Unloved. Forgotten.

Why is she not with Mama and Papa?

The voice in the dark speaks into her ear. She cannot block it out. She presses her fist to her mouth and sobs quietly. It's not just sorrow she feels, it's also rage. They locked her in this room and never came back. Her own mama and papa. She loves them so much, it hurts to remember them.

Jules's and Maisie's voices interrupt her thoughts. They've found the drawings on the wall.

"They tell a story," Jules says.

Yes, they tell a story. Oh, yes, they do. Like everything else Lily's forgotten, the story comes back to her.

21

Lily

The story those pictures tell begins on a sunny morning with the promise of a picnic. Usually Aunt Nellie prepares the food, but when Lily comes downstairs, Aunt Nellie isn't in the kitchen. She hasn't set the table for breakfast. Lily doesn't smell bacon or freshly baked bread or coffee.

"Where is Aunt Nellie?" she asks Mama. "Why isn't breakfast ready?"

Papa is standing at the window, his back to her. Mama is beside him. Lily's question startles them. They turn and look at her, as if they're surprised to see her.

"It's Nellie's day off," Papa says quickly.

"But today is Saturday," Lily says. "Aunt Nellie's day off is Sunday."

"Aunt Nellie had something important to do," Papa says. "So she asked to have today and tomorrow off."

Mama frowns at Papa, as if she wants to say something, but she reaches for Lily's hand instead. Lily senses something between her parents — a worry they aren't sharing.

"What did Aunt Nellie need to do?" Lily doesn't like not knowing things. Surely if she asks enough questions, Papa will tell her where Aunt Nellie is. He must know. The cook is almost part of the family, not really an aunt, but like an aunt. Papa's secretive air is worrisome.

His face reddens. "For heaven's sake, stop asking so many questions. I don't know why she wanted two days off or what she planned to do. And stop calling her your aunt. She's no relation to you."

Lily draws back, shocked at his tone of voice. Papa is never cross with her. Why must she stop calling Aunt Nellie her aunt? She should be quiet, but she hasn't asked the most important question.

She turns to Mama this time. "How will we have a picnic if Aunt Nellie isn't here to fix the food?"

Mama straightens the ribbon in Lily's long hair. "Don't worry. We don't need Nellie. You and I will roll up our sleeves and put on aprons and do the cooking ourselves. Won't that be fun?"

Lily is puzzled. "Cooking is Aunt Nellie's job. I've never seen you cook anything."

Out of the corner of her eye she sees Papa frown, probably because she forgot and said "Aunt Nellie." Mama touches his sleeve, as if to say *Be quiet, let her call the woman aunt if she wants to.*

Papa shrugs, but he doesn't smile. He turns to look out the window, as if he expects to see someone approaching the house.

Mama ties a huge apron around Lily's waist. Aunt Nellie is a big woman, both taller and heftier than Papa. The apron Mama chooses for herself is also too big.

While she and Mama begin to assemble ingredients, Papa fetches his drawing pad and sketches them at work. Neither Mama nor Lily has had much experience in the kitchen. They spill flour and sugar. A pot of melted chocolate tips over on the table, and Lily scoops it up with a spoon, which she licks clean. Mama drops three eggs. The yolks break and run into the whites.

One of the eggs has blood in it, and Lily turns away. The blood means that the beginning of a baby chick was in that egg.

Papa cleans up the eggs and throws the mess out the back door.

When they've finished the cooking and baking, Mama packs a picnic basket with roast chicken, potato salad, green beans, lemonade, and a big, beautiful lopsided chocolate cake.

Before they leave the house, Papa shows them the sketches he's drawn. "I'm calling these drawings *Amateurs in the Kitchen*," he says.

Mama laughs. "How about *Cook's Day Off*?"

Lily says, "I hope Aunt Nellie comes back soon or we'll starve to death."

She notices Mama and Papa exchange another look that she can't interpret. What do they know and why don't they tell her?

Mama holds out a hand for Lily to take. "Come along."

She clasps Mama's hand and decides to put Aunt Nellie out of her mind. For the moment at least.

They take a path through the woods and across a field to a shady spot by a stream. Mama carries the picnic basket, and Papa carries a patchwork quilt. Lily runs ahead. Grown-ups are so slow. Bees buzz in clover growing tall on the edges of the field. Lily sees a monarch butterfly flying ahead of her, as if it's leading her somewhere.

Under the shade of a willow tree, Mama spreads the quilt on the grass, and Lily helps her unpack the basket. She'd eaten only one of yesterday's biscuits and an apple for breakfast because she's saving her appetite for the picnic, especially the chocolate cake. She smells roasted chicken, and her empty stomach rumbles so loudly that Papa looks around and says, "Is that a bear growling?"

Lily giggles. She eats both chicken wings and a drumstick, a big serving of potato salad, a smaller serving of slightly burned green beans, and an enormous piece of chocolate cake.

Her stomach full to bursting, she lies on her back and peers up at the canopy of leaves shushing and fluttering overhead. It's as if the leaves are sharing secrets with each other. She can't remember a better day than this one.

After a while Mama begins to read aloud from *Little Women*. Lily is drowsy from the food and the summer heat. She begins to fall asleep, but she has the oddest feeling that someone is watching her. She opens her eyes and turns her head to the side.

For a moment she sees a dark-haired girl looking at her. The girl says something Lily cannot understand. Lily tries to speak, but her voice is too small for anyone, even herself, to hear. She blinks, and when she opens her eyes, the girl is gone. Too tired to tell anyone about the girl, Lily closes her eyes. Soon she is fast asleep.

When Lily wakes, Mama allows her to take off her shoes and wade in the stream. She steps into the water and shivers at its icy touch. The sand on the bottom is smooth and feels soft under her feet. She splashes and laughs when she realizes that the skirt of her dress is soaked.

The willow casts its shade on a still part of the stream. Small insects with long, skinny legs walk across the water's surface. They move like skaters, darting quickly from here to there, leaving faint circles behind them.

"Papa," she calls. "What are these odd bugs called?"

He squats down and peers at them. "They're part of the Gerridae family," he tells her, "but most people call them water walkers, water striders, pond skaters, and so on. Fascinating, aren't they?"

Lily trails her hand through the water, taking care not to disturb the gerry bugs. "I wish I could walk across the stream on tiny feet like theirs," she says. "It would be fun, wouldn't it, Papa?"

She watches a bird soar overhead. "Flying would be fun too."

"Oh, Lily." Papa smiles. "Such a fanciful child you are."

Mama joins Papa and looks down at her. "Your toes are turning blue with cold," she says. "You'd better come out and put on your shoes and stockings before you catch a chill."

Lily sits on the grass and spreads her wet skirt around her. It's late in the afternoon, and the sun hovers like a golden ball above the treetops.

The happiness she felt earlier bubbles up inside and she smiles at a rabbit hopping across the field. Papa coughs, and the rabbit freezes, as if he thinks no one will see him if he doesn't move. The sun shines through his ears and dyes them pink. His nose twitches. Papa coughs again, and the rabbit bounds away. A patch of weeds quivers to mark his hiding place, but the rabbit is now truly invisible.

The rabbit is smart. No one will catch him. He knows how to be still and how to hide.

Mama wipes chocolate off Lily's mouth with her handkerchief. "The cake is a sorry mess in comparison with Aunt Nellie's creations," she says.

Papa cuts a big slice for himself and divides what's left between Mama and Lily. "The best cake I ever ate," he tells Mama. "Ten times better than any of Nellie's finest concoctions."

Mama smiles and blushes. "Fibber," she whispers.

Papa gives her a kiss on the cheek. "I'd never lie to you."

"Would you lie to me?" Lily asks.

"Never." Papa stretches and gazes across the fields, which are lush with wheat. Cattle moo. Up on the hillside, sheep answer with bleats. A flock of starlings settles in a tree for the night, disturbing the quiet with their harsh cries.

"Then tell me where Aunt Nellie's gone and when she'll be back." Lily is taking a chance. Papa might not answer. He might be cross. But Lily has to know.

Papa looks at Mama, who says, "You might as well tell her, Henry."

"Lily, you know Mr. Bailey is a hard man to deal with. He doesn't do the work I pay him for. He lies. He mistreats his wife and the animals in his care."

Papa looks into Lily's eyes. She knows he's telling the truth.

"Yesterday I caught him stealing money from the cash box — over five hundred dollars that I forgot to put in the safe."

Papa frowns. "I fired him, and the hired hand quit. This morning I discovered that they stole three of our horses last night and rode off. Nellie went with them." He wipes his sweaty forehead. "I hope we don't see any of them again."

"Aunt Nellie didn't want to go," Lily says. "He made her, I know he did. She's scared of him, Papa. She does what he tells her."

Papa takes her hand in his big hand. His love flows from

his hand to hers and warms her. He looks at Lily, as if she knows something she isn't supposed to know.

"He hits her." Lily says this so quietly Papa doesn't hear. He must have noticed that Aunt Nellie's eye was black last week. The week before that, she had bruises all over her arms. Who would have hit her but Mr. Bailey?

With a sigh, Mama gets to her feet and begins to gather up the picnic things. Papa shakes out the quilt, and Lily helps him fold it. The sun is sinking into a bed of pink and purple clouds, and the evening air is chilly. It's time to leave the stream and the water striders behind.

"We should do this every week," Mama says.

"Yes, yes, let's!" Lily claps her hands and laughs. She's glad to have something else to talk about.

"Why not every *day*?" Papa asks.

"Can we start tomorrow?"

Papa lifts her above his head, and her hair tumbles down over his face.

"Oh, Papa," she says, "I love you so!" Turning to Mama, she adds, "And I love you too, Mama, forever and ever and ever!"

By the time they come in sight of the tall stone house on the hill, it's almost dark. The moon lights their way across the fields and along the path. The evening damp breathes out the scent of grass and wildflowers. In the woods, tree frogs call, and in the distance an owl hoots.

Papa carries Lily upstairs to bed. Mama helps her change into her nightgown. She and Papa kiss her goodnight and tuck her in. Lily wants to hear another chapter of *Little Women*, but she's too tired to keep her eyes open.

22

Lily

B ut that's not the end of the story. It's just the end of
the happy part.

The noise of galloping horses wakes her from dreams
of picnics and chocolate cake. She opens her eyes and sees
Mama standing by the bed, her face barely visible in the dark.

Startled, Lily sits up, wide-awake. She grasps her
mother's hand and senses her fear. Why is someone coming
to call so late at night? Who is it? What do they want? She's
frightened.

Mama pulls Lily out of bed. "Quick," she whispers.
"Run upstairs to Papa's studio. Don't make a sound. Lock the
door behind you. Hide in the wardrobe, and don't come out
until Papa and I come for you."

As Mama speaks, someone pounds on the kitchen

door. A man shouts, "Let us in, Bennett, we've got business to settle."

Papa says something, and Lily hears the door burst open and bang against the wall. A man in heavy boots barges into the house, cursing and yelling. Another follows him.

"Get out of my house, Bailey. You're out of your mind with drink," Papa says. "Go home, sleep it off, or I'll report you to the sheriff."

Lily clings to Mama. "What does Mr. Bailey want?"

"Don't worry. Your papa will take care of it."

"I'm afraid," Lily whispers. "Please let me stay with you."

Mama rushes her toward the stairs to the third floor. "Do as I say, Lily. I'll explain later."

Downstairs, something heavy crashes to the floor. Glass breaks. The noise is terrifying.

Mama shoves Lily toward the stairs. "Go," she whispers. "Go now!"

Mama sounds angry. Whimpering with fear, Lily does as she's told. Her legs are weak. Her bare feet make no noise.

In silent haste she slips into Papa's studio and locks the door behind her. The smell of oil paint and turpentine mixes with the odor of Papa's pipe. The familiar aroma makes it seem as though Papa is in the studio, playing hide-and-seek with her.

Lily obeys Mama and hides in the wardrobe. She ducks under Mama's old dresses and curls up in the back, where the shadows are darkest. No one will find her here. She's a mouse, a rabbit, a tiny creature that knows how to be still.

The noise downstairs grows louder. The men's voices rise. Mama screams and screams again. Lily hears explosions, two, three, maybe more. She recognizes the sound of gunfire. There's more cursing, more thuds and bangs.

She whimpers and burrows deeper into the dresses. The fragrance of Mama's scent lingers in the silk, but Lily doesn't feel safe now. Something is terribly wrong.

From the yard, Aunt Nellie cries, "You drunken fools, what have you done?"

"Where's the girl?" Mr. Bailey shouts. His voice comes from Lily's bedroom on the floor below.

He runs up the stairs. Someone is with him. Not Papa. It must be Ellis Dixon.

They stop at the locked door and struggle to open it. They throw themselves against it.

Where is Papa? Why doesn't he stop them? She wants to call him, but she forces herself to be quiet. One sound, and they'll find her.

"Open the door, Lily," Mr. Bailey shouts. "We won't hurt you."

She hears the anger in his voice. He's lying. If she opens the door, he'll hurt her. He'll beat her with his fists the way he beats Aunt Nellie. Her face will be bruised like Aunt Nellie's, both her eyes will be black, her head will hurt, he might even kill her.

Lily presses her hands over her heart in hope that she can keep the men from hearing it beating so fast and loud. Papa will come soon. He must.

Aunt Nellie shouts again. Her voice shakes with fear. "Please, please. You got what you came for. Forget the child. She's done you no harm. Leave her be!"

Why is Aunt Nellie here? Why doesn't she fetch the sheriff?

Aunt Nellie is afraid of Mr. Bailey. That's why she doesn't get help. No matter how much she loves Lily, she'll do what her husband tells her to do. She always does.

One of the men kicks the studio door so hard, it flies open. They're in the room now. She smells tobacco and whiskey and perspiration. She smells anger and hate, too. In the yard, Aunt Nellie cries, "What are you doing up there?"

"She ain't here, Charlie," Ellis Dixon says. "She's probably hiding in the woods or something. Come on. Let's go while we can. We got the money."

Ellis Dixon runs down the steps, but Mr. Bailey closes the studio door and locks it from the outside. "By the time you get it open," he shouts, "we'll be long gone!"

Downstairs, the men drag things out of the house. Large bundles, maybe. She hears thumps.

"Oh, no, no, no," Aunt Nellie cries. "You promised not to—"

"Shut your mouth!" There's a loud smacking sound, and Aunt Nellie cries out in pain.

"You say one word about what's happened here, and I'll kill you," he yells at Aunt Nellie. "You know I will."

"Charlie!" Ellis Dixon shouts. "Give me a hand. I need some help."

Long after the horses gallop away, Lily stays in the wardrobe and waits.

Where are Mama and Papa? Why don't they come? Perhaps the men tied them up. Surely they'll get loose soon and rescue her.

But the house is quiet. No boards creak. No one climbs the stairs. No one speaks. No one calls her name. It's as if no one is here, no one at all—except Lily.

At last the morning sun slants through the window and pokes fingers of light under the wardrobe door. Lily stays where she is. Her body is stiff and cramped from huddling in the same position for so long, but she obeys Mama and waits.

She's hungry and thirsty. She cries. Have Mama and Papa forgotten her?

They do not come that day. But someone else does. More men tramp through the house. They call her name, but she doesn't recognize their voices. She's afraid they've come to harm her.

She doesn't answer the men, and she doesn't open the door. She promised to wait for Mama and Papa. A promise cannot be broken. No matter what.

After they leave, she selects a stick of Papa's charcoal and begins to draw on the wall. Her hand moves rapidly. She tells the story in pictures. It's not her best drawing, but she's in a hurry. She must not forget what happened.

When she comes to the end of the story, she feels as hollowed out as a dead tree. She's also very tired. So tired. She makes her way to the wardrobe on legs that barely hold her up. She crawls inside and burrows into her mother's dresses. She breathes in her mother's perfume. She falls into a deep sleep.

23

Jules

When we'd looked at the last picture, Maisie turned to me and said, "The drawings tell what happened the night Lily's mother and father were killed."

"If she hadn't hidden in this room, Lily would have been killed too."

I reached for Maisie's hand, and she gripped mine tightly. The shadows darkened and closed in on us. For a moment I felt as if we were trapped just as Lily had been. I shared her fear and loneliness. I understood what it was like to wait for someone who never came, to be locked in a room while outside, the world went on, years passing, season after season coming and going, to hear the horses galloping out of the night, ridden by killers who were searching for you.

Behind us, something creaked, and the spell broke. We turned to look at the wardrobe.

Still holding hands, we crept closer. "Lily—" I called. "Don't be afraid."

No one answered.

"Do you remember the day we saw each other? We were in the field near the stream where the willow tree is. You looked right at me and asked me to help you."

"You *saw* me?"

Maisie and I stared at each other in disbelief. Lily had answered us. She was here in the same room as we were, hidden in the wardrobe, close enough for us to hear her whispery voice.

"What did I look like?" She sounded frightened.

It was an odd question, but I answered as best as I could. "Like the pictures your father painted of you—a pretty little girl with long yellow hair, wearing a blue dress. You were as solid and real as I am."

Lily sighed with what sounded like relief. "I was scared I'd be ugly."

"Ugly? How could you be ugly?"

"Never mind," Lily said. "I saw you too, but I thought I was dreaming."

"You asked me to help you," I said. "Do you remember?"

"It was wrong of me to ask," Lily said. "I have fearful enemies, wicked men—fiends from the devil himself—

in search of me. They'll harm anyone who gets in their way."

"But it's not just those men you need to fear," I told her. "Soon the workmen will start working on the third floor. They'll rip out everything. You won't have a door or a wardrobe to hide in. We have to find another safe place for you."

"You don't understand," Lily said. "I promised Mama I'd stay here until she and Papa came for me. I cannot disobey them."

"Lily, do you know why your mother and father haven't come?" I asked.

Lily was silent for so long I thought she'd never answer, but at last she said, "Yes, I know why. But a promise is a promise, isn't it? It would be wrong to disobey."

"Your parents didn't want you to stay in this room forever, Lily." I laid the key on the floor near the wardrobe. "The door is unlocked. Come with Maisie and me. You can't stay here. We'll find a new hiding place."

"Please don't lock your door, Lily," Maisie begged. "Meet us tomorrow in the field by the willow tree. You know the place."

"We'll keep you safe," I promised.

Lily was quiet again. "It would be nice to sit under the willow again and watch the minnows and the gerry bugs in the stream."

"Then come and meet us, Lily," I said. "We'll find a way to help you."

She paused to think about what we'd told her. At last she said, "I'll meet you tomorrow. I promise." Her voice shook, but she sounded as if she meant it.

We pressed our hands against the wardrobe door and whispered goodbye. "We'll see you tomorrow, Lily. Don't worry, you'll be safe with us."

We ran down the stairs and through the house. In my haste, I tripped over an extension cord and landed on my hands and knees. Maisie helped me to my feet. With a bleeding knee, I hobbled into the addition and the safety of our kitchen.

Once I'd bandaged my cut and we were safe in bed, Maisie asked, "Where are we going to hide Lily?"

I took a deep breath. "I have an idea." I looked at her, worried about her reaction. "If you promise not to laugh, I'll tell you."

Maisie stared at me. "I won't laugh, I promise."

I smoothed the Band-Aid on my knee. "You might think I'm crazy, I don't know, but remember when you told me that some people believe alternate worlds might really exist?"

Maisie frowned. "Yes, but —"

"Well, what if Lily could go to a different world, a world where her parents don't die and neither does she?"

Maisie thought about it. "But the world where she doesn't die," she said slowly, "can't exist until she changes what happened that night."

"Suppose she didn't hide," I said. "Suppose she came downstairs and saved her parents?"

"Like she got a gun and shot Mr. Bailey and Ellis Dixon," Maisie said.

"I can't see Lily doing that."

"How about she spills a big bag of marbles on the floor and the men slip on them and fall and her father gets their guns and calls the police."

"What if Lily doesn't have any marbles?"

Maisie frowned and ran a hand through her hair. "Okay, Jules, what do *you* think she should do?"

"In the picture story, Lily drew a woman outside with the horses. She's the one who cries out on the nights I hear the horsemen. Maybe she'd help Lily. . . ."

"Yes," Maisie said. "Lily can run out of the house and cry for help—"

"And the woman can fetch the sheriff or stop the men or something."

"Do you think it will work?"

"I hope so," I said. "I can't think of anything else. Can you?"

"No," Maisie whispered.

Exhausted, we tried to sleep. Above us, Lily's window was dark, but I sensed her pacing around her room, frightened, confused, worried. She must not know what to do. Stay and obey or leave and disobey. For the first time, I realized what I'd asked Lily to do. She hadn't been out of that room for more than a hundred years. It was all she knew, her safe place. Leaving it must terrify her. No mother, no father to comfort her. No familiar places for her to take shelter from Mr. Bailey and Ellis Dixon.

Maybe it was wrong to ask her to gamble her life on a crazy idea that might not work. But what else was she to do?

In the other bed, Maisie was snoring softly, but I was still awake when the morning light crept in through the skylight and chased the shadows from their corners.

24

Lily

After Jules and Maisie leave, Lily opens the wardrobe door and peers out. Sure enough, the key is on the floor. And the door to her room is open.

With some difficulty, she picks up the key. Her fingers don't work as well as they used to. Indeed, she has become rather clumsy.

She studies the key. As Maisie said, she can lock herself in the room again. Or maybe, if she's brave, if she dares, if she trusts Jules, she can leave.

She tiptoes to the open door. With the key in one hand and her other hand on the doorknob, Lily considers. She's been in this room for a long time, hours and days and weeks, and years—too many to reckon up. She's waited for Mama and Papa. She's done what she was told to do.

She knows why they never came back. They're dead;

they've been dead since the night she locked herself in this room. If she stays here, she'll never see them again.

How does she know this? Because they're dead, and now she knows what that means. And she's still alive. Well, not exactly alive. But not exactly dead either. It's as if she's been forgotten, left behind, with no way to go forward or backward. She's trapped in a world that exists for no one but her and the killers who come for her.

What will happen if she leaves the room? She takes a step over the threshold and then takes a step backwards into the room. She wishes she knew what Papa and Mama want her to do, but they've been gone too long for her to ask. They have no more substance than a shaft of sunlight.

Lily looks out the door again. The hall is empty. It leads to the steps. What will she see if she goes downstairs? Her legs tremble, and she holds fast to the doorframe to keep from falling. She's afraid of what she'll find in the house.

While she hesitates, the sun comes up and paints in the colors that night took away. The workmen arrive. Their laughter booms in the empty rooms, their voices bounce from wall to wall, their heavy boots tramp back and forth on the floor beneath her. Doors open and slam shut.

She creeps to the top of the stairs and pauses there. She

holds her breath. Her toes grip the edge of the first step. She's poised like a diver ready to plunge into deep water.

She lowers one foot, then the other, slow baby steps. She's afraid the stairs will creak, but the wood is silent under her bare feet.

On the second floor, she stops and stares about in bewilderment. The furniture is gone. The rugs and the drapes are gone. The pictures are gone. The floor is splintered and uneven. There are streaks and stains and blotches of mold on the plaster walls. The roof must have leaked.

A few tattered strips of wallpaper remain. Pink and blue flowers faded now to gray. Lily remembers helping Mama choose that pattern. She tightens her grip on the banister to keep herself from running back to the safety of the studio, where nothing has changed.

She looks down at the first floor. It's empty, ruined. The noisy men have torn it apart. Dust covers everything. The walls are open wood frameworks. She can see through them into every room.

The workmen are in the parlor. They lounge about, standing in corners, leaning against walls, eating buns and drinking coffee from paper cups. They wear their strange yellow hats and working clothes and heavy boots. One spits on the floor.

She stays in the shadows as she descends, stopping on every step to be certain nobody notices her. No one does.

Lily tiptoes past the parlor. She should be in plain sight, but the men continue talking and laughing as if she isn't there. One man looks right at her, and she can tell he doesn't see her. It's most peculiar.

Moving into a patch of bright sunlight, she stretches out her hand and looks for its shadow. It's not there. She lifts her foot. It casts no shadow either.

She remembers trying to see herself in the mirror on the wardrobe door, how blurred and indistinct she was, more of a mist than a reflection. She'd wondered then if people could see her. Now she's sure they can't. Jules and Maisie won't see her, even with their eyes wide open.

Invisibility gives Lily courage. If she can't be seen, she can't be hurt. She walks right past a man and glides into the kitchen. It's stripped bare, like the rest of the house. Aunt Nellie's stove is gone, her sink too. The shelves have disappeared, along with all the pots and pans.

She notices a new door. It must lead to the addition. She turns the knob, but it's locked. Through it, she hears voices. She smells bacon and remembers its smoky taste. Something in the empty place inside her aches.

She looks out a window and sees a path that leads to the meadow where Papa kept his dairy cows.

Summoning courage she didn't know she had, Lily slips outside through the open kitchen door. If no one can see her, she can go anywhere.

The sun hurts her eyes, and she stumbles, half blind. She doesn't remember how painfully bright sunlight is. She stands still and opens her eyes slowly. At first, she can't see anything but blobs of dark and light. Gradually her eyes stop hurting and her vision clears.

Her surroundings are familiar yet unfamiliar. Most of the trees are gone. What was once a green lawn is now a churned-up field of red mud. Nettles, milkweed, and Queen Anne's lace flourish where Mama's roses grew.

She walks farther from the house. Nothing is left of the barn except its stone foundation. Weeds and brambles grow in the pasture. Honeysuckle smothers sagging fences and broken stone walls.

No hens peck in the dirt. No rooster struts and crows. No cows rest in the grass. No sheep graze in the upper meadow. No corn rustles in the breeze, no wheat rippling like waves. No one works in the fields.

A blight has fallen on the farm.

Once more, Lily is tempted to run back to Papa's

studio and hide in the wardrobe, but in spite of the farm's desolation, the sky is blue and the sun is warm. It's good to be away from dust and dead insects and musty air. It's good to hear birds instead of hammers and saws and men shouting.

At last Lily comes to the field and sees the willow tree. It's much taller than she remembers. She's not even sure it's the same tree. Another might have grown in its place.

Except for the size of the willow, the field looks exactly the same as it did the day she and Papa and Mama had their last picnic by the stream. Wildflowers sway in a breeze. Birds sing. The sky arches overhead, a lovely shade of pure blue — the same blue as Papa's eyes.

A terrible loneliness casts a dark shadow over Lily. She's by herself in this spot where she was happy with Mama and Papa. Nothing has changed. Everything has changed.

Just as she's about to return to the house, Lily hears voices. Jules and Maisie are coming across the field.

Lily hesitates. Half of her longs to be seen. The other half is terrified of being seen. She smooths her ragged nightgown. She touches her hair. It's wild and tangled, unwashed, uncombed, unbrushed. It's grown very long. In truth, it almost touches the ground.

Mama would have a conniption fit if she saw Lily

outdoors in her nightgown, her hair uncombed and her feet bare.

She decides to hide in the willow tree and watch the girls from above. Silently she climbs from branch to branch, higher and higher. At some point she realizes that she isn't actually climbing. She no longer needs to hold on to the limbs of the willow. She lets a breeze carry her to the top of the tree and she perches there. The branches rock her gently.

This must be what it's like to be a bird. If only she had wings. She'd fly high into the sky and look down at the earth. Oh, what sights she'd see.

Lily watches Jules and Maisie brush aside the willow's drooping branches. They sit by the stream and dangle their bare feet in the water.

How small the girls are. How fragile. It breaks her heart to hear them talk and laugh. They do not know what Lily knows. She hopes they never will.

25

Jules

Maisie and I sat under the willow and waited for Lily. The sun splashed the ground with light and shadows. A dragonfly skimmed over the water.

"Do you think she'll really come?" Maisie asked.

"She *promised*."

A breeze riffled the leaves of the willow, and someone laughed. Maisie and I looked up. Sunlight flared in my eyes. I saw nothing but the tree.

"Lily?" I cried. "Is it you? Are you here?"

The willow leaves moved in one place, but the tree was motionless everywhere else.

"Please, Lily," Maisie called, "let us see you."

The willow swayed. Something light and small moved slowly from branch to branch, but I saw nothing except fluttering leaves.

Willing myself to see her, I closed my eyes, opened them, widened them, narrowed them, blinked, and blinked again.

Lily laughed. "I see you, but you can't see me. I'm invisible."

Her voice was right in front of us now. Squeezing my eyes shut again, I pictured the girl I'd glimpsed in the field, the one in the portrait—long blond hair, blue dress, ribbons in her hair. I pressed my eyelids shut until I saw flashes of light. Then slowly, slowly, I opened them, taking care not to look directly at the place where I guessed she'd be.

And there she was, sitting in the willow tree just above Maisie and me. She wore the dress I'd seen before, and her long, yellow hair was held back from her face with blue ribbons.

"Oh, Lily," I whispered. "You look exactly like you did the first time I saw you."

Maisie smiled. "You might have stepped right out of your father's painting—just as we wished you would."

26

Lily

Lily looks down at herself. Instead of a blue dress, she's wearing her disgraceful nightgown, yellow with age and worn almost transparent.

She tries to smooth her hair back from her face, but it's like pushing cobweb strands away. What she needs is a hot bath and a change of clothes. A pair of shoes would also be nice.

But perhaps it doesn't matter. Jules and Maisie see her as she once was, not as she is now.

Sitting quietly in the tree, she watches Papa's gerry bugs parade across the water's surface, tracing their ever-changing patterns of circles, over and over again. Above her head, leaves murmur like children telling secrets.

A bumblebee burrows into a flower. It's so easy to hide, she thinks, and so hard to be found.

"We're happy you came," Jules says. "We were worried you'd be scared to leave your room."

"I *was* afraid," Lily admits. "I've been there ever so long. I went downstairs, and I saw what's become of our house. It's in ruins. Everything we had is gone. The lawn is mud, Mama's garden is overgrown with weeds—the barns and sheds, the chickens, the cows . . . What have they done with it all?"

"Your house was empty for a long, long time," Maisie says.

"This big company hired my father to restore Oak Hill," Jules says. "When he's done, it will look almost like it did when you lived there."

Lily ponders what they have told her. "Please don't think I'm foolish, but when you say a long, long time, I don't know what you mean exactly. When I lived in Oak Hill— my real life with Mama and Papa and Aunt Nellie—it was 1889. What year is it now?"

The girls look at each other, as if they're afraid she won't like the answer to her question.

When Jules tells her, Lily feels as if she's been swallowed up by time. No one from her world is alive now. No one. Not even Mrs. Brown's new baby that was baptized the Sunday before everything changed.

When she can speak again, Lily says, "Reverend Donaldson told us the world would end in the year two thousand. Judgment Day would come, and the dead would rise from their graves, and we'd be sent to heaven or hell."

"In 1999, a lot of people thought the same thing," Maisie says. "They stocked up on food and water and prepared for the end of the world, but on the first day of two thousand, everything was just the same." She shrugged. "And here we are."

Yes, Lily thinks, here we are, but unlike Maisie and Jules, she doesn't belong in the twenty-first century. She belongs in 1889.

"I was born on the ninth of February in 1880," Lily says. "So I'm old now. Impossibly old."

Jules and Maisie nod.

No one is meant to live this long, Lily thinks. She should be dead, really and completely dead. She belongs in her grave, not sitting in a willow tree wearing a tattered nightgown and talking to living, breathing girls.

She looks at them. "I'm not supposed to be here, am I?"

The girls look at each other, their faces solemn. Lily senses that they have something to tell her. She sits quietly and waits for them to speak.

27

Jules

It seemed to me that Lily was thinking along the same lines as Maisie and I. She already knew she was in the wrong time. If we convinced her about alternate worlds, perhaps she'd do what had to be done to set things right.

"Maisie and I've been thinking about the night Mr. Bailey and Ellis Dixon came to your house," I told her. "What if you hadn't hidden upstairs? What would have happened?"

"But Mama told me to hide," Lily said. "I'd never disobey her or Papa."

"But suppose you knew what was going to happen," Maisie said. "Would you still obey your mother?"

Lily frowned and slowly shook her head. "I'd run downstairs after her. When the men came, they'd kill us all."

"That's not a very happy ending," I said.

Lily shrugged. "Don't you see? All I want is to be with

Mama and Papa. Even if we're dead, I'd be happier with them than I am without them."

"Think, Lily," I said. "Could you possibly have gotten help? What if you'd fetched the sheriff? Or a neighbor?"

"They were too far away," Lily said.

"How about the woman with the horses?" I asked. "Would she help you?"

"Aunt Nellie," Lily whispered. "Of course. She was outside with the horses that night. She'd *never* let anyone hurt me. She loved me as if I were her own child. Mama told me so."

"But she's Mr. Bailey's wife," Maisie said. "Would she go against her own husband?"

"Mr. Bailey's a bad man," Lily said. "He drinks whiskey and he hits Aunt Nellie and he stole Papa's money. She'd do anything to save me, even if he told her not to. So help me, if I had a gun, I'd shoot Mr. Bailey dead." She was so angry, her body quivered as if she might break into thousands of pieces and disappear. "I know about guns. Papa gave me lessons."

Maisie and I looked at each other in surprise. Lily was fiercer than she looked. With a temper like that, she might be brave enough to save her parents and herself.

Deciding this was the right moment to explain our

plan, I took a deep breath and said, "I'm going to tell you something you might not understand. In fact, you might not believe it. You might even think I've lost my mind."

When I paused, Maisie said, "Go on, tell her."

"Okay. Suppose this world isn't the only world. Suppose there are lots of other worlds, some almost like this one and others completely different."

"Mars, Venus, Saturn, Jupiter. I learned about them in school. Nobody lives on them. Except maybe Mars."

"I'm not talking about planets," I told her. "I mean worlds that astronomers can't see. They don't show up in telescopes. They exist in another dimension."

From the way Lily looked at me, I guessed she no longer understood what I meant. At this point I wasn't even sure I understood. It sounded too complicated to be true.

I tried again, hoping to convince myself as well as Lily. "It's not easy to explain, but things can happen in one world that don't happen in another world."

"Imagine there's a world where Mr. Bailey didn't kill anyone," Maisie said. "In that world, you and your parents are alive and happy."

"Do you mean heaven?" Lily asked.

"No, not heaven," Maisie said. "Please just be quiet and let us explain. It's really important, Lily."

"I'm sorry. I didn't mean to be rude." Lily folded her hands in her lap and sat up straight.

"It's all right. You weren't rude," I said. "It's hard to understand."

"Just tell her what to do," Maisie said.

"Are you brave, Lily?" I asked.

"I'm as brave as I can be," she said. "I'm not scared of snakes or thunder and lightning. I'm not even afraid of Papa's bull or Mr. Mason's hunting dogs."

"Are you brave enough to run outside tonight when the horsemen come? Are you brave enough to fetch Aunt Nellie?"

She hesitated. "Will you and Maisie be there?"

"Yes," we said together.

"All right then," Lily said. "I'll do it. I'll fetch Aunt Nellie. I'll be with Mama and Papa no matter what happens."

I looked at the child sitting above me in the tree and knew I'd never meet anyone, living or dead, as brave as Lily.

28

Lily

For a moment the two girls say nothing, and Lily is free to drift on the stream of memories time has returned to her. She looks across the field to the woods. The trees hide something in their shadows, something she should see. She can't quite remember what it is, but she doesn't want to be alone when she finds it.

Perhaps Jules and Maisie will come with her. She leans down from her branch, still worried that they might smell her dirty feet, and whispers, "Will you walk in the woods with me? It's cooler there."

"Of course," Jules says. She and Maisie scramble to their feet, and Lily drops down from the tree. She lands without a sound and leads the girls down a narrow path. It's so over-grown with weeds, Lily wouldn't have seen it if she hadn't known it was there.

Somewhere ahead, mourning doves coo, but she doesn't realize where she is until she sees the tombstones hidden in the deep shade. Weeds and ivy cling to them. Trees have grown up around them. The stones tilt and slant. Some have fallen. The graveyard looks very different from the last time Lily saw it.

Jules and Maisie stop. They both look frightened. Have they never seen a graveyard?

"Why have you brought us here?" Jules asks.

"You'll see." Lily drifts ahead of them. Her feet barely touch the ground.

She looks back at the girls. Maisie is making an effort to find a way through the weeds and brambles, but Jules hasn't moved. Is she scared of the dead?

Lily floats ahead. The grave closest to the path belongs to Grandfather and Grandmother Pettifer. Grandfather died before Lily was born, but she remembers Grandmother. Very old she was, wrinkled and worn, like clothing packed away too long at the bottom of a trunk. When her fingers clasped Lily's wrist, she felt as if she'd been caught by a bird with long talons.

Grandmother died when Lily was seven years old. Lily had stood where she is standing now, holding her parents' hands and watching the coffin disappear into the earth.

She'd cried, as much out of fright as of sorrow, for it was dreadful to think of Grandmother in that coffin, her sharp eyes closed forever.

Mama cried too, for the old woman was her mother and she'd loved her. Papa comforted both of them.

Lily walks farther into the graveyard. She looks under the ivy at the small headstones of Pettifer children who died when they were little and at the mossy stones where people older than memory are buried. Pettifer and a few other names appear over and over again. Her family is here, grandparents and great-grandparents, aunts, uncles, and cousins. All dead and buried properly.

At last she spies an angel hiding in the honeysuckle and wild grapevines. Its marble skin is mossy green from age and spotted with lichen and moss. Beautiful in grief, the angel kneels with drooping wings on a tomb. Lily has found what she seeks.

HERE LIE THE BODIES OF

HENRY BENNETT

and his wife, LAURA, *daughter of*

JAMES and SARAH PETTIFER

Struck down cruelly in the midst of life

And in Memory of their Beloved Daughter
Who was taken from us in her Childhood

LILIAN ANNE BENNETT

"Never more to find her where the bright waters flow ...
Her smiles have vanished and her sweet songs flown."

Lily runs a finger over her parents' names: *Henry Bennett and his wife, Laura.* The letters are faded and blurred from years of snow and rain. Even though she knows that Papa and Mama are dead, it's something else altogether to stand here in the green shade and know they lie beneath the mossy earth at her feet.

She touches her own name. Does the inscription mean that she's buried with her parents, or does it mean that she's dead but not buried here? She thinks "in Memory" must mean she isn't here. No one found her. She hid too well.

When she reads what's written beneath her name, she smiles. The words are from a song Mama often sang to her. Lily is pleased to see its words on the tombstone.

"'I dream of Jeannie with the light brown hair...'" Lily sings in a sweet voice. Maisie and Jules sing with her. They stop after the first verse, but Lily remembers every word. She sings all the way to Jeannie's death at the song's ending.

Maisie stands beside her, and Jules stands on the other

side. It's a solemn moment, Lily thinks, like being in church. She wishes she were solid so she could hold their warm hands.

"If Mr. Bailey and Ellis Dixon had found me, I'd be buried here with Mama and Papa." Lily turns to the girls. She's frightened, she needs their comfort. In a whisper, she adds, "Maybe it's where I should be."

"No, Lily," Jules says. "*We* found you—Maisie and me. We'll make sure you go where you belong."

"To that other world," Maisie adds. "Where nobody dies at Oak Hill."

"I thought I was waiting for Mama and Papa," Lily says softly, "but maybe I was waiting for you all along."

"Tonight," Jules says, "everything will be the way it should be."

But Lily isn't listening. She fades silently into the dense shade and disappears. She needs to be alone. Invisible to everyone now, she curls up on the ground and lies still. Willing herself to sink into the earth, she longs to join her parents.

She hears the girls calling her, but she doesn't answer. She'll see them tonight. After a while they leave the cemetery. Their voices are so low she cannot hear what they say. She hopes she hasn't hurt their feelings or been rude.

Day slowly darkens into night. The air turns cold and damp. Nothing happens. Nothing changes. Slowly, she follows the narrow path to Oak Hill.

In the dark, the house looks the same as it did the night Papa carried her home from the picnic. She expects her parents to welcome her at the door, to ask where she's been, but she sees nothing except shadows, hears nothing but the night breeze blowing bits of trash across the floor.

Wearily she climbs the steps and enters Papa's studio. Mama and Papa are not there. Lily is alone.

Jules

I spun around and looked for Lily. "Where did she go?"

"Lily," Maisie called. "Lily!"

No one answered but a mourning dove hidden in the shade.

We called her name again and again. The mourning dove cooed its sad song over and over, but Lily didn't answer, and she didn't appear.

"Where are you?" I called. "Please come out where we can see you."

"She's hiding," Maisie said. "We won't find her unless she wants us to."

Maisie and I stood silently and waited. All around us the trees creaked and sighed, as if they were telling each other secrets. I thought of their roots tangled together under the earth, binding them together in the dark. They held the coffins as well, keeping the dead safe.

The mourning dove cooed, but Lily didn't return.

At exactly the same moment, Maisie and I reached out to touch Lily's name. Our fingers brushed against each other on the rough stone. Friends, we were friends, I knew without asking. Even if I moved to Alaska or Hawaii, Maisie and I would be friends because of Lily.

"We should clean up the graveyard," Maisie said. "It's wrong for Lily's family to lie here forgotten."

"If we tell Dad about it, maybe his work crew will do it."

"And after they finish the hard work, we can plant flowers and stuff for Lily," Maisie said.

"A memorial garden," I said, and she nodded.

Slowly we made our way out of the graveyard and followed the path uphill through the woods. In the damp shade, gnats swarmed around our heads and mosquitoes attacked us.

"Do you think our plan will really work?" I asked Maisie. Now that I knew Lily, I felt as if we were sending a real live child into terrible danger.

When Maisie didn't answer right away, I asked her another question. "Aren't you afraid Mr. Bailey will kill Lily?"

"It's so complicated." Maisie wiped the sweat from

her forehead. "There could be a world where Mr. Bennett didn't fire Mr. Bailey. There could be a world where he hired some other man. There could be a world where Mr. Bennett never met Lily's mother, and Lily was never born. There could be—"

I covered my ears. "Stop it! You're driving me insane."

"Sorry." Maisie squashed a mosquito on her arm. A bright bead of blood popped up and she smeared it away. "Wouldn't it be great to live in a world where nothing bit you?"

We walked on, swatting gnats and mosquitoes, our shirts soaked with sweat despite the shade.

From somewhere ahead I heard voices. "Your mother must be here. Do you think she'll let you stay tonight?"

Maisie turned to me, red-faced from the heat. "She has to. I'm not letting you go in that house alone."

"That's a relief!" I laughed as if it were no big thing, but for the first time, I knew what it was like to have a good friend. I felt like doing a row of cartwheels all the way home, but I wasn't very good at gymnastics. And besides that, it was way too hot to try.

When we came out of the woods, we saw our mothers sitting on the deck, talking like old friends.

Maisie's mom saw us first and waved for us to join her

and Mom on the deck. We collapsed on the picnic table, too hot and tired to take another step.

"How about a big glass of ice-cold lemonade?" Mom asked.

Maisie and I drank ours in about one minute, and Mom poured us seconds.

"Have you girls had fun?" Maisie's mom asked.

Maisie nodded and took another gulp of lemonade. "We've had a great time. Can I stay another night?"

"Of course," our mothers said in unison, and laughed at their unplanned duet.

The two of them went on with their conversation, and Maisie and I went inside to cool off in air-conditioned comfort. We had things to talk about and plans to make.

30

Jules

After dinner that night, we kept ourselves from thinking about our plan by playing a few games of Clue with my parents. I won the first round by accusing Colonel Mustard of murdering Mr. Boddy in the library with a knife. Maisie won the second by accusing Mrs. White of killing Mr. Boddy in the kitchen with a wrench. Mom won the third game, and Maisie won the fourth.

"Poor Mr. Boddy," Dad said. "Always dead before the game even begins."

We started a fifth game, but Dad insisted that we use the British words. We had to call the wrench a *spanner* and the knife a *dirk*.

He also said that Mr. Boddy shouldn't always be the murder victim. "Give the poor man a break, and let that old bore Colonel Mustard be the one to die."

I was already having trouble paying attention to the game. With Dad making up new rules all the time, I was too distracted to keep playing.

I glanced at Maisie and caught her looking at the window, as if she expected to see the horsemen galloping toward Oak Hill.

"I'm so tired," I said. "How about you, Maisie?"

She yawned so widely the fillings in her back teeth showed.

"Oh, girls, for heaven's sake, go to bed before you fall asleep on the couch," Mom said. "We've played enough Clue for tonight."

"More than enough," Dad said. "It's time to bury poor departed Mr. Boddy." He dumped everything into the box and closed the lid. "Rest in peace, old boy."

I kissed him and Mom good night and left them arguing over what TV show to watch.

In my room, Maisie and I checked our flashlight batteries and settled down to wait for my parents to go to bed. After Dad began snoring, we tiptoed into the kitchen and opened the door to the old house. At the same moment, we heard the horses galloping toward us.

"Hurry," I whispered. "We've got to hide."

Darting into the old house, we flattened ourselves

against a wall near the stairs and stared about us in disbelief. Instead of the ruins we expected to see, Oak Hill looked as it must have when Lily lived here. The walls were papered, and the floor gleamed with polish. A kerosene lamp on a small marble-topped table lit a group of portraits—not of Lily and her parents but of people from even longer ago, Lily's ancestors probably, dark with age.

Upstairs, Lily whimpered, and Mrs. Bennett ran down the steps. As she passed us, her long skirt brushed against me, but she didn't notice me or Maisie. It seemed we were invisible witnesses to what was about to happen.

We watched Mrs. Bennett join her husband in the kitchen. Fists pounded on the kitchen door.

"Don't let them in," Mrs. Bennett cried.

But the men forced the door open and entered the kitchen, shouting and cursing.

Mr. Bennett faced the men, his back to us. Mrs. Bennett stood beside him. "Go home," he told them. "You have no business here!"

"I worked for you more than five years. You owe me more than a week's salary." Mr. Bailey was a big man, taller and heavier than Mr. Bennett, and just as ugly as he'd looked in Lily's drawings.

Ellis Dixon pushed his way forward. He looked like a

ferret, short and skinny, with a narrow face and close-set eyes. "Money," he said. "That's what we come for. Give us what's in your safe."

"You're a pair of drunken fools," Mr. Bennett said. "Get out of my house."

"Please," Mrs. Bennett said. "Leave now."

Mr. Bailey pointed a gun at Mr. Bennett. "Don't tell me what to do. I ain't your tenant no more. You listen to me now!"

At the same moment, Ellis Dixon twisted Mrs. Bennett's arm behind her back. "Take us to the safe and open it."

Flattening ourselves against the wall, Maisie and I watched the killers force the Bennetts past us and into the parlor. They were close enough for me to smell the whiskey on their breath and the sour odor of sweat and stale tobacco, but they didn't notice Maisie and me.

Mr. Bennett struggled to free himself, and Mrs. Bennett pleaded with the men to let them go.

We heard a faint noise overhead. Lily stood at the top of the steps. She wore a long white nightgown and her yellow hair hung in loose curls around her face.

For a moment it seemed as if she might turn and run back to the studio.

"Lily," I whispered, "we're here. Be brave."

She didn't seem to see us, but she gripped the banister and inched down the steps. She was pale with fear, but determined.

"Fetch Aunt Nellie. Change what happens," Maisie said.

Holding our breath, we watched Lily take one step down, then another. From the parlor, we heard Mr. Bailey shouting. Mr. Bennett shouted back. Mrs. Bennett sobbed softly.

Lily hesitated at the foot of the steps and looked toward the parlor.

"No, no," I whispered. "If you go in there, you won't save anyone. You'll all die."

She took a step toward the parlor. Her mother was still crying. Her father spoke angrily. The killers shouted about the safe and the money.

Lily was at the doorway now. She paid no attention to us. It was as if we didn't exist—in this world, maybe we didn't.

We had to stop her, but even when I grabbed her arm, she didn't react.

"Lily," we shouted. "Don't let them see you! Go outside. Get Aunt Nellie! Change what happens!"

Sill ignoring us, Lily listened at the door for a few seconds. Maisie and I shouted at her. She didn't hear us. And neither did anyone else.

Suddenly Lily cocked her head like a cat who's just noticed a mouse. She looked at Maisie and me, not exactly with recognition, and backed away from the doorway.

Outside in the dark, a horse whinnied. A woman spoke in a low voice.

"Go," we shouted to Lily, "get Aunt Nellie!"

Without looking at Maisie or me, Lily ran down the hall and into the kitchen. A moment later a door opened and a breath of cool night air stirred the window curtains.

31

Lily

From the top step, Lily watches her mother run downstairs. It's hard to disobey Mama, even though she has a very strong urge to do so. So instead of locking herself in the studio, she clings to the banister. Below her, Mama hurries to the kitchen. The men are in the house now. She hears them cursing Papa.

Mr. Bailey and Ellis Dixon come out of the kitchen and into the hall. With guns in their hands, they force Papa and Mama into the parlor. They want money. Papa's money.

Lily knows the safe is hidden behind one of Papa's paintings. Lily saw it once when Papa opened it to put in a box of money from crop sales. The men tell him to open the safe and give them the money. All of it.

Maybe Papa will give them the money and the men will leave and all will be well.

When Mama begins to cry, Lily creeps slowly and silently down the steps and tiptoes toward the parlor. While Mama weeps, Papa shouts at the men, and they shout back. The angry voices frighten Lily.

Mama and Papa are in danger. Lily must save them, but how is she to do that? Suddenly she's aware that someone or something is trying to tell her what to do. She looks around, but sees no one.

Outside in the dark, a horse whinnies and a woman speaks softly.

Lily knows she must get help, but she's too scared to move. She hears a voice and sees two girls crouching in the hall. They cry, "Don't let them see you, Lily! Go outside. Get Aunt Nellie! Change what happens!"

She doesn't know who they are or where they came from, but almost against her will she does what they tell her. Dashing out the back door, she calls to Aunt Nellie for help.

When she sees Lily, Aunt Nellie drops the reins and runs toward her. "Lily, Lily!" she calls.

Lily seizes Aunt Nellie's hands. "Don't let them hurt Mama and Papa! They have guns."

"Lord God Almighty!" Aunt Nellie cries. "He promised he'd not harm anyone."

Seizing Lily's hand, Aunt Nellie runs toward the house, but before she reaches the door, Mr. Bailey steps outside.

"What's gotten into you?" he shouts at his wife. "Put the girl down and mind them horses like I told you."

He steps toward them, his face like the devil's, ugly with anger and hate.

Lily sees his revolver. Too angry to be afraid, she pulls away from Aunt Nellie and hurls herself at Mr. Bailey. She'll make sure he doesn't hurt anyone.

The man grabs Lily and lifts her off her feet. He holds her under her arms as if she's a dog. His breath smokes with whiskey and his eyes are wicked, like the eyes of the old bull Papa keeps in the pasture.

Lily struggles, she kicks, she flails at him with her fists; she squirms and twists like a cat who doesn't want to be held. If only she had claws, she'd scratch his eyes out.

Her heart pounds with fear and rage, she can hardly breathe, but she's never felt so strong. She, Lily, will save Mama and Papa.

While Lily keeps Mr. Bailey busy, Aunt Nellie ducks around him and runs into the house.

Mr. Bailey follows her. "Get back outside," he shouts at his wife. "What happens in this house ain't no business of yours."

Lily kicks him and strikes him with her fists, but he manages to hold her with one arm and keep his gun pointed at his wife. All three of them join Mama and Papa in the parlor. Ellis Dixon keeps his gun pointed at Mama and Papa, but he looks startled to see Lily.

"What the devil's going on?" he asks. "Where'd the girl come from?"

At the same moment, Mama cries, "For the Lord's sake, put my daughter down. Don't hurt her!"

Papa lunges toward Mr. Bailey. "Let Lily go!"

Lily takes advantage of the confusion. She might not have claws, but she has teeth. With savage ferocity, she sinks them into the hand that holds the gun. She tastes blood.

Taken by surprise, Mr. Bailey drops the gun and loosens his grip on Lily. With a burst of strength, she squirms free and runs to Mama just as Aunt Nellie picks up the pistol and points it at Mr. Bailey.

Mama holds Lily so tightly she can hardly breathe. She kisses Lily's hair, her face, her hands. She murmurs and sighs and starts to cry. "Oh, Lily, Lily, Lily," she whispers.

"Stop right now, Charlie," Aunt Nellie says, "or I'll shoot you dead. Don't think I won't. There ain't a soul in this world who'd blame me."

Lily peeks across the room. Aunt Nellie is aiming the gun right at Mr. Bailey. She looks angry enough to pull the trigger.

"Give me that gun, Nellie." Mr. Bailey holds out his hand. "You won't shoot me. You ain't got the stomach for it."

Aunt Nellie keeps the gun aimed at him. "I'll blow your head off. You been asking for it since the first time you hit me."

Lily hopes that Aunt Nellie will shoot Mr. Bailey soon. If she won't, Lily will grab the gun and kill him herself. Her fingers itch to pull the trigger. She hates him, she wants him dead, dead, dead. She must be the baddest girl in the world, but she doesn't care.

Ellis Dixon stands near Papa. His gun's muzzle touches Papa's head. He looks stunned, as if he's forgotten why he's in the parlor or what a gun is for.

"What are you waiting for?" Mr. Bailey shouts. "Shoot her if you have to. Just get the gun, Ellis."

Lily can't keep up with what happens next. First she hears a gunshot so loud it makes her ears ring. Next she sees Mr. Bailey fall to the floor. His head is bleeding. A red stain spreads across the carpet.

Lily trembles and presses her face against Mama's

shoulder. Even though she's just wished him dead, she doesn't want to see his blood. Her fierceness melts away. She clings to Mama like a baby.

Mama murmurs, "It's all right, Lily. We're safe now."

"Did she shoot him dead?" Lily whispers, afraid to look and see for herself.

"Ellis shot him." Papa drops to his knees beside Mr. Bailey and feels for a pulse. "I believe he's dead."

Ellis Dixon moans and cries. "It's your fault, Bennett. You grabbed my arm. I was aiming at that woman, but I shot Charlie instead."

Pushing Papa aside, he kneels beside Mr. Bailey. "Oh, Charlie, forgive me, I never meant to do it."

Lily lifts her head just in time to see Papa drag Ellis Dixon to a chair and tie his arms and feet with cords from the drapes.

She expects Ellis Dixon to put up a fight, but he just sits there and lets Papa knot the rope good and tight. His face is as white as a dead man's and he's shaking all over.

"Oh, Lord, what have I done?" he groans. "What have I done?"

Aunt Nellie still has her husband's gun. She's sitting down now, so it's cradled in her lap. "I never would have shot him," she mutters. "He was right, I don't have the stomach for such things. But Lord, I'm glad Dixon killed him. I won't miss that man. No indeed."

Mr. Bailey lies on the floor where he fell. Mama covers him with one of her good linen tablecloths. Lily is sure his blood will never wash out of it.

"Mama," she whispers. "Mama, I was scared. I thought they'd kill us all."

"Oh, Lily, I was scared too." Mama hugs her, and Papa embraces them both.

"Thank the Lord, we're all safe." He sounds close to tears.

"How long will Mr. Bailey be lying there? And how long will Ellis Dixon be tied to the chair?" Lily asks. She wants everything to be cleaned up. No reminders of what happened here.

"I'll fetch the sheriff tomorrow," Papa says. "He'll take Dixon to jail and remove Mr. Bailey's body."

Papa turns to Mama. "Perhaps you should take Lily to bed," he says. "This has been a terrible night for all of us."

Lily clings to Papa for a moment. "Don't ever leave me," she begs. She isn't sure why, but she has a strange feeling he might have left her once.

He kisses Lily's tears away. "Don't worry, dearest. I'll never leave you."

"And neither will you, Mama?"

"Never, never, never." Mama gives Lily a kiss for each *never*.

As Mama carries her up the stairs, Lily looks over the banister. For a moment she sees the same two girls looking up at her from the shadows. Or are they ghosts? When they wave to her, she waves back.

"Who did you wave to?" Mama asks.

Lily points at the girls, but they aren't there anymore. She rests her head on Mama's shoulder and closes her eyes. "Nobody," she whispers.

Mama lays Lily on her bed. Her favorite china doll sprawls on its face on the floor. Mama picks it up. "Oh, no. Her head is cracked. She must have fallen off the bed when I woke you."

Lily reaches for the doll. "Can you fix her?"

"Papa's very good at mending china. He'll make her look almost as good as new."

Lilly rocks the doll gently. "I was worried that you might throw her in the midden with the trash."

"Of course not. Whatever gave you that notion?"

Lily has no idea where that notion came from. Mama wouldn't throw her doll away. Yet she's sure she saw the doll in the midden, bald and falling to pieces and ugly. She's glad it's not true. Papa will mend the cracks, and the doll will be almost as pretty as the day Grandmother Pettifer gave it to her.

She lies back on her pillow and clasps her mother's hand. "I hope you aren't cross with me for disobeying you."

Mama squeezes Lily's hands. "If you hadn't fetched Nellie, things might have gone very badly for us." Mama lies down beside her. "Close your eyes and sleep now."

"Will you sing 'Jeannie with the Light Brown Hair'?"

"Of course I will."

Lily falls asleep listening to Mama's soft voice. She's safe now; she's where she belongs.

32

Jules

W e'd watched the scene in the parlor as if it were the
last act of a play seen in dim light through a dingy
curtain. The actors were barely visible, their voices almost
inaudible, and the plot was hard to follow, but it had the
ending we'd hoped for.

Now the play was over, and we were alone in the dark.
Lily was gone. Oak Hill was in ruins again. Moonlight slanted
through the windows of the old house and shone on piles
of rubbish and the plywood subflooring and the skeletal
wooden framework of the walls. Tools and extension cords,
ladders and brooms, paper cups, empty paper bags, and soda
cans lay where the workmen had left them.

"Lily did it," Maisie said. "She saved her parents and
herself."

"I could never be as brave as she was."

"Me neither," Maisie said. "I was worried at first, though, weren't you?"

"You mean when she just stood there like she was frozen or something?"

"And we kept shouting and she couldn't hear us. . . ."

"It was like we were the ghosts instead of Lily."

We sat for a while and listened to the old house. Except for occasional creaks, it was silent. Empty. Lily wasn't hiding in the room on the third floor. I'd never glimpse her at the window again, I'd never hear the horsemen. Their fates were settled.

Maisie yawned and looked at her watch. "It's after four a.m."

We brushed sawdust off our pajama pants and let ourselves into the addition. The Clue game lay on the table where we'd left it. Our ice-cream bowls sat in the sink, rinsed but not washed. The kitchen clock ticked, and the nightlight cast a dim glow on the stove-top.

Moonlight dappled the field behind the house, and the woods lay in darkness. Two deer, followed by a fawn, leaped through the tall weeds and vanished into the trees. On the Interstate, trucks rumbled.

To everyone but Maisie and me, it was an ordinary night.

33

Jules

The next morning, we slept so late that Mom checked
to make sure we were breathing. "You girls would
sleep all day if I let you." Feeling groggy, we dressed and ate
breakfast.

Leaving Mom at work on her novel, we walked down to
the willow tree.

"Last night is so hard to believe," Maisie said.

I tossed a pebble into the stream and watched its rings
spread across the water. "If you hadn't been there, I'd think
it was a dream."

"It seems that way now." Maisie threw a pebble after
mine. "Who'd ever believe something like that could actually happen?"

A breeze rustled the leaves overhead. We squinted at the

sun flashing down through the willow leaves, but this time nothing stirred in the branches. "She's not there, is she?"

"No."

I watched the Gerridae waltz across the water. Beneath them, minnows darted about, turning this way and that in unison. Birds sang, bees buzzed in the clover, and a rabbit studied us from the edge of a bramble patch. It was just like the day before, but because of Lily, everything had changed.

Maisie sat beside me, making a chain of clover blossoms. "Was Lily really in our world?" I asked. "Or was she stuck between two worlds, neither in one or the other, until she disobeyed her mother and went downstairs to save her family?"

Maisie frowned and ran a hand through her hair. "It's just so complicated," she finally said. "In one world, Lily and her parents die, but in another world, she and her parents live."

"Our world must be the world she died in," I said softly. "That's why Oak Hill is in ruins."

"If that's true," Maisie said, "the dolls we found in the midden will be where we left them."

Between the heat and the gnats circling my head, my

brain felt as mushy as a watermelon. Suddenly I was too irritated to think about anything more complicated than one plus one. "I don't know, Maisie. I don't know, I just do not know!"

"You needn't shout," Maisie said. "I'm not deaf, you know." She stood up and started walking toward the house.

Afraid she was mad at me, I ran after her. "Where are you going?"

"To the midden," Maisie said, "to see if the dolls are there."

Without another word we headed across the field and up the hill. Yesterday we'd left the doll and her small companions on the grass by the hole I'd dug. In the excitement of last night, we'd forgotten all about them.

As soon as we came out of the woods, we saw the little china dolls lying on their backs in a row next to the bald doll—just exactly as we'd left them. Except for Lily's absence, nothing had changed.

Maisie knelt in the weeds and touched each doll as if it were a sacred relic from the past. "These belonged to Lily. She's gone, but they're still here."

I stared at the little dolls with some distrust—once, I thought they'd spoken out loud to me, but I must have imagined that. Today they were simply little china figurines, incapable of speech or movement. I turned away from the bald doll. She looked like a corpse dug up from her grave.

"Lily loved that doll," Maisie whispered. "She never would have thrown it in the midden."

"Mr. Bailey and Ellis Dixon probably did it," I said. "They looted the house and left the stuff they didn't want here in the dirt."

From where we knelt by the midden, we heard the noise of hammers and saws coming from the third floor. I looked up as one of the men opened the window in Lily's room.

"Hey, you two," he called down to us. "What are you doing in the trash heap? Go play somewhere safe. You could cut yourself on something."

Gathering the dolls, we ran around the corner of the house. Maisie's mother's car was parked by the back door. Inside, we found her, Mom, and Dad gathered around the kitchen table. Stacked up against one wall were the paintings from Henry Bennett's studio.

"Look what I found on the third floor." Dad pointed at the paintings. "Remember Henry Bennett? This is his work. Isn't it beautiful?"

The bright light of the kitchen lit the colors and details. Portraits and landscapes sprang to life. Maisie and I oohed and aahed, as if we'd never seen them.

"Just look at this one." Dad pulled out the portrait of Lily sitting in the willow tree. "Have you ever seen a more lifelike painting? You almost expect her to jump out of the tree and talk to you."

"Of all of them, it's my favorite," Mom said.

"Such a dear little face," Mrs. Sullivan said. "I wonder who she was."

"I'd guess she's Bennett's daughter, Lily." Dad showed Mrs. Sullivan another painting. "This is his wife, Laura. And here's one that shows Oak Hill as it was when the Bennetts lived here."

"What are you going to do with them?" she asked.

"The Taubman Museum in Roanoke already owns a small collection of Bennett's work," Mom said. "They're bound to be interested."

Dad sighed. "Stonybrook owns the paintings, but I'm sure the corporation will donate most of them to the Taubman or some other museum—another tax write-off for them, as well as a gift for the public."

I pointed to the picture of Lily in the tree. "Is there any way we could keep this one?"

"I'll ask." Dad laughed. "Maybe the corporation will give me one as a bonus for finding them."

Mom set two tall glasses of iced tea in front of Maisie

and me. "You two have been out in the heat too long. Red faces, red noses. I bet you forgot to use sun shield."

While we gulped our tea, Mom picked up the bald doll. "Where on earth did you find this poor thing?"

"In the midden," I told her. "We think she belonged to Lily."

"Yes," Mom murmured. "This must be the doll in several of the paintings."

"Can she be fixed up to look like she used to?" Maisie asked.

Mom sighed. "She's pretty far gone, but I once knew a woman who did wonders with antique dolls. Maybe I'll send her this poor lost soul and see what she can do."

"We found these, too." Maisie and I pulled the little dolls from our pockets and laid them on the kitchen counter.

"Frozen Charlottes." Mom smiled in recognition. "I had one or two when I was little, but I don't know what happened to them. They belonged to my grandmother."

"Why are they called Frozen Charlottes?" Maisie asked.

"They were named after a girl in an old song who froze to death because she was too vain to hide her party dress under an old cloak. Her mother warned her, but—"

"Nice story," Dad said as he picked up the smallest doll. "I thought they were called that because their arms and legs don't move."

Turning to us, he said, "Have you young detectives discovered anything else?"

"There's a family graveyard in the woods," Maisie told him. "It's almost hidden under vines and briars and weeds."

"Can you tell your workmen to clean it up?" I asked.

"It's definitely of historic value," Maisie said.

"Oh, will you show it to me?" Mom asked. "I love old burial grounds."

"I'd like to see it too," Maisie's mother said.

"Let's take a look after lunch," Dad suggested. "I'm sure the graveyard will be included in the restoration plans."

I had to ask one more thing, even though I was scared to hear the answer. "Was there anything in the room besides Henry Bennett's paintings?"

"His easel, some odds and ends of furniture, a big wardrobe."

"Did you look inside the wardrobe?" I glanced at Maisie and saw her eyes widen. She knew why I was asking.

"We pulled everything out in case he'd stashed more paintings inside, but all we found were rags—women's dresses mostly. They probably belonged to his wife."

Maisie and I sighed so loudly that Dad laughed. "What were you expecting? Skeletons in the closet?"

I forced myself to laugh, and Maisie joined in. "No, of course not," I said. "Books maybe, more paintings. I don't know. Just curious."

Maisie's mother stood up. "Now, if you girls will excuse us," she said, "we have some important matters to discuss."

For the first time, I noticed plans and official forms laid out on the kitchen counter.

"What's going on?" I asked Dad. "Are you already planning our next move?"

"I hope not," Mrs. Sullivan said. "My husband and I are on the town council. We've gotten funding for a project to restore the old buildings on Main Street. We're hoping to hire your father to take charge of the renovation work."

"You mean we'll stay here in Hillsborough?" I stared at him, not daring to believe what I was hearing.

"That would be the plan, yes," Dad told me. "Of course, if you'd rather move across the country, I'll tell the Sullivans I can't do it."

I ran around the table to hug him. "Say yes, Dad, say yes!"

Maisie chimed in. "Please, Mr. Aldridge, say yes!"

"Well, now, maybe your mother—"

"Don't be an idiot, Ron. Of course I want to stay in Hillsborough."

Dad spread his arms in a gesture of defeat. "It looks like my roaming days are over — at least for now."

I was too excited to sit still. Grabbing Maisie's hand, I ran outside and began turning cartwheels in the grass. For once, I didn't care what I looked like doing them.

Maisie followed me and collapsed when I did. "Your cartwheels are even worse than mine," she said.

We lay on our backs and laughed. Nothing was funny. Everything was funny.

✦

That evening, while Mom and Dad washed the dinner dishes, I sat on the deck and watched the stars come out. Just the evening star at first, then a few more, and then too many to count. A sliver of moon swung into sight over the mountains.

My thoughts strayed to Lily. I wished I could see her once more. Just once. I needed to know that Maisie's and my plan had worked, and she was safe.

I stared at the field where I'd first seen her with her parents. Would it be possible to see her there again? I concentrated all my mental energy on Lily, willing her to appear. "Only for a moment," I breathed, "that's all."

No luck this time. In the kitchen, Mom laughed at

something Dad said. Out of sight, traffic rumbled like waves pounding the shore. The cicadas made their usual racket in the woods.

The past had closed in on itself. Lily was safe in her world, and I was safe in mine. Most important now, Maisie and I had become friends. We'd be together all summer, and when school started, I wouldn't be alone.